Those Were The Days

LYNDA PAGE
Those Were The Days

HEADLINE

First published in Great Britain in 2017
by HEADLINE PUBLISHING GROUP

1

Cataloguing in Publication Data is available from the British Library

ISBN 978 1 4722 2929 8

Typeset in Stempel Garamond by Palimpsest Book Production Ltd,
Falkirk, Stirlingshire

Printed and bound by CPI Group (UK) Ltd, Croydon CR0 4YY

HEADLINE PUBLISHING GROUP
An Hachette UK Company
Carmelite House
50 Victoria Embankment
London EC4Y 0DZ

www.headline.co.uk
www.hachette.co.uk

For Alex Elizabeth Page-Warburton (Puddy)

Thank you for eight years of pure joy – I am blessed to have you as my granddaughter – and for all the joy you have yet to bring me in the years to come.

All my love, Magga

CHAPTER ONE

A bank of freezing fog rolled in from the sea, twining everything it encountered in its swirling, damp tendrils.

Drina Jolly turned up the collar of her thick winter coat as the world surrounding her suddenly faded into oblivion. When she had set out a short time ago from the general office to walk across to the camp boundary where the dilapidated farmhouse had stood before it was demolished several months ago, a pale sun had been shining down from an almost cloudless December sky.

Others finding themselves in such circumstances would instantly have become panic-stricken and disorientated, fearing to move in case they lost their bearings. Most would have chosen to stay put until the fog thinned or a rescue party could guide them back to safety. But Drina, now fifty-six years of age, had lived here since she was a little girl when the vast area Jolly's Holiday Camp now occupied was just empty fields; she had witnessed its growth from a modest handful of tents to the flourishing site it was today, with its hundreds of chalets, entertainment and administration buildings, outdoor and indoor swimming pools, boating lake, funfair and numerous other recreational activities, catering for up to ten thousand people a week in high season, looked after by an army of staff. A misty day was not going to deter Drina.

She had come here alone on the morning of Christmas Eve for nostalgic reasons, to have one last look around the site where the old farmhouse once stood before it had had to be demolished. Straight after Boxing Day she'd be supervising the landscapers employed to clear away the badly overgrown undergrowth that currently swamped the area, ready for its transformation into a static camper and touring caravan park. While she could, though, Drina wanted to revisit the place where she and her widowed father had settled fifty years before. They were a couple of virtually penniless Romanies then, their only ambition being to find a kindly farmer who would allow them to park their old caravan on his land and give them a chance to put down roots and build a better life for themselves. After a long, fruitless search they finally found a benefactor when Mr Ackers, a landowner, allowed them to settle on his property.

Over time a deep friendship had developed between Drina's father and lonely Farmer Ackers, a source of great comfort to the old farmer who knew companionship and kindness in his last years instead of his previous desolate existence. By way of gratitude for this, on his death Farmer Ackers made it his business to see that Drina's father, much to his shock at the time, inherited all his worldly goods – to the rage and astonishment of the old man's two selfish sons. Drina's father had used the legacy wisely, building up the business they had set up together from a few campers pitching tents in a field to several hundred in several fields. On her father's premature death, Drina's husband, Joe Jolly, had continued the work of building the business into the popular holiday camp it was today, Drina herself taking over the reins when Joe died of a heart attack three years previously.

Drina's attachment to the place remained as strong as ever. She would do everything in her power to keep it flourishing in the manner her father and Farmer Ackers set out to do all those years ago, in order to give working-class people an opportunity to leave behind their regimented lives and the grime of the towns and cities, and have a holiday in the fresh air by the sea at an affordable price.

The winter months were Drina's least favourite time of the year, when the camp resembled an abandoned town, the only sounds the howling of the wind blasting through the bare trees, swirling dead leaves into every nook and cranny, or driving rain against the windows of the empty chalets and camp buildings. Time couldn't pass quickly enough until it was once again filled with the comings and goings of thousands of holidaymakers enjoying themselves under a warm summer sun.

Thrusting her gloved hands deep into her coat pockets, she looked around, hoping to see signs that the fog was to be short-lived. It seemed to her, though, that it was getting thicker, not thinning. A wave of sadness enveloped her then. It seemed she wasn't going to be able to view the area one last time and relive precious memories before it was transformed forever. But then, she reasoned with herself, she knew this area better than she did the back of her own hand and therefore didn't need to be here to conjure up memories of her departed loved ones and of the happy times they had spent together. She could do that at any time, anywhere – and certainly somewhere far more hospitable than the old farmhouse site was at the moment.

She was about to make her way back to the general office when, out of the corner of her eye, she saw a dark shape suddenly materialise only feet away from her. She spun her head to see what it was and simultaneously – for no more than a second or two – the fog thinned enough to reveal the figure of a man before closing in again and obliterating it. Even though he was no longer visible to her Drina froze, staring wildly over at the place where he had suddenly materialised. She felt her legs start to shake as she emitted a gasp of shock.

That man had been her father . . .

. . . except that it couldn't have been, since Drina's dad had passed away nearly forty years ago.

Then a memory returned to her. Her mother had been a

gifted clairvoyant from a long line of seers – a gift she had not, alas, passed on to Drina. She had once told her daughter that the spirits of deceased loved ones paid visits to living family members in order to warn them of imminent catastrophe. Never having had any sign before this that an afterlife even existed, Drina had always taken her mother's words with a pinch of salt. But after her experience just now maybe she should reconsider. She couldn't help but worry. Was this unexpected visit by her father a warning that something terrible was about to happen?

A warning was all well and good but if she didn't know what she was being warned about then how could she try and prevent whatever disaster was about to befall her? Since her father had lived and chosen to reappear here, it must be something to do with the camp. In recent years the business had come under threat several times, mostly thanks to her own son's greed and the terrible things he'd done before his early death, yet her father had never appeared to her to warn her of impending menace at those times. His appearance now must mean something far worse was about to happen.

But what?

As far as Drina was aware everything was running smoothly. Bookings were flowing in for the coming season; in fact, some weeks were already full. The maintenance crew was on track to finish all repairs as well as adding new facilities to enhance the campers' holidays here – such as a tenpin bowling alley and new slides for the indoor swimming pool. Advertisements for staff to replace those not returning next season had been placed in all the national newspapers and the response had been excellent, so there was no fear of not meeting their full complement. A reputable company had been hired to carry out the work required on the old farmhouse site. New deals had been struck with suppliers of goods to the camp and all those suppliers were happy with their contracts.

Yet the niggle of worry escalated. If the camp was under

threat from some unknown source, she needed to know so she could do something about it.

Drina urgently called out, 'Father, please come back. Please, Father? Please tell me what it is you came to say.'

She froze rigid then, as an eerie globe of light suddenly appeared in the fog, in just the same place as the ghost of her father had materialised. It was moving, dancing its way up and down and from side to side the nearer it approached. She held her breath. Was her father about to appear to her again? She wasn't at all frightened of the impending supernatural encounter; she felt quite calm, in fact. Her father had loved her and would never do anything to harm her. But then suddenly the orb of light stopped moving and a voice called out: 'Drina? DRINA? Where are you, love?'

As much as Drina loved Artie Fleming and appreciated that he'd risked life and limb to come and find her in this blinding fog, part of her was annoyed to think that her father would not now reappear and enlighten her. With forced lightness in her voice, she called back, 'I'm over here, Artie.'

He responded, 'Where's *here* exactly? I can hardly see my own feet in this fog.'

'I'll keep calling out, just follow my voice.'

A minute or so later, through a swirl of fog, Artie arrived by her side. He was ordinary-looking, tubby and middle-aged, and his face lit up when he saw Drina. He gave her a hug, clearly relieved to find her safe and sound. 'When the fog came down so suddenly I was worried for you. I know you could find your way back to the courtyard blindfold but I was still concerned you'd fall over an abandoned wheelbarrow or something.' Noticing the expression on her face, he asked in concern, 'What on earth is the matter? You look like you've seen a ghost.'

'I have, Artie. My father's.'

He was visibly shocked by her announcement. 'Eh?'

'Look, I haven't gone mad. I know what I saw and it was

the spirit of my father. When the fog came down I was standing right where I am now. I'd just made up my mind to come back to the office as it was apparent that it was in no hurry to lift, when my father suddenly appeared no more than a couple of feet away from me. It was only for a split second before he disappeared back inside the fog but I wasn't imagining it, I know I wasn't. He was as real to me as you are.' She eyed Artie earnestly. 'You do believe me, don't you?'

Artie looked at her tenderly. He adored the homely-looking woman before him; she was the love of his life, his true soul mate. She had arrived to save him at a time when he was at rock bottom, mentally, physically and financially, had taken him to her generous heart and given him a reason to live. Despite the fact that she could afford to live in luxury, and paying no mind to what others thought of the situation, Drina had chosen to reside with Artie in a small two-bedroomed cottage, furnished comfortably but cheaply. It was all he could afford; his pride would not permit him to live off her money. The pair of them couldn't be happier and were devoted to each other. The only thing to cloud their contentment was the fact that Artie's errant wife had maliciously refused to divorce him unless a large amount of money changed hands – something he was adamant wasn't going to happen, though Drina would gladly have handed it over. In consequence she and Artie were unable to marry. As far as they were both concerned, though, they didn't need a piece of paper to prove to the world their mutual love and commitment. If others looked down on them for what they labelled 'living in sin', then so be it.

Artie always stood by Drina. If she had seen something in the swirling fog that she believed had been the spirit of her dead father, that was good enough for Artie. He leaned over, kissed her cheek and told her with conviction, 'I believe you, love.'

'Thank you, Artie.' She heaved a sigh, though, still looking troubled. 'My mother believed that a visit from the spirit of a loved one meant something bad was about to happen. I wonder what my father was trying to tell me . . .'

Artie racked his brains for something to say that would comfort her. Then an idea occurred to him. 'Maybe spirits don't always pay visits just to warn us about something awful. Maybe sometimes they appear to tell us that they love us and are watching over us from the hereafter, and there's nothing more to it than that.' He took Drina's arm. 'Anyway, let's get you back in the warm. I'm froze to me marrow – you must be as well – and neither of us wants to go down with something nasty this close to Christmas, do we?' He paused for a moment before he added, 'Look, love, I know that neither of us is looking forward to Christmas Day as much as we would have been . . . not with it just being the two of us now . . . but we could still make the day special. And we can make a start by decorating the tree that I got for us in Mablethorpe yesterday.' His eyes twinkled merrily at her. 'I can't speak for you but I've certainly got a few presents ready to go underneath it.'

Setting aside her recent shock, Drina nodded agreement. Her eyes lit up at the thought of sharing Christmas with this man. Before she'd met him, there'd been many festive seasons endured in the company of her husband, Joe. Although he'd been an effective businessman, taking control of the holiday business Drina had inherited from her father and turning it into a force to be reckoned with, Joe Jolly had never been a loving or attentive husband. Soon after their union she was to find out that the handsome Joe had only married her for the lifestyle she could give him. After the birth of their only son, Michael, Joe only visited their marital bed now and again, token gestures to keep his wife sweet, while secretly satisfying his insatiable sexual needs and feeding his large ego with a string of other women. Christmas Day to Joe had been an excuse to show how well he lived, playing host to a wide circle of friends and acquaintances.

For days leading up to it, Drina would be run ragged,

making sure that the house was sparkling and lavishly deco-rated, the pantry filled with only the best food, mostly cooked and prepared by herself with the help of their daily, the drinks cabinet rammed to bursting with the finest wines and spirits of all descriptions. For forty-eight hours she would then play hostess to the army of guests, every one of them wealthy and self-satisfied, people with whom she had nothing in common. And during the festivities she was fully aware that periodically Joe would sneak off somewhere private for an illicit liaison with his latest conquest, usually the wife of one of the guests. By the end of it Drina was exhausted and had derived not one moment of pleasure from all her efforts. There would always be a gift for her from Joe under the Christmas tree, though, always a nice piece of jewellery, but Drina knew without doubt that Joe had never clapped eyes on it before she opened the shop-wrapped parcel, his only involvement in its purchase having been a telephone call to the jeweller's, instructing them to pick something suitable for his wife and deliver it to his office. In complete contrast, the presents that Artie bought for her were always chosen with love and much thought, then carefully wrapped by him.

Christmas Day last year had been far from the happy family celebration it would usually have been. All of them, especially Artie's daughter, Rhonnie, had been in deep mourning over the tragic loss of her beloved husband Dan. This year once again the family would not be together as Rhonnie and her young son were now living in Devon, where she was doing an exceptional job of heading up Jolly's new holiday camp. This one catered for those with plenty of disposable income, who wanted a more luxurious type of stay. Drina's heart really hadn't been in the forthcoming celebrations until Artie had reminded her just now that they still had each other. He was right: the family might not all be together but that didn't mean Artie and she couldn't make the day special for themselves.

She excitedly asked: 'Oh, what have you got me?'

He wagged a finger at her. 'That's between me and Santa . . . and you'd better be a good girl for the rest of today or he won't be delivering them tonight.'

She chuckled. 'Come on then, let's get back and I'll finish up in the office while you go and dig out the decorations from the cupboard under the stairs or Santa won't have anywhere to leave the presents when he delivers them, will he?'

They had barely reached the wide expanse of grass that separated the workers' chalets and maintenance buildings from the main part of the camp when suddenly they both stopped short, staring just ahead of them to where the fog had thinned and the figure of a man had momentarily materialised just a few feet ahead of them, before being rapidly obscured again.

Drina urgently exclaimed, 'You saw him too just then, didn't you, Artie? You did, didn't you?'

Still staring in that direction, he told her, 'For a second or two I did.' He then turned to look at her before adding, 'But, love, I really don't think that spirits in heaven are supplied with roll ups, and the man I saw was smoking one. Nor do I think they leave footprints on the grass.' He pointed just to the side of them where a newly made set were heading off into the fog. Before she could comment, Artie thrust the torch at her, telling her, 'Keep shining this after me so I can find my way back to you.' And before Drina could question him as to where he was going, the fog had swallowed him up, leaving her staring blindly after him.

A moment later she heard angry shouts, then what sounded like a scuffle, before Artie appeared back through the fog, frogmarching another man ahead of him.

Drina was mortified. This man was no ghost but living flesh and blood. The fog had been playing tricks on her eyes as, now she was able to view him properly, she saw he was nothing like her father. For a start her father had been clean-shaven and always wore his shiny black hair short whereas this man had an abundance of thick matted curls springing wildly from his head and his face was completely hidden by a beard as tangled as his hair, except for around his eyes. Under the assortment of tattered filthy clothes he wore was a man who looked to be in his early forties, but living the life of a vagrant as he appeared to be doing would tell heavily on him, so in fact he could be younger than he seemed. One of the man's old work boots had a gaping hole in the front, dirty bare toes sticking out of it, and the worn-down soles of both boots were being held in place by a thick wad of string wrapped tight around them. He didn't have much by way of worldly goods judging by the small sack he was clutching in his gloved hand.

So Drina's father hadn't paid a visit to her after all.

The man was struggling against Artie's grip on him, exclaiming, 'I wasn't doing anything wrong. Please, you have to believe me. If I'm trespassing I'm sorry but I was just trying to find my way back to the main road when I lost my bearings in this damned fog.'

Both Drina and Artie were shocked by how polite the man sounded, both having expected him to be more the uncouth type. Drina then felt ashamed of herself. It wasn't just the people at the bottom of the pile who came to be living the kind of life this man was. One day someone could be rolling in money and the next it could all be gone, through no fault of their own. It suddenly struck her why he had been caught in this particular part of the camp. 'You've been using the old farmhouse for shelter over the winter, haven't you?' she asked.

Through the tangled mass of hair that flopped over them a pair of startlingly blue eyes were fixed on her warily as he said, 'Yes, I have. I've been using it during the winter months for the past few years, even sometimes during the summer when I was around this way.'

Drina had always suspected that vagrants used the abandoned farmhouse for shelter during the winter months but being the kind of person she was had turned a blind eye to it. 'So what will you do now it's been demolished?' she asked him.

The look of wariness in his eyes changed to one of gratitude for this woman's concern for his welfare. 'I'll find somewhere. There are plenty of old farm buildings around to take shelter in, but the length of time I get to stay depends on how often the farmer makes his checks and moves me on, which is generally pretty often. I didn't have that trouble at the farmhouse here as it was only checked on by your security men once in every blue moon and even then they didn't look too closely as I doubt they thought anyone would be stupid enough to risk their life there. But when you're in the position I am, then it's needs must. Look, if it's all right with you, I'll be on my way now to find somewhere else for the night, which will be difficult enough in this fog, let alone when it gets dark too.'

Artie and Drina exchanged a look that signalled they were both happy to let the vagrant go on his way.

Before he could make a move, Artie put his hand in his pocket and pulled out some lose change, which he handed the man while telling him, 'Buy yourself something to eat.'

The man took it, saying, 'Thank you, sir. I much appreciate this.'

After Drina had pointed him in the right direction to get himself back on the main road, he turned away and disappeared back into the fog.

Artie was about to tell her that they too ought to be making tracks when he noticed the look on her face and asked her, 'What's the matter, love?' Then he assumed he knew. 'I'd have thought you'd have been relieved that it wasn't the ghost of your father come to visit you with a warning of impending doom.'

'Mmm,' she said. Then looked at him and insisted, 'Yes, yes, of course I am. Mortally relieved, believe me. But actually

11

I was thinking of that poor man.' She turned her head and peered in the direction he had taken. 'I feel so sorry for him, coming all the way here to bed himself down for the winter, only to find the old farmhouse gone and be left with the problem of finding somewhere else. And did you notice how well spoken he was, and polite too? I got the impression he was an honest sort of man. He had very kindly eyes. I wonder what happened to bring him to living rough?' She turned her head and eyed Artie, looking troubled. 'I won't sleep tonight for worrying about whether he's managed to find shelter or not. I must do something to help him until this fog lifts and he can find himself somewhere else. After all, this is a time of goodwill to those in need.'

If there was ever anyone in need, Drina wouldn't hesitate to do her utmost to help them in any way she possibly could, no matter what time of year it was, Artie thought. He looked thoughtful for a moment before he said, 'Are you thinking of offering him the use of a staff chalet for the night?'

'I was, but then on second thoughts it wouldn't be any good as he can't light a fire in there to keep himself warm or cook any food, and the thin fabricated walls will hardly offer him any more protection from the elements than sleeping out in the open will at this time of year.'

Artie frowned in thought. The chalets were the only accommodation the camp had, all the others having been purpose built to entertain the campers in one way or another. They were in any case shut up for the winter and it would take a lot of work to turn even a section into accommodation for a night, so to Artie it seemed unlikely they could offer to shelter the vagrant if a chalet wasn't suitable. Then a worrying thought struck him. In her need to offer help, would Drina go so far as to offer the man shelter in their own home? Artie himself wouldn't hesitate to help anyone in need, but the little cottage he shared with Drina was his sanctuary and he drew the line at opening his home to a complete stranger, especially the sort

12

with a general reputation for untrustworthiness. But far worse to him than the thought of getting up tomorrow morning to find all his and Drina's valuables missing, was having to endure the stomach-churning stench that had issued from the tramp. Artie doubted a dozen baths would get rid of it or a dozen washes of his clothes . . . though whether his tattered rags would survive washing was debatable.

The trouble was, though, the depth of his own feeling for Drina rendered him incapable of refusing her anything she asked of him so if he himself couldn't think of anywhere to accommodate the tramp, and Drina couldn't either, Artie feared he was going to have to endure him as a house guest for tonight at least . . . and then he couldn't exactly see Drina turning the man out on Christmas Day! He just hoped that she was correct in her appraisal of the man, and he was the honest sort.

He'd steeled himself for her to ask him what he feared she was about to when out of the blue the perfect place to accommodate the tramp hit him and Artie jubilantly exclaimed: 'Donkey Sam's old hut! That would be perfect for him.'

At Artie's suggestion Drina's eyes lit up. 'Of course it would. I'd forgotten all about that old place since we managed to persuade Sam to move out of it into the new cottage we built for him nearer to the beach. While the renovations were being done on the old farmhouse site, I intended to ask the workers to pull it down but I'll hold off on that so I can offer our visitor the use of it over the winter. It will need patching up here and there – I'll get maintenance to see to that. The hut has everything in it he will need. There's plenty of wood to hand to keep the pot-bellied stove going and he can cook himself his meals on top of it. There's a tin bath he can wash in and he's water to hand from the standpipe we had laid for Sam. There's even a bed to sleep in, though I'll need to have the mattress replaced as I suspect the mice have made a good meal of it since Sam moved out. And being as the hut is tucked away out in the boundary woods, he can come as go about his business without anyone being aware of him, so his presence won't affect Jolly's in any way.'

Drina then flung her arms around Artie and gave him a quick hug, telling him, 'I shall rest easy tonight, knowing that poor man is not sleeping under a hedgerow. Come on, let's go and catch him up and tell him the good news. I only hope we can find him in this awful fog.'

They managed to catch up with the tramp as he was halfway up the old farm track heading for the country road at the end of it. To say he was utterly stunned by the offer of using the hut for as long as he wished, providing he kept himself inconspicuous and didn't do anything untoward that would warrant his expulsion, was putting it mildly. When Drina first put her offer to him, he thought it was some sort of malicious joke, definitely something with a catch to it, but finally she persuaded him her offer was a genuine one and his display of profound gratitude brought tears to her eyes.

Later that afternoon Artie arrived in the boss's office to find Drina sitting behind the large mahogany desk poring over a dozen or so application forms spread out before her. She was distractedly tapping the end of a Biro against her teeth.

He was loath to disturb her concentration but then it was Christmas Eve and he knew that if he didn't, she would be here for hours yet. 'Still hard at it, love? I thought you'd have called it a day by now, being as you've let all the other staff go home early. It's coming up for four.'

At the unexpected sound of his voice her head jerked up and she looked across at him, shocked. 'Is it? Goodness, I didn't realise it was that late. Did you dig out the box of decorations from the cupboard under the stairs?'

He nodded. 'Finally, after I'd almost emptied the cupboard out first, and then it took me ages to pile it all back in. I'm sure we don't need half the stuff that's in there. Anyway, then it took me ages to untangle the set of lights.' He went off at a tangent. 'When I put them away last Christmas, I wound them up very carefully so they'd unravel easy this year, yet they were a complete knotted mess. How did that happen, eh, when during that time they haven't been touched? And every year it's the same. It's like the odd sock mystery, isn't it? The way you never find out where the other one has gone. The lights are on the tree now and, thank God for small mercies, they work! Was everyone happy with the presents you bought them and with their Christmas bonuses?'

She smiled and nodded. 'Yes, very. Sandra cried, bless her. Miss Abbott, the owner of the employment agency where she worked before she came here, never even gave her a Christmas card, so she was just overwhelmed to be given a fiver and a gift box of Yardley's smellies. Jill, Eric and all the rest were very pleased with what they received too.'

Artie then fought to hold his tongue, as he was desperate to tell Drina that unknown to her the staff had all clubbed together to buy her a gift, which they had given to him that morning, asking him to put it under their tree for her to be surprised with on Christmas morning. Once she did receive it he knew she would be touched by their thanks to her for being such an appreciative boss to work for.

Drina was continuing: 'Harold and Eileen called in about an hour ago. It was so lovely to see them both. I told them they were bonkers to be journeying out here in this weather but they insisted they wanted to bring us a bottle for Christmas. They asked me to give you their best wishes. Harold told me that his new office is all set up now and ready to receive its first clients in the New Year. He didn't say as much but I know he's wondering if he made the right decision to leave us and start up his own accountancy business, so that he's not working such unsociable hours and can spend more time with Eileen now they're married. But I know he's going to be a great success, and he's already got Jolly's as clients so he's off

15

to a good start. Eileen too, I could tell, is loving her new role as housewife, caring for him, though she's still missing her job here and all her friends . . .' Drina stopped talking for a moment then laughed. 'So I told her that whenever she likes, she can come and do some ironing for us. They're both coming to lunch on Boxing Day along with Eric and Ginny.

'It's Eric's first Christmas of being a father and he's going all out to make it a treat for her. I know I keep saying it, but what a special man he is to take in his brother's illegitimate daughter, making out to her that he's her true father because his brother wanted nothing to do with her when he found out about her. Ginny will never discover the truth of the matter and learn just what Eric has done for her, but thankfully she's a lovely girl so his sacrifices are not at all in vain.' She then asked, 'Were there any telephone calls while you were at home?'

Artie shook his head. 'No.' Then he added knowingly, 'Rhonnie's obviously busy finishing last-minute jobs before she has a couple of days off for Christmas. She'll be thinking the same of you. You see, she'll call tonight when Danny's in bed so you can both have a proper chat and not be interrupted by work matters.'

Drina smiled wanly. 'Yes, you're right. I do want to know that's she got the parcel of presents in time as I'd hate to think Danny would have nothing to open from his granny and grandad on Christmas morning.' She then mused thoughtfully, 'It's strange we've not received a parcel from her. Oh, unless you found it on the doorstep when you went home to deal with the tree . . . or the postman delivered it while you were there?'

Artie shook his head. 'There was no post but that could mean the postman is still doing his deliveries and hasn't arrived at us yet. It'll be there when we get home, you'll see. My daughter won't have forgotten us.'

Drina smiled. 'No, I know she won't have. When I asked her a week or so ago what she had planned for her and Danny for Christmas Day, she told me she hadn't made definite plans.

I expect she'll spend the day making it as special as she can for Danny and maybe Jackie will pop over at some time, them two being such close friends, and other friends she's made while she's been living in Devon will probably call by. At least we both know Rhonnie's not on her own down there, especially at this time of year. I don't regret developing the Devon camp as it's proving a great success but I do wish it wasn't so far away, then we could have popped over tomorrow to see them.'

Artie gave a wistful smile. 'Yes, me too. I'm just glad, though, that she's making a life for herself and Danny after losing Dan. Look, once you've appointed the new manager here and got him or her settled in, we could go and visit Rhonnie for a few days.'

'Oh, yes, I'd like that.'

'Good. Then soon as we can, we'll load up the car and head off for Devon. Anyway, love, waiting for us at home is a blazing fire and I've made us some eggnog, with a good dollop of brandy in it, which might not be up to the standard you make but I've tasted it and it's not bad. I'm sure what you're doing now can wait until after Christmas, so what about us locking up and going home?'

She sighed. 'I've a job I need to do but don't want to do, if you understand me.'

He eyed the application forms for a moment before saying, 'Ah . . . finding a replacement for Harold.'

Drina nodded as she laid down the Biro, rose from her chair and went across to the large window behind her, which looked out over the courtyard. Not that she could see much further than a few feet, as the fog had hardly thinned at all since it had first rolled in earlier that morning. She said, 'I've been silly, trying to find myself another Harold when that will never happened as he . . . Oh!'

At her exclamation Artie himself exclaimed worriedly: 'What's the matter, Drina?'

17

She tutted. 'Oh, this damned fog really is playing tricks on my eyes today. It lifted for a moment and I could have sworn I saw a woman down below by the door to reception and she looked just like Rhonnie. Well, I know it can't be her as she's hundreds of miles away, and at this time on Christmas Eve it won't be anyone else coming here, so this time I'm definitely seeing things. I think next time we have a foggy day I'd be best staying in.' She turned back to face Artie. 'What was I saying . . . oh, yes. I've been trying to find a duplicate Harold for the manager's job, but he was unique so I'm not going to. I'll just have to hope that amongst the applicants is someone who possesses even half his qualities. Harold wasn't just a naturally kind and thoughtful man, he managed to get the best out of the staff, make them feel they were part of a team. He listened to them when they had problems and tried his best to resolve them, never telling them to put up and shut up.'

As she was describing Harold, Artie felt she could just as easily have been describing herself. That was just the way Drina treated the staff and why they liked working for her so much too.

'Do I possess any of those qualities as I wouldn't mind applying for the job?'

Artie and Drina both jumped and spun round to look across to the door at the sound of the unexpected voice. They both stared open-mouthed at the interloper for several long seconds before Drina, regaining her faculties first, joyously exclaimed: 'Rhonnie! It's really you. My eyes weren't playing tricks on me after all. It *was* you I saw down below a few moments ago.' Kicking up her heels, she dashed over to the young woman and seized her in a bear hug. 'Oh, love, it's so wonderful to see you, so very wonderful!' Then Artie was with them, encircling both the women he adored in his arms, too choked with emotion to speak.

It was Drina who pulled away from the embrace first to

look worriedly into Rhonnie's eyes, demanding, 'Where . . .'

Knowing what she was going to ask, Rhonnie cut in, 'You can come out now.' And at that a little boy jumped out from behind her, both hands raised in the air, shouting, 'Boo!'

Artie and Drina pretended to be shocked, crying, 'Oh, my goodness, what a scare you gave us!' Then Drina squatted down and took the child in her arms. Even at his young age he showed signs of becoming as tall and handsome as his father had been in adulthood. She systematically kissed both his cheeks over and over until, fed up, the eighteen month old put both hands on her shoulders to push her off, saying, 'Stop it, Branny.' He couldn't yet pronounced his 'Gs' and called Drina 'Branny' and Artie 'Branpap'.

She laughed and, getting up, told him, 'Okay, young man, for now I will, but I can't promise to hold off for long.' She then focused her attention on his mother and in a scolding tone began: 'This is the best Christmas present ever but why didn't you tell us you were coming so I could get everything ready for you?'

'Then it wouldn't have been a surprise, would it?' Rhonnie laughed. 'I drove halfway yesterday, stayed in a hotel over-night, and would have been here a couple of hours ago if we hadn't hit the fog when we arrived in Lincoln.'

'You're here safe and sound and that's all that matters.' Drina's brain then whirled into action. 'Right, Artie, we need to get cracking. We've got plenty of food, so that's no worry, but we've beds to make and a Christmas tree to decorate and a stocking to put up for Danny and . . .' She paused for a second and, looking worried, whispered to Rhonnie, 'I posted your presents . . .'

'It's all right, I received them two days ago. They're in the car. I didn't telephone to tell you as I was afraid I might spill the beans about us coming up and spoil the surprise.'

Drina looked mortally relieved. 'For an awful moment then I thought I was in for a mad dash about the shops before they shut tonight.' She clapped her hands in excitement and said, 'Let's get you both home and settled. I'll just be a few minutes tidying my desk so why don't you go on ahead and I'll see you all back home?' She fixed her eyes on Danny. 'We've got such a lot to do to get ready for Santa coming tonight and I'll need you to help me and Branpap.' Then a thought struck Drina and, taking hold of Rhonnie's arm, she pulled her aside. 'You were joking, asking if you'd the qualities I was looking for in a manager, weren't you, dear?'

Rhonnie took a deep breath before she solemnly replied, 'No, I wasn't.'

Drina looked quizzically for a moment at the tall, willowy twenty-seven year old, whose shoulder-length, honey-blonde hair framed a pretty heart-shaped face. Drina cared for her just as much as she would have done had Rhonnie been her own biological daughter. Then she affectionately patted the young woman's arm and spoke loud enough for Artie to hear. 'I could do with a medicinal tipple to help calm me after this wonderful surprise I've had, and I bet you could do with one too after your long journey, so will you join me? Artie, will you please take Danny home and feed and amuse him until we join you? Not too many mince pies or biscuits, though, as we don't want to spoil his appetite for his dinner.'

Artie looked from one woman to the other, wondering why all of a sudden the arrangements for going home had been changed. Then it struck him that Drina probably just wanted a quick catch up with Rhonnie over how the camp in Devon was doing before they put work aside to enjoy Christmas. He bent down and scooped Danny up into his arms, saying, 'Let us go and see what Granny has got in her pantry that a little boy would like to eat. I'll see you two in a bit,' he told Drina and Rhonnie as he left the office.

As soon as he had gone, Drina went over to the large drinks cabinet at the side of the office, opened up the doors and took out a half-empty bottle of Glenfiddich and two glasses, which she then took over to the guests' seating area with its two comfy sofas and a Long John coffee table. Putting the glasses and bottle of whisky on the table, she sat down on one of the sofas and poured them each a drink. Rhonnie sat down opposite and picked up her glass. Drina was very curious to learn just what had brought Rhonnie to drive hundreds of miles with her young son in such inclement weather. It obviously wasn't, as she had first thought, just to spend Christmas with them. Drina smiled encouragingly. 'Come on then, love, I'm listening.'

Rhonnie looked at her for a moment before she began speaking in a voice that was charged with emotion 'After Dan died, you and Dad took me down to Devon to stay in that cottage as you believed I was never going to come to terms with things while I was here, surrounded by memories of our life together. You were both absolutely right as getting away from here and not seeing a vision of Dan everywhere I looked, helped me . . . eventually . . . to accept that he was physically gone from me, and that for his son's sake I had to carry on and make a life for him . . . for us both.' She paused for a moment to take a sip of her drink, giving a little shudder as the alcohol hit the back of her throat, then continued, sounding a little brighter now. 'I was overwhelmed, to put it mildly, when you told me that the camp in Devon was mine. I know you'll argue that as Dan's wife I will eventually inherit all the business when . . .' She couldn't say the words because the thought of Drina no longer being here on earth was totally repellent to her. Ever since Dan had arrived in Drina's life, as a little boy, Drina had secretly wished that her own son had been more like him, instead of being the nasty, self-centred man he had turned out to be. On her husband's death, it had come as a shock to learn that Dan was Joe's illegitimate son from an affair he had had before he had married Drina and that Joe had made him his sole heir. At the time Dan had refused to accept Joe Jolly's wealth and business interests, as he felt that, rightfully, it should have all gone to Drina. He had left Drina with no choice but to accept his proposal that he sign over Joe's bequest to her on the understanding that when she was ready to retire Jolly's would be handed back to him and, on her death, he and his family would be her heirs. So, as Dan's widow, Rhonnie was Drina's beneficiary which suited Drina fine, as she looked on Rhonnie as the daughter she had never had. 'But anyway, you did it because . . . well, being responsible for the welfare of a business, its success and prospects, is all about looking to the future, and that was just what I needed at the time. Looking into the past was too painful.

'When you broke the news that as soon as the paperwork was signed and I took over the reins completely . . . not forgetting Jackie's contribution, I could never have managed without her by my side and the wonderful friend she is to me too . . . you and Dad would be moving back up here to Jolly's main camp, I was upset, of course I was, and I knew I'd miss you both dreadfully and so would Danny, but I appreciated that you wanted to go home once there was nothing to keep you down in Devon any longer. I didn't give myself time to miss you both as I continued to throw myself into my job and, with the nanny's help, look after Danny.'

Rhonnie paused to take another sip of her drink before she continued. 'It was the middle of September when it happened. I was making the daily inspection round. Everything was running smoothly apart from a couple of matters I needed to deal with back in the office and most of the guests were clearly enjoying themselves, although you always find those who make it their mission to find something to complain about, don't you?' she said, shooting a knowing glance at Drina. 'Anyway, I was making my way back from the cove where our private beach is, had just climbed up the steps in fact and was taking a breather on the cliff top looking around at the wonderful view, when heading towards me from the cliff-top walk came a young couple of around my age with a child a little older than Danny. They were holding a hand each and swinging him between them.

'I stood and watched them as they rounded the curve in the path that led back up to the main camp. I'd witnessed similar scenes many times since Dan died and why this time should be any different I don't know. Until then I'd always managed not to let it affect me but this time I couldn't help myself. It was me and Dan I was seeing, swinging our son between us on a day out having fun, as if I was reliving a memory. But then it struck me that this was not a memory of me and Dan with Danny and it never would be, as Dan died before his son was born. I burst into tears then, a great flood, like a dam bursting. Thankfully no one was around to see the state I was in or I'd have been mortified. I was finally allowing myself to grieve openly for Dan instead of putting up a barrier to avoid experiencing the physical pain I knew I would feel every time I thought of him. When I had finally cried myself out I realised that I didn't want to be distancing myself from the life I'd lived with Dan because memories of him weren't causing me pain anymore but instead giving a sort of comfort. I now wanted to go places that Dan and I had been to . . . sit on what had been our favourite spot on the beach; wander around the market; live in the cottage we once shared . . . feel his protective spirit around me. Am I making sense to you, Drina?'

A look of pure joy had settled over Drina's face. She leaned forward and laid one hand tenderly on Rhonnie's arm. 'Perfect sense. You're ready to come home, love.' It wasn't a question but a statement.

Rhonnie enthused, 'Oh, I am, and I want to so much! This *is* my home, Drina, where I belong. I enjoy being in Devon, setting up the camp and running it was so challenging and rewarding, but I have never felt at home there.'

Drina's face split into a huge happy smile. 'This is music

to my ears. I didn't dare to hope I would ever receive this news. I've missed you and Danny so very much too. Your father will be over the moon he's getting his daughter back close by him and his grandson too.'

Rhonnie was delighted by Drina's response but regardless was looking worried. 'The last thing I want you to feel is that I am ungrateful for what you did for me, buying the site to build the Devon camp on in the first place . . .'

Drina interjected with conviction. 'I bought the site as I saw its potential. It just so happened that was at the time when you needed to be away from here and have something to concentrate your mind on to help you heal, so it was a perfect marriage so to speak. But now that marriage is dissolved and we have to discuss how we proceed from here.'

A warm glow filled Rhonnie. Drina wasn't being truthful about her reasons for buying the Devon site and building the new camp on it. Rhonnie knew that very well, but she appreciated the way Drina was trying to save her from feeling any guilt about wanting to come home.

Drina asked, 'So when do you want to start?'

Rhonnie looked at her, taken aback. 'Start what?'

'Your new job here as manager, of course.'

Rhonnie gawped at her, utterly shocked. 'You're giving me the job! Just like that? You don't want to interview anyone else who might be better qualified?'

Drina laughed. 'And who else would I find better qualified than you? You know how this camp is run as well as I do. You've more than proved your worth with the success you've made of the Devon camp. The reason I felt free to return home and leave you to it was because you were managing with so little help from me, I was virtually twiddling my thumbs. Oh, this is such a relief to me, Rhonnie. I never thought I would find anyone to replace Harold but in you I have! This means I can make your dad happy, as with you on board I know I can safely take a back seat without any

24

worries and spend time with him doing all the things we want to before we get too old. This will mean I can give all my attention to the new caravan and tourers park, and when that's all done and dusted I will continue doing things in the background, looking at ways to make sure we keep up with the times and such like, but of course it goes without saying I will always be available to come in and help out whenever you need me to. So, it seems we do need to search for a new camp manager, but not for here . . . for the Devon camp.'

Rhonnie said, 'Well, we might not have to. Would you consider Jackie for the job? I know she's only young but she understands how the camp operates as well as we do, she's great with the guests and has the respect of the staff.'

Drina laughed. '*You* are the owner of the Devon camp, Rhonnie, so it's not whether I would consider Jackie for the manager's position but whether you feel that, despite her youth, she's up to the job. It seems you do. And if you're asking for my opinion on the matter, then yes, I think she'd be perfect. I've watched Jackie develop from a scatterbrained teenager into a very competent and considerate young woman. Harold too thinks very highly of her, and if we should ask his opinion on this I feel he wouldn't hesitate to agree with us that the camp would be as safe in her hands as it would in any more experienced manager's.'

Rhonnie looked pleased. 'That's settled then. I haven't mentioned my intention to move back home to her as I obviously wanted your reaction first. I know she'll be upset at the news. But then, nothing gets past Jackie so it wouldn't surprise me if she's already guessed what's on my mind. I doubt, though, that she has any idea she's number-one choice to replace me. It's not often Jackie is struck speechless but I know she will be when I tell her. I've a feeling, too, that if I ask her, Danny's nanny Carrie will move up here with us, as she's loved looking after him. She doesn't get on very well with her parents, hasn't got a boyfriend, so there's nothing keeping her in Devon. I hope she decides to move up with us as she a lovely girl and I can trust her completely with him.'

Drina downed the remains of her drink, topped up Rhonnie's glass and poured herself another, then raised her glass in the air. 'Welcome back home, Rhonnie.'

Rhonnie raised hers and they clinked them together. 'It's wonderful to be here.'

Drina told her, 'Your cottage has been lying empty for over two years so it will need a good clean out but in the meantime you can both stay with us. And workwise, I'll warn you now, you're going to be thrown in at the deep end as several key members of staff need to be recruited before the new season starts . . . amongst them cleaning supervisor and entertainments manager . . . so as soon as you've sorted out matters in Devon, it will be full steam ahead. But first things first, Rhonnie dear. We'll forget all about work and have ourselves a wonderful Christmas!'

Later that evening, warmed by the fire blazing inside the pot-bellied stove and feeling full after a dinner of jacket potatoes he'd bought with the few pennies Artie had given him earlier, Ben Nicholson leaned back in an old sagging armchair and looked around his new abode. At this moment in time he felt like the luckiest man alive. He was allowed to make himself at home in this ramshackle old hut for as long as he liked, without living in fear that at any time the door would burst open and he could be threatened with a blast of shotgun pellets or with being shredded to pieces by a couple of ferocious-looking hunting dogs unless he immediately skedaddled. That or return from a foraging trip to find his belongings, such as they were, reduced to a pile of cinders and the door to the outbuilding or hut where he had taken up residence boarded up against him, no matter that the dwelling in question was unfit for animals to shelter in, let alone a human being.

The owner of this hut belonged to the small minority of people who didn't see him as part of a scourge on society, an object of automatic scorn and mistrust, but simply as a person in desperate need. Out of compassion she had given him the means to make his miserable life just a little more bearable. He certainly owed Drina Jolly a great debt of gratitude for her benevolence when, as the owner of the holiday camp, a woman in her position could so easily have turned her back on him and walked away, but whether he would ever be able to repay that debt he did not know. Regardless, from the short time he had spent with Drina, she hadn't come across to him as the sort of woman who expected any repayment for her benevolence other than the heartfelt thank you he had given her, which was a rare thing in his experience over recent years.

He did wonder though if Drina Jolly . . . Drina, that was a name he'd never come across before and he wondered about her origins. Hungarian, Romanian, somewhere around there, as she did have the look of a gypsy about her . . . would have shown him such generosity had she known that he wasn't, as she might have automatically thought, just a man who had fallen on hard times through one reason or another but because he was a killer and it wasn't just one man whose life he'd extinguished but five who were rotting six feet under because of him.

CHAPTER TWO

'Morning, Jill, Sandra. How are you both today?' Rhonnie asked breezily. Having heard Jill arrive in the general office, she had come out of her own to greet her with the correspondence file in her hand. Inside it were a dozen or so letters that Jill had typed out yesterday that Rhonnie had now signed ready to be posted.

'Morning, Rhonnie,' Sandra Watson, an unremarkable, mousy-haired and chubby sixteen year old, responded before Jill could. She flicked switches on the PBX switchboard on her desk to take it off night service, then proceeded to remove the cover from her Olivetti electric typewriter ready to start work.

Across the room from Sandra, Office Manager Jill Clayton was standing behind her desk, staring down at it with a quizzical expression on her face. Jill was an attractive young woman, at twenty-nine a couple of years older than Rhonnie, her shoulder-length brunette hair tied back at the nape of her neck. She was wearing a long-sleeved pink angora jumper and a pleated black and white tweed skirt, finishing just above her knees, with chunky-heeled black shoes on her feet.

'Is anything wrong?' Rhonnie asked. When the woman still didn't answer her, she prompted her again. 'Jill, what's the matter?'

'Eh? Oh, sorry, Rhonnie. It's just that we all left together last night but I have this feeling someone has been sitting at my desk. I always tidy it up last thing as you know but my typewriter is not in the same position as it usually is, it's been pushed further back, and my notepad is to the side of it and not in front. I always leave a pencil wedged inside the spiral top, ready for use, which I know I did last night, but now the pencil is in the holder with the other pens and pencils. The last thing I usually do is to push my chair right inside the well in my desk but now it's halfway out.'

Rhonnie looked unconcerned. 'We were busy yesterday and late finishing. I remember reminding you that you'd better get a move on packing away for the night or you'd risk missing your bus. Apart from things not being in the place you usually leave them, is anything missing?'

Jill took a look around the office and then shook her head. 'Everything seems to be here. What about you, Sandra?'

The teenager was in the middle of changing her typewriter ribbon and hadn't been listening to the conversation between her two superiors. She looked across at them both, nonplussed. 'Eh? What about me?'

Rhonnie thought Sandra a nice young girl but she had none of her predecessor Jackie's drive to better herself, coupled with an unfailing willingness to use her own initiative, natural inquisitiveness and confidence – qualities that had seen Jackie rise from office junior to manager of the Devon holiday camp within a matter of a few short years. Sandra did not have these advantages, but then she had a pleasant personality, was an accurate typist, albeit a little slow, had a good telephone manner and could be trusted to be left to man the office alone if her superiors had to be elsewhere.

'Anything different about your desk this morning from how you left it last night? Or does anything seem to be missing from it?' Rhonnie asked her.

Sandra glanced over it before responding. 'No, I don't think so.' But then just where she had put everything when she had tidied her desk last night wasn't something she would remember when she had more important things on her mind: such as, the next time she went dancing, would she finally meet a boy who'd want her to be his girlfriend for longer than a few dances and quick kiss and cuddle up an alleyway?

Rhonnie said, 'And nothing has been touched in my office, to my knowledge . . . mind you, I'm not quite as diligent as you are over leaving everything in a certain place. I don't think we've been burgled, though. Maybe you just didn't put everything away as you usually do last night, Jill, and it's as simple as that.'

Rhonnie had to be right, Jill thought. But regardless, no matter how close she was to missing her bus home, right from leaving college with her secretarial qualifications and starting her first job, leaving her desk at night with everything in place ready for her to start work next morning had been a compulsion of hers . . . She smiled at Rhonnie. 'You're right, I must have had an off night last night. I'll deal with the correspondence file for you and then I'll make us all a cup of tea,' she said, taking the file off Rhonnie.

'I'll make the tea as I know you have your hands full today dealing with that pile of bookings the postie bought us yesterday after our newspaper advertising campaign last week. As soon as I've finished a couple of jobs I need to do, I'll come and give you a hand,' Rhonnie told her.

Jill smiled gratefully at her boss. Checking dates requested by potential campers against chalet availability was a time-consuming and somewhat laborious task. It was far easier when two people were tackling it than one on their own and she was extremely grateful for Rhonnie's help. When she'd been informed by Drina on her return to work after Christmas that Rhonnie would be taking up the position of manager, Jill had been a mite worried. Having a woman for a boss or one who was younger than herself was immaterial to Jill. That she was personable and considerate to work for, mattered a lot. It was important to Jill that she enjoyed her work and liked and got on well with the people around her. She considered herself to have been spoiled, having worked for a gentleman like Harold Rose, and didn't think she'd be so lucky again. Her worries were unfounded, though. On being introduced the two women had immediately struck up a good rapport. Rhonnie knew that in Jill she had an office manager she could trust and rely on, and on the personal front found Jill a very nice woman and one she felt she could grow to be friends with. Jill immediately recognised that Rhonnie possessed the same qualities as Harold and concluded that she had struck lucky for a second time in finding a boss who would appreciate the work she did for them as well as one who could be a personal friend once they got to know each other better.

As Rhonnie went off to make the tea, Jill remembered something she wanted to ask her. 'Oh, Rhonnie, Martin announced to me last night that he has invited his boss and a few colleagues over for dinner on Saturday evening. Typical of my husband, not asking me first. Anyway, I had a fondue set for Christmas and I'm dying to try it out so I thought for starters I'd do a cheese fondue with crusty bread. For mains, Coronation chicken, and Black Forest gateau for sweet.' She laughed. 'I'll buy that, though, as my baking skills leave a lot to be desired. I made a cake once that came out so hard it would have made a good house brick! But I wondered if you'd like to come, if you're free and can get a babysitter for your son?'

Rhonnie laughed. 'Getting a babysitter for my son is never going to be a problem while my dad and Drina are still living and breathing. They'd drop whatever plans they had to look after their grandchild.' She paused and eyed Jill shrewdly. 'Drina has told me about your penchant for matchmaking. It was your plan to get Eileen and Harold together, wasn't it? Thank heavens you rescued him from that awful woman Marion, who saw him as nothing more than a meal ticket and

31

would have made his life a misery. But please don't be offended when I ask: you're not trying to match me with one of your husband's work colleagues, are you, and that's why you're inviting me to dinner?'

Jill shrugged this off. 'I'm inviting you to dinner because I like your company. But if a nice-looking chap happens to catch your eye at the party, and you his, and you chat a bit and realise you like each other enough to make a date, then that would be nothing to do with me, would it? Let me know by Friday if you will be coming or not so I know how many I'm cooking for. It should be fun so I hope you'll make it.' She looked across at Sandra. 'Don't be offended by my not inviting you too but I wouldn't have thought a dinner party was your idea of fun.'

Sandra gave a sigh of relief. Sitting amongst people the age of Jill and Rhonnie, trying to mind her Ps and Qs at the same time as using the right knife and fork, plus being expected to chip in now again on topics of conversation she hadn't a clue about as well as not clumsily knocking anything over, would be pure purgatory to Sandra. Tactlessly, she blurted out: 'No, it wouldn't be, definitely not. Thanks for not asking me.'

Rhonnie and Jill looked at each other, both fighting not to laugh.

A while later they were standing before a huge board that ran down one side of the office. It was covered with a chart sectioned off to show every one of the three thousand chalets they had against the weeks of the coming season. They had just finished updating this with the new bookings they had received.

As she scanned her eyes over the chart Rhonnie was looking pleased. 'Well, except for a hundred or so availabilities, that's June and July fully booked already and August looks set to be full soon if bookings continue to roll in as thick and fast as they are. April, May, September and October . . . we need a few more bookings to reach the seventy per cent occupancy target that we're happy with out of high season, but it's still early days yet. Plenty of time for us to achieve that . . . hopefully the nationwide advertising campaign running in the newspapers next week will help.'

Jill nodded. 'If I remember right, this time last year Harold was nervous that April and May weren't looking promising, but a surge of last-minute bookings arrived and put a smile on his face.'

Both of them spun around then to look across at the outer door as it burst open. Sandra too stopped typing out envelopes as a very excited-looking Drina announced, 'Right, ladies, down tools. Sandra, put the switchboard on night service, get your coats on and come with me.'

'Where are we going?' Rhonnie asked the question the other two were desperate to voice.

Drina flashed her a secretive smile. 'The sooner you do as I ask, the sooner you'll find out.'

It was a cold and blustery early-March day. Huddled in their coats, gloved hands stuffed deep inside their pockets, woollen scarves wrapped around their necks, the three women followed Drina. It soon became apparent they were heading for the place where the old farmhouse once stood. As they drew closer the sound of engines could be heard, getting louder the nearer they came.

They'd travelled the path that rounded the large staff chalet complex, which was surrounded by high hedges. Some distance behind it rose a temporary eight-foot-high wire fence. Through this they could all see a fleet of a dozen or so flatbed lorries travelling slowly down the now widened and surfaced farm track, each loaded with a caravan. They were heading towards the area of land that the old farmhouse and its outbuildings had stood on, now transformed into rows of concreted pitches – enough of them to accommodate two hundred and fifty, four-, six- and eight-berth static caravans, with uniform grassed-over spaces between each block of fifty.

Armed with a clipboard, Artie was marshalling the lorries to their respective pitches. Several men wearing boiler suits and holding toolboxes were milling around, waiting for caravans to be offloaded so they could begin securing them and then connect them to the water and electric supply.

As they stood against the fence, looking through it to the scene of activity beyond, Drina said, 'I thought you'd all like to witness the arrival of our first caravans. We're starting with two hundred and fifty statics and if they prove popular then we'll add more pitches. It's very exciting, isn't it?'

They all agreed it certainly was.

Her face pressed against the fence, Sandra said, 'I stayed in a caravan once with my mam and dad and my two sisters and brother, on a site near Skeggy on the coast. It was god-awful! The caravan was small and damp and we were all squashed inside it like sardines. There was no water and each day we had to fetch our own from a standpipe on the site. The toilets were in a wooden block about ten minutes' walk from where our caravan was, so you had to know you wanted the toilet before you did, if you understand me, or you'd wet yourself before you got there . . . and when you did arrive they were usually all in use.'

'These caravans are a bit more upmarket, Sandra,' Drina told her. 'They will all be connected to the electricity and water supply, have a sink, Calor gas cooker and fridge, even a gas fire to heat the caravan if the evenings get chilly. And there will be plenty of toilet facilities and showers as we are having five separate blocks built, so people won't have that long to wait to use them during busy times.' She pointed down towards the sea, which from a distance could be seen as a greyish-looking strip spanning the horizon. 'That's the area down there where the tourers will go. There's room for about five hundred altogether. Let's hope I'm not being too optimistic in hoping we'll be turning customers away when we're full in high season.'

Rhonnie of course knew all of this as since her return Drina had kept her fully in the picture over the new development. So it was Jill and Sandra who asked all the questions.

'What are tourers?' Sandra asked, screwing up her face as if she though they might be a nasty disease or something equally as bad.

'Well, it's self-explanatory really, dear. It's what we call caravans that are towed around by their owners' own vehicles. They can go from site to site, wherever the owners fancy going in fact. Static caravans are permanently fixed to bases on a site and they're the ones that are connected to the water and electric supply, whereas the tourers aren't.'

Sandra was looking thoughtful. 'So a tourer is like a snail, lugging its own house around with it wherever it goes?'

The other three women chuckled. 'That's exactly it,' Rhonnie told her.

Jill asked Drina: 'The people who stay in the static caravans or bring their tourers, will they get to use the main camp facilities?'

'For a daily fee, if they wish to. We are going to introduce a wristband system. One colour will be worn by the main-camp campers and another by the caravan-park campers, so the staff can tell the difference. Those caught not wearing a band will be asked either to pay for their use of the main camp facilities at reception or else to leave immediately.'

'I can't deny it's one great idea of yours to expand the business this way,' Rhonnie told her.

'Oh, I can't take all the credit for it. A great idea is always sparked by something or someone and it was you who sparked this one for me.'

Rhonnie looked taken aback. 'I did?'

'We were driving back to our rented cottage from a meeting with the builders after finalising details for the new Devon camp. The country roads there are hardly wide enough to accommodate one car as you know, and we came face to face

35

with another pulling a caravan. Well, obviously it was easier for me to back up to a passing place than it was for the car with the caravan. I'd not long passed my test so was far from an expert at reversing and kept steering straight into the hedge, which we both found very funny. For me at the time it was a joy to hear you laughing as it was very seldom if ever you found anything to laugh about then. Anyway, eventually I backed into a passing place and as the caravan drove by us you commented on how liberating it must be for those people, to be able to park up wherever took their fancy, have the freedom to explore their surroundings at their leisure and still be able to cook food on their own cooker and sleep in their own bed at whatever time they wanted to.

'It happened just while I was wracking my brains, wondering what to do with the land the old farmhouse occupied. I remembered what you'd said and I thought: why not create a place where people can bring their camper vans . . . tourers too . . . and stay for as short or long a time as they wished? The idea of having static caravans too quickly followed. Thankfully, the bank thought my idea a good one and loaned me the money I needed to get the site up and running.' Drina paused for a moment to smile tenderly at Rhonnie. 'So you see, my dear, it's you I need to thank for being the instigator of Jolly's camp expansion. Now all we need to do is get the right people to run it. We've the interviews for the manager's job next week, so let's hope all those we've invited turn up so we have a good choice.' She gave a shudder. 'Goodness me, this wind is chilly. I expect you could all do with a hot drink now to warm you up, so let's get back to the office and I'll do the honours.'

CHAPTER THREE

Drina looked at Rhonnie, sitting beside her at the desk in the boss's office, and asked, 'Are you ready then?'

Squaring the couple of sheets of paper on which were typed a list of questions to ask candidates for the caravan park manager's job, she responded, 'Absolutely. Let's hope the perfect candidate for the job is sitting down in reception as we speak and we don't have to go through this process all over again.'

Drina smiled. 'I agree.' She picked up the telephone receiver and dialled '0' for the switchboard. When Sandra answered Drina asked, 'Could you please call down to reception and ask Molly to send up the first candidate, a Mr Billings? When he arrives in the office show him straight in here. Thank you, Sandra.'

From inside the boss's office Rhonnie and Drina both heard Sandra talking into the telephone. Seconds later she appeared in the doorway but there was no one with her.

'Sandra, you're supposed to be waiting for Mr Billings at the top of the stairs to escort him in here.'

'Yes, I know, but Molly's asked me to tell you that there's no Mr Billings waiting to be interviewed down in reception.'

Drina looked disappointed. 'Oh, he hasn't shown up. All right, please telephone down again and asked her to send up—' she paused while she looked down her list of interviewees '—Mr Watson.'

Sandra left and moments later returned. 'There's no Mr Watson waiting to see you either. Molly told me to tell you that's there's only a Mr Sampson down there.'

Drina and Rhonnie looked at each other.

'That's odd,' said Drina. 'Only one candidate out of the eight we invited has turned up?' She looked at Sandra. 'The letters inviting the applicants here were given to the postman when he called to collect the post?'

She nodded. 'I stuck the stamps on and gave them to him myself along with the other stuff to be posted that evening.'

Drina turned back to Rhonnie. 'It's usual for a couple of candidates to drop out for one reason or another, but seven! And not one of them with the courtesy either to write or telephone to tell us they wouldn't be showing up either. How rude.'

Rhonnie said, 'Well, at least this Mr Sampson bothered to turn up.'

Drina sighed. 'That's something, I suppose. But what are the chances of him being just what we are looking for?' She addressed Sandra, 'Would you ask Molly to send him up, please.'

Thirty-three-year-old Jeffrey Sampson was just under six foot tall, ruggedly handsome, with a head of thick dark blond hair which he wore fashionably shoulder-length. He was wearing tight-fitting red, green and black striped flared trousers, a black polo-necked jumper, and a black three-quarter-length dark blue topcoat with a vented back and narrow lapels. He strongly reminded Rhonnie of Justin Hayward, the singer with the Moody Blues, for whom she couldn't deny she had a fancy. In fact for a split second she actually thought it *was* him, albeit this man was older than Justin, and had to force herself to close her mouth quickly as her jaw had dropped open in surprise.

Jeff breezed confidently in to the office, smiling broadly, and as he arrived at the desk he leaned over it, his hand outstretched, offering it first to Drina . . . from respect for her as the older of the two women . . . then to Rhonnie. They politely returned the greeting, and he said he was pleased to meet them both. Before he was asked to take a seat he sat down, crossed his legs and reclined in his chair. He launched into speech before they could pose any of their carefully worked out questions.

'Fabulous camp you have here, ladies. I arrived a little early for my interview so had a look around. As you'll see from my credentials it's small camps I've worked for previously, with none of the facilities this one offers, just a club house in a wooden hut and a few swings for the kids, but if it's experience you're after and someone to run a tight ship, then I'm your man.' He looked at them both expectantly. 'I was really excited when I saw your advert for someone to run the new park. Chances like this don't come along very often as usually the owner does it himself, so this is a great opportunity for me. I've worked on sites around the south coast, Southend and Eastbourne mainly, since I left school, worked my way up to be the boss's right hand . . . actually take charge when he has a day off or a holiday. You'll see from my references that the owners I've worked for thought well of me.

'There's nothing I don't know about vans and fixing them if anything goes wrong. In this line of work you have to be prepared to be knocked up in the middle of the night to replace a gas cylinder if a camper wants to make themselves a cuppa and the gas has run out, or let someone in who's lost their keys or just had a few too many and can't remember the van they're staying in. I can handle myself when the occasional fracas breaks out with neighbours not seeing eye to eye. You do get people sometimes who are inconsiderate to others. I'm free and single so have no ties and I can start whenever you want me to.' He paused for a moment and shot a charismatic smile at them both before continuing. 'Anything else you'd like to know about me?'

Drina and Rhonnie looked at each other, obviously thinking

the same thing. Jeff Sampson had seemed to have pre-empted all the questions on their list.

Drina told him, 'I think you've covered everything, Mr Sampson. I expect there are a few things you'd like to know about the job from us.' She proceeded to inform him that it would start in two weeks' time at the beginning of the season and would end in October. An assistant would be employed to work alongside the manager. A caravan was provided as living accommodation, with one for the assistant too. It was a six-and-a-half-day working week, with the free half-day to be taken during the week but not at weekends and never at the same time as the assistant. Then wages and rules and regulations were all relayed to him too.

Jeff Sampson let it be known that he was happy with what Jolly's were offering and would certainly accept the job if it were offered him. Drina then thanked him for coming to the interview and said they would let him know if he'd been successful or not by post by the end of the week.

Sandra was called to show him out.

After the office door was shut behind them, Drina leaned back in her chair, clasped her hands in her lap and asked Rhonnie, 'What did you think of Mr Sampson?'

'He's fond of himself, that was glaringly apparent, and he certainly knows how to use his charm. But he seemed competent enough.'

Drina looked at her with a twinkle of amusement in her eyes. 'He charmed you, did he?'

Rhonnie wanted to deny this but thought better of it. 'A little, I'll admit.'

Drina laughed. 'He charmed me too. I'm not too long in the tooth to appreciate a good-looking man when I see one.'

'Me neither, but looking is as far as it goes with me. I'm nowhere near enough over Dan to be considering another man in my life, and especially not the *big I am* he comes across as being.'

Drina patted her hand. 'One day you will be, love.'

Rhonnie heaved a sigh. 'Yes, one day, maybe.' This conversation was starting to upset her. She knew that Dan would not have wanted her to mourn his loss forever but to find someone to make her happy again, be a good father to his son. At the moment, however, she was far from ready to do anything more than admire a man from a distance. Wanting to change the subject, she said to Drina, 'His references are certainly glowing.'

'Yes, they are. And he made it clear he wants the job. So he's top choice for the position at the moment, do we agree?'

Rhonnie chuckled. 'Drina, he's the only choice if no one else has turned up to be interviewed.'

Drina laughed too. 'Oh, yes, of course. But one of the other applicants might have done since we last checked.' She picked up the telephone receiver and dialled down to reception, spoke into it for a moment then replaced it, shaking her head at Rhonnie. 'No one else has shown.' She frowned in thought. 'So our next decision is, do we advertise again and hope others apply and actually turn up for interview this time, or do we think we'd do better to appoint Mr Sampson?'

Rhonnie frowned in thought as she glanced over his application form and references again. Eventually she said, 'I think we'd be hard pressed to get someone with more experience than he has and such good references.'

'Then that's settled. I'll dictate a letter to Jill offering him the job.' Drina clapped her hands excitedly like a naughty schoolgirl planning to play truant from school. 'Right, this means that we've the rest of the morning free, so how about collecting Danny from Carrie and taking him out to the park? Let's have some fun with him for a couple of hours.'

Rhonnie didn't need any persuading.

Out on the main road, Jeff Sampson parked his seven-year-old Rover 3-litre just past the newly widened and surfaced old farmhouse track, on one side of him a strip of dense woodland, on the other a high strong wire fence splitting the caravan park from the main one. He walked the half-mile down to the park entrance. Above his head was a large metal arch painted red, with metal letters spelling out 'Welcome to Jolly's Holiday Park'. Just through the archway was a small single-storey red-brick building with a sign on it indicating it was the park's reception area. To one side of the office building the boundary woods began. A sturdy wire fence had been erected in front of these and ran all the way down to the sand dunes, to prevent children wandering into the trees and either getting lost or coming to other sorts of harm.

Jeff walked under the arch and a little way further down to where the woods veered off sharply to the right and the area widened out. From where he was standing he could see workmen securing the last of the static caravans to their bases. Several gardeners were filling newly dug beds in grassy areas with shrubs and annual flowering plants. There was a children's play area and a communal area of wooden picnic tables and benches. It wasn't possible from his position to view much more but it did appear that Jolly's owner had put a lot of thought into the layout of the camp, intending it to be both functional yet inviting for those holidaying. At his interview Mrs Jolly had shown him a map of the layout of the park so he knew that further down the gently sloping landscape were the camp supermarket, shower and toilet blocks, and the rest of the land beside the dunes about half a mile away was intended for the tourers.

He took a deep breath and slowly exhaled. He'd gone to a lot of trouble to get this job and from what he could tell up to now the trouble had all been worth it. This job would afford him a way to acquire himself the means to buy some land and open up his own caravan park, somewhere on the coast like this one was, be his own boss, the profits going straight into his pocket instead of him running himself ragged funding someone else's comfortable lifestyle. Jeff was not at all a religious man but he silently offered up a prayer that he'd done enough to land himself the manager's job that would set him on the road to a far more prosperous existence than he led now.

CHAPTER FOUR

Joan Travers looked enviously on at the crowd of young men and women, dressed in colourful bathing costumes, teeny bikinis and swimming trunks, enjoying themselves in and around the outdoor pool. The late-May sun wasn't quite warm enough for her to be wearing such scanty clothing herself but nevertheless she would have walked on hot coals to be one of that group, seemingly without a care in the world as their regimented lives back in their home town and cities was forgotten and all that mattered was how much fun they could cram into their time at the camp.

For a moment, in her mind, she was transported into the middle of the throng. She was dressed in a red polka-dot bikini, her long dark hair flowing free, and was playing a game with a ball partnered by a good-looking man along with another couple. Her partner then scooped her up and swung her around and was just about to kiss her before putting her back down, his reward to her for aiming a good shot, when her dream was shattered by a voice snapping at her.

'Get a move on or we'll miss the start of the film and Nellie and Hilda will be waiting for us. I told them we'd meet them at a quarter to eleven and it's now ten to.'

Twenty-seven-year-old Joan gave herself a shake and apologised to the woman in the wheelchair in front of her. 'I'm sorry, Mother, I . . . er . . . had a stone in my . . .'

Cara Travers cut her short. 'Then hurry up and remove it! I want to see all the film, not half of it.'

Gripping the handles of the wheelchair, Joan shut her eyes and took a deep breath, forcing away a surge of deep resentment. Her mother's illness prevented Joan from having a life of her own as she must instead do all the things her mother couldn't do for herself, which was virtually everything. She felt sorry for her mother for having her life so cruelly turned upside down when an illness struck her without warning. Once an agile woman who had run her own very successful haberdasher's business as well as raising her only child after her husband had died when Joan had been two, Cara was now unable to walk any further than very short distances and suffered constant pain. Her life expectancy had been severely curtailed also – and all at just the time Joan was leaving school and about to make her own way in the world, having won a place at a university in another town, where she'd planned to study English before going on to teach it.

Her disappointment at having her own plans for the future dashed caused her untold grief but it wasn't in Joan's nature to walk away from her responsibilities and abandon the woman who had given birth to her. So since the illness had struck her mother it had been Joan who had run the shop under her mother's watchful eye, and it was Joan who looked after their home as well as seeing to all her mother's personal needs and taking her out to all the social events she wished to attend, it being important to Joan that her mother's final days were as comfortable and happy as she could make them for her.

Caring for her mother meant that Joan had no time for a social life of her own; the only time Cara accepted the offers of friends or neighbours to sit with her was for short spells while Joan saw to the shopping or visited the library to change their books, as Cara insisted she couldn't bear the embarrassment of anyone else but Joan seeing to her intimate needs, which Joan could appreciate as she would feel exactly the same herself.

Her day-to-day life was mundane to say the least, so it came as a great excitement to Joan when in the middle of February Cara announced they were going to take a holiday in May. They had been on holidays before, all of them coach trips to seaside towns, staying in old-fashioned hotels. Joan would be the only young woman amongst a group of middle-aged and elderly people. It was absolutely no fun at all for her, pushing her mother up and down the front, along the pier and around the shops during the day, watching old-time variety shows in the evening or sitting in the hotel lounge with some of the others in the group, listening to talk she had no interest in or watching them play cards. The only consolation was that her mother enjoyed herself.

But this holiday was to be different from all the others. They were going to a holiday camp with a group of other spinsters or widows, women her mother's age, from around their area. Joan had seen advertisements for these camps and heard talk of them through some of their customers who had holidayed at one and they sounded wonderful places with so much going on from morning until night to keep the guests entertained. Joan was hopeful that some of the facilities offered would keep her mother occupied long enough for Joan to be able to slip away and have some time to herself – just an hour or two away from her mother's constant demands on her, to spend as she pleased, would be like finding a pot of gold at the end of a rainbow. But it seemed as if that precious time to herself wasn't going to happen. Just the same as at home, her mother expected Joan to be at her side every minute of her waking hours. As soon as they arrived, with the aid of the entertainments pamphlet given to them by the receptionist upon booking in, Cara had the week's activities planned out for them both. After breakfast they would attend the morning matinee at the cinema to watch the daily showing of a vintage film. After dinner Joan would take her to an event taking place around the camp, Cara insisting her daughter should stay by her side in case an emergency arose, then at four o'clock they'd watch the dancers at the tea dance in the Paradise Ballroom, and after their evening meal and assisting Cara to change into evening wear, Joan would wheel her to the campers' lounges where the girl would be expected to join in the playing of endless games of whist, cribbage or backgammon.

As matters stood this holiday was turning out to be as tedious to Joan as all the others had been, but her mother was a sick woman and Joan herself couldn't imagine what it must be like for her not only to be unable to walk, but with her weakening muscles prohibiting her from doing all manner of simple day-to-day activities a person would normally take for granted. A time would come in the future when Joan would have the freedom to do what she pleased, when she pleased, but until it came it would be unforgivably selfish of her to begrudge her mother doing whatever made her happy.

What would make her mother happy now was forgetting her problems for a while while she lost herself in a film.

As Joan pushed her past the pool and on towards the main courtyard where the cinema building was situated next to the Paradise, she was totally unaware that she was being closely observed.

On the way back from her morning inspection round, taking a detour to check that a hole in the putting green had been cleaned out, as it had been reported that someone had decided to use it as a receptacle to vomit into the previous night, Rhonnie had caught sight of a young woman pushing an older one in a wheelchair. There was nothing unusual about that. Many people who holidayed at the camp were not able bodied. It was the look on the young woman's face as she stared over at the group of men and women having fun around the pool that had caught Rhonnie's watchful eye.

If ever she had seen an expression of longing on anyone's face, then it was blazing like a beacon off that young woman's.

Rhonnie's ultimate job was to make sure that campers left at the end of their stay feeling they could have had no better time. Judging by that young woman's face it was not going to be the case for her. Being as astute as she was, Rhonnie immediately knew the reason why. The person she was pushing in the chair was obviously not able enough to fend for herself in any way and needed a constant companion, meaning that the young woman had no time for any enjoyment of her own. But everyone deserved a little fun now and again. Rhonnie smiled to herself. She was going to see to it that the young girl got a break.

To help her achieve that Rhonnie would need the help of Alan Ibbotson. He was a rotund middle-aged man with a jolly disposition, who had worked behind the scenes in theatres all his working life and was the unanimous choice of Drina and Rhonnie to replace Patsy Mathers as entertainments manager. She had left at the end of last season to get married and help her new husband, met while he too was working at Jolly's, in running a country pub. So far Alan was proving to be a major asset to the camp. He was as much liked and respected by the staff under his charge as Patsy had been, and like her never stopped looking for ways to improve the quality of the entertainment they gave the campers.

Rhonnie was just about to make her way to Alan's small office in the Paradise foyer when the sound of shoes pounding on tarmac made her turn around to see a Stripey, as all the entertainments assistants were known thanks to their striped blazers, heading towards her at speed.

Obviously something was amiss and she put up her hand to stop him as he raced past and asked, 'What's happened, Brian?

He breathlessly responded, 'Oh, sorry, didn't see you there, Mrs Buckland. A woman's got stuck on the Helter-skelter. I've been sent to fetch the nurse.'

'Is the woman hurt?'

He shook his head. 'No, just stuck.'

'Thank goodness for that. Not that being stuck isn't bad enough. But how on earth has she got stuck there? On the stairs going up, got her foot stuck or something like that?'

'No, she's stuck on the slide. Wedged as tight as a cork in a bottle.'

Rhonnie frowned in confusion. 'But I don't see how she could be. The slide part of the Skelter is wide . . .'

'So's she.'

'What?'

'The woman. She's really wide. Huge, in fact. Well, her bottom half is. I've never seen a woman with a bum as big as hers. I think it'll take a crane to shift her.'

Rhonnie stared at him. Surely he had to be exaggerating the size of the woman's backside. Regardless, she couldn't see how the nurse would be of any use in this situation if the woman wasn't hurt. Rhonnie needed to go and assess matters for herself and decide how best to solve the problem. She told Brian to come with her and they set off at a run down the path towards the funfair by the beach.

As usual in circumstances such as this, a noisy throng of spectators had gathered round to watch. Rhonnie saw the woman was stuck on the slide about a quarter of the way down. Due to the side barriers of the chute Rhonnie could only see the trapped woman's head and shoulders and she did indeed seem to be well-made. Regardless of her situation, the woman seemed to be finding the impasse very funny. She was laughing hard and bantering humorously with the crowd below.

Rhonnie turned to address Brian. 'Did you get to her on the slide and try and give her a push from the back, to dislodge her?'

He nodded. 'She didn't budge an inch. I tried to with my hands on her back first and when that didn't work I tried with my feet and shoved as hard as I could, but that did nothing either. She might think it funny . . . she was laughing so hard I couldn't understand what she was saying to me . . . but it ain't funny for us trying to get her off there without damaging either her or the Skelter. So how are we going to manage it?'

Rhonnie frowned in thought. The obvious thing would be for maintenance to take out the section of the side barrier the woman was stuck against, but once it was removed, with nothing to stop her, the woman could topple over the side and come to harm when she hit the ground below. It seemed to Rhonnie that this was probably a job for the fire brigade. Before she called them out, though, she decided to go up and assess the situation at first hand.

Telling Brian what she was doing, she pushed her way through the crowd and then made her way up the steep flight of steps to the top of the ride.

The wooden surface of the slide was slippery when travelled down on a hessian mat and the last thing Rhonnie wanted to do was crash at speed into the woman, which could have severe consequences for both of them. So she decided she wouldn't use a mat. Sitting down on the ledge at the top of the slide, she gripped both edges of the side barrier then gingerly pushed herself forward, her intention being to make a slow descent until she reached the woman, using the heels of her shoes as a brake if her speed accelerated faster than she wanted it to. The crowd below had gathered what Rhonnie was up to and started to egg her on. Good-humouredly, she gave them a wave as she slowly moved forward.

Finally she reached the woman who, not knowing Rhonnie was on her way, thought the crowd below were cheering and waving at her. Still laughing at her own predicament, she was cheering and waving back. As she arrived a little faster than intended, Rhonnie was surprised that her shoes thumping against the woman's backside didn't alert her to someone else's presence, but instead seemed to bounce off her, like a tennis ball bounced back up when it fell to the floor. Now she was right beside her Rhonnie did have to admit that the woman, who looked to be in her early thirties, wearing a loose, flowing style of sundress, did seem to have a very large, doughnut-shaped bottom, which was grossly out of proportion to the rest of her body. A surge of deep sympathy for her washed through Rhonnie. People could be cruel to those whose physical appearance deviated in any way from what was perceived as normal, and no doubt she would have suffered much abuse throughout her life from the narrow-minded sort. To Rhonnie, though, she was a woman in need of help at the moment and she would treat the camper with no less respect than she would anyone else, regardless of shape or size.

Her quick mind assessing the situation, it seemed to Rhonnie that the only way this woman was coming off the Skelter was by being pulled upwards and lifted off, as Brian had in fact suggested, like a cork from a bottle. The fire brigade would have to put a harness around her and pull her out with the aid of a winch. Rhonnie bent her legs and shuffled herself as close to the woman as she could get. She still didn't know Rhonnie was behind her, too caught up in the roars of the crowd and her own responses. Rhonnie gave her a tap on her back to alert her. At this, the woman gave a cry of shock and tried to turn her head to see who had accosted her. She couldn't so instead cried out, 'Who's there?'

'It's me, Rhonnie Buckland. I've come to try and find a way to get you off the Skelter. You do seem to be well and truly wedged, though.'

The woman shouted over her shoulder, 'And I'm Rosie, pleased to meet you. Well, as I tried to tell the young lad who came to help me a while ago . . . only I was laughing that hard about getting meself in this situation I couldn't get the words out, and betime I managed to control myself for a bit before the crowd below started me off again, he'd gone . . .

before I start laughing again and risk missing my dinner as I'm on first sitting, please will you pull the plug?'

Rhonnie was confused. 'Pull what plug?'

'Lift my dress up and you'll see. It's not at the front so it has to be around the back. I can't reach my arms that far round, so I couldn't do it myself.'

Even more confused, Rhonnie pulled up the hem of the back of the woman's dress, having to tug as it seemed to be caught under her massive bottom. As it came up and revealed what lay underneath, Rhonnie herself erupted into hysterical laughter. She laughed so hard, tears rolled down her cheeks. Rosie's unusually wide hips were in fact a rubber swimming ring that her real backside was stuck in the middle of.

Finding the air valve, Rhonnie pulled out the plastic plug. Once the ring was deflated, Rosie pulled it out from under her and both women then slid the remainder of the way down, to the jubilant cheers of the crowd.

As soon as Rhonnie got herself up on arriving at the bottom of the slide, Rosie, now joined by another woman of her age, obviously her friend, looked at her sheepishly and said, 'I'm sorry to have put you to all that trouble.'

Rhonnie smiled at her. 'Well, we've got you off the slide without any mishaps and that's what matters. But can I just ask you, though, what possessed you to attempt to slide down the Skelter sitting on a rubber ring?'

Rosie gave a shrug. 'It seemed like a good idea at the time. You see, me and Kathy had been swimming in the indoor pool . . . well, Kathy was swimming but I can't . . . sink like a stone without anything to help keep me up . . . so before we went in I bought a ring from the gift shop in the court-yard, thinking I'd have a bob up and down while she did her lengths. After we'd had enough of the pool, it was too early to go back and change for dinner, so it was Kathy's idea to go down to the funfair. We had our swimming bags for our stuff but it had taken me ages to blow up the ring and I thought that if I let it down now then, when we went swimming again, I'd have the trouble of blowing it back up, so I just carried it over my arm.

'When I decided to have a go on the Helter-skelter we left our bags of swimming stuff by the pay kiosk and it wasn't until after Kathy had gone down the slide and I was about to follow that I realised I still had the ring over my arm. I was just going to hold it out in front of me as I went down but then I had the bright idea . . . well, I thought it was at the time . . . that it would be fun to sit on it as I went down, like people do when they go down the slides in the indoor pool. At first with me sitting on it, it slid down a treat but then my bum sort of sank down into the middle and that must have pushed the sides of the ring out to wedge against the sides of the slide. I tried to find the plug to let it down but couldn't find it, and I couldn't pull myself out of the ring as I was stuck fast.'

'Well, what you did certainly has given a lot of people a good laugh, including me,' Rhonnie told her. 'I'll leave you to enjoy the rest of your holiday.'

As she walked away to continue her search for Alan Ibbotson, she thought to herself that she really ought to write a book about all the funny exploits the campers got up to. It would certainly be a bestseller.

She came across Alan Ibbotson as she approached the main courtyard and spotted him through the crowds heading towards the outdoor swimming pool.

She hurried to catch up with him.

'Hello, Rhonnie,' he greeted her in his usual jolly way. 'And how is our lovely boss this morning?'

'I'm very well thank you, Alan, and yourself?'

'Tickety-boo, couldn't be better . . . and who wouldn't be on a day like this? I'm just off to check that the stage is set, so to speak, for the pool games this afternoon. I'm glad you're here, though, as it saves me coming to see you in your office. I've had an idea I'd like to run past you.'

Rhonnie eyed him in a manner that told him she was keen to hear what it was.

'I wondered what you thought about including in that pamphlet you give out to all new arrivals a form asking the campers to vote for their favourite Stripey? The top three Stripeys with the most votes that week will get a prize, just a voucher for a drink at the bar, something like that, and then at the end of the season the Stripey with the most votes overall wins . . . ten pounds or whatever you think is appropriate. I thought it'd be a good morale-booster for the Stripeys to see that management notice and reward their hard work.'

Rhonnie readily agreed. 'I think that's a great idea, Alan. I'll ask Jill to make up a form and get it photocopied ready in time to include in Saturday's turn-around.' She smiled and said jocularly, 'Not that the Stripeys don't already do a good job between them, but it doesn't hurt to give them an incentive to do better.' She then told him, 'On my way around the camp yesterday I caught a part of the Glamorous Granny competition and I do like the twist you've put on it, that it isn't the panel that picks the winner but the audience. At least the contestants can't complain of any fixing going on! Also I caught the rehearsals for the Stripey Show and the new sketch with Noddy and Big Ears, I have to say, I found hilarious . . . very naughty though.'

He chuckled. 'The audience love a bit of slap and tickle, as long as it's not too near the knuckle. Bill Rider . . . or Billy Bonkers as we announce him when he goes on stage to do his comedy routine . . . has written some new jokes for his stint in the show and a couple were too rude even for my broad shoulders so they were a no-no. I had to remind him that this is a family holiday camp show, not a sleazy nightclub.'

'You're doing a great job, Alan.'

He looked pleased by her compliment. 'Thanks, it's good to hear you think so. I have to say that Patsy Mathers was a hard act to follow. Some of the ideas for the entertainments that she implemented during her time here are hard for me to improve on.'

'Yes, she did a marvellous job of revamping the entertainments side of the business, which was very stale and old-fashioned when she took over as manager.' Rhonnie realised then that Alan was worried management might not think he was doing enough if he wasn't continually coming up with new ideas for improvements to the competitions and shows, so she put him straight. 'What is the saying . . . don't try and fix what's not broken . . . not until it *is* broken, of course.'

He smiled at her. 'I understand. Thank you, Rhonnie. It's just that I love my job here and don't want to fall down on it.'

Just then a Stripey arrived next to them. 'Sorry to interrupt but we've got a tie in the over-sixties bowling tournament and we've only got one winner's cup to hand out so I need another or I fear we'll have a mutiny on our hands from the winners.'

'Leave it to me and I'll bring one over,' Alan told him. As the young Stripey dashed back off, Alan laughed and said to Rhonnie, 'You wouldn't think a little plastic trophy cup, costing no more than a tanner, would hold so much importance for some people would you?'

She laughed too. 'That cheap plastic cup will be taking centre-stage on the winners' mantelpieces when they get home and will be bragged about proudly to every visitor who calls on them for years to come.' She then remembered that she had something to ask Alan. 'Oh, before you go and get the extra trophy, I just wanted to ask if it would be possible to have the use of one of the Stripeys for a couple of hours a day for the rest of the week? It's just to escort a lady around in a wheelchair . . . give her daughter a bit of time to herself.'

'No problem at all. Let me know between what times you'd like the help and I'll make the arrangements.'

She said she would and they went their separate ways.

Rhonnie had just arrived at the courtyard when she saw the young woman in question pushing the older one in the wheelchair amongst a throng of other campers streaming out of the cinema, all looking like they'd enjoyed the showing that morning. All except the young girl whose face was the picture of misery. Rhonnie changed her route to intercept the pair.

As they met up, a smiling Rhonnie said as diplomatically as she could, 'Hello, I'm Rhonnie Buckland the manager. I'm glad I've bumped into you. You see, I appreciate your situation and assume it must be difficult for you both to divide your time here so that you're both having fun doing what each of you enjoys. I wondered if we could be of assistance by providing a Stripey to accompany you for a couple of hours a day wherever you wished to go . . .' she said, looking at the older woman in the chair '. . . so that your daughter can go off and do something that she enjoys during that time.'

Joan's face lit up at the prospect at having time to herself and not feeling guilty about it since her mother was being taken care of, but then her mood was quickly deflated when she realised her mother would not accept this offer for the same reason she would not accept anyone else's.

She was right, as Cara, without even taking a moment to consider the proposal, said, 'It's very good of you to offer but my daughter and I enjoy doing exactly the same things. We're both having a wonderful time, aren't we, Joan?' Without waiting for her to answer, Cara concluded with: 'Now if you'll excuse us, we don't want to be late for our dinner sitting.'

As she pushed her mother away, Joan flashed Rhonnie a smile of gratitude for her thoughtfulness but she would have had to be blind not to know it was a forced one. The mother might be under the impression that her daughter enjoyed doing everything she did, but that was far from the case. The girl would have jumped at Rhonnie's offer had her mother

56

not asserted her authority and declined it. That was very remiss of her too, Rhonnie thought, without even affording her daughter the opportunity to have her say in the matter. But there was nothing Rhonnie could do apart from console herself with the fact that at least she had tried to bring a little colour and excitement to what was obviously a regimented and tedious life.

CHAPTER FIVE

It was just after twelve when Rhonnie arrived back in the office to find Jill giggling to herself as she sat typing cheques for payment to suppliers. Sandra too was looking amused as she wetted stamps using a sponge pad.

Before Rhonnie could ask Jill just what it was she and Sandra were finding so amusing, Jill said, 'Oh, and here we are, Sandra and me, labouring away in the office while our boss has been enjoying herself down at the funfair.'

Rhonnie replied good-humouredly, 'The speed of the camp grapevine never ceases to amaze me. Our campers can still spring a few surprises too. In this case all ended well, I'm glad to say, and yes, I did get to have a partial ride on the slide once we got the rubber ring out from under the trapped woman. She and I slid down together, which I did most certainly enjoy.' She then thoughtfully eyed each woman in turn before she said, 'Well, seems to me that what's good for the boss is good for the staff. Can you pass me the petty cash tin, please, Jill?'

Wondering what her boss was up to, a bemused Jill unlocked her bottom drawer and took it out, handing it to Rhonnie along with the key to open it. Unlocking it, Rhonnie took out change amounting to a pound. After Jill put the relocked cash tin back in her drawer, Rhonnie gave her the money and told them both: 'I'll man the office for a couple of hours while you two go and have some fun down at the fair. Ten bob each should be enough. Have your dinner first in the restaurant. Be back here by three, not before.'

Both women looked at her in astonishment for a moment before jumping up from their chairs and rushing off towards the door leading down to reception before she changed her mind.

A while later, Drina walked into the general office and frowned quizzically to see Rhonnie sitting at Sandra's desk manning the switchboard. As soon as Rhonnie had finished putting a call through to Eric in the kitchen, Drina asked her, 'Where are the girls? Not jumped ship, have they, as they refuse to work for their tyrannical boss any longer?'

Rhonnie chuckled. 'Their tyrannical boss has sent them both out on a jolly to have some fun down at the fair.'

Drina looked impressed. 'Seems only fair considering she had some herself today.'

Rhonnie shook her head. 'Camp grapevine still in full flow it seems.'

'Carol the gift shop manager told me just now when I popped in to get a Milky Bar for Danny, to give him when me and Artie go and have a play with him later at your cottage. Artie's bought him a swing and is going to put it up in the garden while we're there.'

'You spoil Danny rotten.'

'It's a grandparent's job. So how are things here? No catastrophes . . . well, apart from the woman getting struck on the Skelter, that is.'

'No, I'm glad to say. All the campers are behaving themselves and the staff are doing their jobs. Jeff Sampson seems to be settling down well although we've only had a handful of people staying in the statics, plus a few tourers and a handful of tents, but then it's early days yet as the park's only been open a month. But from what I've observed – and I have had a discreet chat with some people in the statics and tourers about Jeff – they all think favourably of him so I've no reason to believe we were wrong to give him the job. I've not been over to the park for a couple of days as I don't want him to think I'm watching him like a hawk, just like I don't call in the kitchen to see Eric or any of the other department heads every day because we trust that if they have a problem between visits they'll let us know. But I am going later on this afternoon, after Jill and Sandra come back, to collect the bookings paperwork and the weekly tourers' takings. After that I'm just going to go over once a week on a Thursday.

'Then there's the new cleaning supervisor, Lily Dawkins, who replaced Mrs Wright with whom we first replaced Eileen . . .' Here Rhonnie paused for a moment to shake her head ruefully. 'Edna Wright! There was a tyrant if ever I've come across one. She terrified all the chalet maids witless, she was so strict and formidable, but very clever too as she didn't come across like that in her interview, did she? I don't think the staff have ever been so glad to see the back of a boss or ever will be again. Anyway, they all seem to like Lily well enough, I've not heard a bad word yet from any of them about her. I've no concerns over the rest of the new staff either. So all's well at the moment and let's hope it stays that way and we have a non-eventful season for a change.'

Drina said dryly, 'We can live in hope, dear, but we both know from experience that running a business like this, we must always be prepared to face and deal with the unexpected, which can come from the most unusual sources.'

They both looked at each other knowingly as memories of past catastrophes flashed into their minds . . . Drina's own son trying to fleece her out of the business, not once but twice; campers attempting to swindle them out of a free holiday; campers bribing staff to fix competitions in their favour; bank robbers using the camp as a hideaway from the police; even a murder, which only Rhonnie was aware of and then only because the killer told Rhonnie what she had done, knowing she couldn't do anything as she had no concrete proof to go to the authorities with . . . Yes, there was no room for complacency just because nothing major had happened this season. There was still plenty of time.

Drina eyed Rhonnie for a moment before she asked, 'And how are you, dear? I don't need to ask if you're coping with the job, but any regrets about moving back?'

She replied without hesitation, 'No, none at all. I can't deny that I still get a bit emotional when a memory suddenly pops into my mind of me and Dan, when I'm at home in the cottage or round and about the camp, but as time passes the pain is getting less and those memories make me smile not cry. As Dorothy said in *The Wizard of Oz* . . . "There's no place like home."'

Drina smiled tenderly at her by way of telling her she was glad to hear that, before she keenly asked, 'So are your dad and I still on for babysitting Danny this Saturday evening while you go to Jill's dinner party?'

Rhonnie looked at her for a moment before she said, 'I know I should go, make a start on building a social life for myself, but . . .' She paused and heaved a sigh. 'After me and Dan got together I never went anywhere socially without him, and before that without a friend or two. I won't know anyone at Jill's do. I just wish Jackie and Ginger were here to go with me and then I wouldn't feel like a goldfish in a bowl.'

'You know Jill, and I know you haven't met her husband yet but I have and he's really nice. As soon as you arrive, she will introduce you to everyone and before you know it you'll all be chatting like old friends.' Drina eyed Rhonnie knowingly for a moment before she reminded her, 'You didn't know your close friend Carol back in your home town of Leicester, or Jackie or Ginger who've become your bosom buddies since you arrived here, or come to that Dan either, before you were introduced to them all in one way or another. And it's more than likely that some of the people going to Jill's party won't know each other either, and right now they're probably feeling just like you are. You never know, dear, you might enjoy yourself, and it's about time you had yourself a bit of fun after what you've been through. If the worst happens and you really don't, then just make your excuses to Jill and come home. But once you've made the first move to get yourself out and about again, the next time will be so much easier for you, trust me.'

Rhonnie looked at her thoughtfully for a moment as she digested all that Drina had just told her before she smiled and said, 'Oh, I do love you. You have this special way of making me look at things from a different angle.' She leaned over and grasped Drina's hand, giving it an affectionate squeeze. 'My mother, God bless her, was the best mother I could ever have wished for, but if I could have ordered the kind of woman I'd be wanting as my second mum, that woman would be you.'

With a glint of tears in her eyes, Drina responded, 'I can't begin to tell you how much your telling me that means to me, dear. I see you as the daughter I never had and couldn't wish for a better one.'

It was Rhonnie's turn then to feel tears prick her eyes. How she wished that Drina could officially become her step-mother by marrying her father, which she knew both Drina and he would very much like too, but they would never be able to while his greedy second wife was holding them to ransom.

She said now, 'I'm so out of practice I have no idea what to wear to a dinner party.'

'You look lovely in anything you wear,' Drina told her with conviction but then suggested, 'what about that pretty pink, green and blue halterneck outfit you bought the other week when I took you shopping? The one with the wide legs that look like they're a long skirt until you walk in them. What did the shop assistant described the pattern as . . .

psychopathic . . . Oh, no, that wasn't it. Psycho something, though.'

Drina was describing Rhonnie's new catsuit that she hadn't as yet worn. It would be perfect for the dinner party. Laughing, she said, 'Psychedelic. And that's just what I will wear . . . and I have some long pink dangly clip-on earrings to go with it and pink sling-back shoes.' She added with a twinkle in her eyes, 'I shall know exactly who to turn to for advice on how to dress the next time I go out.'

Drina smiled at the compliment, but more important to her was the fact that Rhonnie was talking of a social future for herself and not seeing the dinner party as a one-off. She stood up. 'Well, I'll leave you to get on with it as I have a special date of my own with a little boy and his grandad.'

The very second the general office clock showed the time to be three o'clock, the door burst open and Jill and Sandra charged in. It was apparent that they'd had a good time and were both very appreciative of Rhonnie's generosity.

As soon as they had all had a catch up, Rhonnie left the other two to continue with their work while she went off the caravan park. But she realised she was going to have to postpone the visit because as soon as she arrived in the courtyard her attention was caught by a lone figure standing by the huge fountain dominating the centre with its four dolphin figures spewing water from their mouths.

The young woman's face had the same longing look on it that Rhonnie had witnessed the first time she had seen it, but mingled with that was a sense of desperate loneliness. As she wasn't with her mother Rhonnie assumed that somehow Joan Travers had managed to get some time to herself . . . maybe her mother had realised that she was being unfair, expecting every waking minute of her daughter's life to be dedicated to her . . . but regardless, having no one to share that precious freedom with was just as bad as having none at all. Well,

Rhonnie could fix that. She flashed a look around but unfortunately the Stripeys she spotted amongst the throng were all engaged with other campers. Determined that Joan would have someone to share some fun with, it seemed there was no other answer but for Rhonnie herself to do the honours.

She hurried over to Joan and, smiling at her warmly, said, 'Hello, remember me from the other day? I'm Rhonnie.'

Joan stared at her blankly for a moment before she responded. 'Oh, yes, of course I do. You're the lady who very kindly offered to have my mother escorted around so I could have time to do things by myself. I never got the chance to thank you for that. It was a very nice thing for you to do.'

'It was my pleasure. As you're on your own now, I gather your mother is being taken care of by one of your party so, if you've nothing planned, I wondered if you'd mind a bit of company. I'm at a loose end, you see. All my work is up to date and I was in my office twiddling my thumbs. As it was such a lovely day I thought I'd have a stroll around the camp. But then, it's no fun being on your own, is it? So when I saw you were on your own too, I wandered if you fancied a bit of company. There are lots of activities on this afternoon and I'm easy which one we attend, so you pick, or we could just go for a walk?'

Joan flashed her a wan smile. 'No, it isn't any fun at all being on your own.' She heaved a deep sigh. 'I'd very much like to take you up on your offer but my mother's waiting for me back at the chalet. She wants me to take her to the bowling green to watch others in our party playing in a match but she remembered she'd run out of Mint Imperials and sent me to fetch a quarter from the shop.' She flashed a look at her wrist watch and exclaimed, 'Goodness, I've been gone nearly twenty minutes so she'll be wondering where I've got to.'

Rhonnie knew that Joan no more wanted to watch old people playing bowls than Rhonnie herself did and her heart went out to the girl. 'If you don't mind my asking, just what is your mother suffering from?'

'She did tell me the name when she was first diagnosed ten years ago, something long and hard to pronounce which I can't remember. The disease affects her muscles and nerves and eventually it will destroy her heart. Some days are worse for her than others. The doctors can't do anything for her as there's no cure, just pills to help with the pain. When she first talked of coming on this holiday with the group of other women she knows at home, I thought it'd be too much for us to manage but the coach company said the driver would help get Mother on and off, and with the chalets being ground level and all the other facilities too that she would want to take advantage of, Mother insisted we'd be fine. She's really enjoying herself.'

Unlike you, thought Rhonnie.

It seemed that she was not going to succeed in her wish to see Joan have a chance to meet and mix with people of her own age and have some fun while here at the camp. At least she could offer her a bit of company on her way back to her chalet, though. 'As you're in a hurry to get back to your mother, I'll take you via a short cut if you'd like me to.'

Joan smiled gratefully at her. 'I'd appreciate that, thank you.'

They fell into step together and it was apparent to Rhonnie that the girl was hungry for an insight into the life of another woman her own age who didn't live the sort of cloistered life that Joan herself did. She bombarded Rhonnie with questions about herself and her job and what she did socially. In other circumstances Rhonnie would have found her probing intrusive and bad-mannered but it was obvious to her that Joan was storing up the information to draw upon when she was on her own, imagining herself living the kind of life someone like Rhonnie had, where she was at liberty to pick and choose where she worked and how she spent her leisure time. Joan did show genuine sympathy towards Rhonnie when she briefly explained that she didn't have much of a social life at the moment as she was still coming to terms with the loss of her husband and there was her young son to consider, so any spare time she had was mostly devoted to him. But Rhonnie had the distinct impression that, while outwardly showing compassion, inwardly Joan was thinking that although Rhonnie's story was a sad one, at least she had experienced what it was like to do all the things young people did . . . mixing with friends, going to parties, dancing . . . and to be loved by someone, have married and be a mother. She must have wondered when she would be free to do the same.

As remiss of her as it was, and not that she would wish anyone dead, Rhonnie hoped for Joan's sake that Cara was released from what must be a terrible life sooner rather than later, so at least Joan would still be young enough to achieve all she wanted to in life after unselfishly putting her own on hold to devote herself to the care of her mother.

By this time they were in the campers' chalet area, walking down the path that led to the one that Joan and her mother were staying in. As they rounded a bend, ahead of them Rhonnie could see Cara Travers sitting in her wheelchair outside her chalet, but she wasn't alone. There was another woman sitting with her. Facing the sun, they had their backs to Joan and Rhonnie. Joan didn't appear to have noticed that they were closing in on their destination as she had her head turned towards Rhonnie, soaking up a story about an escapade Ginger had got up to here at the camp a couple of years back.

Fifteen minutes earlier, when Rhonnie and Joan were still back in the main courtyard, sitting outside her chalet Cara was drumming her fingers on the armrest of her wheelchair in annoyance. She had told Joan to hurry as she didn't want to miss the beginning of the bowls match and if her daughter didn't get back soon she would. She was about to turn her head to see if there was any sign of her daughter coming back

66

down the path but was stopped short when a middle-aged, matronly woman from the chalet opposite, came over to her carrying a fold-up deckchair.

'Mind if I join you?' she asked Cara, then without waiting for a response, set the chair down at the side of her, unfolded it, and settled her heavy body down on it. 'Freda Johnson, pleased to meet you,' she said. Cara made to reciprocate but before she could utter a word Freda was going on. 'I take it you've been abandoned too, being's you're sat here on your own.'

'Actually, I haven't been abandoned. My daughter has gone on an errand for me and will be back any minute to take me to watch my friends playing bowls.'

Freda looked at her jealously. 'I've seen you coming and going while we've been here and thought how lucky you are to have a daughter so devoted to you, considering your situation.' She heaved a deep mournful sigh and carried on in a complaining tone, 'I really believed my son wanted me to come on this holiday with his wife and my grandchildren 'cos he wanted his old widowed mother to spend time with them and enjoy herself . . . I should have known that it was just so's they had a babysitter on tap so they can go gallivanting down the Paradise every night and not be worried their good time is going to be interrupted by the camp babysitting service calling them 'cos one of the kids has woken up or needs them for anything. Every day since we got here, straight after breakfast and dinner they've managed to go off without me along, setting off before I'm ready, telling me they'll meet me by the pool or wherever it is they've gone off to, but when I get there there's no sign of them and when I catch up with them later back here at the chalets . . . we've got two next to each other . . . they make out I'm doolally and got the place they told me wrong or use an excuse to explain why they hadn't been where they said they would be but had gone off somewhere else and that's why I didn't find them. Then in the evenings we all go off down to the Paradise together but when it comes time for the kids to go back to the chalet, they always manage to manipulate me into taking charge of that when I'm really enjoying myself and want to stay put.'

She folded her arms under her ample bosom and pulled a disgruntled face. 'Selfish sods my son, Stanley, and his wife are. I only see them when they want something from me, usually to babysit as it doesn't cost them anything like it does when they get someone else in. I agree so I can spend time with the kids as I doubt I'd see much of them otherwise. They live two bus rides away from me so it's not easy for me to get over. I know, though, that once my grandkids are old enough to look after themselves I shall only see them at Easter and Christmas out of obligation, and maybe not even then as they've been dropping hints for a while now that once the kids have finished their schooling they might emigrate to Canada, as my sister's son . . . Stanley's cousin . . . has been filling Stanley's head with how great it is over there and how easy it would be for him to get a good job, paying far more than he gets here.'

Telling Cara this tale was upsetting Freda and she paused for a moment to wipe a stray tear from her eye before she carried on. 'My husband died ten years ago and we only had Stanley. As I told you, my sister lives in Canada and my brother in London, so there's only me left at home. I'm all right at the moment as I've got a job in a baker's and I can do most things around the house myself, but I worry what will happen when I get older and can't manage so well. With no family living close by to pop around each day just to check on me, I don't know what will become of me. You're okay, aren't you? You've your daughter to take care of you, lucky woman you are . . . oh, I don't mean you're lucky to have whatever it is that you're suffering from. But what if I take ill . . . too sick to take care of myself . . . and my son and his wife are thousands of miles away? Well, I'm terrified witless about what the future holds for me.'

Cara said matter-of-factly, 'Then you need to do something about it before it's too late.'

Freda looked at her quizzically. 'Do! Do what?'

A smug smile curved Cara's lips. 'Something like I did when I foresaw this situation happening to me.'

Freda twisted herself around in her seat, giving Cara her full attention. 'And what was that?' Silence prevailed and Freda could tell by the way Cara was looking at her that she was debating whether to take her into her confidence or not. Desperate to hear just what it was that might help her own situation, she urged, 'You can trust me, you have my solemn promise I won't breathe a word of what you're about to tell me. Your secret really is safe with me. I'm just so grateful that someone else appreciates my position and might be able to help me do something about it.'

Cara felt a sudden need to tell someone of her clever plan, receive praise and admiration for it, and as this woman was a stranger whose path she would never cross again once they'd left the camp on Saturday morning, there was no one better. 'All right but you have to appreciate that no one else knows what I've done, not even close friends or neighbours, because if the truth came out I'd be in the same situation as you are but worse – I wouldn't even have any friends, let alone my daughter to take care of me in my old age. They'd all turn their backs on me and then I'd really be on my own.'

'I told you, you have my solemn promise, I won't breathe a word,' the other woman assured her.

Convinced of her sincerity, Cara took a deep breath before she divulged: 'I was thirty-five when I had Joan, my husband and I had almost given up on ever having children so we were overjoyed when I found out I was finally pregnant. My husband died when Joan was two and I was left to raise her on my own. She was a lovely child and I couldn't have wished for a better daughter, it was me and her against the world. By the time she left school I was getting on for fifty and beginning to slow up a bit and get aches and pains as we all do when old age is creeping up on us, but I wasn't worried as I automatically thought that Joan would join me full-time in my business and take care of all the donkey work and I could take a back seat so to speak.

'Since she was a little girl she's helped me in the shop after school and on Saturdays so she knows the business as well as I do. I have a shop selling women's underwear and haber-dashery, knitting wools, patterns, that sort of thing, and very busy it is . . . my customers weren't happy about me shutting down this week so we could take this holiday. Anyway, on leaving school, to my complete shock Joan announced that she had got a university place in Edinburgh to study to become an English teacher, starting the following September. She hadn't told me until she was sure of her place as she had wanted to surprise me. She did that all right!

'At the time I pretended to be pleased that she wanted to make something of herself, but deep down I was worried what would happen to me as I grew older and was not able to do all the things I was doing then. With Joan in foreign parts and a chance that she might like Scotland and decide to stay up there, even meet a Scotsman and marry him, I wouldn't have her nearby to visit regularly and lend me a hand when I needed it. But far more important, who would take care of me in my old age, as like you I have no other family? So I came up with a plan to keep her with me.'

The other woman eagerly urged, 'Ohhh . . . and what was that plan?'

'Well, if I had a terminal illness, Joan would have no choice but to give up her plans to move away, and stay to look after me instead. I went to the library and looked in medical journals for an illness that suited my purpose, that would be easy to play out the symptoms of and difficult to forecast. I went out a few times, being very secretive about where I was going so that later she would think they were visits to the doctor and consultant at the hospital. When I'd set the stage, so to speak, I made sure she found me crying one afternoon and of course Joan insisted I tell her why I was so upset. Believing I was dying, she had no choice but to give up her place at university and stay home to look after me.'

Freda was staring at her, stunned. 'Oh, I don't know whether I've got it in me to deceive my family like that. Don't you feel guilty for stopping your daughter having a life of her own?'

Cara looked back at her, shocked. 'No, why should I? I've looked after Joan since the minute she was born and on my own since her father died, so why shouldn't she look after me in my old age?'

'Well, yes, that's true. So you don't really need your wheelchair at all? Apart from a few old aches and pains, you're otherwise as fit as a fiddle?'

'I am at the moment, yes, but who's to say I will be in a few years' time, next week even, should a real illness strike me down? Or even just the normal complaints of old age that stop me from looking after myself. I can't deny that it's a bind sometimes, making out I can't walk more than a few steps at a time or can't do much for myself. Especially when I want something urgently and Joan doesn't do it immediately, I have to fight not to jump out of my chair and do it myself. But it's a price I'm prepared to pay so as not to face a lonely future.'

Freda mused, 'Yes, you're right, some things are worth making sacrifices for. It's a good plan, I can't deny that . . . very clever. I wonder if I could make it work for me as well as it has for you.'

A slight noise behind them then had both women's heads swivelling round to see Joan and Rhonnie nearby.

A great fear spread through Cara that Joan had been privy

71

to the conversation but as she wasn't showing any outward signs that she had, Cara relaxed and said, 'It's not right to shock a woman in my state of health by creeping up on me like that. Where did you come from anyway? The quickest way to the shops and back is that way,' she said, pointing in front of her.

Joan and Rhonnie moved around to stand before the two seated women. Evenly, Joan responded, 'Rhonnie kindly showed me a quick way back as she knew I was worried I'd left you on your own longer than I intended. I needn't have worried, though, as you've had company.'

Freda rose and as she folded up her deckchair, said, 'I'll leave you to it.' She then looked meaningfully at Cara. 'I'll certainly give some thought to what you told me. Thank you so much.'

As Freda left, Joan asked Cara, 'What did you tell that woman that she was so grateful for, Mother?'

Cara blustered, 'Oh, I was . . . er . . . just advising her on some cream to use for a rash. Now, are you going to get me down to the bowling green before I miss the start of the match?'

Rhonnie too made to take her leave but a look from Joan, begging her to stay, stopped her. She then felt mortally awkward to be an audience to what took place afterwards.

With a look of contempt on her face, Joan said to Cara: 'But you don't really need me to take you to the bowling green, Mother, do you? In fact, you don't need me to take you anywhere or take care of you in the way that I do, as you're quite capable of doing things for yourself. That was no rash cream you were advising that woman about. You were so engrossed in telling her, almost gloating, how you lied to me about having a terminal illness so I wouldn't leave home to make a life for myself, that you didn't hear me and Rhonnie arrive. We heard everything, every sordid detail of your despicable plan, and also that you don't even feel guilty for what you've done.' Tears in her eyes and her face contorted with hurt, she blasted, 'How could you do this to me, Mother? How could you stoop so low as to stop me living the life I wanted, out of sheer selfishness? Now I realise why you wouldn't let anyone else look after you even for a short time while I had a break. Not because you were embarrassed about others having to attend to you but because you were worried they might not be as gullible as me and realise there was nothing wrong with you.

'Mother, don't you know me well enough to realise that no matter where I was in the world, married or on my own, I would always be there for you whenever you needed me? You're my mother and I'd do anything for you, certainly not leave you to fend for yourself in your old age if you weren't capable of doing so. Have you any idea what life has been like for me, believing for this last ten years that my beloved mother is dying, that any day could be her last and doing my best to make sure I made your remaining days as happy and comfortable as I could? It's been horrible, soul-destroying. I used to cry most nights, worrying how it must be for you, never knowing which day would be your last. But do you know what's worse, if that's possible? You never once gave me a thought when you were organising any social events for yourself, expecting me to take you whether I'd enjoy them or not.'

Joan wiped tears from her eyes. 'I could have been a qualified teacher by now, married with a family, and you could have a horde of grandchildren fussing around you. It might be too late for me to study to be a teacher but maybe it's not too late for me to get a job I enjoy and the family I'd love to have for myself.' She paused and eyed her mother meaningfully. 'I hope you've got a good story to tell everyone to explain your sudden miraculous recovery.'

Face the colour of parchment, Cara seemed to have shrunk inside the wheelchair at the realisation that through her need to brag about how clever she had been in saving herself from a lonely future, that was actually what she faced now. She knew without a doubt that there was nothing she could do to recover from this so there was no point in trying. As if it wasn't bad enough for her that Joan had discovered her lies, she had suffered the additional embarrassment and humiliation of the boss of the holiday camp witnessing it too. Damn the woman for taking it upon herself to show Joan a short cut back to the chalets! Had she not done that then Joan would never have overheard her confession to Freda.

Her friends would be returning soon from their bowls match so she needed to get away from here, take herself back home where hopefully she could concoct a plausible explanation for her sudden recovery and Joan's disappearance. She had lost her daughter and the last thing she wanted was to lose their friendship too, so come hell or high water she would come up with a plausible tale. Cara got out of her chair and dashed inside the chalet, minutes later emerging dressed and packed for the off. She paused for a moment to look at Joan and check whether there was any sign that she might be willing to find it within herself to forgive her mother for her appalling behaviour, but any hope she'd had of that was immediately dashed as all she saw in Joan's eyes was utter contempt for her.

As Cara hurried off down the path towards the courtyard, Rhonnie looked with great sympathy at the distraught young woman. 'I can't imagine how you feel, finding out all this.'

Looking like she'd the weight of the world on her young shoulders, Joan sighed. 'I can't begin to describe it to you. But as if it wasn't bad enough what my mother's done to me, she was trying to encourage someone else to deceive their family in the same way too.'

'Well, if that woman has any sense she'll realise that lies always find you out in the end and you are in a worse

74

situation than you were before you told them, just like your mother is now,' Rhonnie mused. 'I can't think how she is going to come up with a good enough reason for her sudden recovery.'

'If she's managed to convince everyone – including me for the past ten years – that she's suffering from a fatal illness, then I'm sure she'll come up with something plausible.' Joan paused for a moment before she added: 'It might sound strange to you but there's a part of me that understands what my mother did. It must be worrying for people who are widowed or alone for other reasons, worrying how they'll manage to care for themselves as their bodies let them down when they get older. Despite what she's done, I still love my mother and would still look after her if she genuinely needed me to, but right now I need time away from her to get over this, and in another town so I don't risk bumping into her. First things first. I'll get myself a place in a women's hostel and a job. I'm experienced in shop work so shouldn't have much trouble. I've always fancied living by the sea so I might try Skegness or Mablethorpe.'

Rhonnie looked at Joan in admiration. The young woman had just been dealt a terrible blow yet she was finding the inner strength to make plans and move on. Just the kind of woman Jolly's liked to employ, in fact! 'Well, if Jolly's camp is situated near enough to the sea then I could certainly do with someone like you working for us for the rest of the season,' Rhonnie told her. 'And of course for staff we provide accommodation. While you're working here you'll have plenty of time to plan what you want to do with the rest of your life and how to go about it.'

Joan's eyes lit up. 'You mean that? Oh, I don't know how to thank you.'

'Well, I don't suppose you want to risk bumping into your mother's friends and having to find an explanation for her departure, so get your stuff packed then come and find me in the office and we'll get you sorted out. For the rest of the week you can lie low and start whatever job we find you as soon as they've gone home.'

Later that evening, sitting at the kitchen table in Rhonnie's cottage, cradling mugs of tea in their hands, Drina was looking at Rhonnie in disbelief. 'I shouldn't be surprised, knowing what I do of the lengths people will go to to get what they most desire, but what that women did to her daughter, just so she wouldn't be on her own in her old age, really was despicable. I'm so glad we've been able to help Joan start on a new future. I'm sure with her experience of shop work she'll be an asset to Carol as an assistant in the gift shop. So, anything else exciting happen today?'

Rhonnie nearly choked on her tea. 'Isn't that enough for you?'

Drina looked sheepish. 'You know what I mean. I should have said anything else out of the norm happen today? I am enjoying my semi-retirement but I still miss being in the thick of it and rely on you to fill me in, so I don't miss anything.'

Rhonnie smiled. 'Well, I'm glad to tell you that nothing else out of the norm happened today . . . in the main camp that is. Because I got distracted by Joan's situation I never got around to visiting the caravan park and collecting the weekly tourers' fees. I assume, though, that all is well there or Jeff would have let the office know. I'll make time to go tomorrow.'

The sound of laughter reached their ears. Putting down their mugs of tea on the table, both of them rose and went across to the kitchen window to look out into the garden beyond. Drina chuckled and said, 'I don't know just who is having the most fun on that swing, your dad or your son.'

'Well, it doesn't seem right to me that it's just those two having fun on it,' Rhonnie said matter-of-factly.

'No, it certainly doesn't.' With that Drina spun on her heel and headed for the door, calling out to Rhonnie, 'Loser pushes.'

They were both squashed together inside the kitchen doorway, giggling as they tried to squeeze by each other to be the first to get to the swing, when the telephone shrilled out.

Frowning, Rhonnie said, 'I wonder who that can be? It won't be Jackie as we've already had our daily chat. It won't be Ginger because she never telephones until she knows I've put Danny to bed. It's not you or Dad as you're both here.' She then gave a groan. 'That means it's got to be one of the managers or security from the camp. But everything was all right when I left not long ago, so what on earth could have happened between now and then that needs my attention?'

Drina said blandly, 'Well, you won't find out who it is or what they want unless you answer it, will you?'

A moment later, receiver to her ear, Rhonnie said: 'Oh, God! I don't believe this! What is wrong with some people? Yes, I'll be there as soon as I can.' Putting the receiver back in place she told Drina, 'Can you believe that some bright spark or sparks thought it would be funny to put shampoo into the fountain and now foam is blowing everywhere? Would you and Dad stay a while longer and put Danny to bed so I can go and organise the clean up?'

Despite the severity of the situation, Drina couldn't stop herself from laughing at the comical scene Rhonnie had just conjured up. 'This I have to see for myself. Your dad can put Danny to bed.'

A short while later Rhonnie drove into the courtyard. It seemed as if she had arrived in the middle of a snowstorm only the snow was foam. To cause this amount, more than one bottle of shampoo must have been poured into the main bowl of the fountain and the resulting foam was still spewing out of the spouts on the four decorative stone dolphins and then being blown in all directions by the evening breeze. A horde of campers were dancing around in it or trying to catch some foam and douse their partners with it. The air was filled with the noise of their screams and laughter.

As they eyed the scene before them both Drina and Rhonnie very much wished they could join the campers in their fun, but when all was said and done they were there to restore order. Even though they were both reluctant to put a damper on the campers' high jinks, as after all the aim of Jolly's was to provide their guests with as much fun as they could, they set about organising the clean-up, disturbing several maintenance men's evening with their families and getting them to come back in, drain the fountain, give it a thorough flush through and refill it again ready to be switched back on in the morning. Meanwhile Rhonnie and Drina calmed down the campers and herded them all off to their original destinations. The culprits behind the foam storm never did own up.

CHAPTER SIX

The next morning was one of those when it seemed everyone wanted to speak to Rhonnie over some matter or another, some serious, some thankfully trivial, but all important to the smooth running of the camp, and she had a constant stream of visitors through her door.

Amongst them was Eric Brown the camp chef. The usually even-tempered huge bear of a man was in a state of panic. His meat stove, an ageing monstrosity of a machine, after years of loyal service, had finally decided enough was enough and refused to work any longer and a mechanic had pronounced it beyond repair, so an urgent and very costly replacement needed to be sourced and installed. Meanwhile Eric would have to struggle to cope without it which, he assured Rhonnie, he would do and they were both very thankful that this had happened early in the season when the camp was only running at half capacity.

Another of her visitors was Carol the manager of the gift shop, first to inform Rhonnie that her new assistant Joan was settling in well, which Rhonnie was delighted to hear, and secondly that the company they bought their sticks and bags of rock from had taken on a new despatch manager, who had inadvertently mixed up orders to several of their customers. As a result the hundreds of sticks of lettered rock they had received today were all spelling 'BUTLIN'S' through the centre. Pontin's in Lowestoft had received their rock with 'JOLLY'S' lettered through it. Rock sent to Warner's holiday camp near Southend had 'PONTIN'S' spelled out through it . . . and so it went on around numerous camps in the country. Carol wanted to know if, while this nightmare of a situation was being resolved by the confectionery company, they should sell the rock that had been meant for Butlin's or should withdraw it from sale? So as not to disappoint their campers, Rhonnie decided to leave it on sale and hope not too many people noticed, leaving Carol and Joan and the other two assistants who worked in the shop making endless explanations.

The new cleaning manager, Lily Dawkins, and Alan Ibbotson, the entertainments manager, for some reason had taken a dislike to each other, judging by the way they kept shooting each other scathing looks and passing snide remarks when one or the other of them had made a comment on a topic that was being discussed at the time. After separately and surreptitiously quizzing each on the other, Rhonnie had come to the conclusion that neither of them actually knew why they'd taken against the other and it was just one of those things that happened between certain people.

Drina didn't like any animosity amongst her staff and especially not senior members. Neither did Rhonnie. As Lily and Alan were both excellent at their jobs and well liked by their staff, replacing either of them wouldn't be easy. Getting rid of one of them to resolve the situation was not something Rhonnie wanted to consider, unless of course the bad feeling between them escalated so as to affect their jobs and the staff under their charge, then she wouldn't hesitate. Rhonnie was adamant that she was going to find a way to get these two people on a better footing with each other but until she came up with an idea of just how to manage it, all she could do meanwhile was to smooth things over in such a way that neither of them thought she was favouring the other.

That morning they had both separately visited Rhonnie to request her intervention in a situation that had developed between them, that they couldn't agree on and resolve. Alan was desperate for the completion of new costumes, as without them he couldn't include the new dance routine he'd choreographed for the Friday night Stripey Show. Lily had not yet handed them over and his complaint to Rhonnie was that he felt that his fellow supervisor was purposely delaying them just to be awkward.

Lily in turn complained that she couldn't seem to make Alan understand that the repairing and making up of new costumes for the entertainments team was only a small part of her department's workload and that he would have to wait his turn in the pecking order, which he was unwilling to do and was constantly badgering her to get them done.

Both, Rhonnie suspected, were purposely causing the other strife just for the hell of it. Had Rhonnie's deceased no-nonsense grandmother been faced with this problem, she would have ordered them both to stop acting like children or she'd bash their heads together.

Alan's need of the new costumes was not as desperate as he was proclaiming, as it wasn't as if the dance routines already in the show weren't a hit with the campers anyway, so the introduction of new ones was hardly urgent. Rhonnie asked him to have patience and, the next time he asked Lily to make up new costumes, he should give her a date by which he wanted to collect them and only then would he have cause for complaint if she failed to do so.

Rhonnie was well aware that Lily's seamstresses were loaded with work undertaking the making of new bedding and curtains for the next wave of chalets that were in the process of being readied after their closure during the winter. The high season started in a few weeks' time and then the number of campers would double overnight, but regardless Lily's team still had room to manoeuvre when it came to undertaking other work that required their attention and so she knew that Alan's claim that Lily was purposely delaying finishing his costumes was more than likely justified. So she asked Lily if just this once she would allocate one of her seamstresses to complete the costumes and the next time Alan requested her to make him new ones they should agree to work to a date.

Hopefully, if both of them stuck to her suggestions, this situation should not happen again. After the meeting Rhonnie came out of her office sighing heavily and raking a despairing hand through her long blonde hair which had she left hanging loose today.

'Anyone want a cuppa?' she asked Jill and Sandra. 'I could certainly do with one after dealing with Lily and Alan. They're both really nice people, of a similar age and seem to me to have a lot in common, I just can't understand why they dislike each other so much.'

Jill, who was in the process of tallying the money in the petty cash tin against receipt for purchases, without lifting her head from her task responded to Rhonnie: 'Can't you? Well, it's glaringly obvious to me.'

Rhonnie's eyebrows rose in surprise. 'Is it? Not to me it's not, so come on, spill the beans then maybe I might come up with an idea of how to get them to mellow towards each other.'

Sandra piped up, 'My mam says you can't make a person like someone they don't. There was a girl at school that was really popular and I was desperate to get her to like me so she'd allow me into her gang. I used to give her me sweets, even did her homework a couple of times for her, but she still treated me like I was dog dirt on her shoe. I never found out why Maxine didn't like me. I've always worried that other people might not like me for the same reason, but not knowing what it was, I couldn't do anything about it, could I?'

Rhonnie looked at her meaningfully. 'Well, that girl sounds like a nasty piece of work to me so she wouldn't have been a good friend to you anyway. To my mind you had a lucky escape.'

82

Sandra thoughtfully mused, 'Mmm, well, Maxine and some of her gang did end up getting expelled for setting fire to the school and now her and some of her mates are in prison for stealing. Even if I had been in her gang, I would never have been part of the school fire or stealing as I'd have been too scared of what me mam would have done to me when she found out I was involved.'

'Well, maybe that girl didn't invite you into her gang because she sussed you weren't the type to be manipulated and it was nothing to do with whether she liked you or not.'

'Ohhh, I never thought of it that way. So it was nothing to do with me as a person – just that she knew I was too scared of me mam to get up to no good.'

'Sandra, you'll learn in life that some people might take umbrage against you, not because you both clash personality-wise, but because there's something in your personality that doesn't suit them, like you having no criminal tendencies didn't suit Maxine's purpose.' Rhonnie could tell that Sandra couldn't grasp what she was trying to explain to her so said, 'You are a lovely girl, Sandra, one most people will like, but as my mother used to tell me, we can't please everyone so just accept that some people won't ever be your friend.' She addressed Jill again. 'You were going to tell me the reason why you feel Alan and Lily can't stand the sight of each other.'

Jill smiled and said with an air of authority: 'They fancy each other, of course, and from the way they're sniping and snarling at each other, I would say a lot.'

Rhonnie scoffed, 'You couldn't have been in the same meeting as me then. If ever I've witnessed two people who loathe each other, it's Lily and Alan. Your matchmaking radar is having a rest it seems to me, Jill.'

She was prevented from responding by the outer door opening as the swimming pool supervisor entered.

As Jason Evers walked over to join Rhonnie by Jill's desk

he said, 'Sorry to bother you, Rhonnie, but I need to speak to you about the new lifeguard, Neil Rogers, who started today. Got a wad of certificates and awards for his abilities in the pool but unfortunately it turns out they belong to his brother, who originally applied for the job with us, only he decided not to take it up after all. Finding out this, Neil decided to pose as his brother and take up the job himself. Only he forgot one matter that's crucial to holding down the job of a lifeguard. He can't swim.'

Rhonnie, Jill and Sandra were staring at Jason, stunned to hear what he'd just told them. It was Jill who started laughing first, quickly followed by Rhonnie, neither of them believing anyone with an ounce of intelligence could have contemplated such a deception.

Sandra's immature brain had not yet quite processed the information that Jason had delivered and she was looking at Rhonnie and Jill in bemusement. 'What's so funny about the fact the new lifeguard can't swim?' Then the significance clicked with her and she exclaimed, 'Oh, yes, I've got it now.' She started laughing then too.

It was the middle of the afternoon before Rhonnie managed to escape the office to pay her overdue visit to the caravan park. The weather was still as warm and dry as it had been the day before so she decided to walk the mile or so out of the main camp gates, down the road a short way, then the half mile or so along the newly widened and resurfaced old farm lane, on one side of her the strip of dense woodland that separated Jolly's land from the neighbouring farmer's, and where Sam's old hut was, and on the other the high wire fence between the main camp and the caravan park.

On arrival she was gratified to see that the park was buzzing with quite a few people . . . some sitting outside their static caravans in fold-up chairs, reading books and newspapers or just enjoying the weather, some sunbathing on the grass, women cooking sausages and hamburgers on primus stoves outside so they could enjoy the weather too. Children were playing on the swings and roundabouts in the designated areas. All the same things were happening down in the touring area, where a hundred or so vans and campers were parked. Some of these guests would be off site down on the beach or else have paid the fee to enjoy the facilities the main camp offered. Now and again Rhonnie stopped to introduce herself to campers and to ask how they were enjoying their stay and if they were happy with the facilities the park offered them, gratified to receive no negative responses. Drina's new venture looked set to do very well indeed, given time.

Having first called in at the small office beside the entrance to find it empty, then at Jeff's own caravan, then in the supermarket – Sally Gibbon, the young woman who ran the shop, telling her she hadn't seen Jeff since he'd opened up and sorted the float out with her at eight that morning – Rhonnie couldn't find any sign of him at first but then came across him at the back of one of the static caravans. He was with his assistant Kevin, instructing him on how to connect a gas cylinder to its housing.

Although most men doing a dirty job like that would have slipped on overalls to protect their clothes, obviously Jeff's ego wouldn't allow him to be seen wearing such items so he was wearing no protection at all over his Jolly's uniform of blue trousers – which she felt sure he'd had taken in as they were certainly fitting him far more snugly than they had been designed to do – and blue short-sleeved sports shirt with 'Jolly's Caravan Park' embroidered over the left pocket. His thick blond shoulder-length hair looked immaculately groomed as always.

On Rhonnie's sudden appearance he immediately stopped what he was doing and looked at her, making no attempt to hide the fact that he was pleased to see her.

'Our lovely boss has come to pay us a visit and isn't she

looking attractive today, Kevin?' he said, undressing Rhonnie with his eyes.

The youth just blushed with embarrassment.

Rhonnie was not averse to being admired by a good-looking man, but regardless didn't feel this was appropriate coming from one of her staff and especially not during working hours with a junior employee present. She cocked an eyebrow and shot Jeff a meaningful look.

He failed to pick up on this. He stepped over to her and, while staring straight into her eyes, placed his hand in the small of her back and said, 'Shall we retire to my caravan where we'll be more comfortable? I'll bring you up to date with the site business and then we can collect the tourers' takings from the office safe and do the paperwork afterwards.'

She stepped aside by way of diplomatically removing his hand from her back and responded matter-of-factly. 'I'm comfortable enough outside in this lovely sunshine, thank you. Don't let me stop you from finishing what you are doing and then you can update me as we have a walk around. I like to see for myself how things are and chat to a few campers to make sure they are happy with what we are offering them,' she told him, although she had already done that.

Jeff shot her a winning smile and responded, 'The lady's wish is my command.' He addressed Kevin. 'You carry on and finish changing this, then get on with fixing that loose cupboard door in caravan sixty-three, while I have my tête-à-tête with Mrs Buckland.' Returning his attention to Rhonnie, he again put his hand in the small of her back. 'Where would you like to go first?'

An hour later, having had her tour and collected the takings and paperwork from the safe in the small camp office, Rhonnie ambled back up the old farm road. She was thinking to herself that she had never before come across a man with such a big ego as Jeff Sampson had. She supposed to many he was irresistible, being so good-looking and charismatic. She couldn't deny she found him attractive herself, but his egotistical behaviour was a source of great irritation to her. Still, he appeared to be very good at his job and the campers certainly seemed to like him . . . especially the women. She hadn't failed to notice the expressions on their faces when she had asked them their opinion of the park manager . . . so it seemed she was just going to have to ignore Jeff's behaviour whenever they crossed paths.

She was halfway between the entrance to the park and the main road when suddenly she felt a sharp stab of pain in the sole of one foot. Wincing, she stopped to take off her shoe so as to shake out the piece of grit that had obviously found its way inside. As it had a strap and buckle fastening she would need somewhere to sit or lean against to remove it. A tree trunk would do.

She limped across to the fringe of the wood and looked around for a sturdy stick to help her flatten some of the undergrowth so she could reach her goal but then she noticed that the undergrowth here was already trampled down in what seemed to be a crude path. She frowned. Someone had been in this part of the woods, and recently. She wondered why, as this unkempt strip of land was not the sort of place anyone could take a stroll through. Then it struck her that the culprit was more than likely a wild animal looking for food, a roe deer or stray dog perhaps. Well, thanks to them she wouldn't have to struggle quite so much through the straggle of undergrowth and protruding roots to get to the tree.

Having shaken the offending article out of her shoe and replaced it, she hesitated. Outside on the road the sun was still beating down. Here under the canopy of the trees it was cool and peaceful, the only sounds those of insects buzzing through the shafts of sunlight that broke through the gaps in the leaves above. Rhonnie felt she was in a completely different world from her usual one, filled with people and problems the whole day long. She pressed her back against the tree trunk, closed her eyes and savoured the moment.

A minute or two later, as she was feeling guilty about playing truant in this way and straightening up to leave, something caught her eye. She automatically looked down at ground where the flash of light had come from. Just by her feet there was a pile of dead leaves and twigs with something metal hidden beneath. It was more than likely only an old metal bottle top but curiosity made her bend down and brush away some of the debris to reveal what it was. It was not just a metal top but something bigger, like a long panel, and it appeared there were two of them. Grabbing a corner of each she pulled them out from their hiding place and realised they were a set of vehicle number plates. As she was wondering how they had come to be hidden here in the woods she heard a twig snap behind her and started to turn her head to see what had caused it, but before she could she felt a heavy thud on the back of her skull and then everything turned black.

CHAPTER SEVEN

Her whole head hurt. The back of it felt like it had been hit with a hammer, the inside was throbbing relentlessly and she was having difficulty opening her eyes. Rhonnie had no idea where she was or how she had come to be here, only that she was lying down on a none-too-comfortable mattress with nasty smells assailing her nostrils: meat cooking, mustiness, damp wood, the sourness of dirty clothes

She yelped in shock at an unexpected touch on her shoulder and forced open her eyes. She screamed hysterically at what she saw looming over her: a terrifying hairy monster of the type pictured in childhood fairy stories.

A voice urgently exclaimed, 'It's all right . . . really it is. I'm not going to hurt you. Please don't be frightened. Can you sit up? I've made you a cup of tea but I've no milk or sugar, I'm afraid.'

The person the voice belonged to might look terrifying, but the voice was kind, soothing, and her terror subsided. She accepted the grubby hand that was being offered to help her sit up, then the tin mug of tea that was held out to her.

The tea was weak – and Rhonnie liked hers sweet with milk – but regardless the few sips she took of it helped to fortify her, though did not ease the throbbing inside her head.

She flashed a glance around her. She was in an old wooden structure, larger than a normal garden shed, and she could see a door over the other side of the small room, which must lead into another. It was vaguely familiar to her but at this moment she couldn't think why. The few pieces of furniture in the room were old and shabby, in varying states of disrepair. There was a pot-bellied stove in the middle of the room, a long rusting black pipe rising from it to disappear out of the roof. On top of the stove was a blackened metal cooking pot, its lid intermittently rising and steam escaping out of the sides. That must be where the meaty smell was coming from. It was in fact quite appetising when considered separately from the other smells around her. There was an old armchair by the stove and a moth-eaten rag rug on the floor by it. On the table was an old tin can with an arrangement of wild flowers inside. The hut might be old and damp, the stuff inside it tatty, but it was apparent that the occupant was doing his best to keep it clean and make it homely.

Rhonnie's eyes then settled on the dishevelled man standing before her. He was wearing a ragbag of grubby old clothes from which a highly unpleasant smell was emanating. Despite his kindly response to her, Rhonnie was immediately on the offensive.

'Was it you who knocked me out? Have . . . have you kidnapped me? You're after money, is that it?' These were the only reasons she could think of for her being here. She suddenly remembered the bag of takings she had collected earlier and her eyes darted around in search of it. For a moment she couldn't see it but then her mouth snapped shut when she noticed it, looking as bulky as it had been when she'd first collected it from Jeff, sitting by the pillow she was resting her head on.

The threadbare creature before her visibly recoiled in horror at her suggestions. 'No, no, absolutely not, to all your questions. I know I look a mess but there's no need to be frightened of me, I'd never harm you, honestly. Please believe that,' he implored her. He was suddenly acutely conscious that he smelled far from pleasant so moved away to take a seat in the armchair by the stove before he told her, 'I was returning from a foraging trip to get some ingredients to add to my rabbit stew. Check my sack if you don't believe me. You'll find some sage, wild garlic and mushrooms. Okay, I did pull up an early potato plant from a farmer's field and got a good yield which will last me a few days, and yes, that was stealing as I never got his permission to help myself, but that's all I'm guilty of.

'I was making my way back to this hut, down the path at the edge of the field on the other side of the woods, when I heard a cry. I thought at first it was an animal caught in one of my traps but when I investigated I was shocked to find a woman . . . you . . . out cold under a tree. I tried to wake you but you were not responding so I carried you back here. You were breathing and I couldn't see any blood anywhere on you, so I thought you'd just passed out. If you hadn't woken up soon, I was going to go down to the caravan park and fetch help. Obviously I was hoping you'd wake up. Because of what I am, people would automatically assume, as you did, that I was somehow responsible for what had happened to you and then I'd have a lynch mob on my hands.'

She looked at him knowingly then as realisation struck. 'Of course. This is Sam's old hut. I thought it seemed familiar. And you're the tra— gentleman of the road that Mrs Jolly told me about, the one she allowed to use Sam's hut.'

He looked at her in surprise. 'You know Mrs Jolly, the owner of the camp?'

Rhonnie nodded. 'I'm the manager there.'

His eyes told her he was smiling. 'Well, it's nice to meet you. I'm very grateful to Mrs Jolly for allowing me to stay here.' His eyes roved around the room and he spoke wistfully. 'It might just be an old hut to most people, but to me it's a palace. The first place I've had to call home in a very long time. It's no fun living on the road, never knowing where you're going to find to sleep next . . . or if you are going to,

91

in fact . . . so it's such a wonderful feeling for me to know I've somewhere to come back to after being out all day, searching for work or foraging for food. Now I have the means to cook that food, a chair to sit in, a proper bed, and can actually have a wash each night with hot water, wash my clothes even, although at the moment I daren't in case they fall completely to bits. I've nothing to replace them with, you see, so I do apologise for the smell but can't do anything about that, I'm afraid.' He eyed her then, looking deeply worried. 'I expect Mrs Jolly will have thought I've moved on by now . . . do you think she'll mind that I'm still here?'

The way of life he'd just described to Rhonnie sounded like absolute purgatory to her, a life she couldn't imagine anyone purposely choosing to live, but she could fully appreciate that this old damp hut, with its shabby assortment of furniture, was like a palace to him and in consequence he was reluctant to leave it. 'Well, we haven't received any complaints about you from our campers or the neighbouring farmers so you haven't given her any reason to evict you. I don't see why she wouldn't continue to turn a blind eye to you living here if that remains the case.'

He looked mortally relieved and told Rhonnie with conviction, 'I assure you that it will.'

His blue eyes, all she could see of his face because of the profusion of hair masking the rest, were brimming with honesty and her every instinct told her that though this man might look fierce, he had nothing to do with the attack on her and posed no threat to her whatsoever. What she was finding intriguing was why this obviously intelligent, well-spoken man had come to be living in such dire circumstances? But more important to her at the moment was how she herself had come to be in the situation she was now in.

He obviously was guessing what she was thinking and asked quizzically: So . . . can you remember how I came to find you like I did?

Rhonnie stared at him as she fought to remember. She lifted a hand and gingerly felt the back of her head, wincing as her fingers touched an extremely tender lump. 'Something struck me on the back of the head. Someone must have hit me. Why, though, I've no idea. I'd been down to the caravan park and was on my way back to the main camp. I had to adjust my shoe so I stepped into the trees for a moment. It was so cool and peaceful there, kind of magical in a way, and after I'd taken the stone out, I leaned back and closed my eyes for a moment. I was about to leave when a flash of light on something metallic caught my eye. I bent down to see what it was. . . . and then I heard a noise behind me . . . the snapping of twigs . . . and that was when I felt a thud on the back of my head and the next thing I knew I was waking up here.'

Without a word he eased himself out of the sagging armchair and went over to the rickety table. There was a ragged but clean-looking piece of towelling there, which he dipped into a bucket of water by the side of the table, wrung it out then came over to Rhonnie, handing it to her. 'I've nothing to give you to help ease your headache but put this on the lump and it might help take the swelling down.'

She gratefully accepted the wet cloth and did as he suggested while he returned to sit in the armchair, where he frowned thoughtfully at her for a moment or two before he said: 'When I found you I did notice a rotting piece of branch by the side of you. It might not have been that someone actually hit you . . . maybe the branch snapped off the tree you were standing under. The sound of breaking twigs you heard just before you were hit could in fact have been the branch snapping off the tree. Wrong place at the wrong time.'

She stared at him for a moment while she digested what he had told her before saying, 'Yes, that could be what happened. It makes more sense than someone attacking me for no reason.' She then added ruefully, 'I wish I'd never gone into the woods now.' She took a couple more sips of the tepid tea before looking at him curiously and saying, 'You're not the normal kind of tramp.'

'Normal? What do you mean by that?'

'Well . . . just that I thought tramps were rough types of people from poor backgrounds, who live a life on the road because they can't be bothered to get themselves a proper job. They rob or con people out of their possessions to pay for what they need. You might look . . . well, like other tramps I've seen, but I can tell you're not the rough and ready sort by the way you talk, and you're certainly not a thief or you'd have taken my bag of takings and left me where you found me.'

Rhonnie could tell by his eyes that he was smiling again. 'That's what most people believe, that tramps are thieves and vagabonds, but not all of us should be tarred with that brush and I'm glad you can see things differently. I've never stolen anything in my life . . . well, anything apart from a few potatoes from a farmer's field, which I am sure he wouldn't have missed. What I eat I pay for from work I've managed to pick up, or I live off what nature provides me with, or I go without. On my travels I've come across all sorts of people living like I am, from all walks of life. I actually met a lord once – he proved it to me by showing me some photos from his past life. And I've met doctors, solicitors, even a bank manager, as well as many people who worked in factories and shops in their previous lives. But I've also come across many like you described, who would steal the boots off your feet to sell for a bottle of meths, even some who would murder for a couple of cigarettes. We all have one thing in common, though. Something happened to us in the past that left us with no alternative but to seek escape in the precarious existence we now live. It's a dangerous life and I wouldn't recommend it to anyone.'

'Did your business fail? Are you a gambler who lost all your money . . . something like that? Is that how you came to be living as you are?'

He looked at her for a moment before he said shortly, 'Something like that. How's your headache now? Would you like some more tea?'

From his evasion of her question Rhonnie deduced that the reason he had come to be living like this was something he was ashamed of admitting: like, he'd cheated on his wife who took him to the cleaners and left him penniless by way of making him pay for his adultery. She smiled at him. 'No, thank you. I must be going. I've some headache pills back at the camp and a couple of those should make things much better. Thank you . . . er . . . what is your name, by the way?'

'People call me Bushy.'

She chuckled. 'I can appreciate why but I prefer to call you by your proper name – the one your parents christened you with.'

He chuckled then. 'It's been so long since I've been called it, I've almost forgotten what it was. It's Ben.'

'Well, thank you, Ben. My name is Rhonda Buckland . . . my friends call me Rhonnie. I very much appreciate your coming to my rescue.'

She got up and picked up the takings bag. As she was about to step through the door, a thought struck Ben. 'Just as a matter of interest, what was it you found beneath the pile of leaves or didn't you manage to see before the falling branch knocked you out?'

She stopped and turned to face him. 'Oh, I'd forgotten about that. Yes, I did. It was a set of vehicle number plates. I'd only partly pulled them out before the branch hit me but they looked newish to me, not old or rusty, so they hadn't been hidden there long at all.'

His eyes looked puzzled. 'Strange thing for someone to want to hide?'

She nodded. 'Yes, it is, isn't it? But people do strange things.'

'Yes, they do. But you just said you had half pulled the

number plates out from under the leaves when the branch snapped off and hit you. When I found you there was no sign of any number plates.'

Rhonnie frowned. 'Oh! Oh, well, maybe the knock on the head has been playing tricks with my mind, that's all I can say. Anyway, I really must be off. It's been nice to meet you, Ben.' And to her surprise she found she really meant that. There was something about this man . . .

Back at the office, on finding out what had happened to her, Jill went to telephone for the duty nurse to come and check Rhonnie over but she said there was no need, insisting there was nothing wrong with her that a cup of sweet milky tea and couple of headache tablets wouldn't put right.

When Rhonnie took Danny for a visit to his grandparents that evening before he went to bed, she decided not to tell Drina about her accident in the woods for the simple reason that Jill had already caused enough of a fuss over it. Instead she told Drina that she had happened upon the tramp who had been allowed to live in Sam's old hut as she had been making her way back from visiting the caravan park . . . Ben, he'd said his name was . . . he had asked her to have a cup of tea with him and, not wanting to hurt his feelings by refusing, she had accepted. Although it was strange talking to someone so out of the ordinary, she had thought him a very nice man, polite and respectful and intelligent too. He was certainly doing his best to make the hut homely.

Drina was pleased to hear this. It made her feel good to know that she was providing a homeless person with a roof over their head and she told Rhonnie that as far as she was concerned Sam's hut would not be demolished until Ben decided to move on.

Later that night, as Rhonnie was selecting clothes to wear for work the next day before she went to bed, a vision of the shabby, very pungent rags Ben had been wearing came to mind. As she had been talking to him it was apparent that he was embarrassed by his appearance and she presumed his dishevelled state would hamper him greatly in picking up any work. Being allowed to stay in the hut might mean he had the means to keep himself clean but that was a largely fruitless exercise when his clothes smelled so badly and were in danger of disintegrating. The only way Ben was going to get anything more decent to wear was if clothes were donated to him.

Rhonnie felt an overwhelming urge to help him. She realised that Drina must have experienced the same thing and that was why she'd allowed him to stay in the hut. Ben just had a way about him that drew people to him, it seemed. Rhonnie had a pile of clothes she could donate to him. Whether they would all fit him she had no idea as it had been impossible to tell under his thick layer of rags, but some of them might at least. The only problem was whether she herself was ready to part with them yet . . . if ever in fact.

She opened the other door to the large wardrobe to reveal Dan's clothes and ran her hand across the row of hanging shirts, pairs of jeans and trousers, his prized leather jacket, then on over the pile of tee shirts, jumpers and underwear neatly folded on shelves down one side. As though it was the most precious, delicate object to Rhonnie, she picked up a tee shirt and held it to her nose, sniffing deeply. Tears then pricked her eyes as she removed the tee shirt and stared at it. She had wanted . . . expected . . . to smell Dan's scent on it but she hadn't, not a whiff. The passing of time since his death had evaporated all traces of him and his tee shirt now just held the musty smell of an item that had lain untouched in a wardrobe for a long time. She refolded the tee shirt and placed it back on the pile. These clothes were still Dan's, though, and the thought of anyone else wearing them, even someone as desperate as Ben, was unthinkable to her. She made to shut the wardrobe door but then remembered once more the man in the woods dressed in garments that were in truth only fit for burning. She gave herself a hard talking to. Knowing Dan as well as she had, she knew he would be cross with her for holding on to his memory like she was. Keeping his clothes was serving no other purpose than providing food for moths and making her sad every time she opened the door to look at them.

Before she changed her mind, she gathered them all together and put them in a holdall, which she then took outside to her car, putting the bag on the back seat, ready for her to take to work the next morning. As soon as she had time she would take them to Sam's old hut and give them to Ben.

At the same time as Rhonnie was bagging up the clothes to give to him, Ben was sitting in the armchair by the stove in the hut, the door of it open so that flames from the wood burning inside could cast some light. Despite his efforts, Ben had not managed to get himself any paid work for a few days so he could not afford to buy any paraffin for the lamp or candles either. This meant he couldn't pass his evening reading any of the discarded newspapers he had found in the village rubbish bins that day as he had passed through on his search of work or any more pages of the dog-eared paperback novel he had found on a bench in the bus station last week: *The Thirty-nine Steps* by John Buchan.

So tonight all he had for company were his thoughts.

At the moment they were of the unexpected encounter he'd had that afternoon. The circumstances in which he had met Rhonnie he would never have wished on her, no matter how starved he was for company, and he was glad it didn't appear the falling branch had caused her any lasting injury. He wondered though if she had any idea of the pleasure that spending time in another's company had afforded him. Even people who were kind enough to give him some work never stopped to talk to him, just seeing him as a dirty nuisance to be avoided like everyone else did. So for a woman like Rhonnie to treat him as a human being and talk to him like she'd talk to anyone else . . . for a short time he had felt as if he was part of the human race again and not an outcast.

He smiled as he thought of Rhonnie. Not only had she been pleasant company, she was also intelligent and a very good-looking woman too, the type that in his previous life he would have been attracted to. He had noticed the wedding ring on her finger, though, so even had he been in a position to pursue her, she was unobtainable on the romantic front anyway. But he could have made friends with her and her husband, invited them along with his other acquaintances to a party he was holding or a dinner he was hosting.

His smile faded. All he was doing by thinking like this was causing himself unnecessary hurt. That previous life was gone, lost forever, along with ever having any kind of relationship with a woman like Rhonnie. The time spent with her today was a one-off.

As he leaned over to pick up a log from the small pile at the side of the stove and place it inside, he wondered if Rhonnie would have been as comfortable in his company if he had told her the truth about his past and the reason why he now lived as he did: he was responsible for the deaths of five people.

At the same time, further down the old farm lane, Jeff Sampson was lounging on a striped deckchair on the grass outside his caravan, long legs stretched out before him, drinking lager out of a tin. He too was thinking about his encounter that afternoon with Rhonnie. He had fancied her the first time he had clapped eyes on her. And what red-blooded man wouldn't want to bed a woman like Rhonnie, with her attractive looks, shapely figure, legs up to her armpits and cascade of long honey-blonde hair? She was feisty too and he liked that quality in his women. He supposed that if he was the type who was looking to find himself a wife and settle down, she was as good a candidate as he would find. Married into the Jolly family, albeit a widow now as he had found out by asking around other staff members, she would no doubt have bene-fitted from her late husband's estate so was in a position to give him a very comfortable lifestyle. But Jeff was the type that liked a different woman every day of the week, so the thought of being tied to one for any length of time filled him with dread, no matter how big her bank balance and how generous she was with it. Besides, very soon he wouldn't need someone else's money to fund a good lifestyle as he would have his own.

That didn't stop him wanting to get Rhonnie into bed and enjoy the delights of her body. He knew she fancied him. What woman didn't fall head over heels for his good looks and magnetic personality? Having been a widow for nearly two years now, she had to be desperate for the physical company of a man. It rankled him that as yet his efforts to charm her had borne no results but he knew she was just her playing hard to get. Some woman weren't so easy to win over but she would give in, in the end, like they all did. It was just a matter of time. Before he left this job with the means to fund his new future he would have bedded Rhonnie Buckland, he was adamant about that.

CHAPTER EIGHT

Rhonnie let out a slow sigh of relief as she eased off her stilettos and in turn gave each of her aching feet a rub. Then, tucking them under her, she picked up the mug of tea she had made herself when she had first arrived home, leaned back in the armchair and took several sips of the reviving sweet liquid. She hadn't been looking forward to Jill's dinner party, her first outing on her own since Dan's death, but now she was glad she hadn't used any of excuses she had come up with not to go as, to her surprise, she had actually enjoyed the evening very much.

Jill could certainly cook. The food she had served up had been delicious and she and her husband Martin were the perfect hosts. The other guests too had been very amiable people: two couples and the other four, including Rhonnie herself, single. Not for a moment since Jill had invited her into her home had Rhonnie felt awkward or out of her depth.

Jill's evasiveness about her matchmaking plans had tipped Rhonnie off in advance. As soon as she'd arrived, Jill had taken Rhonnie by the arm and guided her over to a smartly but casually dressed man of medium height, in his early thirties. Jill introduced him as Colin, a work colleague of her husband's, then immediately excused herself, claiming she needed to go and check the food wasn't burning. Despite being a mite cross with her hostess for putting her in such a situation, Rhonnie realised it had been done with the best of intentions. Rhonnie found Colin to be excellent company and might even have accepted an invitation to dinner with him had he asked her – but early on in their conversation it became plain to Rhonnie that he was interested in only one woman in that house and that woman was Jill. What Rhonnie found amusing was that Jill, who deemed herself an expert where matters of the heart were concerned, seemed to have no idea whatsoever that she had a secret admirer. Rhonnie doubted Martin would have been very pleased had he realised and Colin would not have been invited to another dinner party in a hurry! It seemed to Rhonnie, though, that Jill was losing her fabled ability for instinctively knowing when two people were right for each other, as for the second time recently she had been proved way off the mark, first in respect of Lily Dawkins and Alan Ibbotson and tonight with Rhonnie and Colin.

Then Rhonnie thought of Ben. Earlier that day she had made a visit to Sam's old hut, which in fact she was now thinking of as Ben's, to leave the bag of clothes she had sorted out for him by the door, first making sure he wasn't around so as to avoid any possible embarrassment on his part. She assumed he would have found them by now and hoped they were of use to him.

She leaned her head against the back of the chair as her thoughts then turned to her son. This wasn't just the first night she had gone out socially on her own since Dan had died, but the first time her son and she had been apart over-night since Danny had been born. It felt strange to Rhonnie, as if part of her was missing, her son not being under the same roof as her, but she knew he was safe and secure with his grandparents and they had promised faithfully to telephone her at Jill's should Danny be pining for her or they not able to settle him down for the night. Since they hadn't she could only assume that all had gone well . . . or, knowing her father and Drina as she did, that they had completely tired out their

102

grandson by playing with him and he was probably fast asleep before he had been tucked into his cot for the night.

She caught sight of the clock ticking on the mantel above the fireplace. It was getting on for one and she ought to take herself to bed and get some sleep because in a few short hours she would need to be up and alert to receive her son. It was Sunday tomorrow and unless an emergency arose that needed her managerial intervention she planned to spend the whole day enjoying the company of her son.

Having secured the house for the night, she was just about to put her foot on the first step of the stairs to make her way up to bed when an unexpected pounding on the front door had her almost leaping out of her skin. Her immediate thought that it was either Drina or Artie come to fetch her as for some reason they couldn't get through on the telephone and something was wrong with Danny.

She dashed over to the front door, unlocked it and yanked it open. She just managed to jump out of the way to avoid being knocked over by a body falling through the doorway. It landed heavily on the floor, crying out in shock, 'Bloody hell! Ouch! I've bashed my knee. It really hurts. I think I've broken it.'

A stunned Rhonnie stood staring down at the dishevelled figure lying in heap by her feet. It took her a moment to recognise who it was. 'Ginger!' she finally exclaimed.

Pushing aside her red corkscrew curls, which had dead leaves and twigs sticking out of them, Anita – or Ginger as she was known by all her friends for obvious reasons – looked up at Rhonnie and snapped at her: 'Don't just stand there like a bleddy village idiot, help me up!'

Many questions were tumbling through Rhonnie's mind. What was her very dear friend doing here at this time of night without any warning whatsoever? More to the point, why was Ginger so drunk? The girl Rhonnie knew and loved she had never seen any more than tiddly, so she was extremely worried to see her friend in this state. Not only that but her clothes were covered in mud, her stockings in shreds, and she was barefoot with fresh cuts on her feet. She looked like she'd fallen into a thick prickly hedge and been pulled out backwards.

It took a few attempts to get Ginger up on her feet. Then, with one arm around her for support, Rhonnie hauled her into the lounge and had her sitting on the sofa, or lolling would have been a more accurate description. Rhonnie knew she would have a clean-up job to tackle in the morning, getting stains off it caused by the damp sludge on Ginger's clothes.

Leaving her alone for a moment, Rhonnie went into the kitchen to make her a cup of tea and pour her a glass of water, hoping both would sober her up. When she returned Ginger had fallen into a drunken stupor and Rhonnie had to shake her to wake her up.

Ginger fought for a moment to remember where she was and focus her eyes. Realising what Rhonnie was offering her, she flapped one hand dismissively at her and slurred, 'I'd prefer something with alcohol in it. Anything will do, I'm not fussy.'

Rhonnie told her in no uncertain terms, 'Tea or water, that's all you're getting. You've had enough booze for one night by the look of you.'

'I'm quite capable of knowing when I've had enough or not and I haven't, not until I completely conk out into oblivion. So are you going to get me a proper drink or do I have to help meself?'

Ginger tried to get up off the sofa but failed, falling back on it like a puppet whose strings had been cut.

Putting the drinks on a small table at the side of the sofa, Rhonnie then sat in the armchair close by. Looking anxiously at her friend, she demanded, 'What's going on, Ginger? Getting blind drunk isn't you, not the Ginger I know, so why are you? And looking at the state of you . . . well, I'm worried you've been attacked or something?'

She shook her head. 'No, I haven't been attacked. I fell down a ditch on the way here from Mablethorpe. I was just walking along the grass verge by the road . . . couldn't hardly see a thing as it was so dark . . . then I don't know what the hell happened but I found meself tumbling headlong into a ditch.' She loudly belched and slurred, 'Oh, pardon me for being so rude, it was not me it was the drink.' When Rhonnie didn't find her quip funny Ginger gave a suit-yourself shrug and continued with her story. 'Took me ages to get out, it was all slippy and slimy and I kept sliding back down. I was worried I never would get out and end up spending the night in that ditch until someone came along to help me out in the morning . . . that's if I was still alive to be pulled out and not frozen to death meantime.' She pulled a disgruntled face. 'I lost my shoes. They were nearly new too. But what really pissed me off was that I had some cider left in the bottle and I spilled it when I fell down.'

'But how did you come to fall into a ditch in the first place? Why didn't you catch a bus or get a taxi out here when you arrived at Mablethorpe?'

'Because by the time I'd called in at the off licence after getting off the train in Mablethorpe for the bottle of cider, the last bus out here had gone and there were no taxis in sight and I didn't fancy spending the night in the freezing station waiting room so I decided to walk.' She grumbled, 'I never would have if I'd remembered how far it is to your cottage from Mablethorpe, and especially while dragging all my belongings with me. It felt like I was doing a hundred-mile trek across the Himalayas.'

'Why didn't you telephone me from the station to pick you up in my car?'

Ginger looked at Rhonnie blankly for a moment. 'Oh, I never thought of that. Anyway, you wouldn't have been able to as you wouldn't leave Danny on his own and he'd have been in bed by the time my train pulled in.'

'Danny isn't here, he's spending the night with my dad and Drina.'

Ginger angrily accused her, 'You could have told me that and saved me nearly killing meself!'

'How could I when I didn't know you were coming?'

'Oh, no, you didn't, did you? Well, I'm here now . . . just about in one piece, though I doubt I'll be able to wear these tights again,' she chuckled, looking down at the tattered remains.

Rhonnie was losing patience with her. 'Are you going to tell me the reason for your visit and the state you're in or do I have to wring it out of you?'

Ginger angrily snarled, 'Ask that *bastard* and let him tell you why.'

Rhonnie hadn't any idea whatsoever who Ginger could be referring to. 'And what *bastard* would that be?'

She eyed Rhonnie knowingly. 'Who else but the one I married.'

Rhonnie gasped in shock. 'Paul! But he's the kindest, nicest man I've ever met. I can't imagine him doing anything to upset you so badly that it would drive you out here in the middle of the night.'

The anger seemed suddenly to drain from Ginger then, to be replaced with utter misery. Tears of distress trickling down her face, she whispered, 'Yes, well, I thought he was all those things too until I caught him with another woman.'

'Paul, with another woman? I don't believe it!'

'Nor did I, but then I had no choice to as your own eyes don't lie to you, do they? They were coming out of the pub, both drunk as lords . . . well, she certainly was, draped all over him, hardly able to walk, and she kept kissing him.'

'But Paul doesn't drink, Ginger, not what you'd call drinking anyway. I've never seen him have more than two or three halves of bitter on a night out.'

'And that's all he would have until he was promoted into

the CID.' Ginger had slumped sideways and took a moment to push herself back upright before she miserably went on. 'It was Paul's dream to get into what he called proper policing work and he worked hard at his exams, passing them all with flying colours to get a promotion. He was absolutely over the moon when he finally got the letter telling him he had. It meant a big change for me, having to move to another town where I didn't know anyone, but that's what you do when you love someone, don't you? The first day I packed him off to work wearing a suit not just a plain old bobby's uniform . . . he was so proud, but not as proud as I was of him. Well, you know how I was . . . I drove you mad, ringing you up to tell you how much I admired him.'

She paused just long enough to pick up the cup of tea Rhonnie had made for her and take several sips from it before going on. 'The change in him started that first day. I'd cooked him his favourite for dinner by way of celebrating . . .. roast chicken with all the trimmings, treacle tart and custard for pudding, and I'd splashed out on a bottle of Blue Nun. I even put candles on the table, but by the time he got home after half-past seven the dinner was stone cold and curling up at the edges and he was half cut and could barely stand. I was surprised he'd remembered where he lived. His excuse was that he'd been roped into going for a drink after work with the rest of his colleagues. It was tradition, he told me. Well, I was just glad that that initiation was out of the way, and of course I forgave him and cooked him egg and chips.

'But then the next night he was late again and it was obvious he'd had a drink and when I challenged him he told me that all the team went to the pub before they went home every night, just to wind down after a hard day, and it didn't go down well with the others if one of them cried off. If Paul wanted to be accepted as one of the lads then he had to go to the pub after work every night. Of course I wasn't happy about it but what could I do? Over the next few months Paul would come home later and later and some nights I'd never see him at all when they were investigating an important case. He was also drinking a lot more than he ever used to and he changed, Rhonnie. He became really moody and would snap at me for no reason. I thought this was just due to the pressure of his job. I got friendly with a couple of the other officers' wives and they advised me that being a CID wife was very different from being married to a normal beat bobby. That they were a law unto themselves, the job came before their marriage, and if I wanted to keep mine intact I should just to put up and shut up, the same as all the other wives did. They told me to do like they had done and get myself some hobbies or else have a baby to keep me occupied.'

Ginger's words were spilling out of her mouth in a garbled torrent and she was swaying from side to side, gesticulating wildly with her hands. Rhonnie was having to make a great effort to keep up with her story.

'Well, 'cos I wanted my marriage to work and I loved Paul, I had no choice but to accept the way my life with him would be. I wasn't ready yet to have a baby, I'm not one for hobbies as such – knitting or crocheting, that sort of thing – so I got myself a job as a counter assistant in Boots the chemist. I quite like it and the girls I work with are all nice and I get on with them really well. With both of us out at work all day and Paul working lots of weekends too and most nights, not getting home until after eight, sometimes later, we were like ships passing in the night. At first we used to make love several times a week but it was getting down to barely once a fortnight and when I approached Paul about it, asking him if he'd gone off me or something, he told me not to be so silly, it was because he was working long hours and was tired.'

Ginger stopped talking for a moment to wipe her face before she went on. 'Yesterday it was the birthday of a girl at my work. Her and a few others were going for a drink afterwards. I was asked if I'd like to go. Normally after work

I just want to get home but I thought I'd only be sitting waiting for Paul, hoping his dinner wouldn't be too dried up by the time he did show up, so I decided to go. It was lovely, the girls are really good company, but after a couple of drinks we called it a night as most of them had husbands and children to get back to.

'We'd gone to a pub in town and I was on my way to the bus station when I saw a couple virtually falling out of a pub. The woman was all over the bloke. I remember thinking it was a little bit early for them to be so drunk as it was only just after seven. Then I realised that the pub was the one the coppers all go to after work as Paul had mentioned the name to me once. It's just round the corner from his station. I wondered if he was inside and thought if he was then we could go home together. I was just about to go over to the pub when it struck me that the bloke with the woman all over him was Paul.' Ginger's lower lip trembled, her eyes filled with hurt. 'Oh, Rhonnie, I can't tell you how I felt as I watched a taxi pull up and Paul help the woman into it and then get in after her. I felt like my heart had been ripped out,' she said, banging her clenched fist against it. 'So that was why he was always moody and hardly came near me anymore, because he'd met someone else and wanted to be with her and not me. I supposed it was just a matter of time before he told me he was leaving me, probably waiting for the right moment. So I've saved him the bother.

'I went home and packed up all my stuff, left him a note to tell him what I'd seen and that I was doing his dirty work for him, leaving him free to be with his new woman. I didn't want to be living in hope that he'd change his mind and constantly expecting him to turn up here, begging me to take him back. I mean, he'll guess this is the place I'd come to at a time like this, to be with my best friend, so I told him I was going to Ireland to stay with a cousin who's just married and moved there.' Ginger sniffed heavily and blubbered, 'Oh,

I can't bear all this, Rhonnie, it's so awful. I thought Paul and me were for life and I can't believe he doesn't love me anymore. I don't know how I'm ever going to get over this.' She looked at Rhonnie pleadingly. 'Please promise me that if Paul does telephone you or come here looking for me, you'll tell him you haven't a clue where I am and the receptionists at Jolly's will do the same. I can't ever see him again, I just can't, Rhonnie.'

'But, Ginger, what if . . .'

'There's no what if's, Rhonnie. I could forgive Paul many things, but betraying me with another woman . . . I just couldn't. Do I have your promise to send him packing if he ever shows up here?'

She nodded. 'Yes, of course you do.'

'Thank you,' Ginger muttered. 'Look, I'm sorry I've just dumped myself on you without any warning but will you let me stay until I get myself sorted?'

Rhonnie leaped out of her chair and went to kneel by her friend. Grabbing her mud-smeared hands and giving them a reassuring squeeze, she told her, 'Oh, Ginger, that goes without saying. I'll do whatever I can for you, you know that.'

Her friend flashed her a wan smile. 'And I was hoping you'd give me my old job back as a chalet maid, if you've any vacancies? Then I could move back into one of the staff chalets for the rest of the summer and maybe I'll pal up with some other girls here who'll want to share a flat over the winter like I did before I married Paul.'

'If we've no vacancies I'll make a vacancy for you, don't you worry about that,' Rhonnie assured her. 'Anyway, we can deal with it tomorrow. First things first. You need a bath and those cuts on your feet need seeing to. I'll go and run the bath for you after I fetch in your belongings from outside, so you can sort yourself out some toiletries and nightclothes.'

A moment later Rhonnie returned looking perplexed.

'Ginger, there's no sign of any suitcases and I've just realised you've no handbag with you either, so where are they?'

Her consumption of drink was finally taking its toll. Ginger had toppled sideways on the sofa and was having extreme difficulty keeping her eyes open.

Rhonnie shook her to rouse her. 'Ginger, where did you leave your luggage and handbag? I can't find them outside on the porch.'

'Eh . . . oh . . . er . . . I left them somewhere, Rhonnie . . . I dunno.'

With that her whole body slumped and she passed into oblivion.

Rhonnie looked down tenderly at her. Ginger's cascade of bright carrot-coloured corkscrew curls was covering up the heavy splattering of freckles across her pale cheeks. Her closed eyelids were fringed with golden lashes hiding bright blue eyes, and she had crooked front teeth. Maturity and marriage had filled her out a little from the skinny waif Rhonnie had first met but regardless she was still slim and gawky.

Rhonnie was in no doubt that fate had played a hand in her encountering Ginger in a freezing station waiting room in the early hours of the morning over three years ago. At the time Rhonnie herself was going through a very tough time in her life and that meeting was to change things forever, bringing her to Jolly's and the man she was to marry and then lose so tragically. But through all her highs and lows these last three years, Ginger had been there for Rhonnie every step of the way, her friendship never once faltering. Now it was Ginger who needed a friend to lean on through a painful period in her life and Rhonnie's turn to support her.

She went and fetched a blanket and couple of pillows to make Ginger as comfortable as she could for her night on the sofa. She then remembered the missing luggage. First thing tomorrow she would have to go out and search for it.

*　　*　　*

At just before nine the next morning Rhonnie was in the kitchen at the stove frying bacon when a tap sounded on the back door immediately followed by Drina breezing in, saying, 'It's only me. Artie will be in with Danny in a moment because he wanted a go on the swing. I mean Danny, not Artie,' she adding laughing. Stripping off her coat and hanging it on a hook on the back of the door, she eagerly asked, 'So how did it go then?'

Rhonnie checked the kettle for water, then put in on a hot plate on the range before she turned around and smiled a greeting at Drina. 'It was a lovely night, thank you. I really enjoyed myself and I'm glad I went. And I was right, Jill was up to her matchmaking tricks but this time it backfired on her because the chap she was trying to set me up with only had eyes for one woman at the party and that was Jill herself! She has no idea she has a secret admirer. It was quite funny to watch. How was my son last night?'

'An angel as usual. He went straight to sleep as soon as his head hit the pillow. He was missing his mum when he woke up this morning and that's why we're here early.'

Rhonnie turned and took a look out of the window where her dad was pushing Danny on the swing. 'Seems he soon forgot about me when he arrived and saw his toys. Cuppa and a bacon sandwich?'

'Yes to both, please, and I don't have to ask Artie to know that he'll say yes to both too. I'll mash the tea,' Drina offered, going over to a row of shelves to fetch the tea caddy. As she was filling the teapot with boiling water, with Rhonnie slicing bread at the table, a memory stirred and Drina said, 'Oh, the strangest thing happened on the way over this morning. There was a suitcase abandoned on the verge by the road and when we stopped to investigate Artie found another down in the ditch, covered in mud, and a handbag and a pair of shoes too, but no sign of any owner. Very odd, if you ask me. Anyway, he's going to run them over to the police station later.'

So that's what had happened to Ginger's luggage, Rhonnie thought. 'There's no need for Dad to do that. I know who all those things belong to.'

Drina looked at her in surprise. 'You do?'

Rhonnie nodded. 'Yes, they're Ginger's. She must have forgotten about them when she clawed her way out of the ditch last night after falling in. Mind, she was steaming drunk at the time.'

Drina's eyes were wide with astonishment as she pulled a chair out from under the kitchen table, sat down on it and proceeded to pour out cups of tea. 'I think I'm missing something here. Would you care to enlighten me, dear?'

A short while later Drina was laughing so hard tears were rolling down her cheeks. 'Oh, I know I shouldn't be laughing as what brought Ginger here to us is awful for her, but the thought of her falling down into the ditch and trying to claw her way out in the pitch dark is just so funny.'

Rhonnie was giggling too. 'Yes, I have to agree, it is, and I had a hell of a job keeping a straight face when she was telling me about it last night.'

'I'm having a job believing that Paul has done what he has to her. He's such a nice man. Still, I'm glad Ginger came to us in her time of need, and whatever I can do to help her through this I will.'

'One thing is certain: she's going to need all the help she can get to survive one hell of a hangover. I know she's going to be suffering when she wakes up.'

Drina pulled a face and nodded. 'Sooner her than me.'

CHAPTER NINE

Darren Clarke was twenty-seven, tall and gangling at over six foot three, and rake-thin. He had thinning brown hair and a long straight nose. The scars on his cheeks showed that as an adolescent he had suffered terribly from acne, and detracted from the warmth in his brown eyes. He was shy and lacked confidence at any social gathering he went to. Darren was always the one to be found keeping a tall plant company as he sipped on the same drink he'd had all night, worried that anyone would engage him in conversation and he'd make a fool of himself with his inability to make humorous small talk.

Darren had one great passion in life and that was taking photographs. It had been ignited within him at the age of six when his beloved late father had given him a Box Brownie camera along with several rolls of film for Christmas. Since then, in his spare time he could usually be found out and about snapping shots of whatever caught his eye and then developing them in a makeshift darkroom his father had constructed in an old shed at the bottom of the garden, having learned how to from library books. On leaving school, Darren had been thrilled to be given a job by a local photographer in his shop, where he had learned every aspect of the trade that he didn't already know. He had no great ambitions for himself, didn't aspire to own his own shop or become a great name in the trade, taking photographs for the rich and famous.

So long as he was earning a living doing what he loved doing best, he was happy. Which was what he was doing now as Jolly's camp photographer.

He had seen the job advertised one day in January when he had been reading a national newspaper during his lunch break at work. At the time Darren had been in rather a dilemma. The old man he worked for had announced to him that he was retiring and selling up, and as his long-time employee Darren had been offered first refusal of the business. He would have been delighted to have been in a position to accept the offer, but he wasn't. The two hundred pounds savings he had in the bank, money he'd accumulated over his fourteen years of working, would go nowhere towards buying a business at the price his boss was looking for, and his parents were not in a position to help financially so he'd had to decline. The man who did buy the business made it clear to Darren that once he took over, he wouldn't be needing any help, as his own son would be joining him.

Jobs like he had were become increasingly scarce thanks to cheap instamatic cameras flooding the market, meaning more and more people were taking their own photographs and having them developed by the chain of camera and developing shops springing up in towns and cities across the country. It seemed to Darren that his only option was to apply for a job with one of the high-street stores such as Dixons or Currys. But the thought of being one assistant amongst several stuck behind a counter selling cameras and accessories or dealing with customers' films for developing did not appeal to him one little bit. So the job Jolly's was offering – he was to find out at his interview that he'd be replacing the previous photographer, who had left to take up a position with a big London agency as a society photographer – was like a lifeline to Darren. As the camp photographer he would he be doing what he loved best, actually shooting the photographs then seeing them through every stage of the developing process until he could watch the reactions of people viewing the snaps he had taken of them. The only downside was that the job ran from the beginning of April until the end of October, but if he was lucky enough to secure it then it would give him some much-needed breathing space in which to plan his future. All he had to do was convince Jolly's he was the best man for the job, which thankfully he did.

At the moment Darren was in the back of Jolly's Snaps, as the camp photography shop was called, undertaking the weekly stock check of photographic sundries with his seventeen-year-old counter assistant, Kerry Mullins. Kerry was a pleasant enough young girl and not unintelligent but unfortunately, having no interest in photography whatsoever, she never used that intelligence at work and in truth was more ornament than use. Kerry, like many young girls of her age, had perceived working at a holiday camp as a means to have fun away from under the watchful eyes of her parents and hadn't for a moment stopped to consider that she would actually have to work to earn the means to have that fun. On being given several options at her interview, she had chosen to accept the one of a counter assistant in Jolly's Snaps as it sounded far more glamorous than working as a chalet maid or restaurant assistant.

Thankfully for Darren the two young lads who worked in the backroom developing all the photographs he took were very capable at their jobs and needed little supervision from him.

As Darren was checking the stock levels in the tiny storeroom at the back of the shop, Kerry was supposed to be adding their requirements to the order list, which when completed would be passed to the general office for them to implement. Only, as Kerry seemed to be more interested in the doodles she was drawing down the sides of the order form, Darren wasn't sure she was actually noting down what he told her.

116

'Kerry, did you mark down that we need fifty packs of developing paper, like I just asked?'

Distractedly she responded, 'Yeah!' Then after a pause said, 'Fifty? Oh, I thought you said five.'

He sighed in frustration. Now he couldn't trust that she'd marked any of the previous requirements down correctly either and couldn't risk finding himself without any vital supplies. 'Look, I'll finish the stock check myself. Would you go and make us all a cup of tea . . . oh, and be sure you knock on the darkroom door and wait until either Jimmy or Rodney give you the nod that it's okay to go in. Don't just barge in like you keep doing and ruin the batch of photographs they're in the middle of developing . . . then give the counter in the shop a polish before we open up. Oh, and put the new photos up on the boards, the ones I took yesterday. They're in a pile on the table in the developing room.'

She peeled herself off the wall she was leaning against. 'Yeah, sure.' Then she hesitated for a moment. 'Er . . . Darren, me and my mates are entering the dance competition down in Groovy's tonight and we need to practise a bit. The others work in the restaurant so they finish at eight. I wondered if you'd let me off at that time too? Please, Darren, say you'll let me?' The photography shop opened from ten in the morning until nine at night.

He wished she wouldn't blatantly lie to him every time she tried to persuade him to let her leave early. The last excuse she had used on a Saturday evening was that she was suffering from women's problems and needed to go to bed. Then on his way back to his chalet, he had spotted her all dressed up, running across the wide expanse of grass that split the main camp from the staff chalets and maintenance buildings, with several of her mates, heading towards the main courtyard. And there had been numerous similar occasions before that. As for this latest excuse, well, he might not take much part in Jolly's social scene but he did know that staff weren't allowed to take part in competitions held for the paying guests. But as the kind man he was, he wouldn't want to stop Kerry from having a good time for the sake of making her work her hours. Not to seem too much of a pushover, though, he told her, 'Let's assess the situation at eight and see how busy we are then.'

She took that as his agreement to her getting off early. 'Oh, thanks, Darren. You're the best boss ever, you really are.'

He wagged a warning finger at her. 'Well, you won't be thinking that if you don't go and do as I ask and let me finish this stock check so I can get the order in before I miss this week's deadline.'

He had sounded threatening but Kerry couldn't fail to miss the twinkle in his eyes. She might run rings around him at work but during the time she had worked for Darren he had endeared himself to her in an elder brother sort of way and she had grown quite fond of him.

Over in her office Rhonnie, along with Jill, was looking over a proof copy of the new brochure designed for a mail shot that coming autumn and again early in the year. It would be sent to specially selected households in the country along with a list of past customers by way of enticing people to book their holidays at Jolly's holiday camp next year and thereby beat the competition. The idea was to use some of the material from it in the national newspaper campaigns they ran too. They had been using the same brochure for a number of years but felt that with the advent of the new caravan park and several other facilities, it was time to give it a completely new facelift and had briefed the local printing company they had been using for years to come up with a more modern look.

Ruefully shaking her head, Rhonnie issued a fed-up sigh and snapped, 'Did Mr Coppice not listen to me at all when I gave him the brief? Most of the new photographs he took are no good. That one of the couple frolicking in the pool, yes, it shows them having fun in the foreground . . . but he obviously didn't make a close inspection of the background. There's a couple smooching on the grass by the side of the pool, another pair nearby having a blazing row, and those two young boys right at the back there . . .' she said, stabbing her finger down on the picture '. . . are capering about, pulling each other's trunks down, and one of them is showing his bare bottom!

'As for this photograph of the beach,' she said, pointing to it, 'the caption underneath states: "Sunbathe under the sun on our long stretch of golden beach" . . . but the sun in the picture is about to be covered by a big black cloud! And I'm not happy about all the captions they've come up with either. Would you consider booking a holiday with a camp that proclaims people will be holidaying in a safe environment and shows a lovely aerial shot of the camp in which the medical centre features prominently?'

Jill chuckled. 'I don't think I would.'

'Me neither. Apart from the couples by the poolside, most of the other photos show older people going about, and to me that gives the impression that the campers who come here are middle-aged or older. That could put off young people and families from coming here, thinking they'd be staying in a geriatric facility. The whole brochure has got such an old-fashioned look to it.' Rhonnie looked troubled. 'We've been using Albert Coppice for donkey's years to produce our brochures and posters. Albert's a lovely man, got to be nearing retirement now, but this brochure shows me he's so set in his ways he's not right for us any longer.' She shook her head at the proof and said distractedly, 'I could take better pictures myself than Albert has.'

Jill looked at her thoughtfully for a moment. 'Then why don't you?'

Rhonnie chuckled. 'I was exaggerating. My photos would probably be worse than Albert's are. At least all the heads are on the photos he took.' Then she looked at Jill for a moment before she announced, 'But I do know of someone who could take just the kind of photos I'm looking for: Darren the camp photographer.'

Jill exclaimed, 'Of course. He's very talented. I often call in at Jolly's Snaps when I'm passing and take a look at the latest ones on the board. The way he catches people looking so natural. I wish he'd been around when I got married as I'm sure the photos would have turned out much better than ours did.'

Rhonnie said, 'That's what we'll do then. I'll instruct Darren to take exactly the shots I want, to show the camp off to its best advantage, and surely coming up with suitable captions underneath can't be that hard. We're already got the bumf from the old brochures to play around with and we can give it a more up-to-date ring. Then once we're happy we just need to get them printed. We could still use Mr Coppice to do that so we won't be dispensing with his services altogether. Could you ask Darren to come and see me as soon as he can and we'll get this ball rolling?' With a twinkle in her eyes she then told Jill, 'Your contribution to this new venture will be helping me to come up with some catchy captions to go under the photos so you'd better get thinking.'

Since doing the stocktake that morning, Darren had spent an enjoyable time travelling around the camp taking photos of campers having fun. At lunchtime he returned to deposit the rolls of used film with the developing lads, collect new ones and be ready to go out again after he'd had his dinner. Informed by Kerry of a summons to see the boss in her office, the self-doubting side of his personality had him worrying witless that campers must have made a complaint about the quality of the photographs he had taken of them and he was going to be told to improve or be sacked.

He entered the office and with an anxious quiver in his

voice said to Rhonnie, sitting behind her desk, 'You wanted to see me, Mrs Buckland?'

She immediately noticed his unease and, smiling warmly, beckoned him over. 'Come and have a seat, Darren. And stop looking so worried, I just want to put a proposal to you.' Once he was seated she explained to him what she hoped to achieve in producing their own brochure. 'So I'd like the shots to show the camp off to its best advantage and feature a mixture of the people that come here, not specifically one age group. How do you feel about tackling that, Darren?'

He didn't hesitate in his reply. 'I'd be absolutely honoured to do it. I'm just glad you think I'm up to the job, Mrs Buckland.'

She cocked an eyebrow in surprise. 'I can't imagine why you would question that you would be. We have had some very talented photographers working here for us in the past but I have to tell you that in my opinion your snaps always have something special about them . . . just the way you manage to catch the light and how you encourage people to forget the camera is there.'

He blushed on hearing such praise of his work. 'Thank you,' he muttered. He then focused on the task Rhonnie had given him and told her, 'First I'll have a look at the old brochure, get a feel for the sort of thing you don't want any longer. I'll also get hold of some of the other holiday camp brochures, to see what sort of photos they include, then I should be able to make Jolly's stand out to potential customers as the best.'

Rhonnie was very impressed with his approach to the task she had given him.

At just after eight-thirty that night, Darren sat perched on a stool behind the shop counter, lost in thought. As she had known she would, Kerry had got her way about leaving early and, as the developing lads were up to date with their work,

Darren felt it only fair to let them finish early too. By this time of an evening most of the campers were either getting ready for or already at their chosen venue for their evening activities and it was only the odd customer who came into the shop. Since seven-thirty no one had actually come in and this had given Darren the peace and quiet he needed to put his mind to the task Rhonnie had set him. He was deciding where best to take a shot of the central courtyard when he was disturbed by the shop door opening and looked up to see a young woman enter.

She was about eighteen and dressed tartily in Darren's opinion, in a tight-fitting, short red skirt that barely covered her backside and a snug-fitting low-cut top that showed an indecent amount of her ample bosom. Darren might be on the shy side but he was still a red-blooded man and as the girl sauntered up to the counter and leaned on it, exposing even more of her breasts, he had difficulty dragging his eyes away so as to look her at her face, which he would have thought quite pretty had she not harshened it with far too much garish makeup.

Running a finger around the inside of his shirt collar as it suddenly felt very tight to him, he asked, 'Er . . . come to collect some photographs, have you? If you can give me your ticket . . .'

She shot him a seductive smile. 'No, I ain't come to collect any photos, I've come to see about getting some taken.' She was purposely heaving her bosom up and down, which was making Darren feel very uncomfortable. He wished she would stop it. He was also wishing now that he hadn't allowed Kerry to finish early as then he wouldn't be having to deal with this woman.

He tried to act naturally, not wanting her to know how awkward she was making him feel. 'Oh, I see. Well, I'll be out and about around the camp tomorrow so if you tell me where you and your party will be at a certain time, I'll do my best to be there and take them for you. Or if your party want to come here to the studio and have some themed ones taken, we have lots of costumes you can pick from and I can book you a slot now if you want me to?' He leaned over to grab hold of the diary.

'Those ain't the type of photos I want taking.'

He eyed her in confusion. 'What sort are you meaning?'

'Well, it's like this, you see. I've been told I have the makings of a glamour model.' She eased herself off the counter and placed her hands on her hips, giving him a provocative pose. She then laughed out loud. 'I don't need to ask you if you think so . . . I can see your eyes are just about popping out of your head. Anyway to get myself into that line of work I need a portfolio so my agent can show potential clients how photogenic I am. Photographs that show off my assets to their best.' She eyed him meaningfully and licked her lips in a suggestive manner before she added, 'You get my drift.'

Oh, he got her drift all right. He slapped shut the diary and pushed it back over the counter. 'We don't take pornographic photographs in this studio. And even if I had my own place, I wouldn't as it's against the law.'

She snapped at him, 'Tasteful glamour shots are not pornography.'

'Call them what you like, they would still be unlawful, but I'm sure you won't have any trouble finding someone who will agree to help when you get back home.' Not if you flaunt yourself in front of them like you are to me to further your cause, he thought.

'I'd have to pay for those. The kind of money it would take me years to save up and by that time it'd be too late. I'd be too old.'

'Campers pay for their photos here.'

'But I won't be.' Her lips curled into a malicious smile, her eyes hardened. 'You see, if you don't agree to take them, and for free, then I'll make sure you never take another professional photograph again.'

123

He frowned at her, bewildered. 'And how do you propose to do that?'

She eyed him darkly. 'Well, no one is going to hire a rapist, are they?'

He gawped at her in utter shock. 'You'll accuse me of . . . of . . . *that* if I don't take nude photographs of you?'

'Glamour shots,' she corrected him 'And absolutely I will. I need those photos to get into the business and you're going to take them for me or your life as a photographer is over.' She eyed him knowingly. 'The three friends I'm staying here with will all swear on oath that I came into this shop on my own tonight and if you don't do what I ask, I shall leave here with my top ripped, screaming blue murder. I'll say I came here to collect some photos and you tried to force yourself on me. Don't try and lie to me that the rest of the staff are working away in the back 'cos I've been watching this place every night about this time since I got here last Saturday, waiting for my chance to get you on your own. I was beginning to worry I wouldn't be able to when, lo and behold, you let all the staff go early tonight, so I know no one else is here.' She smiled sweetly at him. 'Shall we get started? Through here, is it?' She headed off into the studio.

Darren's thoughts were racing; he was shaking in panic. Despite his principles, he could take those photographs then send this woman and her threats packing. But what if in the future his name was somehow linked to the photographs and they came back to haunt him, wrecking whatever future he'd built for himself? But if he didn't take the shots and she carried out her threats, he had no way of proving his innocence and could end up in jail, his future in tatters. Whatever he did, he'd have to live the rest of his life knowing he was implicated in the taking of obscene photos. He couldn't stand that, he decided.

His inner panic escalated to fever pitch. He needed to think of a way to get himself out of taking them. But no matter how hard he tried nothing would come to him.

A shrill call to him from the studio cut the air like a knife. 'What's keeping you?'

He called back, 'I . . . I . . . just need to go to the stock-room and get a film and some flashes. I won't be a moment.'

As he said that, like a flash of lightning an idea to stall the taking of the photographs, at least for tonight, occurred to him. And if he forced a delay, he'd have more time to think up a way of refusing to co-operate at all. He went into the corridor off which were doors leading into the darkroom, studio, small kitchen and toilets. Against a wall stood a large metal cabinet where all the photographic sundries were kept. Opening it up, his eyes immediately went to the stack of boxes of flashbulbs. As quickly as he could he gathered the dozen or so boxes and took them back into the shop front, hiding them under the counter. Then, taking several deep breaths in an effort to calm his fraught nerves, he went to join the girl in the studio.

He found her stripped down to skimpy underwear which barely covered her modesty, impatiently tapping her foot against the wooden floor. As he walked in she looked at him expectantly and said, 'I know what poses I want you to shoot me in, so you just get clicking away.'

She sat down on a chaise-longue and put her hands behind her back to unhook her bra. Panic reared within Darren. If anyone walked in now, how could he explain away what they would be witnessing and keep his good name intact? He stopped her by blurting out, 'I can't take the shots tonight. Please put your clothes back on.'

She stopped what she was doing, glared darkly at him and said in no uncertain terms, 'I've told you that if you don't take them, then I run out of here screaming rape at the top of my voice and you'll be finished.'

He urged her, 'Please listen to me. I can't take them. I've run out of flashbulbs. I used the last of them tonight on a family shoot. Without a flash the photos will come out too dark and they'll be no good to you. The new order of bulbs is expected tomorrow. I'm telling you the truth. Go and check the stock cupboard if you don't believe me. We'll have to take your photos tomorrow night.'

She stared at him for several long moments, weighing up whether she believed him or not.

Though terrified she would call his bluff and go scouting around and find the hidden bulbs, he encouraged her, 'Please, be my guest, go and make a search, but you won't find any bulbs.'

'Okay, I believe you. I'll come back the same time tomorrow night, so you'd best let your staff go home early again.' She wagged a finger at him, a look of menace in her eyes. 'Be warned, though, that if you try any funny business then I go straight to the police and tell them what you tried to do to me. If they quiz me on why I never reported it straight away, I shall tell them I was in such a state of shock at what you did, I couldn't talk about it at first.'

It seemed she had every avenue covered, leaving no escape for him. He hurried back outside into the shop, barricading himself behind the counter while she re-dressed, and as she walked past the counter to leave the shop, she shot him a warning look. As soon the door had closed behind her, he dashed out from behind the counter, locked it, turned the sign around to 'Closed' and pulled down the blind. He then slumped down on one of the customer waiting chairs just inside the door and, with his head hung low, he started to cry.

CHAPTER TEN

Rhonnie was deeply worried about her friend. Since turning up drunk in the early hours of Sunday morning, Ginger had spent most of her time in bed. When she was encouraged to get up by Rhonnie, she would sit huddled in an armchair, wallowing in her own misery, hardly eating so that weight she could ill afford to lose was dropping off her. Although Rhonnie had every sympathy with her, she knew from experience that this situation could not be allowed to go on forever. Ginger must be made to climb out of the dark hole she had got herself into, just as Drina and Artie had made it their mission to get Rhonnie out of her despairing state when Dan was killed. This evening she meant to do whatever it took to start Ginger on the road to recovery.

As she walked into the cottage she was greeted by a sight that made her stop and smile. Her young son sat nestled on his nanny's lap on the sofa; she was reading a Noddy book to him. As soon as he saw his mother, the child's eyes lit in excitement and he slid off Carrie's lap and came running over, his arms wide, crying out, 'Mummy, mummy, mummy!'

She scooped him up and crushed him to her. 'Hello, sweetheart. Had a good day?'

'Play horsey, play horsey,' he begged her.

Rhonnie laughed. 'Okay, in a minute, just let me get my coat off.' She put him down and proceeded to take off her coat as she addressed Carrie, who was now on her feet tidying toys away. 'How has he been today?'

The homely-looking girl smiled over at her and in a thick Devonian accent said, 'He's been an angel as usual – well, apart from when he decided to tip a bag of flour all over himself while he was watching me bake a cake to take to the playgroup this afternoon.' She laughed. 'What a mess! No harm done, though, as I'd already weighed out what I needed for the cake. He enjoyed playgroup and is making lots of friends there, especially one little girl who has taken a shine to him. She keeps trying to kiss him and it's really funny watching Danny doing his best to hide from her when he sees her heading towards him. Oh, and he did have a tantrum when I wouldn't let him have his pudding before his dinner but I won out in the end. He ate all his lunch and only left a couple of carrots from his dinner. He's had his bath so he's ready to put to bed.'

Rhonnie looked fondly at her son, who had now climbed onto the sofa and was gleefully bouncing up and down on it, looking far too full of energy to be considering sleep any time soon. Whatever she was doing while away from him, her son was never far from Rhonnie's thoughts. Like other working mothers, there were times when she felt guilty for leaving him in the care of another while she went to work – even though she knew he was safe and flourishing under that person's care – but she was providing a good home for him and building a future for them both. There was also the fact that, although she enjoyed being a mother, that alone was not enough for her.

'Thank you, Carrie. I'll take over whenever you're ready to leave. Doing anything special tonight?'

Carrie had finished putting Danny's toys away and was collecting her belongings together. 'My flatmate is out with her boyfriend tonight so I'm taking advantage of having the place to myself, having a hot bath and watching some telly.

Monty Python is on, then, *The Saint* afterwards. My two favourite programmes.'

'Some of the sketches in *Monty Python* make me ache with laughing but in some I just don't get the joke,' Rhonnie admitted. 'I love *The Saint* though. Roger Moore is rather dishy, isn't he?'

'Oh, he certainly is. I wouldn't mind him investigating me.'

They both laughed at Carrie's quip. Rhonnie then asked her, 'Still no regrets about leaving Devon and moving up here?'

She said with conviction, 'None at all. Best decision I ever made. You're a great boss to work for, Rhonnie, and you know how much I love Danny.' She laughed. 'At first the biggest problem I faced was not understanding what people said up here and they had the same problem with me, but I'm getting the hang of the language now and even starting to sound like you all do. I've made new friends and there's lots to do around here. With having the scooter you bought me to get around on, transport is no problem . . . well, apart from when two of my friends want to go somewhere with me and I've only room for one on the back, that is.'

Rhonnie affectionately patted the young girl's arm. 'I'm so glad to hear this. You know you can always come to me if you have any problems. Well, you'd better get off and I'll see you tomorrow. Oh, as there's no sign of her, I take it that Ginger is in bed?' Then Rhonnie asked worriedly, 'Has she not been up at all today?'

'Oh, yes, she got up about three, had a bath and a slice of toast, got all dressed up and went out not long before you got home.'

'Oh! Did she say where she was going?'

Carrie shook her head. 'She did tell me to tell you that she would more than likely be late back and not to stay up for her. Sorry, I should have said that before.'

Rhonnie frowned, wondering where Ginger had gone. Had

she changed her mind and returned to talk to Paul, in the hope of saving their marriage? But regardless, the fact she had washed, dressed and gone out had to be viewed as a sign that she was on the road to recovery.

Just as she was going out of the door, Carrie stopped and turned back to face Rhonnie. 'Oh, sorry, another thing I forgot to tell you. When I got back from taking Danny to the play-group, I found a bunch of weeds on the doorstep. They were tied up with a piece of string, like you would a bouquet. I thought someone was having a joke and went to throw them away but then I thought I'd better let you see them and decide what to do with them as it was your doorstep they were left on. They're in water in the kitchen.'

Bemused, Rhonnie went and looked at the bunch of weeds Carrie had put in a bucket of water on the floor by the back door. The 'weeds' were actually wild flowers, tree blossom and leafy foliage. A warm glow filled her and she smiled, knowing exactly who had gathered them and left them on her doorstep: Ben. He had obviously guessed that it was she who had left the bag of clothes outside the hut and this was his way of thanking her. She was very touched by his gesture. It was a good walk from his hut to her cottage. With as much care as she would an expensive florist's bouquet, she arranged the wild gathering in a glass vase and put the display on the mantle above the fireplace in the lounge.

Rhonnie had just settled herself on the sofa to watch a drama on the television when the telephone shrilled out. Thinking whoever it was certainly knew how to pick their moment, she rose to answer it.

An unfamiliar male voice asked, 'Is that Roonie?'

'Rhonnie Buckland,' she corrected him.

'Oh, I do apologise but it sounded like she was saying Roonie. I'm the landlord of the Schooner Inn in Mablethorpe. I found this number in her handbag . . . not that I'm in the habit of looking through women's handbags, you understand, but I had to do something before a murder was committed. I managed to get out of her that you're a friend of hers and she's staying with you but, to be honest, she's not making much sense so I'm sorry if I've got this wrong. But if she is your friend then I really think you need to fetch her before she makes any more of a nuisance of herself with my customers and I have no choice but to have the police come and detain her.'

Rhonnie groaned. She didn't need to ask him to describe the woman he was talking about as she knew already it was Ginger. 'Oh, I'm so sorry, really I am. Please don't call the police. My friend is going through a really bad time at the moment. I know that doesn't excuse the way she's behaving but this is so out of character for her. I just have to arrange for someone to come and sit with my son. I'll be as quick as I can.'

As soon as she put the receiver down, she lifted it again and dialled Drina's number. It was Artie who answered and as soon as Rhonnie had explained the situation he told her that he would fetch Ginger and bring her back to the cottage. It sounded like Rhonnie needed to have plenty of black coffee ready for when they arrived.

An hour later, as soon as Rhonnie heard a car pull up in front of the house, she ran out to greet it. Ginger was slumped drunkenly in the back, angrily demanding to be taken to the pub, so Artie had literally to pull her out. Between them he and Rhonnie managed to get Ginger into the cottage and onto the sofa.

Swaying dangerously, she glared at them and demanded, 'What did you go and do that for, making me come home when I was having such a good time?'

'You maybe were having a good time but the people around you weren't from what I could see,' Artie told her.

She slurred, 'The bloke I was with was having a good time. I liked him and I know he liked me. He would have asked me out if you hadn't . . . you hadn't . . . barged in and dragged . . . dragged . . .' With that her eyes closed and she passed out cold.

Artie heaved a sigh, shaking his head sorrowfully. 'Oh, Rhonnie, it was so embarrassing to walk into that pub full of people and find Ginger draped all over this chap . . . and him looking like he wished the ground would open and swallow him. His wife wasn't looking too happy either and was about ready to lose her temper and commit murder. The poor girl is taking this break-up with her husband very badly but getting blind drunk and making such a spectacle of herself isn't the answer.'

'No, it's not,' Rhonnie agreed. She too looked down sadly at her comatose friend. 'I was so pleased when Carrie told me that Ginger had washed, dressed and gone out after virtually not getting out of bed or stopping crying since she arrived. I thought she must have gone to talk to Paul and try and salvage their marriage.' She heaved a sigh. 'All my talking to her, to try and help her through this dreadful time and make her see she does have a future . . . well, it obviously just fell on deaf ears because I don't remember telling her to get blind drunk and throw herself at anything wearing trousers. This is bringing home to me how frustrated you and Drina, my friends too, must have grown, trying to help me start to come to terms with the loss of Dan. Nothing you tried for weeks made any difference to me, but you and Drina never gave up, did you?'

'No, me duck, we didn't. No matter how long it took us or what we had to do, we weren't never going to give up until we were satisfied you were on the mend.'

'Like I won't give up on Ginger.'

Artie affectionately patted her arm. 'You know me and Drina will do what we can to help. We care about Ginger too.'

Rhonnie smiled at her father. 'Yes, I know.' She looked

down at her friend. 'There'll be no talking to her tonight, that's for sure, she's out for the count. I'm not going to risk leaving her alone tomorrow. I won't go into work until I've spoken to her . . . good job I'm the boss and can do that . . . and hopefully I can knock some sense into her. Make her see that what she did tonight was nothing more than starting down the slippery slope to nowhere.'

CHAPTER ELEVEN

Ginger finally surfaced at just after eleven the next morning, groaning at the morning sun streaming through the windows and from the pain in her head, which felt to her as if a steamroller was driving around in it.

Rhonnie was sitting in the armchair opposite her friend's bed on the sofa, reading a book while she waited for Ginger to wake up. As soon as she heard the groans of protest, she slapped shut her book and got up, announcing, 'You'll be needing tea . . . an urn of it by the looks of you . . . and a box of aspirin. Thankfully I have some in.'

Trying to sit herself up, Ginger moaned. 'Please don't shout at me, Rhonnie, my head is killing me. How come I spent the night on the sofa?'

Rhonnie frowned at her, like a disapproving mother at a naughty child. 'You don't remember! Let me get you that tea and I'll fill you in.'

When Rhonnie arrived back carrying a tray on which two large mugs of tea, a glass of water and a box of aspirin, Ginger had managed to ease herself upright. She gratefully accepted the glass of water along with two pills, swallowed them straight down, then started on the tea.

Sitting in the chair opposite, cradling her own mug between her hands, Rhonnie asked her, 'Feeling any more human yet?'

Ginger shot her a feeling-sorry-for-herself look. 'My brain

feels like it's trying to dynamite itself out of my skull and my mouth feels like the bottom of a bird cage.'

'I'm not surprised, the state you were in last night. Don't expect me to have any sympathy as you brought it all on yourself.'

Ginger spoke like every word bought her excruciating pain. 'Oh, don't be like that, Rhonnie. It's not as if you haven't had one too many before this.'

'One too many! Ginger, you must have had a hundred too many, you were that pie-eyed! You could hardly stand and what came out of your mouth was like talking to a foreigner . . . neither Dad nor I could understand a word you were saying. He was so embarrassed when he arrived in the pub and found you pawing a man while his wife was sitting next to him, about ready to do you some serious damage, and Dad isn't the sort to be easily embarrassed as you know.'

Ginger looked confused. 'Artie came to fetch me home?'

Rhonnie shook her head in reproof. 'It was that or the landlord fetched the police and you spent the night in jail, sobering up and facing a charge of making a public nuisance of yourself. According to the landlord, the bloke my dad caught you with wasn't the first you'd propositioned since you arrived in their place last night.'

Ginger gasped in horror. 'You've having me on! Please tell me you are?' she begged.

Rhonnie shook her head. 'Afraid not.'

Her friend cradled her head in her hands and exclaimed, 'I'll never be able to go in that pub ever again.'

Rhonnie said dryly, 'Well, not at least until everyone who was in there last night dies. I can't imagine just why you should pick a backstreet pub to try and find yourself a new bloke anyway. It's an old blokes' pub where they all go to meet their cronies and play dominoes and cribbage. The married chap my dad caught you draped over was at least fifty. Don't you remember any of this?'

Ginger shook her head. 'No. The last thing I do recall is standing outside the pub, willing myself to go in on my own, and then going up to the bar and ordering a double vodka and black to steady my nerves.'

Rhonnie sighed. 'Oh, Ginger, this isn't you . . . drinking yourself stupid and throwing yourself at any man that's breathing. I know you're hurt but this is not the way to get over Paul.'

Tears of misery filled Ginger's eyes and she blubbered, 'I remember someone telling me once that the quickest way to get over someone is to find someone else to replace them. So if Paul doesn't want me, I need to find someone who does. I had a drink to give me some confidence but obviously one led to another . . .' A fresh cascade of sorrowful tears flowed down her face before she added, 'But, Rhonnie, if I was having to throw myself at men, then even those old ones in that pub didn't want me either. Who would want me anyway, a skinny carrot head with crooked teeth, who can't dance 'cos she's got two left feet?'

Rhonnie leaped out of her seat to squat by the sofa and take Ginger's hands in hers. Giving them a tender squeeze, she told her friend with conviction, 'Lots of men would, Ginger. And lots of women would give their eye teeth to be as slim as you and look like Twiggy and have such beautiful hair that doesn't need hours spent at the hairdresser's having to be permed and coloured. And so what if your teeth are a bit crooked? They give your face character – and that face is a very pretty one, Ginger.'

She sniffed miserably. 'You're my friend so you're not going to tell me I'm ugly, are you?'

Rhonnie sighed inwardly. Ginger was feeling so worthless at the moment that she was totally unreceptive to any compliment. 'Ginger, I do think you're pretty but I could tell you until I'm blue in the face and you still wouldn't believe me, the way you're feeling at the moment. Look, believe me when I tell you that I am proud of you.'

'Proud! How can you be after I made such a fool of myself last night?'

'Well, it's not been a week yet since you left Paul but you got all dressed up and took yourself out last night. For the first three weeks after Dan died I hardly got out of bed and the only time I went into the bathroom was to use the toilet, never to wash. I stank to high heaven, Ginger, and I couldn't care less. Drina had to finally drag me, kicking and screaming, to the bath. The first time I've been out socially since I lost Dan over two years ago was to Jill's dinner party last week, and that took a lot for me to do. Whoever it was who advised finding a replacement has a point, but how can you start a new relationship when you still aren't over the old one? All you do is wish the new person you are with was the other one, so the new person doesn't stand a chance, does he?'

Ginger shot her a wan look. 'No. I just wanted another man to make me feel . . . well you know . . . that he found me attractive and wanted me . . . to make me feel better about myself. All I got for my efforts was a banging headache, though. And a sore back. This sofa really isn't that comfortable to sleep on, Rhonnie.'

'Better than a slab-hard mattress in a cell.'

Ginger managed a hint of a smile. 'Yes, I suppose.'

Rhonnie stood up, announcing, 'I'll make more tea and then we'll have a pow-wow on what we're going to do about you.'

A while later she said to her friend, 'I know I've asked you several times but I just have to ask you again. Are you sure that you shouldn't go and talk to Paul, see if you can work out a way to make your marriage work?'

Ginger vehemently shook her head. 'How many times do I need to tell you, Rhonnie? As much as I love Paul, even if he did tell me he'd made a mistake and wanted me back, I could never get that picture of him with another woman out of my head or trust him again. Could you have ever trusted Dan had you found him like I did Paul? Knowing that he must have been lying to you to cover his tracks while seeing her. Sleeping with her. Wondering if they did it in our bed. After that how could I ever believe he was where he said he was or with whom? I couldn't live like that, Rhonnie.'

Rhonnie could have proclaimed that Dan would never have cheated on her but then she would have never in a million years thought Paul would do that to Ginger, something she was still having difficulty believing, but how could she not when Ginger had witnessed him with her own eyes?

'No neither could I,' Rhonnie agreed with her. 'So, you are sure you're up to starting work tomorrow?'

She answered truthfully, 'No, I'm not. I just want to sit around feeling sorry for myself, but I know you're right and that keeping myself busy is the only way I'm going to start making a new life for myself.'

'You don't have to move into a chalet, Ginger, you are welcome to stay with me,' Rhonnie told her.

Ginger laughed. 'Oh, yes, as if it's not going to be bad enough for me, the rest of the staff knowing I'm best friends with the big boss and watching their Ps and Qs around me, let alone them hearing I'm actually living with her.'

Rhonnie smiled. 'Yes, I can see your point. And you're sure you want to go back to chalet maiding?'

'For the time being, Rhonnie. Cleaning I know I'm good at and can do blindfold, even when I'm in the depths of despair, so it's the best thing for me at the moment.'

'Come with me to work tomorrow morning and we'll sort everything out. I'll make sure you're given a staff chalet to yourself so you don't have to put up with sharing with someone you don't know.'

Ginger looked grateful. 'Thanks, Rhonnie.' At least I can cry as much as I want without fear of disturbing my chalet mate, she thought. She said, tongue in cheek, 'When I hold my first chalet party, I'll let you know. Er . . . where's my godson, by the way? I could do with a cuddle from him. There's nothing like a hug from a child to make you feel better.'

'You'll have to wait for a bit. Carrie's taken him to the camp nursery to get rid of some of his energy playing with other children there. He was racing around here earlier this morning, pretending he was a racing car and making so much noise I'm surprised he didn't wake you. Mind you, you were so out of it, I think an earthquake would have passed unnoticed. Anyway, I wanted some peace while we talked so that's why I asked Carrie to take Danny out. Now we've had our chat and I know you are making efforts to get yourself better, I'm going in to work and I'll tell Carrie to bring Danny home so you can have that hug.' She then looked at Ginger meaningfully. 'When Danny's gone to bed, how about you and me having a girly night tonight like we used to? I've a face pack that promises to take years off you.'

Ginger smiled. 'Sounds good to me. Before you go off to work, though, you wouldn't just fetch me another glass of water and a couple more headache pills, would you?'

Ginger watched Rhonnie go off into the kitchen. How fortunate she was that it was Rhonnie she'd happened to bump into in that freezing waiting room one night three years ago. In that very first meeting they'd forged a friendship that many women would give their eye teeth to have, one that saw each of them through good and bad, every event bringing them closer together. Since Ginger's mother couldn't care less about her and her father had disappeared, she had no idea what she would have done had she not had Rhonnie to turn to in this time of crisis.

Meanwhile in the camera shop, unusually for her, Kerry appeared to be taking more than a passing interest in something that had nothing to do with her social life. She was looking over in the direction of the office where Darren had been closeted since she had arrived for work first thing that morning. She was concerned for him.

A huge part of Darren's job was to go out morning and afternoon, when he had no appointments for any studio sessions, to take campers' photographs around the camp. But that morning he did not go out at all.

Usually during the morning Jimmy and Rodney, individually, would come out of the developing room to hand her packets of photographs they had finished processing, ready for to pass on to the customers when they came in to view them and decide which ones they wanted. Usually Kerry and the backroom boys would pass friendly and sometimes downright rude banter if no customers were about. But this morning both young men had kept a low profile; in fact she hadn't seen them at all, except for when she had taken them their elevenses and even then they hardly spoke to her. She could only deduce from this that they too were aware of Darren's most unusual black mood and daren't put a foot wrong in case he uncharacteristically turned on them and gave them the sack.

At one o'clock the shop was shut for an hour while they all went to the restaurant for their dinner, but Darren made it clear that he wouldn't be joining them today. By the time she returned at two, Kerry dearly hoped that whatever was causing his bad mood had somehow resolved itself and the depressing atmosphere in the shop would have been replaced by its usual congenial one. Jimmy and Rodney hoped so too.

But the three of them arrived back together to find the door to the shop locked and had to bang on it several times before Darren came and opened it. He didn't look very happy about being disturbed. The afternoon promised to be as long and tedious as the morning had been and finishing time couldn't come quickly enough for Kerry. She dearly hoped that her boss's mood had lifted by tomorrow and he was back to his normal self as she couldn't bear the thought of another day like today. She'd come to Jolly's to have fun and she certainly hadn't had any on this particular day.

CHAPTER TWELVE

On arriving at the camp after her talk with Ginger, Rhonnie immediately went to the nursery to thank Carrie for taking her lively son out and tell her that she was at liberty to take Danny home whenever she was ready. To her shock Rhonnie was told by Mavis Durham, the nursery manager, that Carrie had suddenly been taken ill a couple of hours ago and had been immediately despatched to the medical centre. As yet she hadn't returned. After checking that Danny was happy playing, Rhonnie went off to find out what was ailing the nanny. She was told by the on-duty nurse that Carrie was suffering from a sudden severe attack of period pains, had been given suitable medication to help ease them, and was at the moment lying on one of the two hospital trolleys clutching a hot-water bottle to her stomach, waiting for the severity of her pains to subside enough for her to return to work. As all women would to another who was suffering the monthly curse so acutely, Rhonnie showed sympathy. She asked the nurse to tell Carrie that once she was able she should go home and that Rhonnie would see her tomorrow so long as she was fit enough. Meanwhile she was not to worry about Danny as his mother would see to him.

Leaving the surgery, it was on Rhonnie's mind to go to the office and telephone Drina to ask if she and Artie would babysit their grandson until this evening, which she knew they would both be delighted to do. But Drina had told her yesterday that she and Artie had planned a day in the garden together today, and as it must have been difficult for her father to get Drina to agree to leave her beloved camp business alone for one day so they could enjoy quality time together, Rhonnie thought better of disrupting them when it was not an emergency. Jill had not telephoned her during the morning with any problems that needed her intervention and Rhonnie knew that there was nothing in the office Jill couldn't see to on her behalf, so she would take Danny with her on her daily camp tour and although it was a day early she might as well make her weekly visit to the caravan park.

Having told Jill what she was doing and collected Danny from the nursery, Rhonnie set off with him on the tour around the camp.

As he trotted, jumped and skipped as young toddlers do, pointing out things that caught his interest, she couldn't help but picture him as a grown man, handsome and tall like his father had been and by then the owner of this camp. Probably he'd do a daily inspection tour and she herself would take a backseat role, just like Drina was now. That was of course if it was what he wanted to do, as she would never force her son to do anything just to please her. She couldn't help feeling regretful that Danny didn't have both his parents enjoying this time with him.

Obviously he could not walk as fast as Rhonnie, and since he decided to run off and explore on his own account several times and she had to chase after him, it took her over twice the usual time to complete the tour. It was well after three o'clock before, having quickly checked in with Jill that all was still well, and pushing a tired Danny in his pushchair now, she began the journey over to the caravan park, but not before stopping off at the sweet shop for a snack and a drink for him.

It was a very pleasant stroll down the long length of the old farm road, away from the hustle and bustle of the main camp, the only sounds those of the birds and insects flitting about in the warm summer sun. It wasn't until she had almost arrived at the entrance to the site that the peacefulness was broken by the sounds of people enjoying themselves, becoming louder the nearer she got.

The small brick-built office by the entrance to the camp was closed when she passed through the gates as she'd expected it to be. The office was only manned on a regular basis on a Saturday morning when coaches or cars carrying people who had booked a week's or fortnight's stay in the static caravans arrived and were booked in, given their keys and directed to their particular van by Jeff or Kevin. Any tourers or camper vans were instructed to leave their vehicles outside the gate and walk down into the camp to seek out Jeff or Kevin, enquiring if any spaces were available and then filling out the necessary paperwork before they were allocated a space.

It was only when she was heading to Jeff's caravan that she remembered it was Wednesday afternoon, Jeff's usual time off. She was cross with herself for forgetting that fact. Should he still be on the premises she wouldn't dream of disturbing him during his leisure time so would need to come back tomorrow. While she was here, though, she might as well have a walk around the park and have a word with Kevin, to satisfy herself the young man was happy in his work. He could talk freely while his boss was out of the way.

As Rhonnie walked around in search of him she was pleased to note that the gardens were being kept weed-free and well-watered and the grass areas neat and tidy. What she wasn't happy about was that there was a blockage in one of the shower blocks as the floor was swimming in water; some of the rubbish bins dotted around the site were overflowing and did not appear to have been emptied that day; and one disgruntled couple who were staying in a static caravan told her they had asked Kevin this morning to put a new gas cylinder in as the other was empty but as yet it had not been done. As a result they hadn't been able to cook their dinner and had had to have sandwiches instead. She apologised for this oversight and told the guests that she would personally make sure the gas cylinder was replaced straight away. The fact that during her visit she hadn't seen any sign of Kevin didn't escape her.

Kevin's caravan was a one-bedroomed one and more basic than the manager's. It was situated on the row in front of Jeff's, which stood on the back row a short distance from the boundary fence. Parking the pushchair containing the still-sleeping Danny by the set of steps leading up to the door, Rhonnie then stepped up them to knock on Kevin's door, and stepped back down to await a response.

None came so she repeated the process, only knocking louder this time. Kevin was nowhere to be seen around the site so must be inside.

On the third knock he finally responded. The door opened to reveal him, not dressed in his Jolly's caravan park uniform, but in a crumpled pair of jeans and tee shirt, hair tousled, loudly yawning and stretching out his arms. 'Yeah, what do yer want?' was his disgruntled greeting to her, it being apparent he was not happy about having his nap disturbed. It was then that it registered with him just who his caller was and his face paled, eyes almost bulging out of his head as he stammered, 'Oh . . . er . . . Mrs Buckland . . . Jeff . . . Mr Sampson . . . it's his day off, so he's not here.'

'Clearly,' she snapped. 'And while the cat's away . . .'

It took him a moment to understand what she was implying and then he blustered, 'Oh, I'd just come back to the van to collect . . .'

She cut in, 'Please don't insult my intelligence, Kevin. You're not wearing your uniform and you've been sleeping for quite a while, judging by the state of you. Sleeping on the job is against Jolly's rules and especially when you are the main staff presence on site and guests are waiting for a change of gas, bins need emptying, there's a blockage in one of the shower blocks and in all three there are toilet cubicles with no toilet paper . . . I could go on.'

He was just staring at her blindly. There was nothing he could argue with. The boss of Jolly's had caught him slacking fair and square. He just said sulkily, 'Didn't really like the job anyway.'

Rhonnie said evenly, 'Well, that's all right then. No loss on either side. I'll wait while you pack your stuff and see you off the premises. If you hurry there's a bus going into Mablethorpe at four-thirty or the next one is just before six. I'll make sure any wages and your cards are posted on to you.'

As he returned inside the caravan to pack, she heaved a worried sigh. The site had been open for several weeks now and if Kevin had been taking advantage of his boss's day off to do as he pleased, leaving the guests to fend for themselves, then that wouldn't have done Jolly's reputation much good. Guests expected to have a member of staff available to deal with any matters they might need help with twenty-four hours a day in the park, the same as they did over in the main camp. Jobs such as Jeff Sampson's, and to a certain extent Kevin's when his superior wasn't around, were based on trust in them by senior management and this was the part of her own job Rhonnie liked least: catching a member of staff red-handed in a sackable offence. But thank goodness it had slipped her mind today that it was Jeff's day off and she had caught Kevin in the act or there was no telling how long he would have carried on like this. And thank goodness she had opted to collect the tourers' takings weekly when the site first opened instead of asking Jeff to bring them over to the office, or sending his assistant. Obviously Kevin hadn't realised she would come today, it being Jeff's day off – to his detriment as it turned out.

Rhonnie knew she would need to organise a temporary

146

replacement for Kevin until someone permanent was appointed. She would use the telephone in the office, she had a key to it on the bunch she always carried allowing her access to all the main buildings. She would telephone Sid Harper, the maintenance manager, to ask him to send one of his men over to take over, after she had seen Kevin off the premises.

Standing by the entrance gates she watched him begin his walk along the lane that would take him up to the main road. She wandered if Kevin gave any thought to the fact that if he didn't change his attitude to work then he would end up in a dead-end job, struggling to give any family he hoped to have more than the most basic standard of living. As he disappeared from view she took a peep under the pushchair's hood to check Danny was still asleep but got the shock of her life to find the pushchair empty. Stupefied, she stared down into the empty chair for several moments while her brain took in what she was seeing . . . or not seeing . . . until it registered with her that while she was occupied in dealing with Kevin, Danny must have woken up, managed to unstrap himself and climbed out.

Heart thundering painfully inside her chest, Rhonnie spun around, calling frantically: 'Danny, DANNY, where are you? Danny, come on, darling, come back to Mummy.' Her son did not come running back to her and neither could she see or hear any sight or sound of him. So where was he? Then it struck her that, assuming he was still asleep inside the pushchair, she hadn't checked he was still there when she had walked Kevin up to the entrance gates to see him off the premises, in fact Danny could have made his escape while she had been occupied sacking the assistant and was therefore still down in the park.

Abandoning the pushchair, she pelted back down the lane into the main caravan park, eyes darting all around as she went, calling out Danny's name, stopping people she happened upon to ask if they had seen a little boy wearing red shorts and a yellow top, but to her dismay no one had. Arriving at Kevin's caravan she searched all round and went down on all fours underneath it and all the other caravans round about too, frantically searching for any sign of her son, but there was none. Several people who had offered to help her and gone off around the park to search came back to tell her they had seen no sign of him either.

Her panic was now reaching fever pitch. If anything happened to Danny she would never forgive herself.

The whole park had been searched, every nook and cranny, nowhere left unchecked. But if he wasn't here then where was he? She began to think the unthinkable, that someone had kidnapped him somehow when her attention had been elsewhere and they were hiding him in one of the vans until it was safe to make their getaway with him. But then through her thrashing thoughts another possibility struck. Had Danny escaped his pushchair when they had been just outside the gates, while she had been watching Kevin heading off down the lane? Danny loved to play hide and seek and while her attention was fixed on Kevin, what if her son had climbed out of his pushchair and toddled back through the gates and been hiding behind the office building? Then when she had discovered him not in his pushchair and come rushing back down here, she had in fact left him alone outside the camp! She froze in horror. If that was the case then by now he could have grown fed up with hiding and found his way up to the main road!

Without a thought for thanking the holidaymakers for helping her search for Danny, like a woman possessed, Rhonnie dashed hell for leather back up to the park entrance. On arriving, she immediately circled the office building but the only sign that Danny had been here was his abandoned pushchair. She was about to continue up the lane to the main road, praying with all her being that she caught up with him before he reached it, but then something made her look instead towards the woods, then again back up the lane, then back towards the woods. What if Danny hadn't gone up the lane but into the trees? She fought to decide which way he would have chosen.

Her woman's intuition, sixth sense, just a pure hunch – whatever it was, she had no idea – but something told her to try the woods. Praying she was right and very mindful of the harm she had suffered previously during her venture there only a short while ago, Rhonnie dashed over to the treeline, shouting out her son's name, and entered the wood. A few yards in, her foot became tangled in a twist of tree roots and she fell to the ground, deeply gashing her knee on a sharp stone. With no thought for the pain it was causing her or the flow of blood running down her leg, she clawed herself up and continued pushing her way through the dense under-growth, yelling out Danny's name, then stopping to listen for a moment for any response before she set off again.

Common sense would have told her that to search every inch of this whole area for a small boy, lying hurt and unable to call for help, would take her days to achieve and what she should have done was call for others to assist her, but common sense had no room in her thoughts as all she could think of at the moment was finding her son and alive and well.

Then suddenly, like stepping through an open door, she arrived out of the woods on a track by the side of a huge field of barley. She had zigzagged her way across the width of the woods and come out the opposite side. She made to turn and head back in when she spotted the figure of a man coming towards her from around a bend in the track. The sun was glaring into her eyes so she could only make out his outline. She immediately ran down to meet him, to ask him if he had seen a little boy on his travels. As she drew nearer she stopped dead as she spotted the man was not alone. Holding his hand, toddling beside him, was a little boy. She would recognise that child anywhere. It was her son.

A burst of sheer relief flooded her and Rhonnie collapsed on to her knees, releasing a flood of grateful tears on seeing her beloved child safe and well. Next thing she knew a pair of arms was encircling her neck and a little voice was saying, 'Mummy . . . my mummy.'

She grabbed him to her, hugging him so tightly Danny yelped in protest. She was about to scold him for running off like he had but realised he was too young to understand, and besides it was her own fault as it was she who was supposed to be watching out for him. She became aware of another presence and looked up, having to shield her eyes from the glare of the sun, to see that the man with Danny was Ben. Still with one hand on her son, fearing he would run off again, she rose to her feet and exclaimed, 'Oh, Ben, I have so much to thank you for . . . I've been searching everywhere for Danny and was beginning to fear the worst until I saw you coming along the track with him.'

He told her, 'I came across him further along with his head almost down a rabbit hole. He must have seen one go in and decided to go after it.'

'Thank God you happened to be walking up there at the time you were! My son escaped from his pushchair when I thought he was sleeping but I'll never let that happen again. In future when we go out, whether he likes it or not, he'll be wearing walking reins and be strapped in so securely in his pushchair he'd have to have Houdini's skills to get himself free. I can't go through that fear that I've lost him, ever again . . . never, never. Anyway, thank you so much again, Ben.'

It was then she noticed there was something different about him. His hair was shorter and his beard, although still a full facial one, was not half so long or bushy as it had been . . . although it was Rhonnie's opinion that whatever he'd used to cut them with he should have sharpened it better as it did look as though the hair had been hacked off with a blunt instrument . . . but there were no pungent smells emanating from him and he was wearing some of the clothes she had given him: Dan's black jeans and grey tee shirt, although they were a little on the big side for him as Dan had been very muscular whereas Ben wasn't, but then she supposed he wouldn't be as he wasn't as well fed. But these small changes had made one hell of a difference to Ben and anyone meeting him now would never put him down as a tramp living in a shed in some isolated woods, just a man who needed a visit to a good barber, but they certainly wouldn't ostracise him just because of that.

Before she could make any comment about the change in him, though, he looked at her worriedly and said, 'That cut on your knee looks nasty to me and needs attending to. I can bathe it in saltwater back in the hut, at least get any grit and mud out of it to try and stop an infection setting in before you get it seen to properly. And you look as though you could do with a cup of tea. I've managed to earn a bit of decent money this week . . . well, decent for me that is . . . thanks to you giving me the opportunity to smarten myself up, I've been helping to stack wood in a timber yard for man whose labourer is off ill, so I've been able to buy some provisions which means this time I can actually offer you sugar and milk in your tea.' He then had a thought and hurriedly added, 'Of course, I appreciate you may just want to take your son straight home after his ordeal.'

She realised that he was giving her a way to refuse his offer should she not feel that his humble abode was a fitting place to bring her son into. Rhonnie would never purposely hurt anyone's feeling, especially not those of someone who had not once but twice come to her aid in a traumatic situation, and besides she was getting a real soft spot for Ben. She smiled warmly at him. 'I could really do with a cup of tea, thank you.'

Once her knee was cleaned as well as possible and her hand-kerchief wrapped tightly round it as a makeshift bandage until she returned to the camp to get it medically attended to, Rhonnie sat on the shabby sofa sipping a welcome tin mug of sweet tea. Danny, seeming none the worse for his adventure and oblivious to the worry he had caused his mother, was lying on the floor near the stove, trying to roll an empty wooden cotton reel into an empty tin can. Rhonnie couldn't help but notice that it wasn't only Ben's appearance that had undergone a transformation. Since she had last been inside the hut it was now decidedly more presentable. The moth-eaten curtains that had been hanging at the window had been replaced by shabby but noticeably better ones and the window itself had been cleaned of its grime. A couple of prints, both Scottish scenic views, hung from nails on the walls and a faded rug was on the floor by her feet. Ben had acquired a few more cooking pots and utensils too, albeit old and well used. It seemed that he hadn't wasted any of the money he had earned since smartening himself on any frivolities but spent it on making his home more pleasant to live in. And if she wasn't mistaken it wasn't quite so dark and dismal in the hut as it had been the last time she was here, which meant he must have cut down some branches outside to let more light in through the window. She had also noticed that he had hacked a path from his hut through the stretch of woods to the track edging the farmer's field, to make it easier for him to come and go unseen by any of the holidaymakers.

It did strike her, though, that regardless of how dire this old hut was compared to her own cottage with its modern facilities and furnishings, she felt just as comfortable here as she did when at home. It wasn't the surroundings that were making her feel like this but Ben himself. He certainly had a way about him of making her feel totally at ease and relaxed in his company.

As he lounged in the old sagging armchair, his long legs outstretched, tin mug of tea in his hands, Ben smiled as he watched Danny. 'Oh, to be a child again with not a care in the world.'

'Mmm, yes, indeed,' Rhonnie mused distractedly. 'I was an only child and very lucky as I had a wonderful childhood. I always felt very loved and protected by both my parents. When I look back to when I was little, I just remember long sunny days and my mother's steak and kidney pudding. She was a good cook was my mam. She could make 'ote out of n'ote, to quote a well-known Leicester expression, which is where I come from. Oh, and gardening with my dad when he was home, as he was away a lot through his job as a long-distance lorry driver.' She looked over at Ben then enquired, 'What about your own childhood?'

It was a moment before he answered. 'Yes, same as you, it was very good. How are you feeling now? Hope that cup of sweet tea has done the trick?'

It was plain by the way he quickly changed the topic of conversation, the same as he had the last time she was here and the subject of his past had come up, that Ben still was not willing to talk about it. Rhonnie was desperate to know just what it was that he was unwilling to divulge but it seemed she was just going to have to remain curious. Anyway she had learned from experience that the past was gone, so there was no point in dwelling on it when it was the here and now and the future that mattered.

'I'm feeling much better, thank you,' she told him. 'My knee still hurts but I'll live. You make a good cup of tea.' She downed the dregs and got off the sofa, saying, 'I'd better get my young man home.' She wondered just how she could show her appreciation to Ben for bringing Danny back to her safe and sound. Money seemed the obvious answer for a man in Ben's position but it would be wrong of her to assume that just because he was a man without means he didn't have any feelings. She worried he might feel offended by her offering to pay him for what he had done, considering it was just what any other human being would do – returning a lost child to its mother. She would think seriously about the matter and felt sure she would come up with something that didn't risk demeaning him.

Having seen her and Danny safely out of the woods and back on the old farm path, ready to set off back to the entrance to the park to collect the abandoned pushchair, Ben said to her, 'I haven't thanked you for the clothes. Well, really I should be thanking your husband as I gather they were his.'

A flash of sadness crossed her face. 'They were, but he was killed in a terrible accident before Danny was born and since then they've been gathering dust in the wardrobe. I know he would be pleased they are being put to such good use.'

'Well, I appreciate how hard it must have been for you to part with them and feel very honoured you gave them to me. As I told you before, it was the clothes you gave me that got me the work in the wood yard this week. Looking like I did before, the boss there wouldn't have given me the time of day, let alone any work.'

'It's not just the clothes that did that, but you look so much better now you've trimmed your hair and beard. You're not half so ferocious-looking now,' she told him with amusement in her voice.

He thought: And a good few baths with carbolic soap to rid myself of years of grime and stop me smelling so vilely did no harm either. 'Well, as I said, I very much appreciate the clothes.'

She smiled warmly at him. 'And thank you for the flowers you left on my doorstep.'

As Ben watched Rhonnie walk away a surge of emotion rushed through him. He had felt very drawn to her the first time he had met her, but believing she was a happily married woman had been enough to prevent his feelings from developing any further. Now he knew she was free and single matters changed for him. He had only been in Rhonnie's company a couple of times but already he knew she was a woman he could very easily fall in love with. Everything about her attracted him. But he was fooling himself if he thought his feelings for her would ever be returned. No woman with a brain in her head would see a man without a bean to his name and no future to offer her as a potential husband to her and a father to her son, but more than that, she definitely wouldn't want a man who was responsible for five other men lying dead.

He should just be grateful that a woman like Rhonnie felt it fitting to have befriended a man like him, and settle for that. Living in hope of any more from her would just be wishful thinking and setting himself up in the future for a lot of pain and heartache when she did find a man who was worthy of her. Issuing a deep sigh of regret, Ben turned back to his hut.

CHAPTER THIRTEEN

Over in the photographic shop, sitting on a stool behind the counter, elbows resting on it, Kerry looked at the clock on the wall and heaved out a huge fed-up sigh, seeing she still had an hour and a half to go before finishing time. Darren's mood hadn't improved at all since dinner time and he had still not left his office, sitting at his desk with a Grim Reaper expression on his face, although when she had taken in his afternoon cup of tea and biscuits, which he had not even bothered to thank her for, the pencil he had been twiddling between his fingers earlier now lay broken in two on his desk and he was using a Biro instead.

Normally at this time in the evening she would be preparing herself to approach him with an excuse she had concocted to leave early, but she wasn't fool enough to risk that today, despite how much she wanted to get back to her chalet and get ready for a party one of chalet maids was having tonight. Kerry had found out that a lad she had a fancy for, who worked in the cinema projection room, was supposed to be going too and if she got her way he would be taking her out on a date on his next night off. Had Darren not been in the frame of mind he was then she would have had plenty of time to get herself looking her best as the party started at ten, but as it was she wouldn't now be finishing until nine, instead of her hoped for eight, so would have to rush her preparations or else risk losing her potential date for Saturday night, his eye caught by someone else before she got there.

Then minutes later she received a shock when Darren emerged from his office, telling her she could go, and Jimmy and Rodney that they could do the same.

Kerry didn't need telling twice and neither did Jimmy nor Rodney.

She was walking down the path across the wide stretch of grass, heading towards the staff chalet complex and sharing a rude joke with Jimmy and Rodney that her friend had told her at lunchtime, when suddenly out of nowhere a vision of Darren popped into her mind, sitting at his desk looking worried to death, and Kerry abruptly stopped her flow as well as her footsteps, looking bothered.

'What's up?' Jimmy asked her.

'Well, it's Darren.'

'What about him?' Rodney asked.

'The bad mood he's been in today. It's not like him at all, is it?'

'No, it's not. He's the best boss I've ever worked for. Really nice bloke. But everyone has an off day now and then,' volunteered Jimmy.

Kerry scoffed, 'Off day is putting it mildly. In foul mood terms he's been off the scale today. Since I've worked here I've never known Darren be anything other than easy-going. But today he's been like a different person, hardly said a word, and when he did he was downright nasty to me. I'm just bothered something awful is worrying him. Well, it's got to be serious for someone like him to be acting like he has today, hasn't it?'

Rodney started laughing. 'It's not like you to be bothered about anything else other than who's holding the next chalet party, Kerry!'

She shrugged. 'So I like enjoying myself – so what? That's what I came here for – to have myself a good time without me mam and dad breathing down my neck.'

'Yeah, me too,' said Jimmy.

'And me,' agreed Rodney.

'You going to Sandy's do tonight?' Jimmy asked her.

She nodded.

'Yeah, so are we,' Rodney told her. 'That chalet maid Marlene is going and I'm hoping to get a snog with her later.'

Jimmy gave Rodney a heavy nudge in the ribs. 'You probably will as I've heard she ain't fussy – she'll snog anything with trousers on, and if yer lucky you might get some added extras.' He then asked Kerry, 'Are you taking any booze?'

She shook her head. 'I've no money left to buy any 'til we get paid on Friday so I'm hoping everyone else does and I can sneak a few swigs of theirs.'

'Me and Rodney ain't got any money either so that's what we were hoping to do. I'm taking a packet of crisps, though, so at least I'm contributing something.'

'You mean that packet of cheese and onion in your bedside drawer?' Jimmy asked him.

He nodded.

'You can't take them.'

'Why not?'

''Cos I ate them last night when you nipped over to the toilet block before we went to sleep.' Rodney then urged them, 'Come on, we'd best get a move on or the party will be finished before we get there.'

They made to resume their journey but Kerry still held back. 'I'll see you both at the party later.'

'Why, where are you going?' Jimmy asked her.

'Back to the shop. I can't stop worrying about Darren. I know you don't think I care about anything else but my social life but I like him, he's been good to me, and I know I won't enjoy myself tonight if I don't at least try to get him to tell me what's wrong with him and see if I can help in any way. He'll probably just bite my head off like he did this morning when I asked him, though.'

158

'You're braver than I am,' Rodney told her, looking at her as though she was stupid.

'Yeah, me too,' said Jimmy. 'I'm not that fond of my job but I wouldn't want to risk losing it as my mother would kill me if I went home and told her I stepped over the line with my boss.'

Kerry didn't fancy having to return home under a black cloud either when she'd had such a hard job persuading her parents to allow her to come and work here in the first place. But even so, the niggle of worry gnawing away in her stomach that her kindly boss was in some sort of trouble and could do with some help, even just someone to talk to, wouldn't go away. Whenever she had a problem and talked to a friend about it, then somehow it never seemed such a big one. Maybe whatever was worrying Darren wouldn't seem so great to him if she could get him to open up about it.

She said to the boys, 'Why don't we all go? He can't sack three of us just for being worried about him, can he?'

Jimmy was resolute. 'I told you, I ain't risking me job. You don't know my mother. She makes Godzilla look like a pussycat.'

Kerry shot a look of appeal at Rodney. 'You come with me, please, Rod? Darren's been a good boss to you too. Or are you going to get out of it by making out you're a sissy like Jimmy, scared of his mother?'

Rodney's ego wouldn't allow anyone to think him a sissy even if he too would sooner face a firing squad than his mother when she was upset about something. He sighed with resignation. 'Oh, okay, I'll come.'

She immediately grabbed his arm and propelled him back towards the courtyard.

On reaching the door of Jolly's Snaps, Rodney held back, telling Kerry, 'I've changed my mind . . . I'm not coming in. I don't want to risk losing me job. At least here at Jolly's I don't have to share a bedroom with my bully of an older brother.

159

I'll have a fag while I wait in the hairdresser's shop doorway.'

Kerry shot him a murderous glare. 'I'll know not to call on you or Jimmy if ever I'm in trouble. Both of you are nothing but a pair of soppy women in men's clothing!'

Looking shame-faced, Rodney scuttled off towards the doorway of the shop next door to wait for her there. Kerry made to open the shop door and noticed that the sign had been turned to 'Closed'. The blind was pulled down so she couldn't see inside, and when she tried the handle she found the door was locked. But the shop wasn't supposed to be closed until nine o' clock and it was only a quarter to eight. The fear of God rushed through Kerry then. Was that why Darren had let them all go extra early? Was his problem so great he was going to do away with himself? Maybe he was in the process of doing that now? Hanging himself maybe from the roof rafters! Not that the roof of the shop has rafters, it was flat. She clenched her fist and hammered on the door. When her summons wasn't immediately responded to, she hammered again, worried to death now that she was too late and he'd already done the deed.

To her great relief she heard a key turn in the mortice lock and the snib on the Yale lock being flicked up. As the door was opening she could hear Darren saying, in a voice fraught with panic, 'You're early, you said eight and it's . . . Kerry! What . . . what are you doing here? You need to go. Go on, off you go before . . . Look, just go, will you?'

She was stunned. Why was he so desperate to be rid of her? Who was he expecting that he obviously didn't want her to see? It wasn't someone he was looking forward to seeing or why was he in such a state of panic?

He started to shut the door on her but she stopped him by pushing her way inside before he could protest. Facing him, she bluntly asked: 'What's going on, Darren?'

He said hurriedly, 'Nothing. Nothing at all. Now why won't you listen to me and leave me alone?'

160

"Cos I don't believe nothing is wrong, Darren. In all the time I've worked for you, I've never known you to be in anything but a good mood. Even when I know I've really annoyed you, you've never so much as raised your voice to me, let alone lost your temper. You've been like a bear with a sore head all day, snapping at me and Jimmy and Rod, and once you were downright nasty to me. It's like you've had a sudden change of personality.' Then something he'd said when she first arrived struck Kerry. 'When you opened the door to me you said . . . *you're early*. Who are you expecting and why are you terrified of them, Darren?'

He frenziedly shook his head. 'No one, Kerry. Really, no one at all. Now please will you go?'

He made to open the door and push her out but she stood her ground by dodging him to dash over to the counter, where she spun around and said defiantly, 'And why don't you pull the other one? It's got a label on it that says *liar*.' Then she softened her voice and told him, 'Darren, I really like you, you've been a good boss to me and I know you're in some sort of trouble. I only want to help you if I can.'

He looked stunned. This was a young girl he had believed only cared about what she would wear that night to catch the eye of the lad who was her current fancy and putting all her initiative into coming up with a plausible excuse to get Darren to allow her to leave work early. The fact that she was now showing real care towards him, instead of thinking only of herself, and sincerely wanted to help him, brought tears to Darren's eyes. He shut the door, placed his back against it and slid down to the floor, cradling his head in his hands. He then uttered in despair, 'But that's just it, Kerry, no one can help me, *she's* seen to that. I'm damned if I do and damned if I don't.' Then he burst into uncontrollable sobs.

Kerry rushed over to him, kneeling down by his side and placing a hand on his arm. 'This woman . . . whoever she is . . . just what is she making you do that is going to cause

161

you trouble whether you do or you don't? Come on, Darren, tell me?'

He lowered his hands and sobbed, 'She's insisting I take photos of her.'

Kerry gave a shrug of mystification. 'But that's what you do, isn't it? Take photos of people.'

'Not the sort she wants me to, Kerry.'

'What sort?' Then it registered and her mouth formed an 'O'. 'You mean those sort . . . rude ones . . . porno?'

He nodded. 'She wants to get into glamour modelling as she calls it and needs a portfolio of photos to give to an agent, for him to tout about and get her work.'

'Well, why don't you just take them, pocket the money and send her on her way?'

He shuddered at the thought. 'Because I couldn't . . . not that sort of thing, I couldn't. Some photographers could and would charge a fortune for doing it as it's illegal, you see, but not me. I couldn't snap away at a woman displaying her . . . private parts . . . in the obscene way she's expecting me to. Call me a prude, I don't care, that's the way I am. Besides, she's no intention of paying me. If I don't take the shots, and for nothing, she's said she's going to report me to the police for . . . for . . . raping her.'

Kerry gasped, astounded. 'She's what! Good Lord, no wonder you've been in a foul mood all day. But . . . but . . . she can't do that. She'd need proof surely that you attacked her, and she hasn't got any, has she, because you didn't.'

He heaved a sigh. 'Just reporting me for rape would do enough damage, Kerry. Jolly's wouldn't tolerate a suspected rapist working for them and would immediately dismiss me. Even if I could prove my innocence, mud sticks and I'd never get another job as a photographer, or much else for that matter, with an accusation like that hanging over me. People believe there's no smoke without fire, don't they? She's got it all planned out.

'She's been watching this place in the evenings since she's been here, waiting for her chance to carry out her plan, and it came last night when I let you all off early and was here on my own. She came in and told me her plan and expected me to do the shoot there and then. I couldn't believe what I was hearing but I managed to fool her into giving me some time to try and find a way out of it by persuading her we'd run out of flashbulbs and the photos wouldn't come out properly . . . too dark without the flash . . . but that we were expecting new stock of them in today. She had no choice but to agree to come back tonight but she warned me that if she arrived and I tried to pull a fast one by having someone here as a witness, she'd claim she'd only returned to warn me that she hadn't reported me the night before because she'd been too traumatised by what I did to her, but now she was thinking clearer she wasn't going to let me get away with it and I could expect a visit from the police.'

Kerry was staring at him in disbelief. This was like a story she would read in a detective novel but never in a million years would she expect it to happen to anyone she knew in real life. 'Look, I know you've told me that you couldn't take the photos but I can't see that she's left you any choice. Just shut your eyes and get on with it and at least then you'd be shot of her for good.'

'But that's just it, Kerry. If I took those photos I wouldn't ever be shot of her. The developing paper we use comes from a supplier who makes it specially for us, with a watermark through it that says 'Jolly's Holiday Camp' and the year the photos were taken, so this year they all have 'Jolly's Holiday Camp 1969' on the back of them and if those photos ever got into the hands of the police they would be traced back to me as the photographer in residence that year and I'd be in very deep trouble, more than likely end up in jail. Or they could end up in the hands of someone who'd use them to blackmail me.'

Kerry pulled a quizzical face. 'But then why did you not think to get hold of some developing paper that hasn't got the watermark and couldn't be traced back here?'

'Don't you think I haven't thought of that? I wouldn't be able to get hold of any in time for tonight. There's no photographic supply shops left now in this part of Lincolnshire. They all went out of business because they couldn't compete with the likes of Dixons and Currys selling their cameras and equipment, and doing developing too, much cheaper. Dixons and Currys don't sell developing sundries as they want you to get your films developed with them. They make far more profit that way. Unless they happen to live in a place that still does have a photographic supplier's, all professional photographers have to order their sundries from a photographic supply company and have them delivered by post.' He heaved a miserable sigh. 'I couldn't sleep a wink last night for trying to come up with a way to get out of taking those photos, and that's all I've been doing all day, but I can't think of anything. She's got me completely over a barrel, Kerry. As I said before, I'm damned if I do, damned if I don't.'

'The bloody bitch,' Kerry hissed furiously. 'Well, *I'm* damned if I'm going to let this woman ruin the life of a lovely man like you.' She jumped up and began pacing the floor, her face screwed up in thought, saying, 'There must be something we can do to put a stop to her disgusting plan. There's got to be.'

Darren got up too, wearily rubbing his hands over his face, his whole body sagging in resignation to his fate. 'I told you, it's all I've been trying to do for the last twenty-four hours and I can't think of anything . . . not a bloody damned thing . . . to put a stop to her evil plan. Well, apart from jumping in the boating lake and drowning myself. Look, she'll be here soon and I really don't want you getting involved in this, so please go, Kerry. As your boss, I'm ordering you to.'

She stood and looked at him meaningfully. 'And when have

I ever done anything you've told me to do?' She glanced over at the clock on the wall. 'We've still ten minutes before she's due. There's a way out, there's got to be, you just haven't thought of it yet. Two heads are better than one, so come on, get thinking.'

Six minutes later, having come up with absolutely nothing herself that would thwart the woman's plan in any way whatsoever, Kerry heaved a resigned sigh and said to Darren, 'You're right, I can't think of anything either and if you had you'd have told me. She has well and truly got you by the short and curlies. It's not fair, Darren, it really isn't, that this woman is prepared to ruin your future for her own selfish ends.'

'I appreciate you trying to help me, Kerry, but you really do need to leave before she gets here. She's a nasty piece of work and if you're here when she arrives I can't promise she won't try and involve you in her scheme somehow. Please, just go and have a nice night with your boyfriend or friends, whatever you've planned for tonight.'

At his parting words to her Kerry stared at him blankly, thoughts tumbling inside her head. Then, to his utter shock, she clapped her hands together and cried out: 'Why, you clever man, that's it.'

He eyed her in confusion. 'What is?' Then his eyes lit up. 'You mean you think you've come up with something to stop her.'

'I think I have, yes. You gave me the idea. She pulled a worried face. You see . . .'

They both jumped and spun their heads to look across at the door as they heard the handle being tried. When the door wouldn't open, someone started to knock on it loudly.

Darren started shaking. 'Oh, God, she's here.'

Kerry spun to face him, urgently ordering, 'You've got to leave this to me, Darren. Now get yourself in your office and don't come in here unless I call you. Got that?'

He was staring at her in total terror.

The shop door banged again and a voice was heard to call out, 'I know you're in there. You can't hide from me.'

In a scolding voice Kerry shot at him, 'Have you got that, Darren? Darren, for God's sake, did you listen to what I told you to do?'

He stammered, 'Yes, yes. Er . . . Kerry are you sure this plan of yours . . .?'

'Just get yourself into the office, quick, before she goes off and reports you because she thinks you're welching on your deal!'

He needed no further telling.

As soon as Darren was safely in his office, Kerry took several deep breaths, went over to the door, turned the Yale lock and opened it. She smiled apologetically at the tartily dressed young woman, plastered in makeup, who was looking far from happy at being kept waiting. Kerry said breezily, 'Sorry about that. The lock on this door is faulty and some-times locks itself. We really should get it seen to. Come to collect some photos, have you?'

The woman followed Kerry inside, looking at her suspiciously. 'What are you doing here?' she demanded.

Kerry responded lightly, 'I work here.'

'But you were supposed to leave early tonight, weren't you?'

Behind the counter now, the other woman standing in front of it, Kerry gave an innocent shrug. 'Was I? I wish someone had told me, I could have done with getting off early. Got a hot date tonight, you see. Have you got your ticket and I'll sort the snaps out for you?' She held out her hand towards the girl.

'I'm here to see Darren. We're doing a photo shoot. Already in the studio waiting for me, is he? I'll just go through,' she told Kerry, about to head off in the direction of the studio.

Knowing what this woman was up to, though not a violent

person by nature, Kerry was having extreme difficulty in stopping herself from lunging at this blackmailer and causing serious damage to her. She needed to keep reminding herself that she had to ignore her own feelings if her plan to thwart this woman was to be a success. 'He's not in the studio. Darren's busy at the moment. There's no appointment in the book for a session tonight . . . you must have made a mistake.'

The woman's face darkened thunderously and she banged her fist angrily on the counter. 'Get Darren out here *now*. We've got an arrangement and he knows what will happen if he doesn't honour it.'

Kerry responded casually, 'Oh, you mean the arrangement to take mucky photos of you and if he doesn't you'll go to the police and report him for rape? Well, he's not going to take them so off you go and report him to the police . . . but be prepared to end up in jail yourself if you do, for making false allegations. It carries quite a hefty sentence, I believe.'

The woman laughed at her. 'He won't be able to prove I'm lying when I tell the police he raped me last night while we were in here on our own. Don't bother trying to make out you or the other staff were somewhere in the back as I watched you all leaving before I came in. And my friends will back me up, saying they witnessed me coming in here for an appointment for him to take some head-and-shoulders shots of me and then a short while later they found me in our chalet in a right state with my clothes all ripped.'

Kerry said darkly, 'Seems your friends are as good at lying and as nasty as you are then. Well, you can tell the coppers whatever you like but they won't believe you as all the staff here at Jolly's will make sure of that. You see, you didn't consider the fact that even kissing a woman, let alone forcing her to have sex with him, is the very last thing Darren would do.'

The other woman gawped at her, bewildered. 'What do you mean?'

167

Kerry took great pleasure in lying to her. 'Darren is a poof, a homo . . . whatever you like to call it. It's men he goes for, wouldn't touch a woman with a barge pole. So you've really been barking up the wrong tree, lady.'

The woman scoffed, 'Think I was born yesterday? You're lying. Now get him out here to take the photos or I'm off to the police station.'

Kerry stared back at her blindly. Oh, shit, she's called my bluff, what do I do now? were the thoughts tumbling frantically around in her head. Her heart began to race, a feeling of doom settling upon her as what she thought was a clever plan to put a halt to this woman's despicable one and save Darren's future, wasn't so clever after all. There was no way she could prove to this woman that Darren was a homosexual . . . especially when he wasn't. Then a thought struck. Or wasn't there?

'Stay there and I'll prove to you that Darren is what I say he is.'

Without waiting for any response, Kerry dashed from behind the counter and over to the door, yanking it open to rush outside and next door. As soon as she arrived Rodney threw down a cigarette stub on the floor and ground it out with the heel of his shoe, saying to her, 'God, you took your time . . .'

She snapped at him, 'Shut up and listen. I haven't time to explain but you've got to go along with anything I say, no matter what. It's really important you do, Rod, as it's a matter of life or death. Got that?'

He frowned at her, taken aback. 'Yeah, okay, but . . .'

She grabbed his arm and starting propelling him out of the shop doorway. 'I said, no time for explanations. Come on!'

Back in the shop, Kerry pushed Rodney forward to stand before the woman. 'Let me introduce you to Darren's boyfriend, Rod. He's been waiting outside for Darren to finish work so they can walk home together. They share a chalet, see. How long have you and Darren been together now, Rod? Over a year, isn't it? It was well after it was made legal for two men to be together in that way so you aren't breaking the law or anything?' She gave him a nudge in his ribs. 'Isn't that right, Rod?'

'Eh? Oh, yeah, yeah, for a year at least.'

'Got lots of friends that will vouch for how long you two have been together, haven't you, Rod? They would swear it on oath if necessary.'

'Er . . . yeah, yeah, loads.'

Kerry smiled triumphantly at the woman. 'Still want to go to the police and report Darren for rape 'cos he's refusing to take those photos of you?'

'Eh! She's reporting Darren for what?' Rodney gasped, shocked. 'Darren would never . . .'

Kerry poked him hard in his ribs to cut him short. '. . . touch a woman in that way, 'cos he only looks at men, doesn't he, Rod?'

'Oh, yeah, yeah, only men. Absolutely. He's as queer as a nine-bob note.'

The woman stared at them both. It was apparent that she was well aware she had been well and truly outwitted and there was no way for her to turn this situation back to her own advantage. Shooting them both a murderous glare, she spun on her heel and stomped out of the door, slamming it shut behind her.

Kerry's whole body slumped in relief and she took several deep breaths to calm her jangling nerves. At least Darren could sleep well tonight, knowing he'd not be going to spend the rest of his life worried that at any time the law was going to come calling. Or a blackmailer either. She clapped Rodney on his back. 'You were great. A born liar if ever I've met one.'

He puffed out his chest, pleased by the compliment. 'Yeah, I can tell a good porky when I have to. I learned when I was young and didn't fancy a clip around the ear. Are you going

169

to tell me what's going on? I know Darren isn't gay so why were you making out to that woman he is?'

She knew that Darren would be absolutely mortified to become the topic of gossip around the camp if this story became common knowledge and felt it was best that it was swept under the carpet and left there, for his sake. She flapped her hand and said in a dismissive tone, 'You wouldn't believe me if I did tell you. Anyway, you've a party to get ready for so you go ahead and I'll see you and Jimmy there.'

As Rodney disappeared Kerry called out, 'It's safe to come out now, Darren.'

A moment later he appeared. Glancing around warily and not seeing any sign of the woman, he looked at Kerry and said, 'She's not here so has she gone to report me to the police or has your plan worked?'

Kerry smiled at him. 'My plan worked a treat. She left here with her tail between her legs, so you can breathe easy again.'

His relief was so great that his legs buckled and he collapsed against the counter, gasping for breath for several moments before he exclaimed, 'Oh, thank God, thank God. I can't believe that this nightmare is over. I could only hear mumbling when I was inside the office and I was worried sick about what was going on out here. I didn't know what to think. But you really got rid of her? You really did, Kerry? She's definitely not coming back?'

'She's not coming back, Darren.'

He threw his arms around Kerry and hugged her so tight she had to beg him to release her as she could hardly breathe.

Leaning back against the counter again, he rubbed his hands wearily over his face before saying, 'I don't want to know how you managed it, Kerry. I just want to forget that woman ever existed and get on with my life.' He smiled gratefully at her. 'I don't know how to thank you. How do you repay someone who's saved your life?' Then the obvious way struck him. 'Oh, I know what would go a small way to doing so. I can let you leave early every night so you no longer have to spend most of the day trying to come up with a good excuse. It's the least I can do.'

She responded in all seriousness, 'Not bloody likely will I ever leave early again while I work here. I'm not going to risk another selfish cow trying to take advantage of you in the way she tried. Or something worse.'

Darren looked taken aback. He had fully believed Kerry would grab at his offer. But how thankful he was that she hadn't and would in future work the hours she was supposed to. Kerry had no idea that all the numerous times he had good-naturedly let her manipulate him into getting off early, he had in fact been worried that either Rhonnie Buckland or Drina Jolly would happen into the shop, enquire why he was manning the counter and not his shop assistant, and he would then be in trouble for being complicit in staff not working the hours they were paid for. Regardless, after his terrible ordeal, tonight it was he who wanted to get away from this place before the official closing time, go to bed and wake up tomorrow with this nightmare behind him.

He put his arm around Kerry's shoulders in a friendly manner and said, 'For tonight though, let's lock up and get off.' He eyed her knowingly before adding, 'If I'm caught by the top brass and need an excuse why we shut up early, I know who to turn to, don't I?'

Kerry laughed. 'I'll start thinking of one, just in case.'

CHAPTER FOURTEEN

At a quarter to nine the next morning, Jill was with Rhonnie in her office having their daily early-morning meeting.

Sliding a leather-bound folder across the desk, Rhonnie said to her, 'That's all the correspondence signed.'

Jill looked at her meaningfully. 'Including the invitation to the Lord Mayor's lunch next month? I keep reminding you that I have to have the RSVP to them by Friday and it's Wednesday today. It won't look good if Jolly's is not represented, considering we're about the biggest business this side of Skegness, if not the biggest.'

Rhonnie sighed. 'Yes, it's in there. I got fed up with you nagging me to do it.'

Jill looked knowingly at her. 'You're about as fond of attending civic functions as Harold Rose was. It was his opinion that they were just an excuse for greedy businessmen to spend taxpayers' money on good food and fine wine and a chance for them to brag about their business achievements . . . or grossly exaggerate was more like it in Harold's opinion.'

'I completely agree with Harold. I dread going to them. I've represented Drina at couple of these dos in the past and was constantly having to avoid the wandering hands of some slimy-toad type while listening to others bragging about their golf handicaps. A lot of the old duffers just can't accept that women are as capable of running a successful business as men are. They're so condescending towards us. But then, having said that, going to these functions can serve its purpose as it's surprising what you get to hear from those who have had too much to drink. That's how Drina found out, through Harold last year, that the council were planning to do major roadworks in Mablethorpe that were to last at least six weeks, probably more if they overran, and some bright spark in the council highways department thought it was a good idea to carry them out during the height of the summer because it would save a few quid!

'Can you imagine the chaos that would have caused, with heavy holiday traffic and especially coaches and buses travelling down diversions along back roads barely wider than single-track and most with ditches on either side! Drina was down in Devon helping me come to terms with Dan's death at the time she found out about this but, regardless, after a few heated telephone calls to other business people it would have affected, and to the head of the council, she got them to change their plans until after the season ended.'

'I remember,' Jill told her. 'Harold was quite worried at the time over the impact the roadworks would have on the camp. He did say to me at the time that if anyone could get the council to see the error of their ways it was Drina. And she did.'

Rhonnie chuckled. 'Well, to look at her you'd just think she was a middle-aged housewife who wouldn't say boo to a goose . . . but how wrong that would be. When anything arises that could damage the camp or lessen the enjoyment of the guests who come here, she's a force to be reckoned with. On second thoughts, give me back the invitation and I'll persuade Drina to go instead of me.'

Jill opened the folder and took out the acceptance letter to the Mayor's lunch. She passed it back to Rhonnie, looking impressed. 'That's as good an excuse as any to get yourself out of going.'

Rhonnie smiled. 'Yes, it is, isn't it? Anything else I need to know about before we get on with the business of today?'

Jill pushed a pile of paperwork towards her. 'This post needs your attention and all that remains is for me to remind you of the managers' monthly meeting at eleven, plus this afternoon you have Mr Coppice coming in to discuss the new brochure.'

Rhonnie groaned. 'Oh, I'm not looking forward to this, telling that lovely old man his work is just not up to our standards any longer and in future we'll be doing our own design. Though I am really excited to find out what Darren will produce and hopefully we'll get to see very shortly.' She eyed Jill meaningfully. 'I hope you've been giving thought to some catchy captions we can use underneath the photos.' She then noticed Jill stifling a yawn and quipped, 'Oh, I apologise for keeping you up.'

A look of mortification filled Jill's face. 'I'm sorry, Rhonnie, it's just that I can't seem to get enough sleep at the moment. It's my husband's fault. His snoring never used to bother me, but recently it must have started doing so as I just can't seem to drop off.'

She frowned in concern. 'Does he snore badly then?'

'That's the thing, he does, though it's more like a cat's purr than a pig's snort.'

Rhonnie mused, 'Dan only snored when he'd had a few too many to drink, which wasn't very often so I was lucky in that respect.' What she would give to hear that drunken snore again. 'Have you tried pinching him so he turns over?'

'I thought about it, and putting a stone in the back of his pyjamas, but I don't like to as it's not really his fault what he does when he's sleeping, is it? If it carries on I will, though. I'm a woman who needs my eight hours. Anyway, you asked me to sort out application forms for those applying for the job of assistant to the caravan site manager. There were half a dozen you asked me to keep on file just in case Kevin didn't work out.' As she passed them over the desk to Rhonnie, Jill gave a disdainful tut and commented, 'It really annoys me that some people would give anything to land themselves such a good job with a company like Jolly's, especially one with living accommodation thrown in, and do all they could to keep it, yet the likes of Kevin feel it's right to pocket the money they're being paid and do as little as they can get away with.'

Rhonnie nodded in agreement. 'Thank goodness his sort are few and far between. I need to find a replacement as soon as possible as Sid Harper is not happy about losing one of his maintenance men to fill in meantime.' Then something Jill had said hit her and she exclaimed, 'Oh!'

Jill looked sharply at her. 'What is it, Rhonnie?'

She pushed the archived application forms back across to Jill. 'Just keep hold of these for the time being. You've given me an idea for a person I'm sure would be over the moon to be given a chance at the job.'

'Oh, who?'

'Ben.'

Jill frowned. 'Ben? I can't think . . .' Her voice trailed off and her eyebrows arched in surprise as she incredulously exclaimed, 'You mean the tramp who's living in Sam's old hut! But you can't be serious about giving the likes of him a job. I know you've told me he's come to your rescue a couple of times, but apart from that what do you know about him, Rhonnie?'

'I know he's a man who's trying to make life better for himself. I know he's honest. Don't forget that when I first met him after he came across me knocked out in the woods, I had the takings on me and he could have taken those before I came round and made out someone else stole them before he found me, but he didn't. Not a penny of those takings went missing from that bag. If Drina had felt there was anything suspicious about Ben, she wouldn't have allowed him to live in the hut in the first place. At times in our lives

175

most of us need a helping hand and as it is I'm in a position to give a man like Ben the break he needs to get himself back on track. I feel in his case it's the right thing to do.'

Jill shot a surreptitious look at Rhonnie. She wondered if giving Ben a helping hand to better his life was the only motive behind her gesture. Jill's instincts were telling her that whether Rhonnie realised it or not she liked the man, and quite a lot by her defensive manner when she had spoken of him just now. Jill hoped that this fact wasn't clouding Rhonnie's judgement of him and she'd come to regret her decision to offer him the job. Jill stood up, saying, 'I'd better go and get the chairs out ready for the managers' meeting or they'll all be arriving and have nowhere to sit.'

At just before noon, all the issues raised by the managers having been satisfactorily dealt with, they started to gather their notes and belongings together believing that the meeting was over, but Drina had other ideas. Even though she had been taking a backseat role in handing over the daily running of the business to Rhonnie, she still attended all the managers' meetings just to keep abreast of what was going on. During the meetings she would sit opposite Rhonnie at the other end of the table, only respectfully adding her input when she was requested by Rhonnie to do so. Once the meeting was over they would always share a cup of tea and Rhonnie would consult Drina on how she thought the meeting had gone and take on board any constructive criticism Drina made as she very much appreciated the older woman's experience and wisdom . . . not that Drina ever found much to criticise her over. This time, though, Drina did have something she very much wanted to discuss with the other managers so, as they began to take their leave, Rhonnie stopped them all by telling them to remain in their seats as Drina would like to address them.

After they had all settled themselves and were looking expectantly in Drina's direction, she smiled and said, 'I don't suppose it's escaped anybody's notice . . . well, you'd have to be blind, deaf and dumb for it not to have as for weeks now it's been constantly in the papers and on the radio and television news . . . that we are all about to be privileged to witness history being made on July the twentieth with the American moon landings. I'm sure you'll all agree that we should celebrate this momentous occasion.'

They all nodded and expressed their agreement.

Drina looked pleased they were all showing support and said, 'I know it won't be possible for all of you to organise a space-related event for your department, but I'd appreciate any ideas for making it a really special fun day for campers and staff alike. The BBC will be televising it all, but the actual landings won't happen until the early hours of the morning, so I thought we could keep the television lounge open for campers who want to stay up and watch it.' She addressed Rhonnie specifically then. 'Could you ask Jill to have a word with the local Rediffusion shop to see about hiring several more sets that we can place in the other lounges, so people who do want to watch are not all sitting on top of one another.'

'We could hang bunting around the lounges showing the American flag and also across the frontage of the row of shops,' suggested Carol from sweets and souvenirs. 'And I could chop into chunks multi-coloured sticks of rock, packet them up and sell them to the kids as moon rock. I could do the same with those sherbet flying saucer sweets too.'

'That's a great idea,' Drina enthused.

'I could make up a new cocktail and call it . . . er . . . oh, I know . . . Moonshine, and another something like Martian Sunrise, Venus Love Potion, that sort of thing,' Bill Johns the bar manager offered.

Alan Ibbotson spoke up next. 'I could organise a kids' fancy dress competition themed on space and also some space games on the field . . . Space Hopper races and moon jumps. I could have a few of the Stripeys going around dressed as characters out of those space shows on the TV, *Star Trek*, *Lost in Space*, and there's another one but I can't remember what it's called off the top of my head. We could also give water pistols to each of the Stripeys in space costumes, and have them squirt the kids as they come across them, shouting out "Kill the aliens" . . . the kids would love that.' He paused and fixed his attention on Lily Dawkins, saying meaningfully, 'If Miss Dawkins will kindly have the costumes made up for us, of course.'

Her look back at him was a murderous one but her tone of voice was sweet when she responded, 'I'd be delighted to, so long as Mr Ibbotson gives me plenty of time to get them made up and does not expect me to do them at the last minute.'

'As I always do,' he said, flashing her a scathing look although his tone of voice was pleasant also.

Rhonnie noticed the looks that passed between the pair of them but made no comment. She knew that Jill had seen too and the look she flashed to Rhonnie was one that said she was resolute in her belief that the pair were passionately attracted to each other but hadn't yet admitted the fact. The one Rhonnie flashed back to Jill told her she was adamant the pair just could not bear the sight of each other. Thank goodness Drina didn't seem to have noticed the looks that passed between Alan and Lily from where she was sitting. She did not at all like any animosity between the staff, in particular management, and Rhonnie did not want her to think her camp manager was falling down on the job by allowing this state of affairs to continue and not doing something about it. But Rhonnie felt she really needed to tackle this situation in a delicate way so it didn't result in either Alan or Lily resigning their post as it would be sad to lose either of these good people for such a trivial reason.

Chef Eric Brown had been sitting thinking about what contribution he could make and volunteered, 'I could serve green jelly for pudding for all the kids and get the serving staff to tell them it's moon slime, and we could give them orange cordial to drink instead of water and call it Moon Juice.'

'What about we end the evening with a firework display?' suggested Rhonnie.

Drina exclaimed, 'Perfect.' She looked around all the staff, pleased that her managers were getting into the spirit of the occasion. 'I'm very impressed with all the suggestions and will be delighted to hear any more you come up with. We have three weeks to make our arrangements and we'll have another meeting next week to formulate everything and discuss any more ideas to celebrate this historic occasion. Thank you, everyone.'

Drina didn't stay after the meeting to have a brief discussion with Rhonnie as she was dashing off to an appointment with the camp hairdresser. Artie and Drina were going out to dinner that night to celebrate the anniversary of their being together for four years. Rhonnie knew that deep down they both wished it was a wedding anniversary they were celebrating but as matters stood that would never be the case for them.

Rhonnie did waylay Lily Dawkins as she was leaving, to enquire after Ginger who had now resumed her job as a chalet maid and had been occupying a staff chalet for several days. Lily seemed to hesitate for a moment before she told Rhonnie that Ginger was getting on well. Rhonnie was very gratified to learn this and hoped her dear friend was now making progress towards rebuilding her life after the devastating end of her marriage. She had invited Ginger for supper on Friday night and Rhonnie was very much looking forward to having a catch up with her.

The meeting later that afternoon with Albert Coppice went better than Rhonnie had expected. In his stiff-upper-lip manner, Albert seemed to accept with good grace the fact that the brochure he had produced was tired and outdated. He seemed very gratified that at least they were still giving him their printing business, so all was not lost for him.

Rhonnie felt it a shame that he couldn't find someone to help him keep his business flourishing, someone younger and enthusiastic with an understanding of how the world was changing and what people were expecting now. They could encourage Albert to modernise his business, which she feared was in serious danger of floundering.

At just after six that evening Rhonnie brought her car to a stop on the road nearby Ben's track to his hut in the wood. She arrived there to find him sitting outside on a stool made out of a thick stump of wood topped with a flat piece; the same technique had been used to make a rustic table. He had a steaming bowl in his hands that he had been so engrossed in eating from he hadn't heard her approach.

She was embarrassed to find she had arrived in the middle of his meal but was here now so might as well do what she had come here for. 'Good evening, Ben. I'm very sorry to call while you're eating,' she said.

He jumped at the unexpected sound of her voice and looked up, frozen for a moment, before he put the bowl of food down on the table, respectfully stood up and told her, 'Oh, I wasn't expecting visitors . . .' which was a stupid thing to say as he never had any '. . . or I'd have freshened myself up a bit.' He looked down at his grubby clothes. 'I was lucky enough to get another few hours this morning in the wood yard and was out this afternoon in the woods checking my traps.'

She stepped forward, looked into the bowl on the table and said, 'And caught a rabbit and made stew with it?'

'Yes. Er . . . would you like some? I have plenty.'

She vehemently shook her head. 'No, thank you. I don't like rabbit, roasted, boiled or in a stew, but I know someone who would love some . . . Mrs Jolly. Her father used to make it all the time, it was his favourite meal and it was hers too, but she's never had it since he died nearly forty years ago as she can't make it like he did.'

'Well, I can't claim mine will be anywhere near as good as

her father's but I'd be honoured to give you some for Mrs Jolly. It's the least I can do for the lady who's done so much for me.'

For a man who had very little, hardly in a position to be giving anything away, his generosity was not lost on Rhonnie. The more she got to know Ben, the more she was finding to like about him. 'She'll be very appreciative. I'll drop it around on my way home. Please don't let yours go cold—'

'Oh, that's okay, I can heat it up later,' he cut in. He then looked deeply worried. 'Have you come to tell me it's time I moved on?'

She assured him, 'No, no, not at all. What I've come to see you about is . . . how you would feel about being offered a permanent job?'

He stared at her, wondering if he had heard her correctly. Finally he said, 'Shocked! No one in their right mind is going to offer the likes of me a proper job.'

Rhonnie smiled. 'Then I must be crackers because I am.'

He gawped at her as she told him, 'Assistant to the caravan park manager. We had to let the lad go as I caught him sleeping on the job while the manager was on his day off. My gut instinct tells me that you would never do anything like that but are the sort of man who'd put all his efforts into it, so the job is yours if you'd like it.'

Ben had to sit down on the makeshift stool while he allowed himself time to accept this was real and not some sort of cruel joke. He didn't know her that well but knew Rhonnie wasn't the sort of woman to have fun at someone's else expense, so her offer was a genuine one. This opportunity was one in a lifetime for the likes of him. Having a job would enable him to pick up the pieces of his life; pay rent on bricks and mortar to live in, with indoor plumbing and hot and cold water; buy new clothes for himself; fund regular trips to the barbers; have a social life – most importantly, be in a position to have a relationship and not live such a lonely existence any longer.

He wanted nothing more than to grab at her offer, start

right now should she want him to, but regardless he couldn't accept. A permanent job with a reputable company such as Jolly's would mean divulging personal details about himself . . . his true name, last proper address and National Insurance number. They'd check his background and in all probability uncover what he'd done. After all, it was splashed over the newspapers at the time. Even if they didn't discover his past and remained oblivious to it, accepting the job would mean he would be expected to smarten up his appearance, trim his hair and shave off his beard, and that could result in his being recognised from his picture in the papers and his past revealed that way. A company like Jolly's, any reputable firm in fact, would never knowingly employ someone responsible for the deaths of five men and risk losing their own good name and business over it. No decent people would stand for a killer living amongst them, even if those people were only here for a short time on holiday.

He had come to think of the humble hut as his home, was starting to feel like he belonged around here and was making friends, Rhonnie included, whom he would be devastated to lose. People no longer crossed the road to avoid him when they saw him heading towards them, out of apprehension of his fearsome appearance. They smiled at him instead, wished him good morning, even stopped for a chat. Should he accept Rhonnie's offer he could be saying goodbye to all the progress he had made recently and be back living as he was before, tramping the roads in all weather, searching for food in rubbish bins if he couldn't get any work, sleeping under hedgerows in bitter cold weather should he not find any shelter for the night. The thought terrified him.

He took a deep breath and, despite his grief over having to do this, told Rhonnie: 'I really appreciate your offer, more than I can tell you, but you see . . .' His mind thrashed for a plausible excuse and he told her the first one that came to him. 'Just this morning I made a commitment to the boss in the wood yard to work for him for the next few weeks as and when he has need of me. He's really busy at the moment.'

It was apparent how disappointed she was by his declining her offer but her disappointment in no way matched Ben's.

'Oh, well, it's a pity I didn't ask you earlier. Our loss is another's gain. I'm just glad you have work.'

He couldn't look her in the eye when he told her, 'I'll fetch a bowl of stew for Mrs Jolly.'

After Rhonnie left he sat back down on his makeshift stool feeling depressed. This was partly due to having to turn down a promising opportunity but mostly it was because of the woman who had offered it to him. Every time he saw her, despite how hard he tried not to allow it to happen, he fell a little more under her spell, as if an invisible magnet was drawing him to her. He was heading for heartbreak, he was aware of that. Feelings were the one thing no one could control. They took over without warning and played havoc with your life. He had no hope, though, of his feelings ever being returned by the likes of Rhonnie. He was just going to have to learn to accept the fact that they would always be unrequited, keep them to himself and get on with it. It was the price he was going to have to pay to continue living here.

Carefully carrying the bowl of stew, Rhonnie made her way back up the farm road to her car. She was hugely disappointed that through his acceptance of other work, Ben had not been able to take the job she was offering him. It would have been far better than the wood yard was in terms of pay, permanency and living accommodation. In view of that, Ben could very easily have broken his promise to the boss of the wood yard and taken up her offer instead. But he hadn't and she deeply admired him for that.

What she couldn't understand was why she felt so disappointed. In fact, quite upset. Then the reason struck her. Was it not simply because she wanted to help a man who was down on his luck, but that she was growing very fond of Ben, more than she'd cared to admit to herself, and giving him a job at Jolly's would have kept him in the area? She had no idea what he actually looked like under that mass of hair but looks were only part of it; it was the qualities a man possessed that were truly important to her, and Ben was continuingly showing her the sort of traits in his character that had drawn her to Dan and made her fall hopelessly in love with him. Was she falling for Ben? Then she scolded herself. No, she was not. She wasn't over Dan by a long way. It was simply pity she felt for Ben, and a desire to help him out of a bad situation, that was all.

Drina was delighted with the bowl of stew when Rhonnie dropped it around to her and proclaimed it to be nearly as good as her father's though not quite, which was always going to be the case as no one's cooking would ever beat her father's. The perceptive Drina did wonder, though, if Rhonnie was getting rather fond of Ben, judging by the way her eyes lit up and tone of voice whenever she spoke about him.

Jeff was not a happy man when he started work the next morning after his day off. He'd told Kevin he'd be visiting his family in Leeds, only to return and discover that his assistant had been sacked for slacking on the job. Not only did this reflect on Jeff's management of him, an impression he would have to work hard to counteract, he now faced the problem of finding a satisfactory replacement. Of the five men he had been sent by top management as suitable for the job of assistant after they had sifted through the horde who had applied, Jeff had chosen Kevin as he had seen him as the least likely to notice what was going on around him or poke his nose into anybody else's business. And he had chosen well as Kevin was naturally lazy and incurious about anything but finding himself an easy berth. Now Jeff just had to hope that amongst the new candidates there was another one cut from the same cloth. The last thing Jeff wanted was for anyone to discover his lucrative sideline as then they might want a cut for keeping quiet about it and Jeff wasn't prepared to share his spoils with anyone.

To his gratification therefore he found amongst the candidates a youngster called Andy Turner, who seemed to be very similar to Kevin. At interview he appeared keen and willing but in truth was exactly the opposite. Jeff sensed that the young man would prove to be far too consumed by his own little world to be bothered what his boss was up to, and so Andy was the one he chose.

CHAPTER FIFTEEN

Three days later Rhonnie was looking over the photographs Darren had taken of the camp for the new brochure. He sat patiently on the other side of her desk as she carefully considered them, her expression giving nothing away. With trepidation Darren watched her put the last one on top of the pile, lean back in her chair and fix him with her gaze. Darren's heart thumped painfully and he braced himself for bad news, so he got the shock of his life when she spoke.

'These photos are just what I was looking for, Darren. Every one of these could be used in the brochure to help sell the camp to future holidaymakers. They're all so good it's not going to be at all easy to pick the best.'

He looked gratified but astonished. 'You really mean that, Mrs Buckland?'

She smiled at him. 'I wouldn't be telling you so if I didn't.'

He sighed inwardly. It was not much consolation being told he'd a talent for taking photographs when as soon as the summer season ended so would his dream job.

Rhonnie was saying, 'Now we just have to come up with some catchy by-lines to put under the shots we choose. Then once Mr Coppice has printed the brochures we can start doing mail shots and hopefully start taking bookings for next season.'

She looked at him searchingly. The photographer Darren had replaced had been very good but, in Rhonnie's opinion, Darren's photos had a special depth of observation to them.

It was obvious he had a great passion for what he did and she found him such a nice man too, so eager to please and unassuming. She wished she knew someone else with need of a photographer who could offer Darren employment all the year round.

Then a thought struck her like a thunderbolt. She did know someone who needed Darren's photographic talents: Albert Coppice. A man like Darren, with his unassuming manner and polite approach, was the perfect person to help the old man bring his firm into the modern era. But how could she bring the two of them together? An idea came to her. As she sent Darren on his way, Rhonnie smiled to herself. Jill's penchant for matchmaking seemed to be rubbing off on her, but whereas it gave Jill pleasure to bring people together romantically, it was giving Rhonnie the same buzz to bring about a good working relationship.

She was just about to ask Jill to come through and help her decide what photographs to choose for the brochure when the woman herself tapped on the door. 'Lily Dawkins has asked if she could have a private word, Rhonnie. She looks worried about something.'

'Please tell her to come in, Jill.'

Lily did indeed looked deeply bothered about something. As soon as she had sat down in the visitor's chair, Rhonnie asked her, 'What is it, Lily?'

She shuffled uncomfortably in her seat before she said, 'When you asked me the other day how Ginger was getting on, I wasn't being truthful with you. I know she's your friend but you did ask me not to take that into account and treat her just as I would any other member of staff . . . but I'm still a woman, Rhonnie, and I know when a woman is suffering terribly over . . . well, it's my guess it's the break-up of her marriage and that's why I couldn't sack her like I would have done anyone else who was acting the same way. Not without speaking to you first anyway.'

187

Rhonnie's whole body sagged. 'Oh, dear, I thought she was starting to come to terms with it all but you're about to tell me otherwise, aren't you?'

Lily said gravely, 'I'm afraid I am. The first morning Ginger did report for work, and I put her with the team of girls cleaning the shops and nursery. Halfway through the morning her supervisor found her out the back by the bins, sobbing her heart out. There was no consoling her, so she was sent back to her chalet. The next morning she was over an hour late reporting for work and again only managed to last a couple of hours before she was found in the toilets crying her eyes out. Again she was sent home. I went over to her chalet to try to talk to her. She wouldn't let me in but I could hear her crying inside. Yesterday she didn't report for work at all. Again I went to try and talk to her but no joy. When she didn't report again this morning, out of respect to you as I know she's a personal friend, I wanted to consult you about the situation.'

Rhonnie smiled at her. 'Thank you, Lily. I appreciate your patience with her and the way you've tried to help her. I'll deal with this now. She's in her chalet, you say?'

'She was when I called around about fifteen minutes ago. She didn't answer the door. There was no crying this time but I did hear movement inside when I put my ear to the door.'

Rhonnie thanked Lily again and sent her on her way. She was deeply concerned to hear that Ginger had locked herself inside her chalet for the last couple of days; she couldn't have eaten if she hadn't come out so twenty minutes later, armed with a flask of tea and a sandwich hastily put together by Eric Brown in the camp kitchen, Rhonnie arrived at Ginger's chalet door. She pressed her ear to it but could hear no movement from inside. She tried the handle but it was locked and the curtains were drawn tight against the two small front windows. Tapping gently on the door, Rhonnie called out:

'Ginger, it's me. Please let me in so I can talk to you.' There was no response, so she tried again. 'Come on, Ginger. I'm really worried about you. I know you're in there so open up and let me in.' Still no response. 'Okay, as you won't open up I'm going back to the office to get my skeleton key, then I can let myself in.'

This time there was a response. The voice that spoke was weak and trembling. 'I'm just having a nap, Rhonnie. I'll . . . I'll come and see you tonight in the cottage.'

It was a useless attempt by Ginger to fob her off as Rhonnie wasn't going anywhere until she had spoken to her friend, face to face. In a warning voice she called out, 'Open up right now or I'll break down the door and have the bill for the repair sent to you.'

There was a brief silence before the door opened just a crack. As soon as Rhonnie clapped eyes on Ginger's tortured face, the grey pallor of it, she determinedly stepped into the chalet.

It seemed Ginger hadn't even enough energy to challenge this uninvited intrusion; she sat hunched over on the bed, looking lost and defeated.

Rhonnie had been prepared for an altercation with her usually feisty friend, not this crushed and grieving individual. Her heart went out to Ginger. Putting down the flask and the wrapped sandwich on the small chest of drawers just inside the door, she went over to the bed, sat down next to her friend and pulled her close, uttering sadly, 'Oh, Ginger. You don't need to be going through this by yourself. You have me. You should have told me you weren't ready to go to work and needed more time.'

Ginger heaved a sorrowful sigh. 'I thought I was ready but I'm not, am I? Why can't I hate Paul . . . all I can think about is how much I want him back, but it's the old Paul I want, not the man he's been since his promotion. We're never going back to the way we were and I need to accept that. But I

189

can't . . .' The tears came then and she sobbed, 'Oh, what am I going to do, Rhonnie?'

'For a start you're coming home with me and I'm going to look after you. Then we'll take it one step at a time. One way or another I will help you through this, you have my promise.'

It seemed to Rhonnie that drastic action was required to get Ginger to face facts or else she'd never start to rebuild her life. If Ginger wouldn't go and see her husband, then Paul needed to come to see her and do the decent thing, tell her their marriage was over because he was in love with someone else. Rhonnie felt in the circumstances she had no choice but to break her promise to her dear friend and let Paul know where Ginger was, so that this sad situation could be resolved. She would write to him, she decided, and there was no time like the present.

Rhonnie had just finished cleaning the kitchen after supper that evening – not that she could tempt Ginger to eat any more than a spoonful of boiled egg and a bite of buttered toast, but she felt at least that was a start – and was about to put Danny to bed when a loud hammering on the front door made her almost jump out of her skin. Before she could catch her breath the hammering came again. As she rushed to answer the summons she couldn't imagine who her determined caller was. If it was anything to do with work, security would have telephoned her at this time of the evening.

Rhonnie pulled open the door just as the person on the other side was about to hammer on it again. She snapped, 'For goodness' sake, you'll frighten my little boy to death and I've a sick friend staying . . .' Her voice trailed away then as she recognised who her caller was. 'Paul!' she exclaimed, stunned to see him. 'But you couldn't have had the letter yet . . . it wasn't posted until an hour or so ago.'

He looked wretched. It was obvious he'd not slept for

days, washed or changed his clothes. Rhonnie's thoughts were in confusion. Paul didn't look like a man in the throes of a new relationship, keeping himself clean and smart to impress his new love. This was clearly a man in the depths of despair. Before she could say anything to him he was blurting out, 'You're her best friend, Rhonnie, so if no one else, Ginger would tell you where she was going. I expect she's sworn you to secrecy, but I beg . . . I beg you with all my heart . . . to tell me where she is so I can go and see her, tell her that she's got it all wrong.'

Rhonnie folded her arms and looked at him sceptically. 'Are you trying to tell me that Ginger didn't see you leaving the pub, the worse for drink, arms wrapped around another woman who was kissing you, and you both getting into a taxi together?'

Paul's shoulders sagged, his face screwed up in distress. 'Well, yes, she did, but . . .'

Rhonnie cut in, 'Oh, you're going to try and fob me off with that old one, are you – that what Ginger saw wasn't what was really going on?'

'So just what *was* happening, Paul, if I got things wrong?'

At the sound of Ginger's voice, Rhonnie spun around but before she could say anything she was unceremoniously pushed out of the way by Paul as he rushed into the cottage to stand just before his wife at the bottom of the stairs. The state of her had him blurting out in shock, 'Oh, darling, you look terrible.'

Ginger cried, 'Don't you dare *darling* me! You lost that right when you broke our marriage vows. And for that matter, you don't look too great yourself. So when I saw you with that woman all over you, getting into a taxi together, my eyes were playing tricks on me, were they?'

'No, your eyes weren't playing tricks on you, you did see me getting into a taxi with a woman . . . but Ginger, I promise you on my life, that it wasn't what it looked like.'

Not at all pleased with the scene that was being played out before her eyes, Rhonnie told them both, 'I'm surprised at you, shouting like this in front of a child. Now could you please hold fire until I collect Danny and take him up to bed, then go into the lounge and discuss this like civil adults.' She told Ginger, 'I'll be upstairs in my bedroom to give you some privacy. Just call if you need me.'

They both looked shamefaced as Rhonnie fetched Danny and took him up the stairs.

A few minutes later, seated opposite her husband in an armchair beside the fireplace, Ginger managed to keep her voice even when she asked him, 'So if what I saw between you and that woman wasn't what I thought it was, what exactly was happening?'

He sat perched on the edge of his chair, his hands clasped tightly together and his face wreathed in misery. 'Just me doing as my boss told me to . . . getting his drunk girlfriend out of the pub. Ex-girlfriend to be accurate as he'd ended their relationship the night before and that was why she was so drunk – because she was devastated. He ended it with her because she had been pushing him to leave his wife and marry her, which he'd no intention of ever doing, despite promising her for months he would and stringing her along. And as if finally telling her it was over between them wasn't bad enough for her, he did it in front of a crowd of people, me included. I felt so sorry for her. She'd come back the next night to beg him to change his mind and had had a good few drinks beforehand to give her the courage. She arrived to find him with his new woman draped all over him and started causing a scene. It was awful, Ginger. My boss treated her like she was nothing to him. He's a good copper, but as a man I don't like him at all. He told me to get her out of his sight and put her in a taxi.

'My boss is not the sort of man you ignore. I hated doing his dirty work, wanted to tell him where to go, but . . . call

192

me a coward, Ginger, that man has the power to end my career, so I was scared too. Maureen *was* trying to kiss me but I was trying to fend her off, honest I was, Ginger. She was so hurt, she was trying to find comfort with another man, any man would have done, it just happened to be me. She was so drunk I worried she might not get home safely so I thought it was the least I could do to make sure she was taken care of . . . and that's why you saw me getting into a taxi with her.'

Ginger was looking at him in confusion. 'But your boss is already married. I met his wife at the Christmas do. They've got three children.'

'Soon to have four. His wife has no idea about his bits on the side.'

Ginger snapped in disgust, *'Bits on the side*? Is that how you men see a poor woman you've led up the garden path with your fake promises and lies?'

Paul fervently shook his head and insisted, 'No, I don't, Ginger. It's just what my boss calls his other women – and sometimes far worse than that, believe me. But what my boss and some of the other detectives get up to behind their wives' backs is nothing to do with me. I've never cheated on you and never will, you have to believe me.

'You know how thrilled I was when I got into CID, doing what I thought was real police work – catching criminals and bringing them to justice. I do enjoy the work, Ginger, but it's the rest of it I can't get on with. The long hours we have to work when we've a case on, which seems to be all the time. Never getting home until you've gone to bed, then getting up and leaving the house before you. And I can't accept the way sometimes things are done to get a case resolved. Pretending I haven't seen anything when a confession is beaten out of a suspect because he won't talk voluntarily, or when I know evidence is being planted to frame a criminal because that's the only way he's going to be made to pay for what he's done. It's not always like that, but it happens often enough

193

to make me lose sleep. I didn't at all like having to go to the pub after work, no matter what time we finished, but all the team were expected to and if you didn't go your life was made a misery by the others.' Tears of distress filled Paul's eyes when he proclaimed, 'I wish I'd never passed those exams and got that promotion now. It's the worst thing I ever did.'

Ginger felt mortified to have misunderstood the situation so completely. 'But why didn't you tell me what was going on with you, Paul? Instead you treated me like a virtual stranger, shutting me out, and I had no idea you were unhappy.'

His expression filled with shame. 'Because I couldn't bring myself to. You'd given up so much for me when we went to Leeds, moving far away from your friends to somewhere you knew no one, and you did that willingly for me. I knew you were finding it hard to settle but you never once complained. I worried if I told you what was happening you'd think I was letting you down. I'd promised you the good life with the extra pay the new job was bringing in and it was great to have that money, but due to the pressures of work and all the rest that goes with the job, we never got a chance to enjoy ourselves together doing the things we wanted to do. I'm not cut out to be a detective, Ginger. I'm a family man at heart, my wife comes first with me, whereas in the CID you're expected to put the job and your work colleagues before everything else.'

'I had no idea you felt like that, Paul. I thought you were loving your job, and I loved you enough to put up with your drinking and hardly seeing you because I thought it made you happy. But then, when I saw you with that woman and it looked as if you were wrapped up in each other . . . well, that I wasn't prepared to put up with, no matter how much I loved you. I just wanted to get away from you as quickly as possible. I couldn't bear the thought of you telling me that you didn't love me anymore and wanted to be with someone else, and probably making a fool of myself by begging you to stay with me. I couldn't bear the thought either of spending every moment hoping you were going to turn up, asking me to come back to you as you'd made a mistake, so that's why I didn't tell you where I really was.' Looking at him knowingly, she said, 'Rhonnie obviously broke her promise to me and told you I was with her. Normally I would be very upset that she betrayed me but now I know what I do, I can't really be upset with her, can I?'

He insisted, 'No, Rhonnie didn't break her promise to you so there's no need to be upset with her. I haven't heard from her at all since you left me. I haven't dared leave the house since I found your note because I was praying you'd realise eventually I'd never deceive you and come home to me. My boss thinks I'm ill with the flu. But as the days passed and you didn't come back, I thought that if anyone knew where you were staying it would be Rhonnie. I suspected you'd make her promise not to tell me where you were, but thought that if I could convince her I hadn't cheated on you then she might agree to help and I could track you down and persuade you to come back to me.'

Ginger looked mortally ashamed. 'I should have listened to Rhonnie when I told her what I'd seen. She told me that you would never cheat on me and I should talk to you, try and sort out what was happening. But I couldn't get that picture of you with another woman out of my head and couldn't see any explanation for it bar the obvious one. Oh, Paul, will you forgive me?' she implored him.

He seemed amazed. 'Forgive *you*? I'm the one who should be asking you for forgiveness after the way I've treated you since I started that job.' He jumped up from his seat, went over and kneeled down before her, taking her hands in his. 'Ginger, all this has only made me see how much you mean to me. Without you in my life, I have no life. I've made a decision. I'm going to see my old boss in Skegness to ask if

I can transfer back to being a regular copper. As you know he was sorry to lose me and told me that if I ever wanted to come back, he would call in every favour he's owed to make that happen. It might take a few weeks for it all to be settled so will you bear with me meanwhile?'

Paul got his answer when he saw the beam of delight that filled her face. She threw her arms around him, hugging him tightly to her.

From the hall doorway a tentative voice asked, 'Is it safe to come in?'

They pulled apart and Ginger shot Rhonnie a suspicious look. 'Were you listening?' she accused her.

'No, of course I wasn't,' Rhonnie vehemently denied, then thought better of her lie since it was obvious she had been. 'Well, not exactly listening . . . but I was on my way into the kitchen to make myself a cup of tea and might have heard that you're going to ask for a transfer back to Skegness, Paul, though that was all I heard.' She clapped her hands together and jumped for joy. 'Oh, it's so wonderful that I'm going to have my best friend living close to me again.'

Ginger grinned too. 'Yes, it is for me too.'

Paul got to his feet. 'Then I'd better get back to Leeds and start making this happen. If I hurry I'll catch the eight twenty-three to Lincoln and be in time to catch the last train to Sheffield and the mail train to Leeds.' He then eyed his wife. 'You are coming back with me tonight, aren't you? I don't think I could bear being apart from you any longer. These past days without you have seemed like a lifetime.'

Ginger jumped to her feet. 'Of course I'm coming with you. It will take me five minutes to tidy myself and pack. Will you call us a taxi, please, Rhonnie, to take us to the station?'

It would be her pleasure. Not that she wanted to see them both leave, but the sooner they did, the sooner they would get their lives sorted and be back where they belonged.

CHAPTER SIXTEEN

Drina and Rhonnie were laughing so hard they were having to cling to each other for support. Finally Drina managed to compose herself enough to say, 'Well, I was hoping that all the stuff we've put on today to celebrate the moon landings would go down well with the campers but I never expected so many of them to be enthusiastic enough to bring their own costumes to wear! That kiddie dressed as a robot looked fantastic. His mother must have spent hours making that outfit out of cardboard boxes . . . and how they got it here on the coach intact I have no idea. That chap in his home-made space suit made out of cardboard painted silver and a colander on his head covered in silver foil for a space helmet was the funniest thing I have ever seen.'

Rhonnie enthused, 'Oh, my favourite was the little boy in the all-in-one sleep suit his mother had dyed green. She'd painted his face green too and put a sign across his chest to say he was a Little Green Martian. But then those two little girls dressed in fairy costumes, calling themselves The Two Moonbeams, were so sweet. Oh, and then there was that Stripey dressed as Mr Spock out of *Star Trek* whose card-board pointy ears kept falling off . . . that was hilarious too. Lily Dawkins and her girls did a fantastic job making up those space costumes for some of the Stripeys to wear. Yesterday I popped in to see the dress rehearsal for the special Stripey Show tonight in the Paradise before the dance and Alan has done a terrific job of theming all the dances and sketches around space travel. I'm sure the campers are going to love it.'

Drina frowned and looked at her quizzically. 'Just to be serious for one moment – this business between Lily and Alan. Have you not got the situation between them sorted yet? I thought you would have by now but then I saw the looks and barbed comments that passed between them at the meeting on Monday, so it's apparent to me you haven't. I've not said anything before now as you're the camp manager and it's your job to deal with matters like this but it's my opinion that bad feeling between managers is not good for staff morale, Rhonnie, so don't let this situation go on for much longer or you might find that you have set department against department because the staff are siding with their managers out of loyalty.'

Rhonnie sighed. She had been a fool to think that Drina had not noticed the animosity between the pair. Drina missed nothing. 'I was just trying to find the right approach to tackle them both in a way that doesn't end up with one of them leaving if they can't resolve their differences, whatever the cause may be. They're both lovely people and good at their jobs and losing either would be such a loss to Jolly's. Jill reckons it's because they both fancy each other rotten but are too stubborn to admit it, but I think it's because they have a personality clash and just don't like each other.'

Drina affectionately patted her arm. 'Well, either way it needs to be sorted before it affects the staff under them. If my late husband had been faced with this situation he would just have sacked them both with no by-your-leave, but thankfully we are more respectful of our employees and show more compassion to them before we resort to such drastic measures.'

Rhonnie smiled. 'And that's why the staff are loyal to you, Drina.'

'Not me now, to you, Rhonnie,' she insisted. 'Right, well, all the world's eyes might be on the Americans about to land on the moon, but ours are firmly fixed on earth. I'm off to the bar to sample Bill John's space-themed cocktails – make sure he's not going to give anyone alcohol poisoning before he launches them on the campers tonight.'

'And I need to have a tour of the camp to make sure everything is still running smoothly considering all the special events we've laid on and the extra people here at the moment . . . according to reception, hearing what we've put on today, quite a few have come from Mablethorpe and surrounding villages and bought day passes to enjoy the festivities here, which is good news for us. And I do have to go over to the caravan park to check all is well there and collect this week's takings. If I don't see you before, I'll meet you in the ballroom tonight before the Stripey Show . . . or I might be a little later as I know Carrie is quite capable of putting Danny to bed but I like to do that myself and sing him his lullaby before he goes to sleep.'

At the vision Rhonnie created, Drina's mind flew back over the years to when she used to sing to her son Michael in his cot, having no idea at all then that her angelic-looking sleeping child would grow up to become the monster he had been. Thankfully, Michael's half-brother's son was showing none of the alarming character traits that Michael had even at an early age with his difficult behaviour and temper tantrums. Hopefully Danny would grow up to be nothing like his half-uncle had been, but just like his honest, hard-working, high-principled father.

Over on the caravan site, Jeff was in his private van kneeling down next to the bench seating under the front window. A section of the padded part was raised, revealing a storage area underneath. He smiled smugly to himself as his eyes scanned the contents. He'd had a very fruitful night last night and his plan for his prosperous future was coming along nicely. If it continued this way, by the end of the season he would have accumulated enough to pay for his own caravan park. He wondered how the delectable Rhonnie Buckland would react if she knew her business was being used to fund the purchase of another. He supposed he had better get back to work because if he was caught slacking and lost this job then his bright new future might never happen.

He had just put the seating back in place and stood up to hide other things associated with his extracurricular activities safely away from prying eyes, when a purposeful knock resounded on his door. Thinking it was Andy Turner, he called out, 'I'll be out in a minute.' He began to make his way over to the table but stopped short in alarm when the door opened and Rhonnie stepped inside.

'Sorry, I can't wait, I'm rather busy over at the main camp since it's moon-landing day today and half of Lincolnshire seem to have descended on us to enjoy the special events. I apologise if I'm disturbing your lunch . . .' she assumed that was why he was in his caravan at this time, even though she could see no sign of it '. . . but if I could just collect the takings and paperwork and have a quick catch up over how things are going, then I'll leave you to it.'

Panic reared within him. If she should notice what was on the table she would be bound to question what he was doing and he would have no plausible explanation. As casually as he could he moved over to stand in between her and the table, blocking the items on it from her line of sight while saying to her, 'Oh, yes, most of the campers here are excited about the moon landings and have bought day passes to take part in the activities. I'd have liked to have gone to the Stripey Show and dance afterwards myself tonight, but someone has to stay and keep an eye on things here and as I'm the manager I thought it only fair to tell Andy he could go as it's such a special occasion.' That was far from the truth. In fact Jeff had a woman coming over, and a choice between a night of passion spent with a very sexy lady or watching an amateur show, pretending he was enjoying it, was not exactly a difficult one.

Rhonnie was wondering why Jeff seemed to have been put on edge by her visit when usually he would be openly showing his pleasure at seeing her, flirting with her, trying to charm her into bed with him. She was glad he wasn't but all the same it was unusual behaviour for him. And why was he so obviously trying to obstruct her view of what lay on the table by moving over to stand in front of it? Now her curiosity was raised and she was determined to find out.

Jeff stepped over to her, putting his hand on the small of her back by way of ushering her out of the caravan. He smiled winningly at her and said, 'As you're in a hurry to get back, we can chat as we go up to the office to collect the takings.'

Outside they had not gone far when Rhonnie suddenly exclaimed, 'Oh, I've left my handbag behind. Silly me.' Before he could question the fact that she hadn't bought a handbag with her, she asked, 'Give me your key and I'll go and fetch it.' He reluctantly handed her his van key. Telling him she wouldn't be long, Rhonnie hurried back to the caravan and let herself inside. She took a good look at what was on the table. There was a folded map with a large red cross on it marking a place called Bolsover. From this ran a red line following various roads, all the way back down to the bottom of the page. She quickly turned over and saw that the line ran all the way back to the area of the map where Jolly's camp was situated. She turned back to the previous page and put the map back on the table. She then looked at an open notepad lying next to the map. On it was written an address in a village near Chesterfield – 56 Laurel Drive, Bolsover – underneath precise directions on how to get there. Altogether there was nothing strange in that. Jeff was obviously planning to visit someone in Bolsover and had sorted out the best route to take. So why then did he not want Rhonnie to see what he had done?

All the time she had been inside his van Jeff had been frantic that while looking for her handbag – which was strange as he couldn't remember her having one when she arrived – Rhonnie would catch sight of the items on the table and take an interest. But then he had reasoned with himself that he was panicking for nothing. All that was there was a notebook with an address in it and a map showing a route. His panic evaporated and by the time Rhonnie came back Jeff had returned to his normal self.

She arrived back beside him and told him, 'Silly me, I didn't bring my handbag with me.'

Jeff cheekily winked at her and in a suggestive tone said: 'Weren't hoping I'd ignore your instruction for me to wait out here and come back and join you, were you, Mrs Buckland?'

She raised an eyebrow at him warningly. 'Please remember I'm your boss. You should treat me accordingly.'

He grinned. 'But only in work time. Outside of work we're just a man and a woman who fancy each other.'

She gave him a disdainful look. 'You presume a lot.'

His grin broadened. 'Oh, come on, Mrs Buckland, what woman could resist this?' he said, pointing one finger of each hand towards himself.

Oh, he really thought a lot of himself and it was *so* annoying, Rhonnie thought. He needed a taste of his own medicine and it would give her great pleasure to administer it. She stepped close to him, gazed deep into his eyes, and in a teasing, seductive manner, whispered: 'Well, Jeff, what I'd like to do right now is . . .' She let her voice trail off, leaving her eyes lingering on him.

'Yes? What would you like to do?' he urged her, excitement building as he anticipated that at long last he was going to receive what he'd longed for since the first time he'd met her.

She took a breath, stepped back and told him in her normal tone of voice, 'To collect the takings and paperwork from the safe so I can get back to the main camp.'

Usually a blatant rebuff like this would see the egotistical Jeff react in such a way as to let the woman concerned know that she had burned her boats and he was no longer interested, but his craving for Rhonnie went too deep to allow him to give up. There was only so long a woman could resist his charms and he had patience.

Jeff held his arms wide open and bent slightly forward, like an actor taking a bow. Looking at her meaningfully, he said, 'I'm your willing follower. Lead the way, pretty lady.'

With takings and paperwork in hand, and having satisfied herself that Jeff was running the site in the manner expected, she set off back up the old farm road towards the camp. As she passed the spot adjacent to where she knew Ben's hut lay deep inside the undergrowth, an overwhelming desire to pay him a visit filled her. She hadn't seen him for a couple of weeks, not since he had declined the job offer. She peered into the wood. It would be quicker to push her way through it than go all the way around to the path Ben had hacked from the track on the field to the hut. But then she remembered that twice before she had ventured inside the wood and neither time come out unscathed. Common sense told her that to avoid further damage to herself she should go the long way round. Regardless she arrived at the hut to find no sign of Ben and the door securely padlocked, the curtains drawn tight. He must be working at the wood yard or perhaps out on a foraging trip. As she left to make her way back to the main camp and the mayhem that awaited her there, it surprised her to realise how disappointed she was not to find him at home and be able to spend some time in his company.

While he had been in the woods checking on his traps, which he happened to have placed adjacent to the back of the static caravan where the manager lived, through a gap in the undergrowth Ben had caught sight of Rhonnie approaching the manager's caravan. Well, Ben assumed he was the manager by the uniform he wore and the way he bossed the younger chap around. And judging by the way he'd been acting on the number of occasions Ben had seen him now, he was an arrogant man, full of himself. It wasn't right of anyone to spy on people in Ben's belief, but because of his feelings for Rhonnie he couldn't stop himself now from admiring her from a distance and smiling wistfully as he watched her arrive at the manager's caravan, thinking how lovely she looked in her pretty summer shift dress, her long honey-coloured hair hanging loose around her shoulders. But then his heart had sunk as he saw her going into the caravan uninvited. Ben assumed this meant something was going on between her and the manager. People who were just acquainted with each other knocked on doors and respectfully waited for a summons to go inside.

Had he stuck around a little longer his spirits would have lifted. Rhonnie emerged from the caravan much too soon for anything to have been happening between her and Jeff but unfortunately he had taken a slow walk back to his hut and returned just in time to see her knocking on his door there. Feeling as raw as he did, believing Rhonnie was having a relationship with the manager of the park when he so longed to be having one with her himself, meant Ben just couldn't face her at the moment. So he hid from her.

Despite her disappointment at not finding Ben at home, Rhonnie was gratified to return and find nothing untoward had transpired at the camp while she had been away, but she wasn't gratified but worried to find Jill fast asleep on one of the sofas in the visitors' area in her office. She looked so peaceful that Rhonnie hadn't the heart to disturb her but it seemed Jill was going to have to find a remedy for her husband's snoring as it was starting to affect her work. She knew Jill would be mortified at having been caught by her boss in such a compromising situation so told Sandra not to mention the fact to her, but Rhonnie would have no choice but to tackle Jill about it should it happen again.

At half-past twelve that night the sparks of the last firework died out in the night sky and a deafening eruption of cheers and claps rang out from campers and staff alike. Rhonnie turned to Drina and enthused, 'Well, I think we can mark today down as an absolute success, don't you?'

Drina smiled. 'I do, most certainly. Let's hope the astronauts up in space are as successful in making a safe landing.'

Artie piped up, 'Well, I'm off to get a good seat in front of a telly before they're all taken.'

Drina looked taken aback. 'But you've already got a ringside seat in your own front room, watching your own television.'

'Not the same, love, as watching it with a lot of other enthusiasts. Would be like witnessing my home town of Leicester win the football league on my own, no one to share the moment with.'

She smiled. 'Oh, I see. Well, don't wake me up when you come in.'

He chuckled. 'I wouldn't dare.'

As he hurried off towards the Paradise, Rhonnie said, 'I'd have loved to join Dad and watch the actual landings but Danny won't care that I was up until the early hours of the morning and will be demanding his breakfast at six-thirty, so I'd best get off home and get my beauty sleep.'

Drina was feeling the effects of the long day too and they were about to say their goodbyes when a conversation between a couple passing by reached their ears and made them stop to eavesdrop.

The woman was saying to the man, 'What a fab day this has been. Jolly's couldn't have done anything more to celebrate the moon landings, could they, Fred?'

'Nope, they certainly couldn't have, Alice. I'm that knackered with all the activities we've taken part in today I'll only be fit enough to sunbathe down on the beach tomorrow.'

'Yeah, me too. Let's hope this good weather keeps up so we can.'

Before either Drina or Rhonnie could make any comment on what they had overheard another couple holding a conversation within their earshot reached them and they couldn't resist eavesdropping on that too.

The man was saying. 'Well, Jolly's put on a decent enough show to commemorate the Americans doing their space whatnot, but it wasn't really fair on those of us who don't give a toss whether them Yankees manage to land on the moon or not. I mean, what's the point of spending all them millions on sending a man up to a place so barren there's not even a Wimpy Bar to buy a hamburger from? Thank God it's over with and I don't have to hear another Stripey dressed in those ridiculous outfits, supposed to be representing God knows who, speaking into a plastic box thing in their hand and saying "Beam me up, Scotty."'

The woman quizzically asked, 'Just who is this Scotty, Malcolm?'

He shrugged. 'No idea, Betty, but after hearing it for the umpteenth time I wished whoever he was had just beamed them up and had done with it.'

Drina and Rhonnie looked at each other. There was no need for words. No matter how much of an effort was made to give the campers a good time, there was no pleasing everyone. All that could be hoped for was that the majority were impressed enough to want to come back and spend their next holiday with Jolly's.

CHAPTER SEVENTEEN

The following Wednesday night the air inside Ben's hut was humid and sticky, no breeze at all coming through the open door. Finally at four o'clock he gave up trying to sleep and got up to cool himself down with a wash in cold water.

It wasn't just the oppressive weather that was causing his sleeplessness. Since he'd last seen Rhonnie several days ago, try as he might, as soon as he closed his eyes he just could not get the vision of her going into the caravan to meet the handsome manager of the caravan park out of his mind. He was haunted too by regret for what had happened in his past, preventing him from making his feelings known to her now while someone else claimed her affections.

Only seconds after he had thoroughly washed himself down, his whole body was clammy again. Worst of all was the way his face burned under his thick bristly beard. His facial covering was a blessing in winter, protecting him from the bitter weather, but in the warmer months it was nothing but a bind that often led to his suffering from painful bouts of heat rash. But that was part of the price he must pay to remain incognito.

It would be cooler out in the wood than it was in the hut so Ben decided to go for a forage in the hope of finding himself some mushrooms to go with the sausages he had bought from the butcher's yesterday for his breakfast. The work he had been getting at the wood yard had dried up now so until he secured himself some more work he would need to keep a tight rein on his spending.

A while later, he was stooping down by a tree gathering a patch of penny buns when above the serenade of the dawn chorus another sound reached his ears. He stood up and listened. A car was driving into the caravan park. It was a strange time in the morning for a vehicle to be arriving. A worrying thought struck him then. Could the driver of the vehicle be up to no good?

Leaving his mushrooms, Ben pushed his way over to the fence and peered through the wire. From where he was, he had a view of the back row of a section of the static caravans and although he couldn't actually see the car, he could deduce from the noise the tyres were now making that it had turned off the main site road and was travelling over grass. Then he heard the engine die and negotiated his way further along the fence, skirting several trees and clumps of shrubs, until he saw a red car parked by a van. Someone was getting out of it. He instantly recognised the manager of the caravan park. Ben assumed that the man was just returning from a late night out . . . albeit the fashion these days was for flamboyant clothes in bright colours not the black jeans and sweater he was wearing. But his worry that possibly someone was up to no good was unfounded so he was about to return to gathering mushrooms when what the manager did next made Ben stand still and watch him inquisitively.

Over the other side of the fence, having got out of his car, Jeff Sampson took a quick look around to check he wasn't being observed – thankfully he didn't look in the direction of the fence or he might have seen Ben watching him – then went around the back of the car and opened the boot. Taking out a large and clearly heavy black holdall, he heaved it over to the steps leading up to his caravan and put it down on the ground in front of them. He then returned to the boot of his car and rummaged around for a moment before he took out a screwdriver and shut the boot. He crept around the back of his caravan, kneeled down and scrabbled in the grass beside the concrete pad on which his caravan stood. He grabbed at what appeared to be two clumps of grass and began to heave up a rectangular-shaped piece of turf, but before he could fully pull it up and take out what he was after, there was the sound of a caravan door opening close by then someone loudly yawning and a match being struck obviously to light a cigarette. The noise startled him and like a scalded cat he dropped the clump of grass back into place, scrambled up and hurried back around the caravan. He grabbed the heavy holdall by the steps, hurried up them and disappeared inside the caravan.

Still standing behind the fence, Ben thoughtfully raked his fingers through his mass of beard to scratch at an itch on his chin and pondered on what he had just seen. But no matter how many times he went over it, he couldn't come to any other conclusion but that the manager of the site had been acting very suspiciously. Ben wondered what had been inside the holdall, but not as much as he wanted to know what Jeff had been hiding under the grass behind his caravan. He was intrigued. Whatever it was, it had to be something the man didn't want anyone else to see or why go to the trouble of making himself a secret hiding place? Ben would very much like to have found out what was in it by sneaking into the camp and having a look, but if he was seen then it would be he who would be reported for acting suspiciously, which could result in him losing his right to stay in the hut.

Should he report what he had seen to Rhonnie? But report what exactly? All he had seen was the manager of the caravan site acting suspiciously – that wasn't a criminal offence. But as he returned to gathering his mushrooms, he couldn't stop the desperate need building within him to find out just what that man had been keeping in the hole at the back of his caravan that he obviously didn't want anyone to know about. All Ben's instincts were telling him that the other man was up to no good, and *that* he couldn't ignore.

CHAPTER EIGHTEEN

The last week of July and the first week of August had been a complete washout for the whole of the country as a ridge of low pressure settled, bringing nonstop rain and below-average temperatures. Some ignorant people blamed the Americans for sending a rocket into space!

Bad weather, though, brought bad tempers. The holiday-makers were free to vent theirs and frequently did on the entertainments team, who were doing their utmost, in the camp's undercover facilities, to keep spirits high and the holidaymakers amused from the moment they got up until bedtime, because as far as they were concerned Jolly's had promised them a holiday under the sun and they were breaking that promise. But despite the conditions and the extra work they caused, the fraught nerves and the campers' displeasure, it was the entertainments team's job at all times to display smiles and cheerfulness, so there were no happier people than them when finally the skies cleared and the sun shone down once again, bringing harmony to the camp.

Stuck inside her stuffy office on the first rainless day for what seemed an age, Rhonnie would have liked nothing more than to find an excuse to take a walk outside under the warm summer sun, but she had important work to deal with before she could even consider doing anything of the sort. She was slightly cheered by the fact that it was her day to visit the caravan park and collect the takings after a catch up with Jeff.

The rain had prevented her from walking over to the caravan park for the last two weeks. She had been forced to drive around in her car, leaving her no excuse to offer Ben for calling in on him. But today the sun was allowing her to do that and this time she just hoped that he was in. During all the bad weather Ben hadn't been far from her mind as she knew that finding work wasn't an easy thing for him to do and the rain would make it virtually impossible. She wondered how he had fared during this time, if he had been able to afford food or if the bad weather had worsened things for him by hampering his foraging trips. She wanted to satisfy herself that he was all right.

Mid-morning she was sitting behind her desk closely watching Darren for his reaction as he cast his eyes over a piece of paper, pasted both sides with photographs and captions, the dummy for what would later become Jolly's trifold brochure.

Darren could see that Rhonnie's efforts to revitalise the camp's publicity material had paid off. He felt an immense sense of pride to be part of this new effort, but what was giving him the most gratification was the fact that his photographs were going to be seen by many thousands the length and breadth of the British Isles. Rhonnie had even credited him by name on the last page of the brochure along with Albert Coppice for printing them. For Darren that was like seeing his name lit up in lights on the front of a theatre.

She was saying to him, 'I wanted your opinion since you've been involved in the project, Darren, but by the look on your face I don't think I need to ask if you approve of the new brochure?'

He enthused, 'I do, most certainly, Mrs Buckland. I can't tell you how . . . well . . . honoured I am to have my photos included in it.'

Rhonnie felt the honour was all hers, to have such a talented staff photographer to call on. The world of photography would lose a gifted man when his time at Jolly's ended, but then that might not be the case if her plan to bring him and Albert Coppice together worked out as she hoped it would.

She said to Darren, 'I really need to get the new brochure over to Mr Coppice as soon as possible but I'm snowed under at the moment and can't spare any of the other staff either. So I was wondering if you'd kindly take it for me so Mr Coppice can start the printing process as soon as possible? I'm sure the campers can do without having their photos taken for a couple of hours. I'll telephone Sid Harper and tell him you have my permission to use one of the maintenance vans.'

Darren's enthusiastic response was genuine. 'I'd be delighted to, Mrs Buckland.'

Rhonnie saw him on his way, thinking all she could do now was wait and see if her plan had worked and those two people could make a go of working together.

It was Jill's turn to do the camp inspection round that morning and Rhonnie went out to ask her not to forget to call in at the souvenir shop and ask Carol if the new delivery of rock had arrived and the lettering was correct this time. Since she had found Jill asleep on the sofa a couple of weeks ago, Rhonnie had been keeping a close eye on her and she was gratified that nothing similar had happened since; in fact, these last couple of days Jill seemed to be absolutely full of energy and racing through her work, in complete contrast to her previous lethargy.

She found Jill bashing away on her typewriter, wading her way through a pile of correspondence from Rhonnie and the other managers. Although she had planned her afternoon out, that still didn't stop Rhonnie wanting to find an excuse for a walk out in the sunshine this morning so she was secretly hoping that Jill was going to tell her she was too busy to do the inspection round, then Rhonnie would have to do it herself. She was to be disappointed, though, because as soon as she arrived at Jill's desk, the office manager stopped typing, pushed back her chair and jumped up, saying, 'I'm just going to the loo then off to do the camp round. I shan't forget to call in on Carol.'

Rhonnie hid her disappointment, smiling at her and saying, 'If you make that your last port of call, you can bring us all back an okey pokey.'

Jill looked at her blankly. 'A what?'

Rhonnie laughed. 'It's what we who come from Leicester call an ice cream.'

Jill laughed too. 'Three okey pokeys it is then.'

Sandra, who had been listening to the exchange, piped up, 'Can yer make mine a strawberry Mivvi, please?'

'And I'll have a Flake in mine too, please,' Rhonnie told her. She then lowered her voice and asked Jill, 'I haven't asked you lately as I didn't want to appear to be interfering in your private life, but I take it that you've resolved your husband's snoring problem?'

Jill leaned towards her and whispered, 'Well, it's very strange but suddenly this past week Martin's snoring has stopped bothering me and I've gone back to sleeping like a log.' She then looked at Rhonnie for a moment, as if weighing up whether to take the other woman into her confidence or not, then obviously decided to as she continued: 'When you were married, did little things your husband did suddenly start to irritate you when they never did before?'

Rhonnie frowned in thought for a moment before she answered, 'No, I can't say they did, but then I wasn't fortunate enough to be married to Dan for as long as you and your husband have been. Is there any reason why he's stated to get on your nerves, do you reckon?'

'What, like I've gone off him, you mean? No, definitely not. I love him as much as I've always done, couldn't live without him. But just this past week, he's only got to do the slightest thing, such as not putting the milk bottle back in the fridge or not pushing his chair back under the dining table, and as for leaving the toilet seat up when he's used it, well . . . Anyway, I have to fight with myself not to have a go at him because I know I'm being unreasonable, but sometimes I can't and the poor man can't understand what he's done to annoy me so badly. I can't understand it either, Rhonnie, why trivial things like this should get me so cross when they never bothered me at all before.'

Rhonnie shrugged. 'I've no idea,' she chuckled. 'When my mother couldn't explain anything away, she'd blame the weather. Until today the last fortnight has been awful. The poor Stripeys have had their patience tested to the limited, keeping grumpy campers happy, and even my Danny has been tetchy at not being able to play outside.'

Jill's face brightened. 'Yes, it could be that, couldn't it? Last Sunday Martin had planned to take me on a pleasure boat trip with friends then to lunch afterwards on the front, but it had to be called off due to the rain and I was very disappointed as I'd been so looking forward to it. I was annoyed about that. Yes, your mother was probably right, Rhonnie, and it's the weather that's making me testy, but hopefully it won't any longer now we have the sun back . . . long may that be the case!'

Just over an hour later Jill arrived back from her inspection tour, reporting nothing amiss except that the electrics to the Tunnel of Love ride down at the funfair had temporarily failed and maintenance were there now fixing it . . . one camper was causing a rumpus as her sixteen-year-old daughter was inside the tunnel with a boy she had met here at the camp and the woman was frantic about what they were getting up to unchaperoned in the dark together. As promised Jill was carrying an ice cream with a Flake for Rhonnie, which was beginning to melt and run down her arm . . . and a Mivvi ice lolly for Sandra.

Greedily taking it off her, Rhonnie asked, 'Where's yours?'

'Oh, I suddenly didn't fancy one.'

'But you never turn down the chance of an ice cream . . . well, not since I've known you.'

'Yes, strange that,' Jill said as she returned to her desk and resumed work.

At just before twelve o'clock Rhonnie was beginning to think that Darren was never going to come back when Sandra telephoned to say that he was here to see her. Hoping that the length of time he had been away was a good sign, she eyed him expectantly as he came in and gave her an invoice for the first five thousand print run of the brochures, telling her that Mr Coppice would have them ready by the end of the month. Rhonnie made a mental note to ask Jill to call the agency and request a couple of temporary clerks to come in then for a week, to threefold the brochures, put them in envelopes then run them through the franking machine ready for posting. It was too big a job for Rhonnie, Jill and Sandra to fit in with their already heavy workload. After informing Rhonnie that he had returned the van and keys to the maintenance department, Darren started to take his leave and for a moment Rhonnie's heart sank. Maybe her plan had not played out like she had hoped it would. But then she realised that he seemed to be hesitant about going.

She put him out of his misery. 'Just telling it straight is the best way, Darren.'

He looked worried. 'But I'm afraid to, Mrs Buckland, in case it's not real and I'm in the middle of a dream. But if I'm not in the middle of a dream, then miracles do happen and wishes come true.' Evidently her plan had worked. But she would have to play dumb and listen to every detail to convince Darren this was all his idea. She got up, went around and gave him a pinch on his arm.

He cried out, 'Ouch! Why did you do that, Mrs Buckland?'

As she returned to her seat and sat back down, she told him, 'To prove to you that you're wide awake.' She clasped her hands in front of her and urged him, 'So are you going

215

to put me out of my misery and tell me what has just happened to you?'

He took a deep breath and launched in. 'Well, I arrived to find Mr Coppice in a right state, trying to answer the telephone while setting up his printing machine to do a run of posters he'd promised he'd have ready for collection at four this afternoon. Plus he'd negatives he was trying to finish off in his darkroom. So I took it upon myself to finish the developing for him while he dealt with his customer on the phone and then finished setting up his printer ready to roll, which he was still doing when I'd finished off the developing . . . and that was when he let slip that he hadn't had a cup of tea since he started work at seven that morning as he'd not had time to make himself one, so I did it for him. Seeing Mr Coppice struggling like that made me realise that working with him would be the perfect job for me, taking over the photographic side of his business and maybe helping him look at ways to modernise it before it went under. I knew how rude it would be of me to say so, though. Anyway, as Mr Coppice was drinking his tea, he was looking over the new layout for the brochure and I could tell he was comparing it to the one he'd put forward and obviously realising just how out of touch he was, and . . . well . . . that's when it happened.'

'What did, Darren?'

'Well . . . have you ever had an idea at the same time as someone else has and you both come out with it together? That's what happened with me and Mr Coppice. As I said to him, *You really need help, don't you, Mr Coppice? . . .* hoping he would say yes and then I could ask him to consider me . . . he said, *I could do with a man like you working for me, to help me modernise before I lose everything. I don't suppose you would consider it, would you?* I didn't need to consider it, Mrs Buckland. This job with Mr Coppice, is heaven-sent for me. It's the miracle I've been praying for.

'My family tried to persuade me not to take the job with

Jolly's as it was only temporary and I'd be living away from home amongst people I didn't know, but I'm so glad I didn't listen to them as then I wouldn't have met Mr Coppice and been given this fantastic opportunity to carry on earning a living doing what I love best. And not only that but learning the printing side as well. He did mention the fact that if all goes well between us . . . and I've no reason not to think it will, as we seem to get on so well together . . . when the time comes for him to retire, we'll come up with some sort of arrangement so that I can buy him out gradually. I've dreamed of this happening since I lost my last job but I never believed dreams could come true. This proves they do. You're not to worry though, Mrs Buckland, I won't be joining Mr Coppice until my contract here comes to an end at the finish of the season.'

Rhonnie was relieved to hear that. She told him how pleased she was for him and Albert, and as she watched Darren jauntily depart the office, Rhonnie thought to herself that heading up a company that employed as many staff as Jolly's did there were bound to be problems for employees that needed to be resolved by a caring employer. She had thoroughly enjoyed helping Darren sort out his problem but there was another staff predicament she had to smooth over. Lily Dawkins and Alan Ibbotson must somehow settle their differences and reach an understanding on how they could work harmoniously together in the future.

A while later Rhonnie was standing by Jill's desk, discussing with her where they would put the temporary desks in the general office ready for the brochure temps, when Sandra came bounding in at the end of her lunch hour. She looked fit to burst with excitement when she blurted out, 'Oh, guess what? Very soon I'm going to meet the lad of me dreams and we're going to get married and have three kids.'

The other two women were staring across at her blankly while she imparted this exciting news.

Rhonnie said to her, 'That's good to hear, Sandra. I'm very pleased for you.'

'Me too,' Jill told her. 'Just . . . er . . . how do you know this if it's not happened yet?'

''Cos the fortune-teller told me. She's ever so good and only charged me ten bob for me reading.'

Rhonnie was looking at her enquiringly. 'How did you manage to get to Mablethorpe and back in your lunch hour?'

'Eh? I never went to Mablethorpe to have me reading with that woman on the pier, if that's who you're on about. Me mam reckons she's really good, told her she was going to come into money and she did. Had a win on the bingo . . . only thirty bob but still money at the end of the day. She charges a quid for her readings and I can't afford that. I had my reading here in Jolly's.'

Rhonnie looked at Jill. 'Jim Davis never mentioned he was installing a fortune-teller down in the funfair. He shouldn't do anything like that before okaying it with me or Drina first.'

Sandra piped up, 'Oh, no, this woman's not working here, she's on holiday and doing readings from her chalet. I was going into the restaurant for my dinner when I overheard Gaynor and Cindy talking about the reading they'd just had with her and that's how I found out about her.' She grumbled then, 'Trouble was, I went to see her instead of having me dinner and now I'm starving.'

Rhonnie was shocked. 'This woman is doing what! But she can't do that, come here on holiday and set up shop, hassling our campers to use her services to make money for herself.' She addressed Jill. 'We need to put an end to this or next thing we know we'll have coachloads of suitcase salesmen arriving, thinking we turn a blind eye to this sort of thing and they're on to a winner. What chalet is this woman in?' she asked Sandra.

The young girl gave a shrug. 'On a row somewhere near

the bottom. You'll know which one as you'll see a queue of women waiting outside.'

Ordering Sandra to man the fort, Rhonnie and Jill set off to put an end to this woman's use of Jolly's to line her own pockets.

They found the chalet easily enough, exactly the way Sandra herself had told them they would, by the queue of women waiting their turn outside. Rhonnie got a shock to see at least twenty women, some with babies in their arms or young children clinging to their skirts – all, she guessed, hoping to be told how rosy the future was going to be for them. Their reception of the new arrivals was far from friendly as they saw Rhonnie and Jill heading straight for the head of the line.

'Oi, you two,' shouted a buxom blonde woman, halfway down the line, drawing heavily from a cigarette. 'Who do yer think yer are? Get to the end of the queue like we've all had to or else me and me mate here will see you both do.'

The woman behind her pulled a warning face and shouted over, 'Yeah, we will.'

Murmurs of discontent were heard coming from the rest of the women waiting their turn and, fearing a lynch mob was about to form, Jill moved closer to Rhonnie for protection. At the head of the queue now, Rhonnie faced the queue, raising her hands to get their attention. 'I'm the manager of the camp and I suggest that if you want your fortune telling, you visit the lady on Mablethorpe pier. There'll be no more told in this chalet.'

'But we want to see this lady here! I've heard she's ever so good,' piped up another woman.

'Well, she might be, but we can't have people come here on holiday, see a way to make money for themselves and decide to set up in business. Now all the afternoon entertainments are about to start so you'd better get off. I'm sure you don't want to miss the fun.'

Seeing Rhonnie meant business, the crowd began to disperse with murmurs of 'Bloody spoilsport' and 'Who's she . . . Lady Muck?'

Rhonnie, followed by Jill, stepped up to the chalet door and knocked on it.

A voice inside called out, 'Please wait your turn with the others. I won't be a minute, I've just about finished this reading.'

Rhonnie opened the door and she and Jill went inside. Sitting opposite each other on the single beds were two women, one middle-aged and the other in her twenties. The older woman had her eyes closed and was rubbing something between her hands. The young one meanwhile was staring at her expectantly. As they approached the older woman was saying, 'You're coming into money . . .'

Rhonnie interrupted her by saying: 'That will be the money she doesn't hand over to you for your so-called glimpse into her future.'

Both women glared over at the interlopers.

The older one snapped, 'Who do you think you are, barging in on a sitting like this? Now you've broken me concentration.'

'Well, that's fine as you won't be needing it any longer, not to read people's fortune's here you won't. We're Jolly's management come to tell you to stop doing what you are immediately or we'll have no alternative but to ask you to leave the camp.'

Seeing a chance to escape without paying for her reading, the young woman got up and sidled her way out.

The fortune-teller shifted uneasily on the bed. 'Well, you can't blame a woman for seeing an opportunity to make herself a little money when she realised her holiday funds were getting low.'

'Are you a bona fide fortune-teller?' Jill asked her sceptically.

She said defensively, 'Well, dearie, that depends what you

mean by bona fide. You can't go to university and learn to be a clairvoyant, you've either got the gift or you ain't. If I hadn't I wouldn't have so many people willing to pay me for a reading, would I?'

'I suppose not,' Rhonnie agreed. 'Well, so long as we have your promise that you won't be charging for any more readings while you're here, we'll leave you to it.' And just in case the woman thought she might ignore the warning, Rhonnie added, 'We will be keeping our eye on you, though, just in case.'

As both women made to leave the fortune-teller got up, caught Jill's arm and said to her, 'I can tell by the way you're looking at me that you're not a believer are you?'

Jill didn't hesitate in her response. 'No, I'm not. People like you just tell gullible fools what they want to hear and throw in a few random things for good measure, then charge them for the privilege.'

The other woman smiled knowingly at her. 'Oh, well, in that case I won't bother to tell you that you need to warn your husband that shortly he'll be vying for your attentions with someone else, but he'll be very happy about it.'

Jill frowned at her in bewilderment. 'What do you mean by that?'

The woman shot her a contemptuous look. 'You don't believe in the likes of me so why should I waste my time explaining to you what I mean?'

They had arrived back outside and the woman was just about to shut the door on them when she unexpectedly said to Rhonnie, 'You've suffered much heartache for a young woman of your age but there is love for you again. It's hiding from you at the moment but a car will show you that it is possible to fall in love once more.' With that she shut the door, leaving Rhonnie and Jill staring blindly at it.

Rhonnie spoke first. 'Now I don't understand what she meant by that.'

Jill gave a disdainful tut. 'I shouldn't even try to, Rhonnie.

I can tell you for nothing, there is no way my husband would be happy vying for my attentions with another man. Now if she'd said he'd kill a rival, I might have believed that!'

Rhonnie did not respond. Drina's mother had been a clairvoyant but apparently Drina herself hadn't inherited her gift and as they'd never really talked in depth about it Rhonnie wasn't sure if Drina was a believer or not. She herself had been tempted several times when she had come across a fortune-teller's booth while at the seaside but decided she didn't want to know what lay in store for her, and knew of no one else who had had a reading from a fortune-teller either, so she had no argument ready to challenge Jill with. Instead she said, 'We'd better get back to the office.'

They were just approaching the main courtyard when, amongst the throng of campers coming and going or just moseying about, they simultaneously spotted a couple having a very animated argument.

Jill commented, 'Goodness me, that couple are having a right go at each other.'

Rhonnie said, 'Yes, they are. It's the couple in question, though, that's really bothering me. That's Lily Dawkins and Alan Ibbotson.'

Jill recognised them then and spoke gravely, 'Oh, so it is. Having a lovers' tiff is my guess.'

'That is no lovers' tiff they're having, Jill, more like two warring neighbours going at it hammer and tongs. But whoever is in the right, I can't have two of my senior staff brawling in public. I need to put an end to this situation.'

Lily and Alan were so engrossed in their argument they did not sense they had company and both jumped and spun round in alarm to face Rhonnie when she said to them in no uncertain terms: 'I'd like to see you both in my office now, please.'

Faces reddening in embarrassment, they both gulped and looked horrified as she turned away and headed off with Jill towards reception.

CHAPTER NINETEEN

Ten minutes later, behind a closed door, Lily and Alan, both shamefaced, were seated in front of Rhonnie's desk looking like pupils called before the headmistress.

She said to them, 'You both know that any members of staff found acting inappropriately in front of the campers are in contravention of Jolly's code of conduct. It is even worse to find two managers behaving so sloppily. It's bad enough having to put up with your behaviour towards each other in meetings, which I was about to warn you about, but arguing in public like this . . . well, I'm well and truly shocked. Just what was the cause?'

Lily erupted, 'I found out he was trying to pinch one of my staff behind my back.'

'And I keep trying to tell her, I wasn't. The girl approached me and I told her that if Lily was in agreement then I would give her an audition.'

She barked at him, 'That's *not* what Nicola told me. She said you'd approached her and asked her if she'd like to join the entertainments team.'

'Well, that's what she *would* tell you because she wouldn't want you to think she was angling to leave you for a better opportunity. Then you'd know her heart wasn't in her job with you, and might have decided to finish her.'

Lily looked insulted. 'I would never . . .'

Rhonnie erupted: 'Enough! My goodness, can't you two

223

even hold a civilised conversation? I should sack you both with immediate effect.'

'Oh, please don't, Rhonnie. I love my job here,' Lily pleaded with her.

'So do I,' mirrored Alan.

'And you're both very good at them and I wouldn't like to lose either of you.' Rhonnie sat back in her chair and studied them for several moments before she leaned forward and asked, 'You're such nice people, so what is it that you find so offensive about each other that you can't even be in the same room without passing snide remarks?' She heaved a sigh. 'You remind me of a bickering married couple.' She could not fail to miss the look that flashed between them then and her eyes widened, jaw dropping open as she uttered, 'You two are married!'

There was a long silence for a moment before Lily spoke. 'Coming up for twelve years and I thought we were happy until he left me five years ago.' If looks could kill, the one she then flashed Alan would have seen him drop dead instantly.

He shot back at her, 'I didn't leave you! Well . . . not like just up and left you, that kind of leaving, Lil, and you know it.'

She glowered at him. 'Accepting that stage manager's contract for twelve months with the travelling theatre company, and no wardrobe mistress job for me, meant we'd be apart for a year . . . and that wasn't leaving me in your eyes then? When we both knew we were serious about each other, we made a pact that we came as a package and would never take a job that didn't offer one for the other person. By taking that job you broke our pact.'

He glared at her. 'I agree I did break our pact but I had to take the job as I knew it could lead to better things for both of us. The theatre company had shows up and down the country and especially on Drury Lane. The sorts of people I would have been mixing with, where that could have led . . .

I was thinking of our future, Lil. I loved my job with the Huddersfield Players but when all's said and done it's just a backwater theatre in a provincial town up north that hardly anyone of importance in the theatre has ever heard of. If I wanted to better myself, I had to get out and get myself known in the business. That job with the travelling theatre company was the best way to do it.'

'But you never even sat down and discussed it with me first, found out how I felt about it, just told me you were taking it and leaving that very night.'

'But what was there to discuss, Lil? It was a chance of a lifetime for me . . . for us . . . and I thought you'd appreciate that. I had to make an instant decision, as the company's stage manager had landed himself a part on a television show and they needed a replacement quick since their first performance was in Glasgow in two weeks' time. My agent had to telephone them at five that evening with my decision, and if it was yes then I'd to be down in London at the rehearsal rooms at ten the next morning.'

She folded her arms and set her mouth tight. Seeming to forget that the manager of Jolly's was privy to their conversation she snapped, 'Yes, well, the job certainly led you to fame and fortune, didn't it? Introducing you to all those influential people in the business landed you with the prestigious job of entertainments manager at a holiday camp!'

He eyed her darkly. 'Well, if you'd not taken that job as head of laundry on that cruise ship for six months, I would have been able to tell you that I loved the job, but loved you more, and had handed in my notice to come back to you.'

She was looking confused. 'I never went to work on a cruise ship! Who told you that?'

'Your father. On giving in my notice, I immediately packed up my belongings and travelled back to Huddersfield. As soon as I got off the train I went straight to the theatre and got a shock when I was told you'd left, so I went to the lodgings we were staying in at the time and was told by the landlady that you'd packed up and gone back to your parents in Carlisle. I went there to see you, only to be told by your father you'd taken a job with the cruise ship and were halfway across the world by then. He took great delight in telling me too, didn't bother to hide his joy that our marriage was over. You know he never liked me, felt you could do much better for yourself than a bit-part actor and stage manager.'

Lily frowned, even more confused. 'But why would my father tell you such a lie when . . .' Her voice trailed off and she issued a loud, despairing groan, slapping a hand on her forehead. 'Oh, because that's what I told him and Mother to tell you, should you try and contact me in any way. I was so upset at the time that I never wanted to see you again. But Dad never mentioned a word to me about your visit. When you called, I was probably in my room sobbing my heart out. I stayed with my parents for three months and, not having heard a word from you during that time, thought our marriage was over. So I tried to get on with my life without you.'

He looked astounded. 'And meanwhile I managed to get my job back in Huddersfield and for those three months was spending all my spare time contacting the cruise companies, asking if you worked for them . . . of course now I realise why none of them had ever heard of you. But with no clue how to get in touch with you, and knowing you wouldn't be able to contact me in London, I had no choice but to think our marriage was over and try to get on with my life without you. I couldn't believe it when I saw you in the restaurant at breakfast time the first morning I started here with Jolly's. I thought I must be seeing things.'

'Yes, so did I when I saw you.' Lily heaved a forlorn sigh. 'I had such a job stopping myself from rushing over to you, throwing my arms around you and telling you how much I'd missed you, that I should never have acted so childishly when you told me about the job but seen your side about the potential it had. But by then I hated you for leaving me like you did and making no effort to make up for the pain and disappointment I've suffered since, so every time I saw you I couldn't help myself from lashing out so as not to let you know how I felt about you.'

'That's just what I did too,' he told her.

They both seemed to have forgotten that Rhonnie was present so she decided it was time she reminded them. 'Well, it's obvious to me that you still love each other, so will you be moving into Alan's chalet, Lily, or will Alan be moving in with you?'

They both looked at her blankly for a moment before Alan said to Lily, 'I do still love you, Lil, even though I acted like I hated you.'

'And I love you too.'

'Do you think we could make another go of our marriage?'

'I'm willing to try if you are.'

'It wouldn't take me long to pack up my stuff and move into your chalet. If that's what you want, of course, Lil?'

A huge smile lit her face. 'Do you want any help packing or can you manage by yourself while I make room for you in my place?'

As soon as they'd left the office, Jill came dashing in and said in a triumphant manner: 'I was right about them, I knew I was! If ever I've seen a couple in love it's Lily and Alan. They went walking out of the office hand in hand just now.'

'Don't be so quick to proclaim yourself the winner, Jill. We were both right about them. When they walked in here, what they felt for each other then was far from love. It's said there is a fine line between love and hate and those two just proved to me that the old wives' tale is true. On the surface they hated each other while deep down they adored each other.' Knowing that she did not need to remind Jill that anything she heard now was strictly not to be repeated, Rhonnie proceeded to tell her Alan and Lily's history together.

When she had finished Jill blew out her cheeks and exclaimed, 'Well, I'll be blowed. Married! I'm just so glad that fate has brought them both here to Jolly's, to give them a chance to sort out their differences and mend their marriage.'

Rhonnie smiled. 'Yes, me too.' She looked enquiringly at Jill. 'Talking of loving couples, how are things between you and your husband?'

Jill sighed. 'Great . . . well, apart from little things he does that still manage to irritate the life out of me when I can't understand why as they never did before. He's just gone away on a business trip to Scotland for two weeks. His boss was supposed to be going but he broke his leg so he elected Martin to go in his place. He's only been gone a day and I'm missing him already. Hopefully by the time he gets back, I'll be so glad to see him that his irritating little ways won't bother me anymore.'

Rhonnie smiled. 'I'm sure they won't. Anyway, I've got the Lincolnshire head of children's services coming in soon to discuss how many weeks' holidays we're prepared to give the orphan children in the area next year. I'd better go and have a tidy up so I at least look professional to him.'

Jill smiled. To her Rhonnie never looked anything other than professional when she was at work.

As a mother herself the meeting with the head of the Lincolnshire children's services department proved very emotional for Rhonnie, who felt mortally sorry for all the little mites being looked after in homes without the love and support only parents can provide. The social worker didn't have a hard task persuading Rhonnie to agree to give them six separate weeks for twenty children at a time to holiday at Jolly's. In the past they had only given away four weeks.

Feeling the need for a breath of fresh air after the meeting was over, Rhonnie went outside to sit on a seat in the court-yard and eat an ice cream. She became lost in her surroundings, watching all the children laughing and joking as they went around with their parents, unaware how fortunate they were to have them when so many others did not. An unexpected deep voice speaking beside her made her almost leap out of her skin when it said in a London accent: 'Giz us a quick kiss, darlin', and a lick of your ice cream.'

She spun round to reprove whoever it was who had accosted her and instantaneously erupted into laughter to see Ginger sitting beside her, wearing a Kiss Me Quick hat, face thrust out, lips puckered. Holding the cornet out of her dear friend's reach, Rhonnie spluttered, 'Get your own, but I'll give you a kiss!' Which she did, a smacker, on Ginger's cheek. Then she enthused, 'Oh, it's so great to see you. Is this just a quick visit or are you staying for a bit? Have you got any more news since we last spoke on the telephone and you told me that Paul was going to be speaking to his old boss the next day?'

'To answer your first question, I'm staying, but I won't need a bed as I've got my own.'

Rhonnie looked at her for a moment until the significance of what Ginger had just said registered and she blurted out, 'Does that mean Paul has got his transfer and you've moved back?'

Grinning, Ginger nodded. 'We're in the process. When Paul went to see his old boss, he was told that there wasn't a vacancy at that time in his old station in Skegness but one of the local village bobbies was retiring in a couple of months' time and they were just about to advertise for a replacement. Paul's old boss told him he'd pull a few strings. The job will be based in Threddlethorpe, just down the road from here. He starts in six weeks' time but they've let us have the house early so I'm here to lick it into shape while Paul works his notice in Leeds. The pay for a village bobby isn't bad either so I won't have to work unless I want to. I can't see myself being a lady of leisure for long, so I might be coming to you for a part-time job in the future.'

'And I'm sure I'll find you something.' Rhonnie threw her arms around Ginger and hugged her fiercely. 'Oh, I can't believe I've got my friend back. I have missed you. Phone calls are all well and good but not the same as putting the world to rights face to face over a glass of wine. Or going shopping with you . . . there's nothing like a best friend for being truthful about a dress.'

Ginger told her, 'Well, I'm just as pleased too, but I need to tell you that your ice cream is dripping down the back of my neck.'

Rhonnie freed her friend from her embrace and looked at the offending article in her hand. 'Oh, sorry, I forgot about that in the excitement of your news. This is such a special occasion that I'll finish early, then we can go back to mine, relieve Carrie of Danny and have some dinner, then we'll all drive over to your new house in Threddlethorpe and you can show me and Danny around.'

'Sounds good to me,' enthused Ginger.

Early that evening, over in the hut in the woods, Ben was frying two trout for his supper that he had managed to catch with a makeshift rod earlier that day. He was feeling rather rich at the moment with £2 in his pocket that he had worked hard for over the last two days after a desperate farmer had recruited him to help harvest his fields of cabbages and ripened corn. The journey to and from the farm had meant a walk of twenty miles a day for Ben, but had it been three times that he would have done it for the work at the end of it.

He knew he needed to get in as much work as he could from now until the winter set in, as jobs during the bitter cold months would be very few and far between. But as he poked his fish around in the battered, blackened old frying pan on top of the pot-bellied stove he wasn't thinking of how he was going to survive the winter months but of the caravan site manager and his odd behaviour.

Since the night that Ben had seen the man acting so suspiciously, it had become an obsession with him to find out just what the man was hiding. He couldn't shift the feeling that in some way or other the manager was up to no good. Until he had found out Ben wouldn't let it go and in any spare time he had, at differing times during the day and evening, he would wait in the woods, hiding near the wire fence, directly opposite the back of the man's van, keeping watch on him. So far he had not discovered what was happening but he was determined. That man worked for Rhonnie and Drina, two women who between them had done so much to better Ben's life, and he owed them a debt of gratitude. If he saw something that could cause them or their business harm, then he would do his best to bring it to their attention.

One thing he had found out during his observation of the man was that he had something about him that drew the ladies and in consequence there were not many nights he slept alone. Apart from a Wednesday night that was. Wednesday seemed to be his regular weekly half-day off and he would go out in his car just after it got dark in the evening and not return until the early hours of Thursday morning. It had been on a Thursday morning that Ben had seen him acting suspiciously and he realised this was the best time to catch him at it again. So far he'd not managed to catch the right moment but tonight, a Wednesday, Ben was determined he was not going to miss the man either leaving or returning. He was going to be in his hiding place before it got dark and would watch everything the other man did.

CHAPTER TWENTY

Much to Ben's disappointment, though, he wasn't going to achieve his aim that night as, unbeknown to him, Jeff's car wouldn't start when he had tried to use it to go into Mablethorpe during his lunch hour. The fault was the sort only a garage could fix so his Wednesday night out that week wasn't going to happen.

Jeff was not happy about it. Thanks to his car failing on him he now had to kiss goodbye to whatever he would have made himself tonight and a whole long evening stretched ahead of him, stuck here on the park with nothing to fill the time. He'd already managed to have his way with all the women staying at the moment that had caught his eye. But then an idea struck him. If he could get a certain lady he'd been chasing for a while finally to give in to his charms, then his evening might not turn out to be a complete failure after all. It would need some planning, though. He'd need to give his van a clean and especially to change the bed sheets, but if at the end he managed to entice the delectable Rhonnie Buckland under them then it would certainly help to soften the blow of missing out on tonight's outing.

As Jeff was putting his plan into place for adding Rhonnie to his list of conquests, over in the office, over a pot of tea, Drina was saying to her, 'Times are forever changing, love, and we have to keep changing too if we want people to continue flocking to Jolly's for their holidays in the future.' She paused to take a sip of tea and then with genuine sadness said, 'At least three camps to my knowledge have closed down this year. They were much smaller operations than the likes of us, Pontin's and Warner's – Butlin's being the biggest of all of course – but it's a warning that package holidays are a threat to holiday camps and we need to do our best to make sure we keep people wanting to take their holidays with us. We might not be able to promise the sun will shine every day like these foreign holiday operators do, but we can promise better accommodation, food, fun facilities, and that no holidaymakers will be better looked after elsewhere than they will be by our staff here at Jolly's.

'We've made a start, opening the new caravan and touring park to give people an alternative to the all-inclusive chalet package, and I'm so pleased with the way it's taking off, but now we need to look at ways of improving the main camp. I've given a lot of thought to this and the first thing we need to consider making improvements to is the accommodation we offer. The chalets are getting rather old now and are desperately in need of modernisation so I've decided to go ahead and give them a facelift.'

She took a sip of tea before she continued. 'The work will have to take place over a two- or three-year period, a section of chalets at a time, as we can't afford to close down the camp to do all the work in one go. As each section of new chalets is finished we can start taking bookings for them and charge a higher rate too as they'll be much more comfortable than the old ones are. It'll take a big cash injection but I'm sure I can persuade the bank that to take the camp into the seventies and beyond, we need to do this.'

As Drina was speaking, Rhonnie had put down her cup and picked up a pencil drawing Drina had sketched out of what she proposed the revamped chalets would look like, both outside and in. They were twice the height of the

233

one-roomed chalets on the camp now, and were partitioned inside to have a small lounge and a bathroom downstairs, with upstairs two bedrooms large enough to hold one double bed, small wardrobe and chest of drawers in one room, and two singles and bedroom furniture in the other. The main change, though, was that the new-style chalet would be centrally heated.

'Obviously it's just a rough sketch and the chalets need designing by an architect, but what do you think of my idea?' Drina quizzed her.

Drina never ceased to amaze Rhonnie. She might have given up the day-to-day running of the camp but behind the scenes she was still busily working away, protecting the future of her beloved Jolly's. Rhonnie said, impressed, 'Staying in one of these chalets instead of the old ones would be like the difference between a cheap bed and breakfast and a first-class hotel. And having them heated . . . when all the chalets have been finished, we'll be able to extend the season by four weeks at each end, won't we?'

'My thoughts exactly. Eight extra weeks a year adds up to a lot of revenue, which will help pay for the improvements.'

Rhonnie put down the plan on the Long John table then looked at Drina meaningfully. 'I know you signed over the Devon camp to me, but it goes without saying that as soon as it's showing a profit after the building loan has been paid off, then those profits are yours to help out with this.'

Drina smiled warmly at her. 'I appreciate that, love. The way it's going, Devon will soon be making a profit. Eventually the Jolly's empire will all be yours and Danny's. I'm just making sure it's a legacy worth having.'

When that happened it would mean Drina was no longer with them and that thought was unbearable to Rhonnie. 'And you know, Drina, that as long as I'm living and breathing, both Jolly's camps and any more we have in the future will always be run along the lines that your father and Farmer

Ackers started off with over forty years ago – giving people a holiday to remember at an affordable price.'

Drina leaned over and affectionately patted her hand. 'I know that, love. I just hope that Danny will grow up to want to take over from you when you decide it's time to step down. Or if not him then any other of your children.'

Rhonnie gave a distant smile. 'I'd like more children, of course. Just need the right man to have them with.' It shocked her to realise that a vision of Ben had popped into her mind when she had said that.

Drina was pleased to hear this as it meant that Rhonnie was well and truly coming to terms with her loss of Dan and realising that it was possible to find room in her heart for someone else.

Jill knocked on the door and popped her head around it, smiling at them. 'Just wondered if you'd like a refill of drinks and I also need to tell you that Jeff Sampson telephoned and left a message with Sandra to say that he really needs to speak to you privately, Rhonnie, and wondered if it was possible for you to go to his van tonight about seven-thirty. He can't make it before as he has a couple of tourers booked in due to turn up about six this evening and he needs to get them settled in first, but what he needs to talk to you about can't wait.'

After they had told Jill they did not want any drinks and she had returned to the general office, Rhonnie frowned and said, 'Oh, I hope Jeff's not thinking of leaving us. He's doing a good job of running the park. And remember when it came to interviewing, he was the only one who bothered to turn up so it's not going to be easy to find a replacement for him if he is about to hand his notice in. But then if he is surely it could have waited until tomorrow.'

Drina mused, 'That was rather a strange state of affairs when no one else turned up for the interview but Jeff Sampson, wasn't it?'

Rhonnie nodded. 'But at least he did and we weren't left flat.' She then said, 'I'd better put a call through to the cottage and ask Carrie if she can stay on while I go over to see Jeff. And I do hate missing Danny's bedtime,' she said a mite crossly, 'so this had better be a matter of life or death.'

Drina hid a smile. She wouldn't like to be in Jeff's shoes if Rhonnie felt he had kept her late for no good reason. 'No need to call, Carrie,' she told Rhonnie. 'There was another reason I wanted this meeting – I needed to tell you your father and I are going away to have a few days on the south coast.'

Rhonnie laughed. 'Bit of a busman's holiday for you both!'

'Yes, it is, but we both love the coast and it's nice to explore somewhere new. And as your father keeps reminding me, I am supposed to be semi-retired so agreeing to go away will stop him from nagging at me to take things easier. Anyway, we were both wondering if you'd let us take Danny with us? We're setting off early tomorrow morning so it would be best to have him to stay with us tonight, which leaves you free to have your meeting with Jeff and not trouble Carrie to stay late.'

Being apart from her son for several days was going to be hard on Rhonnie but it was good for him to spend quality time with his grandparents. She smiled at Drina. 'Yes, of course you can take Danny. I'll call Carrie and asked her to pack a case for him and she'll be delighted as it'll give her a few days off too. Remember to bring me a stick of rock back,' she told Drina.

'And you can't get rock whenever you wish from our own shop?'

'Ah, well, it tastes different with another town's name running through the middle.'

At just after seven that evening, Ben settled himself into as comfortable a position as he could in his usual place behind the site manager's caravan. He was glad to see that the red car was still there so he had not missed the man's departure.

As Ben took a chunk of wood and a penknife out of his pocket and began whittling, fashioning a peg to add to the others he had made to hang up his washing, his eyes settled on the car parked the other side of the fence. Ben knew a little about cars, he'd owned several in his previous life. This one was a 1963 Rover 3-litre. The bodywork looked a little rusty but otherwise it was solid enough. Ben knew this model had wide leather benchseats and, given the owner's eye for women, he wondered if that was why this particular make had been chosen as the seat would prove very comfortable in more ways than one. His eyes settled on the car's number plate: BIA 974. Ben snorted in derision. A very apt plate for the likes of the caravan park manager. BIA for Big I Am, which was how the man acted, strutting around the park like a peacock.

Ben returned his attention to making his peg, ears pricked for any sounds coming from the caravan a few yards away.

After waving her son and his grandparents off on their holiday, Rhonnie got in her car and drove over to the caravan site, parking just inside the site entrance. She walked the rest of the way to Jeff's caravan for her meeting with him.

Inside his caravan, Jeff had a final look round to make sure all was as he wanted. Satisfied it was, he put a Marvin Gaye LP on the record player as background music to create the atmosphere he wanted, then for the umpteenth time checked his appearance in the mirror in the bathroom. Making sure every strand of his long blond hair was in place, he rubbed a liberal amount of Brut aftershave over his face and neck, wet his fingers and ran them across his eyebrows, then stood back to admire his reflection. Smiling broadly, he held his arms wide and smugly said aloud: 'Now what dame could resist that?' Fully believing that no woman ever could, he went into the living area to await the arrival of the one he was convinced would be his latest conquest.

Ben heard someone approaching the caravan, light steps, a woman's . . . He was shocked to see Rhonnie arrive at the steps leading up to the van and knock briskly on the door. His thoughts raced. A woman visiting a man at home at this time of the evening had to mean they had a prearranged date! So he had been right, Rhonnie was having a relationship with the blond-haired lothario.

Ben wanted to warn her that the man she was courting was a serial womaniser, and it was very likely she was no more special to him than any other of the string of women Ben had seen entering that van recently. To do so, though, would leave him with a lot of explaining to do as to why he was spying on the site manager's caravan in the first place. Emotions raged through Ben as he saw the door open and the philanderer himself appear in the doorway, sporting that rakish smile Ben had seen him giving many women before Rhonnie. He couldn't believe that an intelligent person like she was had not seen through the man's fake facade to recognise him for the shallow predator he was, but instead, like all the others who had gone before her, had fallen for his looks and patter and become his willing victim. Ben fought with himself not to scale the fence, charge into the caravan and save Rhonnie from making a huge mistake, dragging her out kicking and screaming if necessary. At least he would be saving her from the humiliation she would suffer when she discovered that one night of sex was all that man was after with her.

But then reason began to filter through his anger and he realised that other man could not fail to see Rhonnie for the special woman she was. Jack the Lad though he might be, he'd be sharp enough to recognise she was the type to hang on to. Perhaps at this very moment he was trying to prove to her what a good catch he was and what a good husband he'd make.

Realising that his own vigil would not pay off since the site manager was going nowhere, and that by staying here he would only cause himself misery, Ben went on his way.

Inside the caravan Jeff was giving Rhonnie one of his most charismatic smiles while lying shamelessly to her. 'Quite a while since a pretty lady has graced the inside of my van. Actually the last time was when you were here before. Take a seat. Would you like a drink . . . glass of wine?'

The fact that the caravan was immaculately clean and tidy considering a single man lived here, and that Jeff himself had obviously made a very special effort with his appearance and his manner towards her, was not lost on Rhonnie. He had not asked her here to discuss an urgent private matter but to seduce her, Rhonnie had no doubt about that. She was insulted he would believe she would fall for such a cheap trick, and furious that his selfishness had prevented her from putting her son to bed.

She wanted to tell him that he had wasted his time, but there was a spark of devilment in her that also wanted to teach him a lesson. He needed to know that not every woman he met considered it an honour to have his attention bestowed on them . . . or not this woman at any rate.

Smiling sweetly at him, she sat down on the horse-shoe-shaped seat that spanned the front of the caravan under the window and said, 'Just a small glass would be nice, thank you.' Watching him closely as he went into the kitchen area and took a bottle and glasses from a wall cupboard, she didn't miss the twitch of a satisfaction that curled his lips. If this went the way she intended he wouldn't be wearing that smile when she left.

Glasses filled, he came over and sat down beside her, a little too close for her liking but she did not show him that. Handing one of the glasses to Rhonnie, he clinked his against it and, resting his free arm along the sofa behind her, said in a seductive tone, 'Now this is nice, isn't it?'

She took a sip of her drink and batted her eyelashes at him. She knew he wasn't referring to the wine but regardless replied, 'Yes, it's a good drop of plonk. Now what was it you wanted to speak to me about so urgently and why couldn't it wait until tomorrow?'

He inched himself even closer to her, looked at her meaningfully and replied, 'Oh, come on, Rhonnie, you know very well why I asked you here.'

She feigned surprise. 'Do I?'

He took his arm from the back of the seat and put his hand on her knee. 'I know a woman who has the hots for me when I see one. And I can't deny what I feel for you. You're a very attractive woman.'

She wanted to smack his hand off her but, keeping in character, she smiled back at him and said shyly, 'I appreciate the compliment.' Not that she felt it was one, coming from him. Jeff just spoke the right words, with no sincerity behind them. 'So what makes you think I have the hots for you then?'

His hand moved up her leg to her thigh. 'You think I haven't noticed the way you undress me with those come-to-bed eyes of yours every time you look at me?'

Fighting not to show him that his uninvited pawing of her was in fact turning her right off, she feigned surprise. 'Do I! I hadn't realised.'

He told her with conviction, 'I think you know very well you do.' He took a sip of his drink before adding, 'We both know what we want, so why are we wasting time playing games with each other?'

She eyed him teasingly. 'And you know what I want, do you, Jeff?'

'Oh, yes. This,' he said, gesturing towards himself. 'And

it's yours for the taking.' He lifted his hand off her thigh and ran a finger down the side of her face, saying huskily, 'Shall I lead the way or will you? I'm just as comfortable here if you are.'

He didn't need to spell out to her that he meant lead the way to his bedroom. A wave of disgust swamped Rhonnie. This man was egotistical enough to believe that he needn't do anything by way of wooing a woman into his bed, she would just feel so privileged he was choosing her to share it with him that she would jump straight in without a second thought. He very much needed bringing down not just a peg or two but a dozen or so, and she would take great delight in doing it. Fluttering her eyelashes at him again, she told him, 'Well, I'm very flattered that you're offering yourself to me *but* . . .' She let her voice trail away as she downed the remains of her drink, stood up and matter-of-factly announced, 'I have to go.'

Before he could fathom just what was happening she was over at the door letting herself out.

He was so shocked by what had just transpired that he sat and stared at the closed door, utterly astounded that for the first time ever a woman had not taken him up on what he was offering. Then fury rose within him. What was wrong with her? She had missed out on having the best sex ever, something no other man could ever equal. But then a thought struck him. Just what had she meant by that 'but' she had added, after telling him she was flattered by his attentions? Was that her way of telling him she thought that as she was a boss and he an employee he wasn't good enough for her? Condescending bitch, he inwardly fumed. He was better than good enough for any woman. And to think he'd wasted good money for a quality bottle of wine and got nothing in return! If he had ever felt any guilt at all for using her business as a way to feather his own nest, he felt absolutely none now. He supposed there was one consolation and that was that Rhonnie had only consumed a small glass of the expensive wine so he still had the majority of it left for himself.

But he faced another problem. He had been under the impression that his sexual needs were going to be well and truly satisfied tonight and Rhonnie's departure meant that wasn't going to happen, not with her anyway. Of course, that didn't mean to say another woman wouldn't rise to the occasion. He'd finish his wine then take a stroll around the park to see what was on offer, and the way he was feeling now, he wasn't fussy who he spent the night with, any woman would do.

As Rhonnie halted her car at the top of the lane she paused for a moment, looking over in the direction of the path Ben had made. She felt a strong urge to pay a visit on him and spend time in the company of a man most unlike the one she had just left, someone who showed a great deal of respect and courtesy towards women. It would help take the nasty taste out of her mouth after the attitude Jeff had displayed and restore her respect for the male of the species. But it was a bit late for a casual call and she didn't particularly want to explain to Ben what she had just been doing, so she turned the car and headed home.

Had Rhonnie decided to brave the dark and pay a visit on Ben she would have had a wasted journey anyway, as at that moment he was taking a brisk walk along a deserted stretch of beach, trying to take his thoughts off what he believed was going on inside a caravan a mile or so away.

CHAPTER TWENTY-ONE

Two days later, around mid-morning, Rhonnie replaced the telephone receiver and smiled at Jill as she arrived in the office.

'Having a good time, are they?' Jill enquired.

'A whale of one, in Southend-on-Sea, staying in a very nice hotel on the front and Danny is being as good as gold.'

Jill chuckled. 'Well, a granny will tell you that. I remember being a little monkey to my gran on more than one occasion, that bad sometimes she threatened to murder me, but she always told my mum I had been her little angel when she took me back home. You should be enjoying this freedom from being a mum, Rhonnie, pampering yourself and doing things you don't otherwise have time for.'

She flashed a wan smile. 'I should be, I know, but I just miss him so much and can't wait until they come back, so all I'm doing is willing the time away.'

'Well, if you're at a loose end tonight, why don't you come around and I'll cook us a meal? As you know Martin is away in Scotland so I would enjoy the company. Ask your friend Ginger if she'd like to come too. I'd like to get to know her. From what I've gathered she seems a lot of fun.'

Rhonnie chuckled. 'Oh, yes, Ginger does have her moments. I'm sure she'd love to.'

Just then Rita from reception tapped on the open door and came in.

Rhonnie could not fail to notice the perturbed expression on the young woman's face. 'Anything wrong, Rita?' she asked.

Screwing up her face, she replied, 'I'm not sure, Mrs Buckland. It's just that there's a woman down in reception demanding to see Mr Fleming. I phoned over to maintenance to ask Sid Harper if Mr Fleming was on site today and he said he's gone away with Mrs Jolly for a few days. I told the woman that but she wouldn't listen, said I was lying and shouted at me to get him now or we'd be sorry. She was causing a bit of a scene in reception so Kate told me to come and tell you and ask you what to do about her.'

A woman who wasn't the well-mannered sort was demanding to see her father . . . Rhonnie was beginning to feel uncomfortable about this. To confirm her suspicions she asked Rita, 'What's the woman's name?'

'I didn't get as far as that. But she was acting like she owned the place.'

Rhonnie's suspicions were escalating rapidly. 'What does she look like, Rita?'

'Er . . . well . . . she's got a good figure on her for her age . . . late forties I'd guess, and wearing a lot of make up. What's she's dressed in . . . well, she reminds me of Elsie Tanner off *Coronation Street* . . . yer know . . . the brassy sort.'

At this information Rhonnie knew exactly who the woman was. She groaned, 'Oh, God no! What the hell could she be wanting?'

Jill eyed her sharply. 'Do you know this woman, Rhonnie?'

She slowly nodded. 'Unfortunately, I do. Thank you, Rita, I'll deal with this now.' After the young woman had left Rhonnie said to Jill, 'Would you go and fetch her up here, please? And don't tell her that it's me she's coming to see. In fact, don't speak to her any more than just to ask her to come with you to the boss's office, and when she's here shut the

244

door behind her, please, and make sure I'm not disturbed while she's here.'

Jill was desperate to ask just who the woman was but it seemed she was going to have to be patient until Rhonnie decided to enlighten her. She asked, 'Do you want me to send in any drinks?'

Rhonnie snapped, 'Absolutely not. I will not be doing anything to encourage this woman to stay any longer than necessary.'

While Jill went to fetch her, Rhonnie got up and began nervously pacing the space behind her desk by the large picture window with its view of the courtyard below, trying to work out just what it was that could have spurred the woman to travel all the way here. Then it struck her that the last thing she wanted her visitor to realise was that she was making Rhonnie feel on edge, so she sat back down and made herself look efficient and in command by appearing to be looking over some papers. She continued to do this when she heard the woman enter and the office door shut. She then slowly lifted her head and, although inwardly quaking, fixed her eyes on the woman and said matter-of-factly: 'What can I do for you?'

The woman sneered back at her and in a gravelly smoker's voice snapped, 'Fine way to greet your stepmother, Rhonda. You could offer me a drink. It's a long journey here from Leicester. Had to catch three trains.' She said this like it was Rhonnie's fault.

'You won't be stopping long enough to drink it. What are you here for, Mavis?'

Mavis Fleming strolled over to the desk on her scuffed high heels, sat herself down in the chair before it, crossing her still shapely legs and resting her handbag in her lap before she replied. 'Well, I didn't come to see you. It's yer dad I'm after. That silly bitch downstairs tried to fob me off that he weren't here but, as I told her, you either get him here now or you'll

245

be sorry.' She said this while opening up her handbag to take out a packet of Park Drive cigarettes and box of matches.

'The receptionist told you my father's not here and he's not, Mavis, so either tell me what it is you want to see him about or get yourself out of my office and off this camp. You are not welcome here.'

Striking the match, Mavis lit a cigarette then drew deeply on it, blowing out a plume of smoke before smirking sardonically. 'Oh, *your* office, is it! Come up in the world a bit since I last saw yer.' She got up and took a look around while saying, 'Well, if yer not going to offer me a drink, it seems I'll have to help meself.' Her eyes settled on the large ornate cupboard against the side wall. 'Ahhh . . . this looks interesting,' she said as she went over to it and opened up the two highly polished mahogany doors in the top section. 'Woooh!' she exclaimed as her greedy eyes took in the assortment of bottles lining the glass shelves. 'Got more booze here than the Shoemaker's Arms stocks. I'm spoiled for choice.'

As Mavis decided on what drink to help herself to, Rhonnie studied her. The three years since she'd last seen her hadn't been kind to her stepmother. She was still as tartily dressed but her clothes were shabby now, market quality against the chain-store sort she had worn when she was being funded by Artie, and her years of drinking and smoking had taken a huge toll on her face, the fine crow's feet around her eyes and mouth now deepened into gorges which she was failing to disguise under a layer of thick foundation. From her attitude it was apparent that she hadn't softened at all, was still the same vulgar, hard-faced woman who had fooled Rhonnie's father into marrying her, only to fornicate behind his back while he was out working all the hours God sent, driving a lorry up and down the country to earn the money to put a roof over the head of Mavis and her daughter.

The reason Rhonnie had ended up at Jolly's in the first place was because she had caught Mavis red-handed with another man while Artie had been away working, confirming suspicions she'd had for a long time that her stepmother was cheating on him. Unable to bring herself to break her father's heart by informing him of his wife's betrayal, Rhonnie left home after leaving a note for him to say she was going away to recover from a broken heart after ending a relationship with her then boyfriend, praying that her father never discovered the truth. But only months later he had turned up at Jolly's, a shadow of his former self, believing he'd nothing left to live for as he'd discovered for himself what Mavis was doing behind his back. It was only through the love and care of Rhonnie and Drina that he had recovered from Mavis's betrayal of him and now led a very happy new life with Drina. The only thing that marred it was the fact that so far Mavis had refused to agree to a divorce unless she was paid handsomely to do so.

Now armed with a full glass of Drina's five-star Napoleon brandy, Mavis sat back down, took a gulp of it, and said, 'I expect you're wondering why I'm here?'

Rhonnie answered sardonically, 'I was hoping that you'd come to do the decent thing at last and give my dad a divorce, out of the goodness of your heart, so he can finally be free of you.'

She scornfully replied, 'Nothing in this life comes for free, Rhonda. Your dad knows how much I want to give him his freedom but until he pays up then he stays married to me.'

Rhonnie inwardly sighed. It was Drina's one wish to marry the man she adored but it didn't seem she would ever be granted it while Mavis was alive. Rhonnie eyed her suspiciously. 'So why are you here?' Then the reason occurred to her. 'You're after money, aren't you? Why else would you be here.'

Mavis slyly smirked. 'Oh, yer not as thick as you look, Rhonda dear. It certainly is money I want and not just a few coppers either. I want five grand.'

Rhonnie was astounded. 'How much! That's more than a working man would earn in a year.'

Mavis grinned wickedly. 'Yeah, but nothing compared to what my dear husband has at his disposal now, thanks to him shacking up with the rich bitch he has.'

Rhonnie erupted, 'Don't you dare speak about Drina like that. She's a good woman, worth a million of you.' She wagged a warning finger at Mavis and insisted, 'Now you look here – my father owes you nothing. He paid you more than he should ever have done to leave his house, which you didn't at all deserve, but that is all you're getting out of him and not a penny more.'

Mavis's eyes darkened thunderously and she stabbed a nicotine-stained finger at Rhonnie. 'I'm his wife and he's a moral duty to look after me and my daughter, who he took on as his own when he married me. I want five grand and I ain't leaving here 'til I get it. And cash. I ain't accepting no cheques for you to cancel as soon as I leave here. Besides, I haven't a bank account. If you refuse to pay me then I'm going to the newspapers to sell my story to them.'

Rhonnie frowned in bewilderment. 'And what story is that? How you broke my father's heart by sleeping with other men behind his back while he was away working to keep you and your daughter in clover?'

Mavis gave a throaty cackle. 'I'm sure they'll pay hand-somely for the story about the owner of a popular holiday camp who set her cap at another woman's husband and stole her off him, throwing her and her daughter out of their home without a penny to their name. And I expect I can think of a few other juicy things to tell them as well. So good for business that will be, won't it? That husband-stealer Artie is living with won't ever be able to hold her head up in public again after I've finished with her. I'll make sure of that, trust me.'

Rhonnie was horrified. 'But that's all lies,' she cried out.

Mavis sneered at her. 'You prove that. Once the story is printed there's no point in trying to retaliate . . . the damage is already done. No smoke without fire, eh? So, come on, open that safe and hand over the money. I want to get out of here just as much as you want to see the back of me.'

Rhonnie's thoughts were in upheaval. She knew Mavis of old and the woman wasn't bluffing. Rhonnie was just mortally glad that neither her father nor Drina was here at the moment to hear this. The awful woman had blighted their lives enough already. Mavis was right about one thing, though. A story like this headlining the local and national newspapers could cause irreparable damage to the good name of Jolly's, who promoted themselves as a family-oriented business.

Mavis had certainly put a lot of thought into her plan to fleece her husband again and at right this minute Rhonnie had no way of thwarting her. There was enough cash in the safe to put a stop to her despicable plan, but to hand over such a huge amount without putting up a fight was unthinkable. Rhonnie needed to come up with a plan and settle this business before her father and Drina came home.

She needed time to think, and to afford herself that she needed to lull Mavis into a false sense of security. Smiling sweetly she said, 'Okay, you've got us over a barrel. I've no choice but to give you the money.'

Mavis's face lit up with triumph. 'So what yer waiting for? I've a train to catch . . . ain't got time to dilly-dally,' the woman snapped

Rhonnie made a great show of looking astonished. 'You must realise that we don't keep amounts of money like that on the premises. It will take me a couple of days to get my hands on that sort of cash.'

Mavis's moment of triumph vanished. 'Oh!' She was visibly annoyed. 'Well, you'd better get cracking then. You've two days, no more, else I go to the papers with my story. And as I doubt you're gonna offer me a room in your place, I'll need money for a hotel and some to spend, a decent amount an' all, as I'll need a change of clothes and some toiletries as well.'

Rhonnie eyed her in disgust. She had said she needed money for a place to stay for herself but hadn't mentioned her thirteen-year-old daughter. 'Where is Tracy? Have you left her at home alone?' Rhonnie asked, worried.

Mavis scoffed, 'You was never bothered about my daughter when I was living with yer dad, so it's a bit late to start now.'

That was not true, Rhonnie inwardly fumed. The then nine year old had been a difficult child with her lying and cheating ways, taking very much after her mother in that respect, and had made it clear she only wanted Rhonnie to be sisterly towards her when there was some advantage to herself in it.

Mavis was enlightening her. 'Yer don't need to concern yerself with our Tracy, she's quite capable of teking care of herself.'

No, she isn't, she's only thirteen, Rhonnie wanted to shout at her, but then the Tracy she remembered took better care of herself than Mavis ever showed towards her child. Rhonnie leaned down under her desk to retrieve her handbag, out of which she took two £5 notes, which she handed over grudgingly, telling her stepmother, 'I'll be docking that from the five thousand.'

Mavis snatched the money and put it inside her handbag, saying ungraciously, 'I'm sure I won't miss a paltry ten quid considering what I'll be putting in my purse shortly.'

She got up and eyed Rhonnie meaningfully. 'I'll be back this time the day after tomorrow . . . and just remember what will happen if you fail to deliver.'

As soon as she'd left, slamming the door behind her, Jill arrived looking bothered. 'You all right, Rhonnie? Only that woman left looking none too pleased and I was worried about you as she . . . well . . . comes across as a bit of a character.'

Rhonnie leaned back in her seat and heaved a sigh, before

smiling wanly. 'That's putting it mildly, Jill. She's not a nice woman at all. Anyway I'm fine, thank you. This is just personal business that I'd sooner not have to deal with.' She picked up her handbag and got up. 'Can you manage for a while as I have to go out? Anything urgent will have to wait until I come back.' Despite the worry she had on her mind she managed to say lightly, 'If there's a fire, you know the drill.'

Jill smiled at her. 'I do. Take as long as you need.'

A while later Rhonnie was sitting in the back room of the police station in the small village of Threddlethorpe, nursing a cup of tea between her hands. Considering that Ginger and Paul had only moved in a few days ago, Ginger had made the place looked as homely as it would have had they been living here for years. 'You've got the place looking great,' she told her friend.

Ginger took a glance around. 'It's like stepping back into the nineteen-twenties in here, isn't it? When there's talk about modernising the force they don't even give a thought to the houses the men have to live in. Did you see the gas cooker in the kitchen? My old gran had one like that when I was a little girl. Paul and I don't care how old fashioned the house is though, it's a small price to pay for us to be back here.'

'Does it feel strange at the moment having Constable MacAvey waltzing in and out like he still lives here?'

'A bit. But I can't expect the bloke just to stay out front all the time when he's on his breaks or not dealing with police business. He's a bit of an old woman, set in his ways, but I get on with him all right and it's not for much longer.'

'Where is he now?' Rhonnie asked.

'Out on a call to see a woman in the next village about her lost dog. She reckons the neighbour took it as they're having a dispute over the number of chickens she's keeping. According to the neighbour she doesn't keep them that clean and they're

251

encouraging rats. He's holding the dog to ransom, she says, until she gets rid of the chickens. The neighbour is swearing that the woman is doolally and he hasn't touched the dog. It's his opinion it ran off to find someone that'll look after it better. I get to hear most of the police business back in here.' She chuckled. 'Far cry from the sort of crime that Paul had to deal with in Leeds . . . murders, bank robberies, that sort of thing. I'm starting to make friends with the locals. Me and Paul have been invited to the neighbours' house for dinner when he comes to join me here.'

'And you've been invited to dinner tonight with Jill and me if you fancy it? Her husband is on business in Scotland at the moment, and she thought it would be nice for us all to get together. I could pick you up on the way as she lives in Mablethorpe.'

Ginger looked delighted to be receiving the invitation. 'Yeah, sounds good. We'll stop at the offy on the way, get a bottle or two of nice wine.' She then looked across at her friend, one eyebrow raised. 'Anyway, why's a big business-woman like you calling on me in the middle of the day with a face on like it's a wet weekend? Not a social call, is it?'

Rhonnie heaved a sigh. 'No, it's not. I need your help, Ginger.'

'And you've got it, you know that without asking. Only if it's money you're after I'm a bit boracic at the moment, but I could stretch to ten bob if that's any good. But I can't imagine it's money you need my help with?'

'It is about money, Ginger, but ten bob isn't even a drop in the ocean against what she wants. My stepmother Mavis turned up out of the blue this morning, demanding five thousand pounds or she goes to the newspapers with a trumped-up story that Drina set her cap at my dad then stole her off Mavis, kicking her and her daughter out of the house to walk the streets without a penny to their name. You can imagine what the papers would make of this if they got hold of it,

252

considering how well known the two Jolly's camps are. Reporters are always on the lookout for a sensational story and wouldn't bother to check their facts before it was printed. It could cause Drina and the business a lot of damage, which they might never recover from. I can't just hand over that kind of money and especially not to someone who doesn't deserve a penny of it. I came to talk this over with you, see if between us we could come up with something to put a stop to Mavis's disgusting scheme . . . well, I've tried on my own but I can't think of anything so I'm hoping you can.'

Ginger was looking back at her incredulously. 'This is the woman who was playing around behind your dad's back, hurt him so much you feared he might do something stupid to himself? The woman who caused you to leave home?'

'The very same. I can't believe the gall of her, considering my father had already paid her a good amount, far more than she ever deserved, to get her and her daughter and her then fancy man out of his house so he could sell it to buy the cottage for himself and Drina to live in. And I doubt she'll stop here, Ginger. As soon as she's desperate again, she'll pop back up with another rotten scheme to squeeze money out of my father, and it will keep going on until she dies.'

Ginger frowned angrily. 'Then we need to put a stop to her once and for all,' she said with conviction.

Rhonnie looked at her helplessly. 'But how?'

Ginger shrugged. 'I dunno.' She paused thoughtfully for a moment then exclaimed, 'We need to turn the tables on her, tell her we've got something on her that we'll go to the papers with that would . . . oh, that's no good as the papers wouldn't be interested in her since she's not a prominent figure like Drina, just some bloody lowlife out to fleece people out of their hard-earned money . . . but the police . . . yes, that's it, we'll go to the police and have her put in jail for a long time.'

'Go to them with what, though?'

Ginger blew out her cheeks in exasperation. 'That's the

million-dollar question, Rhonnie, me old ducky. But a woman like Mavis, well, don't tell me she's not got a rail full of skeletons in her wardrobe. Finding just one will do us nicely. It's a case of asking the right people the right questions then putting what you learn from each of them together. Don't forget, I'm married to a copper and one thing I've learned is that most cases are solved by someone who knows the criminal letting something slip to the cops that they didn't mean to. The likes of Mavis have to have done something they'd sooner no one found out. Something like, she was already married when she married your dad . . . that's the sort of thing I mean, Rhonnie. If I can help catch a wily drug dealer carrying on his despicable business at Jolly's the summer before last, then getting someone to dish the dirt on that nasty piece of work your dad had the misfortune to marry will be a piece of cake.'

Despite the severity of the situation Rhonnie couldn't help but laugh. 'You sound like Detective Harry Hawkins in the new television show *Softly, Softly.*'

Ginger looked at her keenly. 'Oh, I haven't seen that yet. Been too busy to watch television recently. Cops and robbers programmes are my favourite. Is it good? Mind you, my Paul says that if the police really went around trying to collar criminals like they do on these shows then the jails would be empty as that's not how real policing works. Anyway, this is getting away from coming up with a way to deal with your problem.' She paused thoughtfully before she asked Rhonnie, 'How long have we got before the deadline for handing over this money to that miserable excuse for a woman?'

'She didn't like it at all, but I managed to fob her off for a couple of days. She's coming back at twelve the day after next.'

'Then let's hope it's long enough. That dinner with Jill tonight will have to be postponed for me at least as I think a visit back to our home town of good old Leicester is called for. I ain't seen me mam for over two years now so it's about

254

time I did. Mind you, whether she remembers who I am is another matter. "Out of sight, out of mind" just about sums up my mother. I can stay with my sister, be nice to see her and her kids. Her husband is a bit of a waster but I get on with him well enough. Anyway I'll do a bit of sleuthing and see if I can rattle Mavis's skeleton enough to give us something to blackmail her back with.'

Rhonnie's eyes lit up with hope. 'If anyone could dig up the dirt on someone it's you.'

Ginger looked at her sharply and said, 'I'm not sure whether that's a compliment or not.'

'It was a compliment,' Rhonnie assured her friend. 'You're really good with people and if anyone can get them talking it's you. I should come with you . . .'

Ginger cut in, 'Well, you can't, can you? You've a holiday camp to run. Anyway, one woman enquiring after an old friend is just that, isn't it? Two could look suspicious, especially to the type of people I guess the likes of Mavis rubs shoulders with.'

Rhonnie looked gratefully at her. 'I really appreciate you doing this, Ginger. I'll keep everything crossed that you find out something, for my dad's and Drina's sakes. Where will you start? I don't even know where she's living at the moment.'

'I bet if I went into any corner pub around where she used to live with your dad, someone in there will know where she's living now. Anyway I don't really need to know where she lives, I just need to find people who knew her in the past and are willing to divulge anything she might have done back then that we can use against her.'

'Sounds easy,' mused Rhonnie. 'Let's hope it proves to be.'

Ginger downed the rest of her tea, uncurled her legs from under her and stood up. 'Right, let's get this show on the road. I'll go and throw a few clothes in a bag and leave a note telling Constable MacAvey that I've gone to visit me mother for a couple of days, then you can run me to the station. If

I time the trains right I'll be in Leicester early this evening. I'll just need you to give me the address of yer dad's old house where you all lived together and I'll make my start looking for gossipy chums of hers around there.'

Later than evening, after making her excuses to Jill and saying she must have an early night, Rhonnie arrived back in her cottage to the sound of the telephone ringing. Dashing over to it, she snatched up the receiver and spoke urgently. 'Is that you, Ginger? Have you any news?'

But all she heard back was the beeping sound of a telephone call box before Ginger's voice asked, 'Rhonnie, you there?'

'Yes, it's me. Have you any news?'

Ginger snapped back, 'Oh, for crying out loud, Rhonnie, give me a chance, I've only just got here. Well, about an hour ago. I settled meself at me sister's first before I came to the phone box to check in with you, in case you was worried I'd survived the journey.'

Rhonnie heaved a sigh. 'Oh, I'm sorry, Ginger, it's just that I'm so on edge.'

'Yeah, well, it's understandable. I'll call you tomorrow night with an update of how I've got on.' More beeps sounded down the line. 'Oh, that's all me change . . .'

Rhonnie didn't get to hear any more as the call cut off.

As she put the receiver back in its holder she heaved a sigh. All she could do now was pray that Ginger's gift of the gab reaped the results they needed to send Mavis packing empty-handed and if possible never to return again.

CHAPTER TWENTY-TWO

As she stood outside the Golden Hind public house, a red-brick building situated on the corner of a street of terraced houses in a rundown area on the outskirts of Leicester, Ginger scraped a hand through her mop of bright curls and took a deep breath. It seemed that every other street in this area had at least two pubs on it and she had visited so many since yesterday that they were all beginning to look the same. Although in many of them the regulars all knew of Mavis, no one would admit to knowing her well enough to chat about her to an old 'friend' searching to reacquaint herself after living away from the city for several years. Hopefully Ginger would fare better here.

Time was beginning to run out. Tomorrow afternoon the woman would be paying Rhonnie a visit in the office and if Ginger couldn't uncover any of Mavis's past misdeeds then she would be returning to Leicester far richer than she had left it and at liberty to resurrect her blackmail at any time in the future. Artie and Drina might never be free of her.

Twenty minutes later Ginger came out of the pub with nothing to show for it apart from a lighter purse. Three pubs later she still had not found one person who would admit to knowing Mavis before she had married Rhonnie's father, and as it was now approaching ten-thirty Ginger was seriously doubting that she was going to and would be returning home tomorrow, the whole trip a wasted one. Just time to pop into one more pub before she had finally to concede defeat.

During her trawl of the pubs, some of the interiors had been modernised and were bright and welcoming but some were decidedly seedy and the Merry Monk was definitely in the latter group. As she pushed open one of the two peeling entrance doors and walked inside, Ginger felt like she'd stepped back into the nineteen-thirties, to a time when land-lords still scattered sawdust on the floor to soak up spills. Metal spittoons were still placed strategically around and the beer pumps were the old-fashioned pull type. The air was thick with smoke from pipes and roll ups. Shifty-looking men sat huddled together in the darkened recess at the back of the room, no doubt planning their next robberies and, filling the seats at tables by the wide bay window, were an assortment of hard-faced, tartily dressed middle-aged and elderly women, their menfolk all lining the bar and the majority all acting the worse for drink. It was the women Ginger was interested in. She had never met Mavis personally but from Rhonnie's description of her, these were the sort she would definitely mix with.

In her effort to act like an old friend of Mavis's, Ginger laughed off the sexual innuendo of the men lolling at the bar while she waited for her drink to be served to her by a slovenly-looking barmaid, probably the wife of the brute of a landlord. He was standing knocking back a pint of beer by the counter flap, raucously laughing at a joke a customer was telling him. Armed with her glass of lemonade Ginger went over to the tables the women were sitting around and addressing the one nearest to her, said, 'Excuse me, but I'm looking for anyone who might know Mavis Fleming.'

A woman on the other side of the table erupted: 'Don't you dare mention that thieving cow's name to me! She borrowed two quid off me four weeks ago, told me some cock and bull about the tally man threatening to send the heavies in if she didn't pay off at least some of her arrears, and out of the goodness of me heart I lent it to her 'cos she promised faithfully she'd pay me back at the end of the week once that useless sod she's shacking up with gets paid for a job he's done . . . but did she hell as like. Still had the brass neck to come in here every night drinking and have a skinful.'

The woman next to her scoffed, 'More fool you, Glenda, for falling for one of her sob stories. She borrowed ten bob off me two years ago and I'm still waiting to get it back and all I get is promises that next week she will. Next week never comes in her case.'

Another woman piped up, 'She owes me a pound an' all, I lent her it a couple of months ago.'

'And me five bob,' said another.

The woman Ginger had first addressed spoke up again. 'She's always bin the same from the moment I met her on our first day at school. Always trying to cadge something or other off me and her classmates, and like prats we all ended up giving her what she was after and never, ever got it back. That first poor sod she married who's the father of her daughter ended up disappearing one night, never to be seen around here again thanks to the debt she landed him in – and she was carrying on behind his back with any Tom, Dick or Harry that'd take her on. But it was the second poor sod she married that I feel most sorry for. Nice man was Artie Fleming, too nice for Mavis that's for sure. Don't know what happened to him. I just know that he arrived back from work unexpected one night and found her in the pub, draped all over another bloke, and no one's seen him since. I heard he'd hung himself, he took what she'd done to him so badly.' She paused for a moment and frowned thoughtfully. 'Come to think on it, I ain't seen Mavis in here for a night or so. She'd have to be knocking on death's door to miss a night at the pub. Do you think she's kicked the bucket and news ain't got around yet?'

The blowsy-looking woman opposite her sneered, 'Nah, she's more than likely found another pub as her local now that there's no one left in here for her to borrow money off.' She then looked up quizzically at Ginger. 'Why are you asking after Mavis anyway? You look a nice gel to me, not the sort that'd be seen dead with the likes of her.'

Ginger realised that these women wouldn't be looking on her favourably if she told them she was an old friend of Mavis's. 'Er . . . she owes me mother money and I was sent to try and get it off her.'

All the women almost choked on their drinks. One of them spluttered, 'You'd have more luck gettin' blood out of a stone, ducky. Anyway, if she has any money to be paying back debts there's a whole queue in front of you first.'

'Oh, well, I'd better tell my mam that the best thing she can do is put it down to experience and not to fall for a sob story from that woman again.' Ginger inwardly sighed. Owing money to a load of different women wasn't a police matter. Judging from what they had said, Mavis more than likely had no close friends. It was a long shot but maybe the neighbours where she lived might know more about her, as she could have found a kindred spirit amongst them and talked about her past . . . got drunk one night and said more than she meant to. 'Er . . . I might pop a note through her door and warn her to keep away from my mam in future or she'll have me to deal with.'

All the women laughed at that and one spluttered, 'Tek more than an army of you to frighten Mavis Fleming. Got skin on her as thick as cowhide. But if it meks you feel better, she lives on Wheat Street. Look for the house with the muck-iest step and yellowest nets and you've arrived.'

Ginger nodded a thank-you to her, then downed her drink and placed the glass on the table nearest her and said to all the women around the tables, 'Nice to have met you.'

Outside in the street she decided that no neighbours of

Mavis's would appreciate her knocking on their doors at this time of night, so she would come back first thing tomorrow morning. Rhonnie had told her that Mavis was coming to the office at twelve o'clock tomorrow so she had until then to put a telephone call through to her with anything she managed to discover in the morning. Ginger just prayed that she got lucky then as things didn't look promising.

At just after nine the next morning Ginger stood at the top of Wheat Street by the corner shop and looked the length of it. Leicester City Council had made huge strides forward over the last couple of decades in ridding the town of its slum housing but this street and several surrounding it seemed to have been forgotten about. The houses were the two up, two down, flat-front type built over a hundred and fifty years ago to accommodate incoming workers in the boot and shoe industry, and as Ginger looked down the street now the crumbling properties looked like a pack of cards ready to collapse. To be living here meant that Mavis could not have fared at all well since she had brought about the ending of her marriage to Artie. He hadn't lived in the best of areas but it was a damned sight better than around here. The women had told Ginger to look for the dirtiest step and nets to tell her where Mavis lived, but the nets at all the windows were grubby and yellowing with age and nicotine and all the steps had discarded rubbish piled around them and an abundance of weeds growing in cracks. The only way to find out which one Mavis lived in was to knock on doors and ask outright. Ginger was just about to begin when a thought struck her. Stupid me, she thought. The owner of the corner shop would know.

The windows of the shop didn't look like they had been cleaned for years and the display inside showed some products Ginger knew were no longer available. The prices on the likes of a tin of Ajax or a packet of Weetabix were grossly out of date. It was dark and dingy inside the shop and a smell of

261

must and decay lingered in the air. Ginger felt that she would have to be in dire need to buy anything in here.

The shop was deserted and as she arrived at the counter and made to knock on it to attract the owner's attention, she jumped in shock to see a shrivelled old lady sitting on a chair behind it busily knitting.

On the arrival of a customer the old lady struggled out of her seat, beaming a welcome and exposing badly fitting false teeth. 'Morning, ducky. What can I get yer?'

Before she began to quiz the old dear, Ginger felt obliged to buy something. She scanned her eyes over the shelves at the back. 'Er . . . tin of peas, please.'

'Garden or processed?'

'Oh, er . . . garden will be fine, thank you.'

The old lady shuffled around and picked a tin off the shelf, which she placed on the counter before Ginger. The lid of it was full of dust. 'Anything else, lovey?'

Ginger scanned her eyes over the shelves again. 'Er . . . packet of plasters.'

'Waterproof or fabric?'

'Fabric, please.'

As the old lady shuffled off to oblige, she said, 'I ain't seen you around here before. Just visiting or moving in?'

'Just visiting. Actually I'm looking for an old friend. I know she lives in this street but I'm not sure which house.'

'Oh, well, yer've come to the right place to enquire as I knows where everyone lives around here.' She chuckled and leaned forward to wink at Ginger. 'Could tell you a thing or two about most of 'em an' all what'd mek yer hair curl, so I could. What's yer friend's name?'

'Mavis Fleming.'

The old lady scowled. 'You're a friend of the likes of 'er!' Her whole attitude changed, gone was friendliness to be replaced by hostility. 'That'll be one and thruppence,' she snapped, holding out a gnarled hand.

Mavis had obviously upset the old shopkeeper very badly. Ginger remembered the story she had used last night. As she fumbled in her bag for her purse she said, 'When I said a "friend" of Mavis's, I wasn't being exactly truthful. She owes money to my mam and I've come to try and get it back from her as she isn't giving it voluntarily.'

The old woman's attitude immediately softened. 'Get in the queue, love. She owes most of the folks around here and she ain't paid anything off her tab with me for weeks now yet still has the gall to send her daughter in most nights, asking me to add what she wants to it, promising faithfully she'll be settling up at the end of the week, though she never does. Well, as I told that idle little so and so of a daughter of hers last night when she came in asking for some bread and cheese to put on her mam's tab, show me yer money and you can have it. If not, sling yer hook, I don't run a charity.' The woman took Ginger's money, and rang up the sale. She then said, 'Come to think on it, I ain't seen Mavis around this past day or so and it wouldn't surprise me if she ain't come into some money and scarpered off on holiday, leaving her daughter to fend for herself. She's that sort of woman if you know what I mean.

'I do know that the bloke she had living with her . . . and a right lowlife he was . . . well, they had a big bust up last week and he's not been seen around these parts since. Betty Shrivens, Mavis's neighbour, told me she heard an almighty row coming through the walls just before she saw him leave with his suitcase. Anyway, I personally think yer wasting yer time trying to get yer mam's money back, but if you want to pursue it then you could always go and ask the daughter when her mother's due back, save you coming back and forth until she does.' She pulled a face. 'That gel is turning out to be as bad as her mother, nasty piece of work she is, got a mouth on her worse than a fishwife. Lost count of the times I've caught her trying to rob from me shop. She'll be at home as she ain't at school. She hardly goes when her mother's there so she ain't going to get herself up and off when her mam's not after her to. The board man is never off their doorstep.'

'Er . . . do you know if Mavis is pally with any of the women in particular around here?'

The old lady looked at Ginger as though she was stupid. 'That sort don't mek friends, lovey. You've only got to be in the company of a woman like her for a few minutes to see that she's sizing you up to see what you're worth to her. Best give her a wide berth, if you've got a morsel of intelligence that is. Number fifty-nine, ducky.'

Ginger put her change and purchases in her bag, thanked her and left.

Outside the shop, she looked at her wristwatch. It was a quarter to ten. Would it be worth her talking to Mavis's daughter? Could she know something about her mother that Mavis wouldn't want becoming common knowledge? Children were always listening behind doors, hearing things adults didn't realise they had. From what Rhonnie had told her about her stepsister and what that old lady had just said, Tracy sounded the type to eavesdrop on adult conversations and store away anything of value she could use at a later date. But how did she get the girl to spill any damaging information? Ginger stood and mulled over the situation. Mavis hadn't expected to be staying over in Mablethorpe for any length of time, just to make her demand, be handed her illicit gains, then on her way back to Leicester. Believing she would only be away for hours, not days, had she left provisions for her daughter? The shop owner had told Ginger that the girl had visited the shop only last night for bread and cheese, requesting they be put on her mother's tab, so obviously she'd run short. The girl must be starving by now.

Ginger went back into the shop, buying bread . . . and it was yesterday's by the feel of it . . . plus a tin of Fray Bentos corned beef and a half pound of best butter, a couple of bags of Walker's crisps, a packet of custard creams, a bar of Cadbury's milk chocolate and a bottle of White's lemonade . . . the sort of food all youngsters preferred to eat and that might help loosen the tongue of a famished young girl.

She knocked purposefully on the door of number fifty-nine. There was no response so she knocked again. After waiting a couple of minutes still with no response, she made her way back to the end of the street, turned the corner and walked a little way along to the jitty that accessed the back of the houses. The rotting gate that led into the little cobbled yard of number fifty-nine was barely hanging on its rusting hinges. She went into the yard and had to step over and around a jumble of discarded items including a rusting mangle minus its rollers, the remains of a rotting tin bath, pots of long-hardened paint, old tyres, plus a pile of crumbling bricks that had fallen off the dividing wall with the yard next door. The curtains at the window were pulled across but not tightly. A gap of about an inch or so in the middle allowed her a partial view of the room beyond. In front of the old-fashioned black-leaded fireplace Ginger could see a sofa and over the arm of it hung a pair of feet. It seemed Tracy had slept on the sofa last night – was still sleeping on it, in fact.

Ginger went over to the door and hammered on it, then peeped back through the gap in the curtains to see if Tracy was responding. The feet were in the same position. She hammered again on the door, this time for longer. When she peeped back through the window she was gratified to see a girl sitting upright on the sofa, rubbing her eyes. In case she thought she had dreamed she'd heard something, Ginger hammered on the door again. A moment later she heard a key turning in the lock and the door flew open. Tracy stood there wearing a crumpled skirt and jumper, obviously the clothes she had been wearing yesterday that she hadn't both-ered to take off last night. Her long hair was a bird's nest around her head. If she hadn't had such a sullen look on her face but a smile instead, Ginger would have thought her pretty.

When she had opened the door the girl's eyes held a look of hope in them, but that faded to dullness when she saw her caller wasn't who she was waiting to see. 'Oh, I thought you was me mam. Anyway, wadda yer want? If yer after me mam she ain't in and don't bother asking me where the bloody hell she is as she told me she was only gonna be gone a few hours and that was nearly two days ago.'

Ginger smiled a greeting at her. 'My name is Anita . . . well, everyone calls me Ginger for obvious reasons. It's your mother who sent me. She's been detained where she is, won't be back until later this evening, and was worried about you so sent me around to see if you're okay. Your mother is an old friend of my mam's, you see.'

Tracy was looking at her incredulously. 'Me mam bothered about me! That's one for the books. And I didn't think she had any friends. Full of surprises is me mother. Anyway, as you can see, I'm fine.'

She made to shut the door but Ginger stalled her by saying, 'I've brought food.'

The girl's face lit up. 'Chocolate and salt and vinegar crisps?'

'I've chocolate but the crisps are plain.'

She pulled a face. 'Oh, well, better than nothing, I s'pose. Yer'd better come in.'

Mavis was no housekeeper and neither was her daughter. The old pot sink was filled with dirty dishes, and used pans jostled for space on top of the gas stove. The back room was no better. The table was littered with the remains of a meal from when Mavis herself had been here as there were two dirty plates along with bottles of tomato and brown sauce, the tops of the bottles caked in a thick gunge where the sauce had not been wiped off, salt and pepper in their original shop-bought containers, used cups and a near-empty milk bottle whose remains were turning rancid. A pile of ash surrounded an overflowing ashtray. On the floor by a threadbare sofa was a plate with dried up crusts of toasted bread on it and an empty used cracked mug, obviously Tracy's last meal, whenever that had been. The rest of the room was furnished with an assortment of ill-matched shabby furniture and on every available surface, looking like they'd just been thrown there, were items Ginger would class as junk. The whole room smelled of damp, general decay, stale food and cigarette smoke.

Acting as if every house she walked into was as squalid as this one, Ginger said breezily, 'If you clear a space at the table I'll make you a sandwich. I hope you like corned beef.'

As Tracy threw herself back on the sofa, pulling an old blanket over herself, she told Ginger, 'There's plenty of room on the table if yer move the other pots aside. I like ham better but corned beef will do.'

Ungrateful little madam. And lazy too, not even offering to help her saviour prepare the food or even offer her a cup of tea, Ginger thought to herself. Regardless, if she wanted to gain this girl's trust then she needed to ingratiate herself to her. As she spread butter on a slice of bread, to start making inroads with Tracy, now idly thumbing through a popular teen magazine, Ginger said, 'Me and you have a lot in common.'

Tracy looked up from her magazine to shoot her a look. 'I don't know how. You look ancient to me, so we can't have.'

Ginger laughed. 'Ancient? I'm only in my early twenties. I didn't mean our ages. I meant that when I was young, I hated school too.' A lie as Ginger quite enjoyed learning and had got on well with her schoolmates and teachers alike.

Tracy looked at her, taken aback. 'How do you know I do?'

'Well, if you did you'd be there now, wouldn't you? Whether your mother was here or not.'

'Mam sez I'm old enough to mek up me own mind what I do. She sez what yer learn in school don't do n'ote to help yer survive in the big wide world anyway.'

Children like Tracy with mothers like Mavis had no hope of ever reaching their potential and Tracy would more than likely end up in a dead-end job, probably getting pregnant by the first man who looked at her, and end up in a slum like this with a dozen kids hanging on her skirts, old before her age, Ginger thought sadly. Still, the girl must be won over. 'Well, it is said that you don't learn about proper life until you're thrust on your own into the big wide world. We've another thing in common too, though. Our mothers were close friends when they were young women.'

Tracy had gone back to glancing through the magazine. 'I didn't know me mam had any friends,' she said in a bored-sounding voice.

Ginger was fiddling with the tin of corned beef, trying to get the small opening key to fit onto the protruding piece of metal in order to open it. 'Well, she certainly had one in my mother. Thick as thieves they were according to my mam. They met at work and used to pal around together, going dancing, that sort of thing. And got up to no good a few times but thankfully managed to get away with it! Oh, that's caught it,' she said as she finally managed to fit in the key and began twisting it around to open the tin, careful to avoid cutting herself on the razor-sharp edges. 'Has . . . er . . . your mam told you about all the trouble her and my mam got up to together? My mam often jokes that she's worried one day her past will catch up with her and she'll be made to pay the price.'

'Nah. Mam never really talks to me like that. Anyway, it's not the past catching up with her she's bothered about at the moment but the heap of trouble she'll be in now if she don't manage to get it sorted in time.'

Ginger looked over at her sharply. Her heart began to thump in anticipation. So that was why Mavis needed money. She was in trouble – and a lot of it, if she needed five thousand pounds to make it go away. Ginger had to find out just what this trouble was and vehemently hoped it was the sort that could be used against Mavis in some way. She wanted to demand that Tracy tell her but knew that if she pushed the girl on the subject, seemed too interested in it, then she could become suspicious. Fighting to keep her patience, Ginger finished preparing the sandwich and then took the plate, along with a packet of crisps and drink of pop, over to Tracy. 'There you are. I hope you enjoy it,' she said, handing it over.

The girl snatched the food off her and began tucking in like she hadn't eaten for weeks. Through a mouthful she said, 'Yer make a good sandwich. Could you do me another? I'm that hungry I could eat a scabby cat.'

'Be delighted to,' Ginger said as she went back to the table. She waited a moment before she ventured: 'Er . . . this trouble your mam's in. Anything I can do to help? Only I know for old times' sake my mam would want me to offer.'

Tracy finished gulping back some of the lemonade before she responded. 'Not unless you've a couple of grand going spare.'

Ginger stared at her thoughtfully. So Mavis had got herself in debt to the tune of two thousand pounds! What on earth had she been buying to amount to that much? Nothing by way of making improvements to the inside of this house, that was evident. And she was actually demanding five thousand from Rhonnie, so the dreadful woman was not only using blackmail in order to clear her debt but also pocketing a substantial amount to fund her in the future. Considering the sum involved, Mavis could only owe this money to unscrupulous sorts, like loan sharks, and was being threatened by them to pay it back or suffer their form of retaliation. But even if that was the case, it wasn't clear how it could help Rhonnie. Regardless, Ginger needed to find out the story behind the debt. She took a glance at her wristwatch. It was coming up for half-past eleven. Time was rapidly running out.

Pretending to be shocked, she exclaimed, 'Oh, my God! If

your mother's after that sort of money then she certainly is in a pile of trouble.' She put on a worried look. 'How on earth did she get herself into debt like that? Oh, well, of course, she wouldn't tell you something like that . . . wouldn't want to worry you about it, would she? I expect you don't know.'

A malicious glint sparked in the young girl's eyes as she smugly told Ginger, 'Oh, I know all right. Every bloody detail of how me mam got herself into the pickle she's in. I heard her arguing with Harry about it before she threw him out last week. She didn't know I'd come home and was listening behind the door.'

Forgetting about the other sandwich, Ginger picked up the bar of chocolate and went over to the sofa where she sat down beside Tracy. Handing her the chocolate bar, which Tracy grabbed off her and began tearing into, she said in a coaxing manner, 'Just what was it you heard, love?'

Meanwhile in Jolly's Holiday Camp Rhonnie was pacing back and forth behind her desk, stopping every few moments or so to look worriedly at her watch. She had tossed and turned all night and what sleep she had managed had been fitful. From the moment she'd woken this morning tension had been building inside her. There was so much at stake – this might be her last chance to free her father from his money-grabbing wife. But it was now three minutes to twelve and Ginger knew that Mavis would arrive promptly, expecting to receive her blackmail money. In fact Rhonnie had already been informed that she was down in reception now, demanding to be shown straight up and not at all happy about being kept waiting. As Ginger hadn't made contact by now, it didn't look like her trip had paid off.

Rhonnie stopped her pacing and looked at her watch again. It was a minute to twelve. She heaved a forlorn sigh. Last-minute miracles only happened in stories so it was best she got this over with. She was not at all a violent woman but in these circumstances she knew it was going to take all her willpower not to launch herself at Mavis and beat the smug smile off her face when she laid hands on her ill-gotten gains.

She had just reached out to pick up the telephone receiver when she jumped back in shock as it shrilled out. Knowing it would be reception asking her what to do because Mavis was causing a scene, Rhonnie picked up and reluctantly said into it, 'You can send Mrs Fleming up now, please.'

But it wasn't reception and what the voice at the other end told her had Rhonnie listening intently.

It was several minutes later when she flicked the button to clear the line, then dialled down to reception, asking them to send Mavis up.

Not long afterwards the woman stomped angrily into the office. As soon as Jill had shut the door behind her, she snarled angrily at Rhonnie, 'I've been holed up in this godforsaken place for nearly two days, waiting for you to get my money, and then you have the nerve to keep me waiting like I was just another of the common rabble that come on holiday here. As Artie's wife, I should be treated with the respect I deserve and you make sure that happens next time.' At the desk now, she flapped her hand impatiently at Rhonnie and demanded, 'Right, I've waited long enough, give it to me.'

From her calm and controlled persona, Mavis would never have guessed the turmoil Rhonnie was in fact feeling. She had no idea how her stepmother was going to react to this. She politely asked, 'Would you like a drink, Mavis?'

The other woman looked at her as though she was stupid. 'No, I don't want a fucking drink. I just told yer, I want me money. I need to get back to Leicester as I've urgent business to see too. Now stop shilly-shallying and hand it over.'

Rhonnie took a deep breath before informing her, 'I'm not prepared to give you five thousand, Mavis. The two you need is my limit – but only if you sign a statement saying you're in agreement to my dad divorcing you on the grounds of your infidelity.'

Mavis gawped at her incredulously. 'You what! I ain't never going to divorce yer dad, not while it pays me not to.' Then she screwed up her face. 'And just what did you mean, you'll only give me the two grand I need?'

'Well, that's all you really do need to get you out of the trouble you're in, Mavis, isn't it? The other three is for you to live the high life on.'

She eyed Rhonnie darkly. 'I ain't in no trouble. All that money is to support me and my daughter, like your dad promised to do when he married me.'

Rhonnie pursed her lips. 'Oh, so when Derek Potter gets out of prison tomorrow early for good behaviour, after a three-year sentence for his part in a robbery, and comes to collect his share of the proceeds that he paid you to take care of for him while he was inside, and finds two grand missing because you've not managed to replace what you and Harry "borrowed" between you, you won't be in any trouble then?' Rhonnie laughed sardonically. 'From what I've learned about the nasty sort he is, I wouldn't have thought it likely he'll take what you've done lightly. I think you'll be lucky to escape his form of payback without a lengthy hospital stay and then you'll be lucky ever to get another bloke to look at you again. They don't go for women with scars, do they? A bit of advice, Mavis. In future you need to be careful who you tangle your-self up with.'

She leaned back in her chair and looked at the older woman scornfully. 'Must have been a real shock to hear Potter was getting out early and you had only days to replace the money you'd helped yourself to . . . and not only you, Harry as well, the two of you helping yourself to a pound here, ten bob there. Over a couple of years it added up to . . . well, in this case, two thousand pounds. So that's when you came up with your despicable plan to fleece Drina.' She leaned forward and fixed Mavis with stony eyes. 'Well, I'll tell you something for nothing. If Drina had been here and it was her you were dealing with, she'd tell you to go to hell and do your worst, she doesn't care what people think of her . . . so be thankful it's me you're dealing with and I *do* care what people think of Drina and my dad. That's why I'm willing to do a deal with you, but only on the terms I've already told you. There is no room for manoeuvre. Either accept the two thousand and confirm you're willing for my dad to divorce you or leave here empty-handed. What you do then is up to you, but if you do go to the newspapers they'll not pay you anything near two thousand for your trumped-up story and time is running out for you fast. Derek Potter will come straight to you from prison, won't he?'

Mavis was staring dumbfounded as she considered all that Rhonnie had told her. From Rhonnie's own experience of dealing with Mavis in the past, when the woman wasn't getting her own way and had no choice but to concede defeat, that's when her temper would ignite. In a matter of seconds there would be an outburst of volcanic rage and quite possibly violence too. Rhonnie had been on the receiving end of that before and was not prepared to be victimised again. She warned, 'Don't even think about it, Mavis. I am not that young girl any longer, reluctant to upset my dad by telling him how you were really treating him and me behind his back. One scream from me will have my staff running in here and in another minute the security guards will be called and you will be being carted off to the local police station, to be charged with assault.'

If looks could kill the one that Mavis shot her then would have seen Rhonnie drop stone dead. For several long moments Mavis continued glaring murderously at her then suddenly it seemed to Rhonnie that her stepmother was shrinking before her eyes, like a tyre slowly deflating from a puncture, as it finally registered on her that she had been outmanoeuvred and it was now a case of accepting Rhonnie's offer or suffering the consequences. As she sank down on the chair in front of the desk, the smug look of superiority Mavis had worn when she arrived in the office had been replaced by one of defeat.

She demanded, 'How did you find out all this? No one else knew I was keeping that money for Derek, 'cept of course Harry. When he found it he thought it was mine and I was holding out on him. But it couldn't have been him as he scarpered quick sharp from Leicester when I told him what Derek would do to him for nicking his money. So who was it, eh? I deserve to know who's bin spying on me and grassed me up to you. One thing is for certain, they'll deeply regret crossing me by the time I've finished with 'em.'

Rhonnie declined to tell her. Mavis would discover soon enough that it was her daughter and Rhonnie wouldn't like to be in Tracy's shoes when she did. But then, Tracy was wily and a practised liar. There was every chance she'd realise the seriousness of what she had done and lie her way out of trouble. Then Mavis would forever be in the dark over the matter.

Rhonnie took a piece of paper out of the top drawer of her desk and pushed it and a Biro across the desk to Mavis. 'Head your letter "To Whom It May Concern", and when you've finished I'll get the two ladies outside to come in and witness your signature. As soon as it's signed and witnessed and in the safe, you'll get the money.'

The woman didn't even blush when she asked Rhonnie, 'Could you make it a couple of pounds more than two thousand as I've not got my fare home?'

As a very subdued Mavis left the office a short while later, Rhonnie let out a huge sigh of relief. That was one person she was glad to see the back of. No need ever to see her again but more importantly, Rhonnie's father was now free. She couldn't wait to see the looks on his and Drina's faces when she told them.

Drina was to learn of this incredible news a couple of hours later when she arrived in the office hand in hand with Danny, who was toddling beside her. As soon as she saw who her unexpected visitors were, Rhonnie let out a whoop of delight, jumped up from her chair and dashed over to her son, to swoop him up in her arms and hug him to her tightly. 'Oh, I missed you so much, my little man. Have you been good for Branny and Branpap?'

Drina told her, 'Like I said every day I telephoned you, he's been as good as gold.'

Rhonnie put her son down and he immediately went off to play with the box of toys his mother kept in the office for him. Rhonnie laughed. 'Jill told me the other day that no matter how badly she behaved for her gran when she was little, her gran always told her mother the same as you just did me.'

Drina smiled. 'Well then, Jill's grandmother is a woman after my own heart. I just popped in to let you know we were back. I knew you'd be desperate to see Danny but I'll take him back now and you can come and pick him up after you've finished work. I've left Artie unpacking and if I know him he'll try and help as much as he can . . . I fear he'll put some washing on and mix whites with colours and we'll both end up with dingy grey underwear.'

Rhonnie grabbed her arm. She was bursting to tell Drina her news, and grey underwear or not it just couldn't wait. 'Have you a minute for a chat?'

Drina frowned at her. 'Oh, has something happened while we were away?'

Rhonnie fought to contain her excitement. 'Yes, something did. Sit down, Drina,' she told her. 'I just have to fetch something and I'll get you a whisky while I'm at it as I think you're going to need it.'

Moments later she was sitting beside Drina on the sofa. After first checking that her son was still happily playing with the box of toys, Rhonnie said, 'What is your dearest wish, Drina?'

She took a sip of her drink while frowning quizzically. 'You know very well what that is, Rhonnie dear, and we both know it will never be granted, so why are you asking?'

'Well, you're wrong, because it has been granted!' Rhonnie was holding out an envelope.

Looking confused, Drina put down her drink on the coffee table and took the envelope off Rhonnie. She took out the folded piece of paper and read the words written on it. She had to read them over twice more before what was said hit home. Looking at Rhonnie, utterly mystified, she said: 'This is no joke, Rhonnie?'

She smiled. 'Would I make a joke out of what I know is the most important thing in the world to you? Mavis paid a visit here. Obviously she wanted to see Dad but as he wasn't here she agreed to speak to me. She wants to get married again and to do that she needs a divorce. That's her letter of authorisation for Dad to go ahead.'

Drina was staring at the letter dumbfounded, like she expected it to disintegrate between her fingers.

Rhonnie reassured her, 'It's real, Drina.'

Drina lifted her head and asked, 'Mavis came to you voluntarily, didn't demand an extortionate amount of money in return for giving your dad a divorce?'

'No, she didn't demand anything,' Rhonnie lied.

Drina shook her head, mystified. 'I don't understand it. Has she had a brainstorm, do you reckon?'

'She seemed fine to me,' Rhonnie lied again.

'Well . . . wonders will never cease. But isn't this just wonderful? Me and your dad can finally get married and what a day to remember that will be!'

Drina started to cry then and Rhonnie joined her. After a while Drina pulled a handkerchief out of her cardigan pocket, wiped her eyes then jumped up, declaring, 'I need to go and tell your dad. If you hear shouting, it'll only be him yelling for joy that he's got rid of that woman once and for all.'

In her rush to tell Artie she hurried out, completely forgetting to take her grandson with her. Rhonnie didn't mind a bit, though, and said to her son, still playing happily with a set of Dinky cars, 'How do you fancy helping me look over the accounts then?'

Ginger was given a hero's welcome by Rhonnie when she greeted her at the train station at just after six-thirty that evening. Ginger wanted no praise or recompense in any way for what she had done as she was only too glad that her trip back to Leicester had proved so successful. But after they had discussed everything Ginger had found out, she and Rhonnie made a pact that it need never be spoken of again, for fear that Drina and Artie should find out the truth of just how Mavis's agreement to divorce Artie was actually obtained.

CHAPTER TWENTY-THREE

B en swung the axe down on a log, then brought it down again on the offcut to split it in two, before adding the wood to a pile he'd cut previously. He wiped sweat from his brow and looked up through a gap in the leafy canopy to see the position of the sun in the sky so he could judge the time, something he'd had to learn to do several years ago when out of desperation for money he'd been forced to pawn his watch.

It was around five and very possibly a long night stretched ahead of him. If he wanted to eat before settling down for his vigil watching the caravan site manager, then he'd better finish up here for today and get back to his hut. He had enough logs now to fuel the stove for several days anyway. His meal tonight was a bowl of the thick vegetable soup he'd made yesterday that just needed heating up. He meant to be at his observation place in the woods just as twilight was falling that Wednesday evening, which was usually about eight o'clock at this time of year.

Unfortunately Ben timed his arrival in the woods behind the fence just as the manager's car was pulling out of its parking place beside the caravan so Ben did not see him remove anything from his hiding place. He watched it drive off, annoyed with himself for missing the man's departure yet again. Now there was nothing for it but to await his return.

As he settled himself down to whittle yet another clothes peg to add to his collection something struck Ben and he stopped what he was doing to stare thoughtfully over to the space where the car had stood before it had driven off. Something about the car had been different. But what? There was nothing tangible he could pinpoint . . . it was the same colour, no new dents or broken wing mirror or suchlike . . . yet something was different about the car since he'd seen it last time.

Over the next few hours, despite the various noises drifting across from the caravan park as people came and went about the business of enjoying their holiday, his thoughts kept travelling back to the question that haunted him. As the site lapsed into virtual silence when all the residents retired for the night, he must have dozed off himself for a while as an unexpected sound in the otherwise still night air woke him with a start. He toppled off the old tree stump he was sitting on, landing in a heap in the undergrowth below and only just managing to stop himself from yelling out as one hand landed in a bed of nettles, which violently stung him. Scrambling up as noiselessly as he could and vigorously rubbing his painful hand with his other one, he looked through the wire holes of the fence several feet away and saw what had woken him. It was the car backing into the space it had been driven away from a few hours before. Only the sidelights were on so it was apparent the driver didn't want the full beam of the headlights waking any of the caravan dwellers up as he drove past. Was that out of thoughtfulness or did he wish to remain unobserved for some reason?

Then the engine was switched off and the lights went out, plunging the side of the caravan into almost pitch darkness as there were no lights on at all in the caravan next door. Ben then saw the shadowy figure of a man appearing out of the car and heard the creak of a car door opening. Instinct told him that the man was taking something out of the back. He then saw the silhouette of the man moving around the car, heading for the steps of the caravan, and could tell by the way he moved and his ragged breathing that what he was carrying was heavy. Next he heard a thud followed by an expletive and assumed the man, through lack of light, had missed his footing on the steps leading up to the caravan door and fallen.

Ben then heard the sound of a key being scraped around the lock and the sound of it being inserted then saw the outline of the door opening and a shadowy figure disappearing inside the caravan. A moment later the man returned and stealthily made his way down the side of the caravan and around the back of the car where he lifted the boot, rummaged around inside for a moment, pulled something out, and then quietly shut the boot again. A surge of expectation flooded Ben. Was he finally going to find out just what the man hid in his secret hiding place?

But then to Ben's surprise he made his way to the front of the car where he disappeared completely from view. Ben began to wonder if he'd gone off somewhere when he saw a silhouette suddenly become visible again as it sneaked its way down the side of the car to the back of it. He was carrying something that Ben couldn't make out but it was rectangular. He kneeled down behind the car and put the object down on the grass beside him, then with his back to Ben he began doing something by the back bumper. Ben strained hard to see just what he was up to and what the object was that had been put on the grass, but to his frustration it was too dark.

When the man had finished what he was doing, he appeared to be holding something – again oblong in shape. Picking up the object that he had temporarily put down beside him on the grass, he put both items together then, still with his back to Ben, stood up and crept over to the back of the caravan, squatting down by the place Ben knew was his makeshift hiding place. Ben held his breath. This had got to be what he'd been waiting for so long. Then he remembered that for this stage of the operation he would need his torch. He thrust his hand into his jacket pocket. It wasn't there. Panic reared in him. It must have fallen out when the noise of the car returning had woken him from his doze and he'd toppled off the tree stump. Acutely conscious that he was in danger of yet again missing his chance to discover just what that man was hiding, he squatted down and felt frantically around on the ground by him. Thankfully his hand knocked against a metal object and he had to stop himself from whooping. He snatched up the torch and, whether he was timing it right or not, flicked the switch and shone the beam directly over at the man crouched by the back of the caravan, just as he was in the middle of retrieving something from the hole and replacing it with something else.

As the unexpected beam of light illuminated him, Jeff let out a shocked yelp, dropped what he was holding and jumped up, shielding his eyes from the blinding light and blurting out, 'What the hell's going on?'

Immediately flicking off the light, Ben responded in a deep gruff voice, 'Sorry, sir, I'm chasing a couple of thieves hiding in these woods who've burgled a farm up the road. I heard a noise and thought it was them. Again, sorry for disturbing you.' He was confident Jeff would not be able to make him out, dazzled by the recent light and peering into darkness.

The relief in Jeff's voice was most apparent. 'Oh, that's okay, officer. Hope you catch the blighters.'

As Ben moved off he thought to himself: Oh, I've certainly caught the blighter all right. Trouble was, he wasn't sure right this minute what he'd caught the blighter actually doing. At least now, though, he'd had his question answered: he knew what was different about that car tonight from when he'd last seen it.

By the time he got back to his hut Ben was certain there was only one explanation for what he had witnessed. A man who swapped his car number plates for a false set when he went out and then changed them back when he returned, hiding the false set away until the next time he intended to use them, had to be up to something with which he did not wish his own car to be associated. Judging by the heavy holdall he had seen the man lugging into his van on his return tonight, it was Ben's guess that it contained items he felt sure the police would be interested in.

As he came to this conclusion, something else occurred to him. The first time he had met Rhonnie she had told him a strange story about seeing something in the undergrowth just before she'd suffered the injury to her head – and afterwards believed they had been car number plates. He himself had assumed a falling branch had struck her and as there had been no sign of any number plates when he'd discovered her, they had both assumed she had imagined seeing them as a result of the blow she'd suffered. But what if she had not? What if they had been stored there and Rhonnie had been struck to prevent her from making any sort of enquiry about them?

The thought of anyone purposely attacking her made his blood boil. He'd have liked nothing better than to pay back that smarmy manager in kind but as yet he had no concrete evidence to back up his suspicions. Regardless, all Ben's instincts told him that in other respects at least the site manager was definitely a guilty man who needed to be stopped and made to pay for his crimes, and Ben meant to make sure that this happened.

He knew from Rhonnie herself after he'd come to her rescue that fateful Thursday afternoon that she visited the caravan park weekly on that day to do a tour of the site, check everything was operating in the way Jolly's expected it to and also collect any fees taken between her visits, so she was due today. Ben would wait in the woods and waylay her, either on her way to the site as she made her way down the old farm road or on her way back. The only problem was that he had a chance to earn some money that morning . . . was supposed to be starting it in a couple of hours' time in fact, so he was going to have to do without any sleep. It was only a morning's farm work but Ben needed the money. He just had to hope that Rhonnie paid her visit today during the afternoon and not the morning or he would have to make the long trek to her cottage that evening, as he felt it was his duty to let her have this information as soon as possible.

Men with egos like Jeff Sampson didn't usually take kindly to rejection in any form, especially by a woman, so Rhonnie was prepared for their weekly meeting that Thursday afternoon to be on the frosty side on his part. And she was not wrong. Although he was courteous towards her as she was after all his boss, there was an underlying coolness in his manner and he rushed her around the site on her inspection tour. Not once did he try to flatter her in any way. It was clear to her that he wanted to get their meeting over and done with as soon as possible, so he could get back to being surrounded by people who fed his ego, not starved it.

Jeff might have character faults but regardless she was gratified to find no fault with his management of the park. Having collected the weekly takings, she was just about to take her leave when a man tapped on the open door of the office and said to Jeff, 'You the manager here?'

Rhonnie hid her annoyance. Why was it that men always assumed another man must be the one in authority? She wondered how this bigot would react if she informed him that Jeff was the manager of the park, but that the woman dismissed as being incapable of holding down such a position, was in fact the manager's boss.

While the other man then launched into a lengthy tale of how he'd heard favourable reports about the park from other campers he'd come across on his travels and had called by on the off chance, to see if there were any pitches going for a few nights' stay, Rhonnie made her escape.

From his hiding place a little further up in the woods, Ben

saw Rhonnie come out of the office and begin walking back to the main camp.

Contrary to the site rules, which requested all new arrivals to leave their vehicles in a temporary parking place just inside the park, the new arrival had parked his car and touring van on the farm road. As she walked past, Rhonnie saw a woman sitting in the back seat with a young toddler on her knee. Rhonnie smiled politely at her and passed by.

Further up the lane in the woods, Ben was keenly watching Rhonnie's progress, ready to waylay her when she drew level with him.

Just then Rhonnie heard a shout coming from the back of the car, automatically turned around to investigate – and to her astonishment saw that the car was slowly rolling forward. She frowned. How come the vehicle was moving when the driver was in the office with Jeff? Then the truth hit her like a thunderbolt. The car's handbrake had either not been put on before the driver had got out or else it had failed. The woman in the back was shouting frantically now as the car picked up speed and headed under the park entrance arch.

Inside the office, the woman's husband and Jeff were unaware of what was happening, both engrossed in dealing with the booking the man wanted to make.

Rhonnie froze. There were dozens of men, women and children down in the park enjoying the facilities, oblivious to the potential catastrophe heading their way. The car was gathering more speed now as it rolled on down the gently sloping terrain, the van being towed at the back beginning to sway from side to side as it hit uneven patches in the road. That car needed to be stopped. Rhonnie could think of only one way to do it. She would need to get herself inside it and apply the brakes.

With no thought for her own safety, she threw the heavy bag of takings onto the wide grass verge to the side of her then began to run, screaming out a warning to people she could see further down in the park to get out of the way of the driverless vehicle. She had just about reached the driver's side door and was stretching out her hand to grab hold of the handle when someone grabbed her shoulder and she was pushed aside, to fall heavily on the gravel road. Dazed from the unexpected attack on her person, it took her a moment to gather her wits. She did so just in time to see a man running beside the car. He grabbed hold of the door handle, wrenched open the door then took a headlong dive inside.

Rhonnie didn't have to see the man's face to know who he was as she would have recognised Ben's thatch of hair anywhere.

Scrambling up, she ran after the car, yelling out a warning to people still going about their business oblivious to the danger hurtling towards them.

Inside the car, Ben struggled frantically to right himself in the front seat and get behind the wheel. He'd just managed to do so when to his horror he saw that the car, having now travelled past the rows of static caravans, had left the road and was on the grass heading directly for a row of tourers. There were people outside these sunbathing or cooking meals, transistor radios blaring out their favourite music. But what most worried Ben was the group of a dozen or so young children playing a game of football only a hundred or so yards away. The runaway vehicles were pointing straight at them . . . he *had* to get the car under control. He slammed his foot down on the brake pedal. To his horror the pedal hardly budged. Then Ben realised that of course it wouldn't because the engine was not on to power the brakes. He then frantically yanked up the handbrake which caused the car to skid slightly and slow a little but then to Ben's horror, the car began to pick up speed again, rising from twenty to twenty-five miles per hour in a matter of seconds and continuing to rise as it travelled down the now steepening sloping terrain.

He frantically bashed his hand against the car horn to alert people to the runaway vehicle but to his horror nothing happened, the horn wasn't working for some reason.

With no brakes to stop the car Ben knew the only thing he could do was try and steer it out of harm's way then bring it to a stop by crashing it into something solid that wasn't another vehicle, though what that might be he had no idea at the moment.

Then the sound of a child whimpering behind him froze Ben rigid. For the first time he realised he wasn't alone in the car. He flashed a look in the rear-view mirror and saw a petrified-looking young woman, clutching a toddler to her for dear life.

He yelled at her, 'You and the child get down on the floor . . . put the child underneath, yourself over the top then brace yourself. Now! Do it NOW.' He just had to hope that she had because his attention was then taken up with trying to steer the car out of the way of the children and then the row of tourers and campers beyond. He was also conscious that if he pulled too hard on the wheel in his effort to turn it, the van at the back would jackknife and could topple over on top of the children as the car swerved by them.

The distant sound of urgent shouting had managed to reach the ears of a couple of the campers down at the row of tourers, who had seen the car lurching out of control over the grass. Someone had realised the danger the children were in and had started running frantically towards them, bellowing at them to run for their lives.

Further back, Rhonnie was racing after the car, screaming out as loudly as she could to warn whoever could hear her of the impending danger. Some campers were so shocked they were just staring blindly after the car as it travelled past them; others had joined Rhonnie and were racing down the field behind her, yelling warnings to get out of the path of the runaway vehicles.

Inside the car Ben fought to steer it away from the children without causing the jolting van at the back to jackknife. They were now travelling at thirty-five miles per hour. Gently does it, gently does it, he kept telling himself as he pulled down on the steering wheel. Only yards away from the children now . . . who, despite the efforts of Rhonnie and the other campers, were still happily playing their game in ignorance of the danger. Ben began to fear the worst but then to his relief the car began to swerve away from the children and head to one side of them, the violently tossing van at the back thankfully remaining upright. As he sailed past the children he said a silent prayer of thanks to the Almighty but then gawped in shock to see that he was now heading straight for another huddle of touring and camper vans, a few tents too, further down the park, the occupants of these all going about their business unaware of what was heading towards them.

With a surge of panic rushing through him, Ben flashed a glance around but everywhere he looked there were rows or huddles of vans and tents, with not enough space between them for a car towing an erratically jolting van to pass safely through. It was far more congested with vehicles down near the bottom of the park as it was not so far from here for the campers to access the beach. A feeling of impending doom flooded through Ben. He was already bearing the burden of five deaths on his conscience and it looked very much as if he was going to be bearing the guilt of many more very shortly . . . that was if he survived, which he thought doubtful.

The car was travelling at over forty miles per hour now. Yelling at the woman in the back to prepare herself, he was just about to brace his hands against the wheel and shut his eyes in preparation for the impact when out of the corner of his eye he spotted it.

Spanning the whole bottom of the park was a roughly grassed over sand dune, about ten foot high, that acted as a natural boundary line with the beach and also served as a windbreak.

A near-continuous row of touring vehicles and tents stood against it but in several places gaps of approximately two van widths had been left so that campers could access the beach. Dips in the top of the bank had formed where hundreds of pairs of feet had tramped over it.

If Ben could manage to steer the car towards the gap nearest to him and crash it into the bank, although that could well bring harm to himself and his passengers, he would at least save the lives of many innocent bystanders.

With adrenalin rushing through him, the sound of his own heartbeat pounding in his ears, he coaxed the steering wheel to the left while managing to keep the jolting van behind upright. Once the bonnet of the car was in line with the gap, he used all his strength to keep the car heading for it.

As the bank rushed towards him, Ben shut his eyes and prayed. Then everything seemed to move in slow motion. First came the thumping jolt of the car hitting the sand dune that seemed to jar every bone in his body, then the sledgehammer-like punch in his chest as he bounced forward against the steering wheel, followed by another heavy blow to the back of his head. There was the sound of breaking glass shattering around him. It seemed to Ben that he was sailing through the air, then falling down, and he instinctively put out his arms to break his fall. He landed hard, the impact knocking all the breath from his body, and as he heaved in air to replace what had been driven from his lungs, everything went black.

By the time Rhonnie arrived on the scene, breathless and near collapse herself from the sheer physical exertion of running a mile or so from the other side of the camp to the sea, other campers were already swarming around the crash site. The buckled front of the car was buried in the dune and the van had become separated from the car when it had crashed and was lying in a crushed heap on its side, items having burst out of it to lie scattered around. One man had already discovered the woman and child in the back of the car . . . Rhonnie could see them moving about so they were alive at least . . . and was heaving at the passenger door, trying to get it open.

Barging her way through the throng, Rhonnie arrived at the front of the car by the driver's side and bent down to look through the side window, praying with all her might that she didn't see what she feared she was going to: Ben slumped against the wheel, either seriously injured or dead from his injuries. But to her shock the front of the car was empty. Then she saw that the front windscreen was almost obliterated, except for shards of glass jutting out of the frame, some of which had blood on them. She froze. The impact must have thrown Ben clear through the windscreen – to land where? She spun around and started searching for him, pushing people out of the way in her urgency to find him. But there was no sign. Then it struck her that as the car was facing the beach on impact, Ben could have been thrown clear over the dune. She scrambled up it and at the top stopped long enough to take a glance around. She saw his body immediately, lying in a crumpled heap at the bottom on the far side. People who had been previously sunbathing on the beach were rushing towards him.

Scrambling down the bank, she threw herself on her knees beside him. His mass of beard and hair were matted with blood and the skin she could see around his eyes were starting to blacken from bruising. What remained was a deathly white. 'Oh, Ben,' she cried as she gently eased up his head to cradle it on her lap. Stroking it, with tears rolling down her face, she sobbed, 'Please don't die on me, Ben. Please, please. I couldn't bear to lose you.'

Just then a voice made her jump. 'What the hell happened here, Rhonnie?'

She lifted her head to see Jeff looming over her, panting heavily from his race down from the park entrance. She cried, 'Go and telephone for an ambulance. Tell them to hurry! I

289

think he might be . . . be . . .' She couldn't bring herself to say she feared Ben was dying.

Jeff was looking down at him in confusion 'But who is he? I've never seen him before . . . he's not one of our campers, that's for sure.'

'Jeff!' she bellowed at him frenziedly. 'Just go and telephone for an ambulance.'

A while later Rhonnie watched solemnly as the ambulance, its siren blaring, drove away. She had very much wanted to travel with the still-unconscious Ben but there had been no room for her in the ambulance as the woman and child from the car had to be taken off to be checked by doctors also, although they only seemed to have sustained cuts and bruises.

The woman's husband was beside himself when he saw what had happened and readily admitted that it was his fault for forgetting to put on the handbrake when he had left the car to go to the site office. His gratitude towards Ben for his quick thinking and bravado in saving the lives of his wife and son was immeasurable, as was his grief at what Ben was suffering as a result. After seeing them off in the ambulance, Rhonnie had had the man escorted to the camp nurse, to be treated for shock. Once the nurse was satisfied that he was over the worst, Rhonnie had requested a taxi to be called to take him to the hospital so he could be with his wife and son. Also, since the family was now without shelter or transport, the man had been told that Jolly's would provide his family with chalet accommodation and meals while he arranged for their journey home. All the other campers had now gone back to getting on with their holidays.

Despite feeling shaky herself, and suffering from a thumping headache that was making her feel sick, Rhonnie could not do what she had advised everyone else affected by the upsetting incident to do – take a painkiller and have a lie down – as she was in charge and needed to keep going until the situations had been satisfactorily dealt with. She said to Jeff, 'I need to get back to the office to organise getting the wreckage cleared and the dune raked together. I'd appreciate it if you'd run me back in your car as I walked here, but first could we stop by your caravan as I really need a glass of water and if you have any headache tablets I'd appreciate a couple too? Oh, and as we arrive at the park entrance, could you stop for a moment as I need to retrieve the bag of takings I threw on the grass verge before I chased after the car.' She couldn't understand why he was looking at her as though she had just ordered him to hang himself from the nearest tree and asked, 'You don't mind, do you?'

He didn't mind at all running her back to the main camp in his car but as for her coming into his caravan for a drink of water . . . that was another matter entirely. After switching the plates on his car when he had arrived back at just after four o'clock this morning from a very successful trip out, he'd left his haul from that night and other evidence related to it on the dining table while he poured himself a drink and stretched out on the seating, intending to rest for just a moment as he was feeling the physical effects of his labours of earlier. The next thing he knew he was being woken from a deep sleep at a quarter to seven by a holidaymaker from one of the static caravans needing him to fix a wardrobe door that had come off its hinges . . . a trivial matter at such an ungodly hour. From then on a succession of campers had vied for his and his assistant's attention, presenting them with jobs ranging from unblocking a sink to changing a gas cylinder as well as fitting in the booking in and marshalling to their pitches of new arrivals, seeing away those leaving, accompanying Rhonnie on her weekly inspection tour . . . and then the incident with the runaway car had happened so he hadn't yet had time to return to his own van and tidy away all the incriminating evidence of his nocturnal activity. His illicit gains of the night had been great enough that he hadn't been able to close the holdall so all was plain for anyone to see.

His mind raced frantically for an excuse to stop Rhonnie coming into his caravan. Thankfully he had a naturally devious mind. 'Of course you can, why would I mind?' he told her. 'I was just thinking, though, how done in you look and you've got to be suffering from shock too. It's a long way back up to my caravan, so I was going to suggest that you stay here while I run and fetch my car and I'll grab a bottle of water from my van and a couple of Aspros while I'm there. I'll be back before you know it.'

She was grateful for his consideration. The way she was feeling at the moment the long walk back up to the top of the camp seemed like a marathon. 'I appreciate that, Jeff, thank you.'

Thank God for that, he thought, then belted off before she changed her mind.

CHAPTER TWENTY-FOUR

Desperate to find out how Ben was, Rhonnie waylaid a harassed-looking young nurse just as she was entering the sluice room with a covered kidney dish and urgently asked, 'Excuse me, I'm sorry to bother you, but I'm hoping you can tell me where the man is who was brought in a couple of hours ago after a car crash. His name is Ben.'

'Are you a relative?' the nurse asked her.

'No, I'm not. Ben hasn't any family that I know of. I'm his friend, the only one he's got really.' She crossed her fingers as she said this, knowing that Drina too could be classed as Ben's benefactor and friend.

'If you'd like to wait here while I deal with this then I'll fetch Sister,' the girl told Rhonnie, and immediately went into the sluice room.

Since arriving in the hospital, anxiety over Ben's welfare was making Rhonnie feel nauseous. Along with that she still had a thumping headache, which medication had not seemed to shift. So far she had asked after Ben in three different places in the hospital and the wait while they went to check always seemed to last for hours rather than the actual minutes it was. Finally a sister joined her who did seem to know Ben's whereabouts and condition.

She was a small, plump, efficient-looking woman, wearing a starched blue uniform, who clasped her hands in front of her and addressed Rhonnie briskly. 'I understand you're enquiring about the gentleman who was brought in after the accident at Jolly's Holiday Camp?'

'I am, Sister. How is he?'

'I can only discuss a patient's condition with a family member, I'm afraid.'

Rhonnie implored her, 'But as I told the nurse who came to find you, Ben has no family that I know of and I'm the only friend he has too. Please can't you break the rules just this once, Sister? I'm really worried about him and I won't rest until I know how he is.'

The sister looked at her for a moment. This young woman was showing genuine concern for her patient and although hospital rules were in place for good reason, in some circumstances there was good reason to bend them. She told Rhonnie, 'I'm glad to tell you that all he's suffering from is cuts, bruises, a couple of broken ribs and concussion, so considering the type of accident he had, he got off very lightly. He regained consciousness about an hour ago but understandably was in a lot of pain so Doctor ordered he be dosed with morphine. You won't get to speak to him until tomorrow at least. We'll be keeping him in for a few days' rest but once he's home he'll need to take it easy for some weeks until his ribs heal properly. Now why don't you go home and come back tomorrow afternoon at visiting time, when he's fully awake and more comfortable?'

Rhonnie's whole body sagged in relief. 'Oh, thank God he's all right and no permanent damage has been done.' She then pleaded, 'Please let me see him and sit with him until he wakes up. I hate the thought of him believing that no one cares about him. Please, Sister?'

The older woman looked at her for a moment before she smiled kindly and said, 'All right. Before you go in to see him, though, could you come into my office and give me some details about him? We only have his Christian name.' She smiled then. 'Quite a hero, so I've been informed. Saved the lives of a woman and her child.'

'And many others too by his brave actions, Sister,' Rhonnie told her. 'I'm sorry but I haven't any more details about Ben. I don't even know his surname, I'm afraid. He's the loner sort, keeps himself very much to himself.'

'Oh, I see. Well, we'll just have to wait until he's awake and can us tell himself. He's in the room at the bottom of the corridor on the left. I'll send a nurse along with a cup of tea for you.'

'Thank you, Sister, thank you so much. Oh, how are the woman and her son who were brought in at the same time?'

The sister smiled. 'Both just bruised and shaken. They've been discharged.'

Rhonnie was greatly relieved. 'Oh, I'm so very glad to hear that. Thank you again, Sister.'

She then hurried off down the corridor and quietly opened the door of Ben's room where she slipped inside and tiptoed over to the bed. She looked down at the man lying there, his face covered in bruises with black ones around both eyes. There were bandages around his chest. This sleeping man had been in an accident too by the looks of him but the nurse had directed her to the wrong room as this was a stranger. Unlike Ben, with his mass of hair and bushy beard, this man's hair was very short and he was clean-shaven. The man wasn't handsome nor was he ugly, just ordinary-looking. But it was a face that would immediately instil trust in people. Although she had no idea who he was, she hoped that his injuries were no more life-threatening than Ben's were.

She left the room as quietly as she had entered it and went off in search of the sister. She found her at the other end of the corridor in her office, sitting at her desk dealing with paperwork. 'I'm sorry, Sister, but I must have misheard you when you told me which room Ben was in.'

She frowned. 'I'm sure I told you right. He's in the room on the left at the end of the corridor, and that's the one I directed you to.'

'That's the room I went into but it's not Ben in the bed. That man has short hair and is clean-shaven. Ben has bushy hair and a beard.'

The sister chuckled. 'Fancy you not recognising your friend without them! We had to cut his hair and shave his beard to check for hidden injuries. Thankfully we found none except for the bruising, which I doubt would have been the case had he not had all that hair and beard. They protected him from the flying glass when he smashed through the car's windscreen and quite possibly saved him from terrible scarring.'

Oh, so that pleasant, kindly-faced man was Ben. Now Rhonnie finally knew what he looked like, she saw that his face reflected the essence of the man she knew. 'Thank you, Sister,' she said, and returned to the room she had just left.

Ben was still asleep four hours later when Jill arrived.

As she crossed over to the bed she said to Rhonnie in hushed tones, 'Nurse said I can come in for a few minutes but to be quiet as Ben is still sleeping.' She put a heavy-looking shopping bag on the floor and stood holding a bunch of flowers. 'When I got home tonight I called the hospital and they told me you were still here and hadn't been home yet. I thought Ben might need some things bringing in, which I know would have been the last thing on your mind when you came here, so when I went home I got a couple of pairs of Martin's clean pyjamas and some toiletries together . . . soap, a flannel, that sort of thing. And a bottle of cordial.' She held out the flowers, wrapped in a piece of newspaper. 'I picked these from my garden to brighten up the room for him. I'll go and find a nurse in a moment to ask for a vase to put them in. Also there's a flask and a sandwich in the bag for you as I doubt you've eaten since breakfast this morning after all that's gone on.'

Rhonnie smiled tiredly up at her. 'Thank you, Jill. You're right, the last thing on my mind was bringing anything in for Ben as I was just too desperate to find out how he was. I didn't realise I was hungry until you mentioned food,' she said, delving in the bag to take out the flask and sandwich.

Jill was looking at her in concern. 'You look shattered, Rhonnie. It's been some day for you, hasn't it?'

She smiled wanly. 'Not one I'd like to repeat. I'm fine, Jill, it's Ben I'm worried about. I know the sister told me that he's going to be fine but I won't rest easy until he wakes and I can see for myself that he will be.'

While Rhonnie poured herself a cup of tea and unwrapped the sandwich, Jill went around the other side of the bed and looked down at Ben. 'So this is what our man in the woods looks like. Of course I've not met him personally before, but from what you told me, you didn't know what he looked like either because of his beard. I expect he'll get a shock when he wakes up and finds the hospital has shaved it off for medical reasons. He's got time to grow it back again before winter sets in, though, as I bet he kept it so long to help keep him warm.' She sat down on the visitor's chair opposite Rhonnie's and relaxed back in it. 'Well, he's no Clint Eastwood but he's got a nice enough face. Sort of kind-looking, isn't it? The nurse wouldn't tell me anything about his condition. He's going to be all right, though, isn't he?'

Through a mouthful of cheese and pickle sandwich, Rhonnie told her, 'Yes, thank goodness.' She then told Jill about the injuries Ben had sustained. 'He was very lucky that was all he suffered . . . after an accident like that he could be dead. They said that him landing on the soft sand was what saved him. Hard ground would have been a different matter. He was in a lot of pain from his broken ribs so the doctor had him dosed with morphine and I was told he could be out for hours yet. I'm not leaving, though, until he does wake up as I'd hate him to think that no one cares about him, especially after what he did.'

It's apparent to me just how much you care about him, Jill thought to herself.

Just then a young nurse arrived and told the women not to mind her as she was only going to check Ben's blood pressure and pulse.

'Everything is fine at work,' Jill told her boss as the nurse carried on with her business. 'I checked in with Sid Harper before I left and he told me that the local scrap yard had been down and collected the wreckage of the touring van. A local garage towed the car away and will deal with the owner directly from here on, and the maintenance men have done the rest of the clearing up. On your behalf I called by the caravan park before I went to catch my bus home and had a word with Jeff Sampson. He reported that everything at the park has gone back to normal and the campers are all getting on with their holidays. I telephoned Drina like you asked me to and she was really shocked when I told her what had happened and said that she was going straight over to the park to see that all was in hand with the clear up, even though I told her it was, but she wanted to check for herself that all the holidaymakers were all right and make it known that Jolly's nurse was on hand to see them if they showed any signs of shock. She told me to tell you not to worry about Danny as she was going to pick him up from Carrie and keep him for as long as you needed her to. Apart from that everything else is running smoothly. Oh, the new brochures arrived this afternoon from Coppice's and they look great, Rhonnie. I called the agency to check that the two clerks and typist are still scheduled to come in on Monday to do the mail shot and they are.'

Rhonnie was looking impressed. 'You've been busy, Jill. I appreciate all you've done, thank you.' She then gawped at the other woman in astonishment. 'What on earth are you doing?'

Jill looked back at her, confused. 'What do you mean?'

'You're picking the petals off that marigold and eating them.'

Jill's eyes widened when she looked down at the flower in the bunch minus most of its petals and then at the petal clamped between her fingers. She exclaimed, 'Oh my God, so I am. I have to say, they do taste rather nice though.'

In the process of taking Ben's blood pressure, the nurse piped up matter-of-factly, 'With my friend it was nibbling on coal. My sister it was aniseed balls. I've heard of all sorts of cravings but never marigold petals, so that's a first. When's it due?' She directed her question at Jill.

Jill frowned. 'When is what due?"

The nurse looked at her as though she was stupid. 'Your baby, what did you think I was referring to?'

'My baby! I'm not pregnant,' she snapped at the nurse as if she was offended that the girl would think she was.

'Are you sure?' queried the girl.

Rhonnie was looking at Jill quizzically. 'Yes, are you sure you're not, Jill? Come to think of it, several things have been going on with you this last couple of months that have not been normal behaviour for you. Your husband was irritating the life out of you with his snoring and doing other little things that never used to bother you before. You went through a stage where I was always catching you yawning . . . I actually found you asleep on one on the visitors' sofas although I never told you about it as I didn't want to embarrass you . . . but you said that you were sleeping well at night so there was no reason for your tiredness at the time. Then I came for dinner that evening and you said you'd been really looking forward to the spaghetti bolognese you'd cooked as it was your favourite meal, yet when you sat down to eat it you couldn't face it. Now this with the marigold petals. And those are only the things I know about.' Then she suddenly exclaimed: 'That fortune-teller told you that soon you'd have someone new in your life but your husband would be happy about it. Was she trying to tell you you were having a baby and it would be a boy!'

Jill was staring at her open-mouthed. 'Oh, my God, do you think I could be? But I haven't had any other symptoms to suggest I am. I'm sure my monthlies haven't stopped so I can't be!'

'Some women's don't for the first few months so that's nothing unusual. Some women sail right through their pregnancy and haven't a clue they are pregnant until they go into labour,' said the nurse. She then announced, 'Well . . . Mr . . . er . . . Ben's blood, pressure and pulse are normal, so I'll be back in hour to check them again.' Before she left she said to Jill meaningfully, 'If I were you I'd go and visit the doctor to have it confirmed one way or the other, but I've been a nurse long enough to know an expectant mother when I see one and I'm looking at one now.'

Rhonnie said to Jill, 'Oh, wouldn't it be wonderful if the nurse is right and you are having a baby?'

But far from being delighted, Jill looked decidedly worried. 'Well, we weren't planning to have children for another couple of years yet and were looking to move . . .' Her voice trailed off as it seemed to hit home that in a few months' time she could be a mother and her eyes began to shine with excitement. 'I was about to say that it would scupper our plans to move to a bigger house . . . but a baby . . . well, what is a bigger house compared to a baby? Oh, Rhonnie, I so hope the nurse is right, I really do. Martin will be over the moon if I am expecting, I know he will. Now I come to think of it, I had noticed my bras were getting tight on me recently and the waistbands on my skirts, which I put down to eating too many sweets. I shall make an appointment to see the doctor when I finish work tomorrow night. Oh, I shan't sleep tonight, I know I shan't, and neither will Martin until we find out one way or the other. It's going to feel like forever waiting for the test result to come through.' She got up. 'I don't really want to leave you here on your own . . .'

'Just get off home and tell Martin what you suspect . . .

what the nurse suspects at least.' Rhonnie knew that she was going to be as impatient as Jill and Martin were to get the results of the tests.

After Jill had gone, Rhonnie finished the sandwich and drank the rest of the tea in the flask, then settled back in the high-backed visitor's chair to wait for Ben to wake up, occupying her time by reading out-of-date magazines she collected from waiting areas.

Over the next few hours nurses came and went after checking on Ben's status, each time satisfied he was stable and showing no signs of any undetected injuries. It was beginning to grow dark outside, the noises from the corridor lessening as the hospital settled down for the night. A thoroughly exhausted Rhonnie couldn't stop her eyes from drooping and she fell asleep. Then the sound of a voice broke the silence in the room and had her jerking wide awake to look over at Ben, expecting to see that he had finally woken up. But his eyes were still closed and the voice she had heard was him talking in his sleep.

He was agitated, head thrashing from side to side, his face wreathed in anger as he mumbled incoherently at first, but then the sense of his words became clearer. 'Need . . . need to tell her . . . he's . . . he's up to . . . no good. Saw him hiding . . . hole in ground.' There was a long pause before he cried out, 'Bag! What . . . in bag?' Then his voice rose hysterically and he shouted out, ' No . . . NO . . . don't go in there!' His head thrashed from side to side for a moment before it suddenly stopped moving and he went quiet for several long moments. Rhonnie thought that whatever nightmare he was having was over and he had drifted back into peaceful sleep again but then she nearly jumped out of her skin when he unexpectedly cried out, 'Please, no . . . no . . . mistake . . . big mistake . . . he . . . he . . . many women, he . . . not for you. Don't . . . don't go in there! Oh, Rhonnie, I . . .' There was a long pause before he added '. . . love you.' His voice trailed off then, the anger left his face and he began to snore gently, signalling the fact that now his nightmare was over he was peacefully sleeping again.

She stared at him. Had she really just heard him announce that he loved her? And why did the thought of him having such feelings make her feel warm all the way through? But then it struck her that he was delirious from the morphine and didn't know what he was saying. But it was said that if you want to get the truth from a man, get him drunk, so did the same go for a man who was under the influence of a drug like morphine? Then other things Ben had said came back to her. Who did he need to tell that someone was up to no good? And what did he mean about a hole he'd seen someone hiding something inside? And the bag? What bag, and why was he desperate to find out what was inside it? Who did he not want to go inside somewhere as they were making a big mistake? And the many women? Nothing Ben had said made any sense whatsoever to her.

Then before she could think any further he suddenly started groaning and tossing and turning. It was obvious he was in excruciating pain. She jumped up and pressed a button on the wall to summon someone. Within seconds a nurse arrived followed by a doctor and Rhonnie was asked to wait outside. A moment later the nurse came rushing out again to dash into a room down the corridor. She came back out pushing a trolley with a tin box with a sloping lid on top, which she took into Ben's room. A great fear of the unknown filled Rhonnie. She started panicking that an undetected injury had suddenly shown itself and Ben was far more seriously hurt than the medical staff had previously thought. Tears of anguish pricked her eyes and it was then that she realised this man that she knew so little about meant so very much to her. Love? Yes, she did love him. *Oh, dear God,* she silently prayed, *please don't let Ben die. Please, Lord, please.* A memory struck her then. The fortune-teller they had discovered plying her trade without permission on the camp had told her that a car would make her realise that it was possible for her to love again. It had made absolutely no sense to her then but now it did. Ben had been in a car crash and the thought of him not surviving it had made her realise that she loved him. Maybe she should not have been so hasty in branding the woman a charlatan after all.

It seemed an age before the doctor came back out, followed by the nurse with the trolley, who pushed it back to the storeroom.

A small, wiry Asian doctor smiled at Rhonnie kindly and said to her, 'The morphine we gave Ben earlier is wearing off and his broken ribs are causing him a great deal of pain, so I've decided to keep him sedated for the next twenty-four hours at least to give his ribs a chance to start healing. If he dislodges one of them there's a possibility it could puncture a lung, which could prove fatal. There's really no point in your being here so why don't you go home and get some rest and come back tomorrow evening at visiting time? Hopefully by then Ben will be on milder medication and at least he'll know you are here.'

The doctor was right. There was no point in her waiting at his bedside while Ben was being kept in a coma. And at this moment her bed had never beckoned so invitingly. Before Rhonnie left she urged the doctor, 'If you do allow Ben to wake up properly before I come back tomorrow, will you please tell him that I have been here? I don't want him to think he's been left here on his own and no one cares about him.'

The doctor smiled and gave her arm a reassuring pat. 'Don't worry, we'll make sure he knows.'

Despite how exhausted she was, sleep evaded Rhonnie as she was far too worried about Ben's health, her confusion over what he had said during his bout of delirium, but most especially his astonishing declaration that he loved her. She was shocked by how much she wanted that to be the truth and hoped it did not turn out that the powerful drug had made him say things with no substance behind them. She had never thought that she would find room in her heart again for a man after she had lost Dan, and what was so surprising was that it was for one who was so different from him . . . Ben, with his ordinary looks and quiet personality, against the devastatingly handsome and outgoing Dan, with his own house, well-paid job and, unknown to them both at the time they married, the life-changing inheritance he was to come into on the death of his father. But the two men also shared some personality traits . . . their honesty and kindness. It was those qualities that had made Rhonnie fall in love with them both.

She did worry, though, that she herself was a woman of substance and Ben a man with nothing, so he might deem himself not worthy of her. She felt extremely lucky that twice in her life she had met a man she knew without doubt she could be happy with, and should she find out for sure that Ben did return her feelings then she was damned if she was going to let him walk away from her out of his misplaced pride. She meant to let him know that it was he she loved and that what he had or hadn't got materially was of no consequence to her.

With so many things playing on her mind along with extreme fatigue from lack of sleep it was a wonder Rhonnie managed to get to work the next day, let alone be at her desk at just after eight in the morning. She prayed the time passed quickly so she could go and see Ben, ease her mind that he was recovering well and would soon be back on his feet, and somehow find the courage and right words to let him know how much he had come to mean to her.

Normally Jill would have been showing great concern over the dark rings under Rhonnie's eyes and general air of distraction, but she was far too consumed with her own exciting situation to notice today. Sandra too was in a world of her own. It seemed that the fortune-teller's prediction to her that she would meet the man of her dreams could come true, the same as Jill's and Rhonnie's seemed to be doing, as a new maintenance man had arrived to replace the one who had left to join the armed forces, and he had asked her out on a date on Saturday night.

Since the day Rhonnie had come to work for Jolly's the time here always seemed to fly past, so much did she enjoy her job. She still loved it, but today time seemed to crawl by, each moment seeming like several minutes, each minute at least an hour. Finally home time arrived. Rhonnie very rarely left on time but today she was first out of the door, asking Jill to lock up for her so she could go home, ready herself and be waiting outside the ward door to be first in when they opened up at visiting time.

She still hadn't quite got used to seeing Ben without his profusion of hair and for a second after she had stepped into his room she did a double take when her eyes fell on the short-haired, clean-shaven, pleasant-faced man propped up on pillows and looking back at her. Her relief to see him looking so much better than he had a few hours ago was immeasurable and she had to fight to restrain herself from throwing her arms around him and giving him a tight hug. But apart from the fact that such an action could cause him much pain and possibly damage his healing ribs, she wasn't at all certain yet that such a display of affection from her would be welcome. She had to find out from him whether his declaration of last night was a true statement of his feelings for her or just the ramblings of delirium. She did know he was very pleased to see her by the way his eyes lit up when she walked in.

He still seemed slightly dopey and she supposed that was due to the fact that the heavy doses of morphine had not completely worn off yet. She sat down in the visitor's chair, putting a laden carrier bag on the floor beside her, then looked at him earnestly and asked, 'How do you feel, Ben?'

A nurse had told him that Rhonnie was coming in to see him that evening and since then he had not been able to suppress feelings of excitement at being in the company of the woman he adored. Now she was here all he wanted Rhonnie to do was lie on the bed beside him so he could feel her close to him, and even though it would cause him excruciating pain to hold her in his arms he would gladly suffer that if he could kiss her long and passionately. But to answer her truthfully about how he felt right this minute was out of the question, he feared she'd be insulted even if he said it in a jesting manner. Instead he told her, 'Like I had a head-on collision with a speeding train.'

She flashed a look at him. His face was still covered with black, purple and yellow bruises and under the pyjama jacket she knew his chest from his waist up to his armpits was encased in thick bandaging. When she brought her eyes back to look into his she grinned and said jocularly, 'Well, if I didn't know better I'd think that you had.'

He smiled at her joke. 'Sister told me you sat with me until the early hours of the morning. I really appreciate you doing that considering you've a son and how busy you are with work.'

He had said that in a way that implied he didn't think he was worth wasting her time on, and she needed to put him right about that. 'I was so worried about you, the last thing I wanted was for you to wake up here on your own, thinking you'd just been abandoned.' She then saw a chance to let him know how much he had come to mean to her since she had got to know him. but just as she opened her mouth to do that she snapped it shut as the door swung wide and an elderly lady, a member of the local WVS, came bustling in pushing a tea trolley.

'Tea or coffee, chocolate digestives or rich tea?' she offered them both cheerfully.

Despite being annoyed by the old dear's untimely entrance,

which meant she now had to wait for another opportunity to present itself to make Ben aware of her feelings for him, Rhonnie nevertheless smiled back and asked for tea and Ben requested the same.

After the lady had left, Rhonnie told him, 'I've brought you in a few things.' She picked up the carrier beside her, taking out the items inside one by one and putting them on top of the cabinet beside his bed. 'I hope you like grapes and oranges and there's a packet of custard creams and a couple of paperbacks of the type I saw you reading when I was in your hut, so I hope I made the right choice.'

The two books she had brought him were by his favourite authors and she couldn't have chosen better for him. He couldn't remember the last time he'd had a biscuit so being in possession of a whole packet made him feel like a child would after being denied sweets for a while as punishment for being naughty – he wanted to rip the packet open and greedily gobble them all down. And the same went for the fruit. He told her, 'I haven't read either of those, thank you. And thank you for all you've brought in already and for what you did yesterday too.'

'Oh, I didn't bring you anything in yesterday. That was Jill, our office manager. She knew I was too bothered about how you were to think about what you might be in need of while you were in here so she brought in the toiletries and pyjamas. She hoped you wouldn't be offended that they're her husband's.'

He had to swallow a lump of emotion that stuck in his throat at all this kindness being heaped upon him. How could he be insulted by a woman's thoughtfulness towards him, and one who'd never met him at that? 'Please tell Jill from me that I'm not at all offended. I shall make sure I return them in the state they were lent to me.'

Other men in his position wouldn't even consider giving the pyjamas back, let alone making sure they were in the same condition. He really was a very considerate man. As she had done many times before Rhonnie wondered how such a man as Ben had come to be in this position. If he had fallen on hard times, surely even if he had no family he would have had friends to help him through his bad times and get him on his feet again?

'Oh, I need to tell you that you're quite a local hero as everyone is talking about what you did and the local paper want to do an interview and take pictures of you once you feel up to it,' Rhonnie told him. 'And I wouldn't be surprised if the nationals did as well once they hear of it.'

At this news a look of horror filled his face and he blurted out, 'No, no, I want no publicity over this! Please call the paper and tell them not to come here as I won't see them if they do. You will, won't you, Rhonnie, make sure they understand I'm not interested?'

She could understand Ben not wanting a fuss made over his heroic actions since that was the unassuming sort of man he was. She assured him, 'Yes, of course, if that's how you feel.'

'Thank you,' he said, relieved.

'Well, even if you don't want any public praise, you'll still get it from me. I'm just so very glad that fate brought you to the woods near the office at the time that car begin to roll down the slope as I doubt I would ever have managed to steer it like you did and save the lives of so many people. You're definitely my hero, Ben.'

The look that flashed across his face made Rhonnie think he didn't consider himself a hero at all.

He looked uncomfortable when he told her, 'Well, that's just it, you see, Rhonnie, it wasn't anything to do with fate why I was in the woods at the time. I was waiting to waylay you as you made your way back to your office as I'd something to tell you.'

Her heart sank. Not that he was moving on! 'Oh, and what

was that, Ben?' she asked trying not to look as anxious about the answer as she actually was.

He looked awkward. 'Well . . . this is rather difficult since . . . well, as far as I know you're going out with this man and you won't like what I'm going to tell you about . . .'

Frowning, she interjected, 'Going out with what man?'

'Er . . . I don't know his name but he's the manager of the caravan park.'

Her frown deepened. 'Why on earth would you think that I was going out with Jeff Sampson?'

He looked at her uncomfortably. 'I was . . . well, in the woods opposite the back of his van one evening and I saw you going in.'

'And from that you presumed I was going out with him? You presume wrong, Ben. I'm Jeff Sampson's boss and nothing more.'

She then went to tell him that there was a man she was very fond of, hoping he would ask her just who that was so it gave her the opening to tell him, but Ben was already saying, 'Oh, thank goodness for that because from what I've witnessed that man has a different woman in his van most nights! Well, knowing this makes it much easier for me to tell you what I found out about him. I think . . . actually I'm positive . . . he's up to no good, Rhonnie.' Ben proceeded to tell her what he had seen Jeff doing in the early hours one morning and how he had made a point of returning to the caravan several times after that to try and find out what was going on. He told her about the heavy holdall Jeff had taken inside and the way he'd switched number plates, which couldn't be for any innocent reason.

Rhonnie sat looking at him gravely while he spoke. 'I have to agree with you, Ben. What you've just told me makes sense of all you said last night. You were rambling in your sleep – none of it made sense to me at the time but now some of it does. You were going on about needing to tell someone that someone else was up to no good. And you mentioned the bag . . . wanting to know what was in it.' She felt this wasn't the right time to tell him that he'd also declared his love for her, so just said, 'You rambled on about other things but nothing to do with this.' Her face was wreathed in worry. 'If it comes to light that one of Jolly's employees is up to no good, and that management suspected he was but did nothing about it, then it would badly damage the business. People won't want to come to a holiday camp worrying that a load of crooks are looking after them.'

'Are you going to go to the police and ask them to investigate Jeff?'

Rhonnie thought about the prospect for a moment but then shook her head. 'If I do and it turns out Jeff is completely innocent, that means we have done him a terrible injustice. Anyway the police will want me to produce proof to back up my claims before they'll take any action.'

Ben said with conviction, 'I know that man is up to no good, Rhonnie, I'd stake my life on it. I'll be out of here in a couple of days. If you give me your permission to be on the caravan park, I'll get you your proof.'

She scolded him, 'Ben you will be in no fit state to do anything for a few weeks while you heal properly and anyway you've already done enough. You could have turned a blind eye to what you saw Jeff doing that first time, but you didn't. Now I know about it, I'll deal with this from now on. You need to concentrate on getting yourself better.'

She got up.

'Where are you going?

'To find out for definite if Jeff is a bad 'un or not, and if he is put a stop to it pronto. What if it's not just on his nights off that he's doing something he shouldn't be – what if he's fleecing our customers in some way? Since I've worked for Jolly's we've discovered several staff using ingenious way to make money for themselves at the expense of our campers so

310

this doesn't come as such a big shock to me as you might think. We employ hundreds of people and the majority are as honest as the day they were born but you get the odd one or two that see an opportunity to line their own pockets and don't hesitate to take it. The problem for management is spotting those corrupt ones. Thanks to your eagle eye we know to look out for Jeff Sampson.'

She paused in thought for a moment before she went on, 'I'll think of a way to get him out of his caravan for a while then I can have a look inside. And I'll check for the spare number plates in his hidey-hole outside. I'll take it all to the police and let them carry on from there. I'll come and see you tomorrow afternoon at visiting time and tell you what happens tonight.'

As she dashed over to the door, Ben was terrified that she could be unwittingly putting herself in a dangerous situation, and he frantically shouted to her: 'Rhonnie, wait . . .'

His voice trailed off as she had already gone.

CHAPTER TWENTY-FIVE

On her drive home Rhonnie wracked her brains for a plausible excuse to get Jeff out of his caravan for just enough time for her to search it and leave before he came back and caught her. She rejected several ideas, then one that she couldn't find fault with presented itself, the only downside being it would mean her deliberately damaging Jolly's property.

First she went home to change into dark clothes. She picked up a torch and on her way out collected the lump hammer from the coal shed. At just after nine with it pitch dark outside, she set off to drive to the caravan park. She was not at all worried for her own safety or anxious for what she was about to do but fired up with anger at the thought that Jeff Sampson was using the cover of his position at Jolly's to hide his own dishonest activities.

If Jeff was hiding ill-gotten gains inside his van then he would lock the door before he left to deal with the problem she was going to create for him, so she would pay a visit to the park office first where a copy of all the static caravan keys were kept in a locked wall cupboard. As the boss she had her own keys to the office and the lock up cupboard, along with one for the safe.

Having retrieved the skeleton key from the park office, she left her car outside it and took the hammer with her. She crept around the perimeter of the camp until she came to the back of Jeff's caravan. She stopped long enough to check that the lights were on at the front of the van and could hear the faint strains of music playing. She hoped that this signalled he was inside. She then carried on skirting the back fence until she reached a clearing where the first of the shower blocks was situated. From where she was she could hear more strains of music, but this time coming from the direction of the touring van area. Someone was playing a guitar, others singing along, and for a moment she wished she was with them enjoying herself. Shutting out these thoughts, she stood and listened for any noise coming from within the shower block.

Happy that it was clear, she dashed inside, made straight for a shower cubicle, raised the heavy lump hammer high then brought it down as hard as she could just where the taps were positioned halfway up the tiled wall, joining two water pipes. It took two blows to achieve what she'd hoped for. The cold tap flew off, the top part of the hot along with it, leaving the rest hanging. From both, water gushed out and began to flood the floor.

Running out of the shower block, she again skirted the perimeter fence as far as the back of Jeff's caravan. Leaving the hammer by the fence, she crept over to the steps by the door, then leaned up and thumped her fist on it several times before leaping back into the shadows created by the caravan next door whose occupants were out, thankfully.

It wasn't the caravan door that opened to her summons but the side bedroom window. A bare-chested Jeff leaned out and looked around. 'Who's there?' he called out in an annoyed tone.

Assuming she had woke him up from a sleep, from the shadows and disguising her voice as best she could, Rhonnie shouted out, 'Me mam sent me to tell you that she went to take a shower in block four and a pipe's broke. Water is pouring out all over the place. You'd best come quick.'

She heard him curse before he called out, 'Okay, I'm coming.'

Rhonnie swiftly hid herself behind the caravan next door, peeping around the corner to watch for Jeff to leave. He hadn't shut the bedroom window and from the conversation she heard coming through it, Rhonnie realised that it wasn't sleep she had disturbed him from but entertaining a woman.

'I have to go out, got an emergency to see to.' This was Jeff speaking and his tone implied he wasn't too happy about it.

A female voice responded, 'Well, hurry back and we can carry on where we left off.'

He laughed scornfully. 'And leave you here to have a rummage through my stuff? Not bloody likely. Now get that lovely arse of yours out the bed and make yourself scarce. If I'm still in the mood when I've finished fixing the leak, I'll come and find you.'

'You promise?'

'Yeah, yeah, 'course,' he responded with a hint of irritation in his voice.

A couple of minutes later the woman came out, still in the process of dressing herself. By the light cast through the door Rhonnie could see she was a pretty girl, sixteen or seventeen at the most and obviously the sort to be easily swayed by an older man. She felt disgusted that it didn't seem to bother Jeff how young and innocent a girl was so long as he had his sexual appetite satisfied and his ego fed. As the girl slipped on her shoes, Jeff came out and locked the door behind him. He joined the girl who told him, 'I'll be with my friends at the camper van so you will come and find me as soon as you're finished, won't you?'

Jeff snapped back at her, 'I said I would, didn't I?' He gave her a slap on her backside and laughed as she reluctantly went off. He then picked up a toolbox from beside the steps and went off.

With adrenalin flooding through her, Rhonnie emerged from her hiding place and crept over to the back of Jeff's caravan where she flashed the torch around the grassed area by her feet. At first she couldn't find it but then she noticed a rectangle of grass was raised slightly higher than the rest. She kneeled down and grabbed hold of clumps to both sides, heaved it up, put it to the side of her then shone her torch inside the hole she had revealed. There lay a set of number plates just as Ben had told her. She replaced the turf, switched off the torch and then crept around the side of the caravan, stopping for a moment to shine her torch at the number plate on the back of Jeff's car to satisfy herself that the screw heads holding the plates in place there showed the tell-tale signs of having been unscrewed and screwed back up many times. Once she had checked this, she went up the steps of the caravan and let herself inside.

As soon as she had locked the door behind her, she took the torch out of her pocket, switched it on and shone the beam around. She pulled a disgusted face at the sight that met her eyes. Jeff obviously hadn't tidied or cleaned the van at all since she had been in here a couple of weeks ago. He certainly was a slob and she supposed she should feel honoured that he had bothered to clean the place for her benefit, but she didn't, just insulted that Jeff Sampson could ever think she would lower herself to his level. Dirty dishes overflowed the small sink, the top of the cooker was piled with crusted pans, and he obviously had a penchant for Newcastle Brown Ale as several full and empty bottles littered the work surface by the sink. The dining table was covered with old food containers, mainly Vesta beef curry packets and Fray Bentos steak pie tins, that he hadn't bothered to put in the rubbish bin after he'd prepared himself a meal.

Despite the fact that as the boss she had a right to be in the caravan, Rhonnie still felt the guilt all honest people feel on invading someone else's private space uninvited. She wanted to do what she had come for and get out of the van as fast as she could.

Hurriedly she searched every conceivable place she could find where items might be hidden. She discovered that most of the wall cupboards were empty. She did find a suitcase under the metal-framed bed but when she pulled it out and opened it up it was empty. There was nothing hidden under the small bed in the other bedroom and no place in the tiny bathroom to hide anything at all. Back in the kitchen area she flashed her torch around one more time to check there was nowhere she had missed. Her whole search had unearthed nothing incriminating, and definitely not the black holdall Ben had seen Jeff take out of his van and carry inside. If Jeff was up to no good, as the number plates indicated he was, then it seemed he didn't keep his spoils here in his caravan.

She was just about to leave when a memory surfaced. When the fleet of static caravans had first arrived, never having been inside one before, Rhonnie was keen to explore. Drina was her guide and during their tour had shown Rhonnie some concealed storage places: two separate cavities under the seating area at the front of the caravan that could be transformed into a double bed. Most people put the bedding in these before turning the bed back into a daytime seating area.

She went across to the left side of the seating area, moved aside the detritus on top, pulled up the seat padding, which she put on the floor, took out the panel of wood, then shone her torch inside.

Rhonnie gasped, stunned by what she saw. In the hoard were numerous silver objects, the type passed down as heirlooms from generation to generation; china ornaments and figurines; several small framed oil paintings. There was a large wooden box, which Rhonnie opened. She shone her torch inside and gasped again to see precious and semi-precious stones set into gold necklaces, rings, bracelets and earrings. These jostled for space with gold and silver cigarette cases and lighters, glinting in the torchlight. Her eyes then settled on a Crawford's biscuit tin. She reached inside and picked it up, surprised by how heavy it was. Taking off the lid she stared into it, shocked to see that it was half filled with an assortment of coins and, tied together with an elastic band, was a thick wad of banknotes, a few hundred pounds at least by Rhonnie's reckoning. She put the lid back on and replaced the tin where she had found it. Squashed flat on top of some of the items was the capacious black holdall Ben had described seeing. Rhonnie decided she didn't need to open up the other storage space – what she had revealed here was more than enough to incriminate Jeff.

She was just about to put the seating back into place when she noticed something sticking out of the top of the holdall. She leaned over and saw a spiral notepad with writing on it, along with a folded map of the British Isles, a corner of which she had seen protruding from the top of the bag. There was also a pile of A to Z maps, which upon examination she found were of various towns covering the Midlands, across to Manchester and Liverpool and northwards up to Leeds. Intrigued, she took everything out of the bag and shone her torch on the notepad. On it was written a name and address for somewhere in Derbyshire and underneath directions on how to get there. She flipped over the pages and found many more addresses and instructions. She put down the notepad and opened up one of the A to Z maps for the town of Sheffield, seeing a red line drawn from an entry road into the city towards a destination marked with a cross.

A memory then stirred of the way Jeff had tried to hurry her out of the van once when it had been evident he hadn't wanted her inside. On the table there had been a notepad similar to the one in her hand now with an address on it along with a map with a route outlined on it. She had thought no more than that Jeff had just preplanned a visit to a friend or family member . . . how wrong she had been. But all these addresses . . . how did he pick the properties he burgled, and why over such a wide geographical area?

317

Then a further horrifying truth dawned on her. Of course . . . Jeff would know that these particular houses would be empty because all the owners were staying on Jolly's site at the time in their camper and touring vans. His victims could only be from that group of people as he wouldn't know the private addresses of those staying in the static caravans as those bookings were dealt with by the general office, whereas Jeff himself booked in the tourers when they arrived seeking a vacant pitch. And he would have a good idea what those holidaymakers were worth judging by the make of car they drove and touring van they towed.

Anger flared up in her as she put the notepad and maps back inside the holdall. Not that Jeff would be needing them again where he was going next. Rhonnie just hoped that all the items he had stolen could be reunited with their rightful owners. But how terrible for all of them to have arrived home from their holidays to find their houses had been burgled – and how could they ever have guessed, the police either, that the culprit was not as they assumed someone local but the very congenial, charismatic manager of the holiday camp they had stayed at.

After checking around that she had replaced all Jeff's belongings, she switched off her torch, her intention being to head straight for the park office and telephone the police. Then she froze rigid on hearing a key in the lock and the next thing she knew the door opened and light flooded the room.

Rhonnie and Jeff stood staring at each other. It would have been impossible for an onlooker to say who was the more shocked to see the other.

Rhonnie's heart was thudding so loudly in her chest she could hear it. She started trying to come up with an excuse for her presence. She couldn't understand why he was back within ten minutes when it was a job that should have taken him a couple of hours at least.

It didn't seem, though, that she needed an excuse as Jeff

318

himself gave her one. With a smug smile he said, 'Well, Mrs Buckland, what a surprise. A very nice one, though. You obviously realised the big mistake you made last week and what you missed out on, so you've come back hoping I'd give you a second chance.' He walked over to her. Stroking his hand up and down her arm, he looked at her seductively and said, 'Shall we go straight into the bedroom or would you like a drink first?'

He totally repulsed her but to shove him away would immediately alert him to the fact that she had another reason for being here than the one he assumed. She took a step sideways to evade his hand and lied. 'Look, I really like you, Jeff, but coming here tonight was a mistake. I thought I was, but I now realise I'm not yet ready to go to bed with another man. I'm still not over my husband. I'm sorry, Jeff, really I am.'

She made to head for the door but he barred her way. Grabbing her hand, he started pulling her towards his bedroom. 'I'll show you you're ready. Deep down it's what you want, you know it is or you wouldn't be here.'

She was so angry that he was ignoring her wishes to satisfy his own selfishness, she snapped furiously at him: 'I told you, I'm not ready. Now I want to go home.' Or to get out of here at any rate and summon the police to deal with this egotistical monster.

He held up his hands in mock surrender. 'Okay, okay, you've made your point.' He shot her a look of contempt and mumbled something derogatory beneath his breath. He wouldn't come straight out with it, she thought, because with the lucrative sideline he'd got himself here, the last thing he would be wanting was to lose his job. He stood aside to allow her to leave but then eyed her questioningly as a thought struck him. 'How did you get in here? I locked the door when I left.'

She searched for a plausible answer but the only thing she

319

could think of was to tell the truth. 'I got the skeleton key from the cupboard in the park office.'

'Oh, I see.' Then he frowned as another thought struck him. 'But how did you know I'd be out so you'd need the skeleton key to get in?'

She stared blankly at him. 'Well, I, er . . . it struck me you might not be in, could be off dealing with a camper for some reason, so just in case you did happen to be out, I got the key. Thought I could wait for you inside instead of out in the dark. And it was getting chilly,' she added, hoping that added weight to her excuse.

He was just about to accept her reason when he noticed that a pair of trousers he had taken off earlier and left where they'd fallen on the floor were now on the seating, and the magazines he'd left strewn about were neatly piled together. He looked at her suspiciously. 'Have you been rummaging through my stuff?'

'No, of course not,' she blustered.

All his instincts told him she was lying. Then he looked at her more closely. He knew all about women and this wasn't one who'd dressed to make herself attractive to a man. Who came to seduce someone dressed in plain black trousers and a dark Sloppy Joe jumper? Then he remembered the damage to the shower. 'It was you who broke the taps,' he accused her. 'Don't bother to deny it, I know you did. You got the skeleton key from the office on your way here to let yourself into my van as you knew I'd be out.' He then scowled quizzically. 'And you wanted me out for a while judging by the damage you caused to the shower, which you knew would take me a couple of hours at least to fix. As it was I couldn't be bothered tonight, so I just switched the water off at the stopcock and put an "Out of Service" sign on the door.' He eyed her darkly. 'Just what were you looking for?' Then he suddenly realised just what and his face screwed up in fury as he lunged towards her, grabbed her jumper and pulled her towards him. His nose almost touching hers, he hissed, 'Find anything interesting, did you?'

She placed both hands on his shoulders and with as much force as she could muster pushed him away from her. This unexpected attack caught him off guard and he tumbled backwards, only just managing to keep himself upright. Defiantly she hurled at him, 'Yes, as a matter of fact, I have. I know exactly what you've been up to and how you've gone about it. You disgust me . . . stealing off Jolly's customers while they've been holidaying here. When you were ransacking their homes did you not care how devastated they'd be to find all their valuables gone . . . things that had sentimental value to them and that they could never replace?' The look he shot her told her he didn't give a damn. She glowered at him. 'I just hope to God that one day someone steals your most precious thing and you get to know what it feels like. I rue the day we gave you the job here.'

He laughed and gloatingly told her, 'You never gave me the job. I made sure you never had a choice *but* to give it to me. Didn't you think it was odd that none of the other applicants turned up for the interview? That was because I made sure they didn't. I broke into your office and went through your files until I found the addresses of the other candidates. I typed out a new letter telling them not to bother turning up as the job had gone, photocopied it, forged your signature, and sent it out to all of them. By the way, you need to have a word with your security guards as I was in the office when they came in to do a check around. If they'd bothered to look in the well under the desk they'd have seen me, but they didn't. This job had far too much potential for me to risk you picking someone else for it. All rather clever of me, don't you think, eh?' he smugly sneered.

So Jill had been right that morning when she'd come into work and said the things on her desk were not in the same place as she had left them. They had put it down to her being mistaken.

321

Jeff was going on, 'Oh, and I should tell you that Jeff Sampson isn't my real name. It's the name of a bloke I once worked for on a van site down south. And my references are all forged because if you knew my real name and background you'd never have employed me.' He paused for a moment before he asked, 'I was so careful not to get caught, how was I sussed?'

She took great pleasure in telling him, 'Because you're not as clever as you think you are. Someone saw you changing the number plates on your car in the early hours of the morning and then hiding the false ones. And while we're on the subject of number plates . . . at first you hid the false plates in the woods, didn't you? And when I accidentally uncovered them you attacked me, not giving a damn if you killed me or not.'

He nonchalantly shrugged. 'I thought the woods would be as good a place as any to hide them in but as it happened I was wrong. I'm just thankful I happened to see you going in that afternoon. A man's got to do what it takes to protect his interests.'

'You're despicable,' she hissed in disgust. 'You're going to jail for a very long time for what you've done. I'm going to telephone the police right now.'

He laughed. 'By the time they get here, I'll be long gone. It's been good here while it lasted. I've made a decent enough amount already, more than enough to get me started, so all's not lost. Now, if you'll excuse me, I've packing to do. Oh, and if you're thinking of leaving to go and raise the alarm, you can forget it as you don't go anywhere until I do.' He shot her a warning look. 'Make one move and you'll regret it. I've laid you out once – and that time I was being careful.'

As she stood staring at him he pushed past her and headed for the seating area, his intention she knew to collect his illicit gains before he made his escape. He wouldn't waste time packing up his belongings – why should he when he'd plenty of money to buy new? In a few minutes he would be gone, free to live the rosy future he had planned for himself. With no idea of his true identity, how would the police trace him? Appearances could always be altered as Ben's transformation proved.

She could not stand by and do nothing to try and stop him getting away. But she was one woman against a strong man. She had no hope of ever restraining him while she went to call the police. Her thoughts raced frantically for something else she could do and another idea occurred to her.

Jeff, or whatever his real name was, had thought nothing of knocking her out in order to stop her taking his precious false number plates from him. Although she abhorred violence in any form, in these dire circumstances she could think of no other way to stop him.

She flashed a glance at him, glad to see that he had his back to her, bending over the storage place under the sofa, piling all he could from inside it into the capacious holdall. She flashed another look around the rest of the area for something heavy enough to do the job. At first she could see nothing but then her eyes settled on the full bottles of Newcastle Brown on the work surface by the sink. One of them would do nicely. So she took a breath and said, 'I need to get a drink of water. Please can I go to the sink to have one?'

Without turning around he replied in no uncertain terms, 'Make sure that's all you do.'

Heart pounding painfully, she went over to the sink and turned on the tap, all the time keeping her eyes on him in case he turned around to see what she was up to. With the tap still running, she leaned over and picked up a bottle of the beer, which she then secreted behind her back. She turned off the tap and returned to where she had been standing previously, which was about three feet away from Jeff. Then, holding her breath, she took small side steps closer to him and, as soon as she was within reach of him, raised the bottle high. Just as she was about to bring it down with full force on the back of his head, he jumped up, spun around and grabbed her arm, squeezing it like a vice and forcing her to drop the bottle.

Fear rushed through her when he thrust his face into hers and hissed, 'You stupid bitch! Did you think I wouldn't realise you were up to something?' Then her fear escalated as he added, 'I need to do something about you, don't I? You obviously can't be trusted to do as you're told.' He raised his arm and balled his fist. She screwed her eyes shut and steeled herself for the blow to her face she knew was imminent, but then she heard the caravan door burst open and to her shock saw a pyjama-clad Ben dive inside. He bellowed, 'Lay one finger on Rhonnie and I'll kill you myself.'

Shocked by the unexpected intrusion, Jeff hesitated. Before he could gather his wits Ben was on him. He threw a punch and knocked Jeff flying into the storage space he was busy emptying. He passed out cold. Ben then clasped his hands to his chest and collapsed to the floor, rolling from side to side, groaning in agony.

Dazed by what had just transpired, it took Rhonnie a moment to gather her own wits. She cried out, 'Oh, Ben, what on earth did you think you were doing? The doctor warned you that any sudden movement could dislodge a piece of broken rib . . . And how on earth did you get here?'

He could barely speak for pain but managed, 'Tie . . . him . . . comes round . . . Jam . . . cord.'

'Jam cord?' she repeated, perplexed. 'I don't understand.' Then the penny dropped. 'Oh, pyjama cord.' She wasted no time in untying the knot of the cord threaded though the top of his pyjama trousers, pulled it out and went over to Jeff, who was starting to make guttural noises signalling that he was coming round. She pulled both arms behind his back and twisted the cord tight around his wrists, finishing it off with a firm knot. She then realised it would be safest to tie his feet together too, rendering him completely immobile. Scanning her eyes around the debris-strewn room, she spotted a pair of women's tights, obviously left behind by one of his string of female visitors. Snatching them up, she wasted no time in tying them tight around his ankles. Satisfied that Jeff wasn't going anywhere, she went back to Ben, who was still groaning and rolling about in excruciating pain.

She laid her hand tenderly on his arm and told him, 'I'm going to the office to ring for an ambulance for you, and the police to deal with Jeff. I'll be as quick as I can.'

He let her know he understood by blinking his eyes.

Rhonnie was to find out just how Ben had travelled the distance to the caravan park from the hospital when she found a parked taxi by the entrance, the driver of it leaning on the door smoking a cigarette. When he saw her he asked her if he'd seen a man wearing pyjamas anywhere around. Apparently he'd found the driver waiting outside the hospital and said he'd pay him double his usual fare if he did the journey double quick. At the park the man had jumped out and run off and the driver hadn't seen him since. As soon as she'd telephoned for the police and an ambulance, Rhonnie gladly settled his bill and added a generous tip.

Thankfully Ben hadn't caused any further damage to his ribs. He had, though, torn a chest muscle while hitting Jeff full force. The doctor had prescribed more pain relief and the sister in charge had administered a good ticking off. Ben was told he had been foolish and reckless in absconding from the hospital, but now he was resting comfortably.

As she sat by his bed Rhonnie thought that it must have been something far stronger than just normal pain relief the doctor had prescribed as Ben appeared comatose to her. She smiled at him tenderly as he lay peacefully sleeping. She knew it was good for him, as while he slept his broken body would be healing, but how she wished he would wake up so she could tell him just how grateful she was to him for coming to her rescue.

As she laid her hand on his arm and gently stroked it, she didn't realise that she was speaking her private thoughts out loud. 'Oh, Ben, what a lovely man you are. I think I fell in love with you the first time I met you. I never thought I would after losing Dan. How lucky can a woman get, meeting two wonderful men during her lifetime, when some woman aren't able to meet one? I don't care that you haven't a bean to your name. It's you I love, the man you are.' She laughed softly. 'And you can never accuse me of falling for your looks as I didn't have a clue what you looked like, did I, thanks to that bush of a beard you wore? I know you care about me. I can just tell by the way you look at me and the way you are with me. And if you didn't care, you wouldn't have risked your life to come and save me like you did, would you?' She heaved a deep sigh. 'Oh, Ben, I hope you feel the same way about me as I do you. I know we'd be happy together. Why don't you wake up so I can tell you all this?' She smiled down at him. 'If a nurse came in now I'd be carted off to the madhouse for talking to myself.' She got up, leaned over and kissed his cheek. 'I'll be back tomorrow afternoon at visiting time and hopefully you'll be awake by then and I'll hear you tell me what I so desperately want you to. Sleep well, my love.'

After he'd heard the door click shut, Ben slowly opened his eyes, and with a look of utter misery clouding his face, heaved a deep sigh. He had been asleep when Rhonnie first arrived but her gentle touch on his arm had roused him. Before he could open his eyes she had started to speak and what she was saying was both music to his ears but also shattering to learn. Tomorrow Rhonnie would visit him and reveal her feelings to him and there was no way he could look her in those beautiful eyes of hers and blatantly lie that he didn't feel the same. He had thought he had been so clever in keeping his feelings for her hidden but obviously he hadn't. He couldn't bear to disillusion her by telling her the sort of man he truly was. As much as it devastated him, he was left with no choice but to leave this place and resume his old life on the road.

A while later a worn-out Rhonnie was sitting at Drina's kitchen table, cradling a cup of tea between her hands. The older woman was giving her a scolding.

'I love you dearly, Rhonnie, you know that, but what you did was utterly thoughtless and could have got you killed, or seriously hurt at any rate.'

'I know, I know, Drina. Please don't be cross with me. But I never thought I was putting myself in any danger because as far as I was concerned I was only going to be searching the van for evidence. How was I to know that Jeff would shirk his responsibilities and leave repairing the shower until tomorrow morning? All I could think of was that if Ben was right, this man needed stopping before he stole anything else. And I was thinking of Jolly's reputation too. According to the police that man won't be free for a very long time and there's a good chance they'll be able to trace the owners of the stolen property from the addresses on the notepad.'

Drina said, 'Seems we have a lot to thank Ben for, doesn't it? He spotted that man was up to no good and saved you from . . . well, I dread to think what. Astonishing considering the state he was in because of his brave actions a couple of days ago.'

Rhonnie nodded and said, 'He's a very special man.'

Her tone and the look on her face when she said those words had Drina looking at her quizzically. 'You like Ben very much, don't you, Rhonnie?'

'I do, Drina. I feel a lot for him.'

More than that even, was Drina's guess, judging by the dreamy expression in Rhonnie's eyes. Now that she had had her wish to marry Artie granted, Drina was eager for Rhonnie to find happiness again. She asked her, 'Does Ben feel the same for you?'

Rhonnie paused for a moment before she responded. 'I think he does . . . I'm sure he does . . . but I worry he won't admit it because he's not got anything to offer me.'

'Then you need to tell him that.'

'I plan to, tomorrow afternoon when I go and visit him. Just keep your fingers crossed, Drina, that I'm not wrong about his feelings for me as I'll be devastated if I am.'

'I'll cross everything for you.'

Rhonnie gave a yawn. 'I'd best get off. Carrie will be over in the morning to collect Danny about nine. Thank you so much for looking after him for me.'

'I keep telling you, you don't need to thank me for looking after my own grandson. He's a pleasure to have and it certainly keeps me and your dad fit, running after him. Did I tell you that Artie is going to build him a climbing frame in our garden with a little hut on top that Danny can use as a den?' She laughed. 'I suspect that your father will have as much fun playing Cowboys and Indians on it when it's finished as Danny will.'

Rhonnie chuckled. 'I agree with you.'

CHAPTER TWENTY-SIX

It was a nervous Rhonnie who walked through the door with the rest of the crowd when a nurse announced that they could all come in at visiting time the next afternoon. Outside Ben's room, Rhonnie took a deep breath to steel herself for what she was about to do, before she tapped on the door and went inside.

The smile on her face vanished when she saw the bed was empty. Frantic that Ben had taken a turn for the worse after his ordeal of last night, she dashed out of the room to seek a nurse. She found three of them together having a cup of tea in the small kitchen next to the sluice room.

'Ben . . . he's not in his room. Where is he?' Rhonnie asked.

One of the nurses told her, 'He discharged himself this morning. I suppose he's at home. Sister did try to persuade him not to go as he's far from well enough to leave here but he was most insistent.'

Rhonnie was stunned. What did Ben think he was doing leaving hospital before he was well enough? Having thanked the nurse, she dashed off.

The drive back to Jolly's seemed to Rhonnie to take forever. Abandoning her car by the track, she ran all the way to his hut. When she arrived she didn't stop to knock at the door and be invited inside but thrust it open and charged in.

*   *   *

The few coins Ben had on him – all that was left from the small sum he had earned a few days before by helping to harvest potatoes – was just enough to pay the bus fare from Skegness to Mablethorpe. The bus driver had been a careful one but regardless potholes and bumps in the road had Ben biting his tongue so as not to scream out through the pain the jarring vehicle brought him. The six-mile walk from the bus station to the hut in the woods had been slow and painful too and by the time a shattered Ben reached his hut he'd had to lie down for a couple of hours before the dagger-like pain in his chest had subsided enough to allow him to endure it while he packed up his belongings in a merchant seaman's canvas bag. He wanted to be off on the road before Rhonnie discovered he was missing and came in search of him. He was trying to hurry now but his injuries were greatly hampering him. Regardless, he still felt that time was on his side.

He got a shock therefore when she burst into the hut.

Before he could utter a word, Rhonnie was demanding, 'Ben, why did you discharge yourself from the hospital when you're nowhere near well enough to look after yourself?' Then it sank in just what he was doing when she saw the bulky canvas bag lying on the floor by his feet. 'Are you going somewhere?' Her eyes filled with horror. 'Ben, are you leaving?'

'Yes.' He spoke bluntly.

'But why, Ben? I thought you liked living here?'

'I do, but all the same, I can't go on abusing Mrs Jolly's kindness any longer. It's time for me to move on.'

'You know you're not abusing Drina's kindness. You don't need to leave, Ben.'

But he did, away from the woman he loved, the one he knew he could be deliriously happy with, but did not dare to stay with because of what he'd done in the past. 'Look, I've really enjoyed living here but it's time for me to go. Please tell Mrs Jolly that I'm very grateful to her for allowing me to live here.' He paused for a moment to clear his throat before he said softly, 'And thank you for being a friend to me.'

Her heart felt as if it was being ripped in two. If Ben was leaving she must have been wrong about his feelings for her. If he loved her he wouldn't be able to walk away from her, would he? She felt a great sense of loss and sadness as she realised her future with him had been a figment of her imagination. With forced lightness she said, 'Yes, of course I'll tell her.' And then she had to clear her throat before she could add, 'All the best, Ben.'

He picked up the bag and fought not to show the pain it brought him to be holding such a heavy object. He collected his jacket and began to make his way over to the door.

As Rhonnie stood watching him go, an overwhelming need to tell him she loved him filled her. She couldn't let him go off without being made aware of how much he had come to mean to her. She cried out, 'Ben!' He turned to face her and she ran across to stand before him and blurted out, 'I need to tell you . . . that . . .. that . . . I love you, Ben. I just needed you to know that. Please take care of yourself.' She kissed his cheek before she stepped away from him.

He stared blankly at her for several long moments then, to her shock, tears filled his eyes and his face crumpled. 'I wish you hadn't told me that, Rhonnie,' he said hoarsely.

'Why?' she implored. 'Tell me why? Is it because the thought of me having feelings for you repulses you, is that it?'

He looked aghast. 'No, of course not, don't you ever think that. I'm honoured that you care for me, truly I am.'

She frowned in bewilderment. 'But why do you wish I'd never told you I love you?'

He heaved a miserable sigh. 'Because it will make it so much worse when you decide you hate me instead.'

She told him with conviction, 'You're a good man, Ben, and there's nothing I can imagine you doing that would make me not love you.'

He blurted out, 'Could you love a murderer, Rhonnie?'

She stared at him aghast. 'What? No, I don't believe you. You're not a man who could kill someone.'

'Not someone, Rhonnie, five men.'

Her mouth dropped open in astonishment. 'You killed five men in cold blood!' She shook her head. 'No . . . no . . . I still don't believe you. You haven't got it in you.'

'Not cold blood, Rhonnie, but it's my fault five men are dead, so whichever way you look at it I killed them.' He dropped the bag and jacket on the ground and hung his head as he told her his story.

'It happened eight years ago. I was orphaned when I was six, both my parents were killed when Coventry was blitzed in the war and I went to live with my only living relative, my father's brother, my uncle William in Leamington Spa. He was a lot older than my father and due to an accident when he was a young man classed as unfit to join up, though he still did his bit by becoming a member of the Home Guard. That's why he was in a position to take me in at the time. He never married so lived on his own. He was a lovely man and very good to me, treated me like I was his own son. He had a scaffolding business, just a small one, a couple of employees besides Uncle William, but it provided us with a decent living. When I left school I naturally went to work for him.

'From the very first day, time and time again, my uncle instilled in me that we never cut corners and always used the best quality steel for the tubes and wood for the battens . . . they're the platforms the workers stand on . . . and got all our ironmongery from reputable firms. We must always be meticulous in our work as we must never forget that men's lives were at stake. In all his time running the business not one accident happened that was due to his firm's negligence in any way and nor did it under my watch . . . well, not until . . . Anyway, when he died twelve years ago, my uncle left the business to me. Over the next four years I worked hard to keep it a success and built it up enough to take on another couple of men and an apprentice. And during that time I met Rosamund . . . Roz . . . and we got married, were very happy and planning to start a family.

'We had a contract to put scaffolding up for a firm that was retiling the roof of a factory. The job went like clockwork and after I had inspected it I informed the roofers they could start work first thing the next morning. Next day we were just loading the lorry to set out on another job when Betty, who ran the office for me, came tearing across the yard to tell us she'd had a telephone call from the owner of the roofing company, to say that the scaffolding had collapsed and men were injured. I went racing straight over there. I'll never forget the sight that met me. The scaffolding was in pieces, all in a heap, it had gone down like a pack of cards. The fire brigade was trying to get to the men trapped underneath and ambulances were waiting to take the injured to hospital. The police were taking a statement from the foreman and another worker, who'd been on the ground at the time and witnessed what had happened. It transpired that five men were up on the top deck and just beginning to start work when without warning the whole scaffold collapsed. When the men were finally taken out, two were already dead and the other three seriously injured. One of them died before he got to hospital and the other two over the next couple of days.'

He abruptly stopped for a moment and it was apparent to Rhonnie that even though eight years had passed, the memories of this incident were still painful for him to recall. Finally, taking a deep breath Ben continued. 'I'd thoroughly checked the scaffolding over before I signed off the job so all I could think of was that someone must have tampered with it. The police told us that there would be an investigation into why the scaffolding had collapsed and we would be informed of the outcome at the inquest. I was confident that no blame would be attached to me. But it seemed that the relatives of the dead men weren't going to wait for the coroner's verdict. As far as they were concerned, their husbands and sons were dead because of my faulty scaffolding, so it was I who had killed them. The local newspaper had a field day. My picture was on the front pages and the story that followed implied I had used sub-standard materials and caused the collapse. Then the nationals picked it up and the headlines in all of them were similar. It was untrue but mud sticks and immediately all the jobs we had lined up were cancelled. Everywhere I went people were pointing the finger at me. Someone even daubed "Murderer" in red gloss paint on my doors at home and at work. Until the investigators had done their job and the inquest had taken place and the coroner reached his verdict, there was nothing I could say or do to clear my name. Because I'd no money coming in I had no choice but to lay off my employees and close the business, but I was convinced it was only temporary and as soon as the inquest was over my life would go back to normal. I had some savings so managed to pay off our suppliers. I felt that if we were careful me and my wife would get through on what was left until I was in business again.

'But investigations and inquests take time and over the next few weeks me and my wife's lives were made hell by all those that had branded me guilty without trial. We couldn't go anywhere without someone hurling abuse at us and the relatives of the men who'd died made sure that the local newspaper ran a story every other week to keep it fresh in the public's mind. They made up all sorts of stuff about me, like that they heard rumours from reliable sources I'd been drunk when I was working on the scaffolding, or one of my men was, that sort of thing. It was terrible. It got to the stage where we daren't go out of the house and became prisoners in our own home. Friends stopped calling on us and neighbours too. Finally my wife couldn't stand it any longer and left me to go and stay with her friend in Birmingham. I was distraught but still convinced that once the inquest was over and the truth came out, I would be free to restart my business and my wife would come back to me.' He heaved a miserable sigh. 'But it turned out I was living in a fool's paradise. My life was never going to be the same again.

'At the inquest it came out that the investigators had discovered that on some of the tube joints the wrong sized bolts . . . a size smaller than they should have been . . . had been used to bolt them together, so when the weight of the five men pressed down on the scaffolding the bolts weren't strong enough to cope and snapped, causing the scaffold to collapse. When the investigators made a search of my premises they found a box with several bolts missing out of it that had a label stating the bolts were one size while the ones in the box were a size smaller. It was impossible to determine whether the fault for this lay with the supplier putting the wrong bolts in the wrong box or if we'd possibly done it ourselves . . . knocked two boxes over and put the bolts back in the wrong box when we'd picked them up . . . although if that had happened then the investigators should have found some bigger bolts in a box intended for smaller ones. They didn't, and my men and I all swore we had not put any bolts back in the wrong box. Finally the coroner decided that the men's deaths were accidental.'

Ben stopped abruptly to wipe tears from his eyes before he carried on speaking. 'But when all's said and done the men's deaths weren't accidental, were they? I was the boss of the firm and it was my responsibility to make sure that all the materials we used were the best there were. I never thought to check that the boxes had the right bolts in them.

'So it was my fault that five women were widowed, children would grow up without their fathers, and fathers and mothers had lost sons, siblings their brothers. The guilt was unbearable. There was nothing I could do to bring those men back to their families but I could try and ease the financial burden a little. I had no money left, no business to sell, but I did have the house that my uncle had left me in his will, which was worth a few thousand. I instructed my solicitor to sell it and put the contents in an auction as my wife by now had made it clear there was no going back for her. She was divorcing me and didn't want anything from the house. I instructed that the proceeds were to be divided equally between the families of the dead men. It was the least I could do. So with nowhere to live and no money, I've been living like I am now ever since. And even now the guilt never leaves me because, had I checked those bolts before we used them, five men would still be alive.

'When you offered me a job I badly wanted to accept it and be able to build myself a future, but you'd obviously have expected me to smarten up my appearance and cut my hair and shave off my beard, which would have meant I risked being recognised by someone from my home town or just a newspaper reader who remembered the case. It wouldn't have done your company any good if it became known you'd employed a man who was responsible for the deaths of five others. I couldn't expect you to choose keeping me on against risking the business. If it had all come out I'd have been back living on the road again in all weathers instead of staying in the hut, and the thought of living that life again unless I had no choice . . . well, I daren't risk it.'

He lifted his head and looked at Rhonnie. 'Now you know I was responsible for five deaths, do you still feel the same about me?'

She took his hands in hers. Fixing him with her gaze, she said with conviction, 'Those deaths were an accident, Ben. You didn't plan to kill them so you're not a murderer. You'll never know just how those bolts got to be in the wrong box

336

and maybe you should have checked they were the right ones before they were used on the job, but you didn't because you trusted your materials. You can't go on forever blaming yourself for that one mistake. It's a rare person who goes though life without making any – we're only human after all. And anyway, Ben, in truth you've more than repaid your debt to society, if indeed you ever did owe one, as the number of lives you saved the other day with your bravery far outweighs the five who died through simple human error, so if that doesn't take away your guilt, I don't know what will.'

She paused to smile at him tenderly. 'You asked me if now I know what I do about you, I could still love you. If anything I love you more. You didn't need to sell the only asset you had left to give to those bereaved families, but could have used it to fund a future for yourself in another town, under another name. You chose to put others before yourself. Ben, you've carried that guilt for long enough. Now it's time to let it go and live life with your head held high. Jolly's has tens of thousands of holidaymakers through the gates every year. Should any of them recognise you after all these years and choose not to holiday here again because they don't like the fact we employ a man they don't approve of, then that's their decision and it's their loss of a good holiday here with us.'

He looked at her for a very long time before he said, 'Yes, you're right. I never planned to kill those men and it's time to put it behind me.' His shoulders lifted as if a great burden had been eased off them and he smiled at her. 'Oh, Rhonnie, I can't tell you how I feel right now. It's like I've been set free from a big black hole and allowed out into the sunshine. If you offered me that job on the caravan park now, I'd take it.'

She smiled. 'Well, since it was you who instigated me getting rid of the previous park manager, it just so happens that I intend to do that. It's yours. You can start as soon as you're

337

well enough.' She eyed him searchingly. 'So, now you've come clean about your past, when are you going to come clean about your feelings for me? Mind you, you've already told me you love me, so I know you do anyway.'

He frowned at her quizzically. 'I don't remember telling you that.'

She laughed. 'Well, you wouldn't, but you did all the same. You were actually delirious at the time after the amount of morphine the doctor had given you, so in all honesty, I'm not sure whether you meant what you said or not.' Her face grew serious and she pointedly asked him, 'So now you're not under the influence of drugs, did you mean what you said or not?'

He looked at her tenderly. 'Oh, I meant it, Rhonnie, very much so. I fell for you the first time we met and fell in love with you a little more every time I saw you. But how on earth could I ever expect a woman like you to want to be with a man . . . well, I saw myself as a murderer, didn't I? And besides that I had nothing to offer you, so as far as I was concerned my feelings for you were futile.'

'You have yourself, Ben, and that's good enough for me.'

'Yes, I heard you tell me that. I wasn't asleep last night when you thought I was – I heard everything you said. I wanted to jump for joy when I heard you say you loved me and that it didn't matter to you that I hadn't a bean to my name. But I couldn't face seeing that love you felt for me turn to disgust, hatred even, when I told you what had happened in my past. So to avoid that I decided to leave, only I didn't get away quickly enough, did I? You caught me still here so I couldn't avoid telling you my secret anyway.'

'And I so glad I did catch you, Ben, otherwise I wouldn't now be looking at the man I'm going to marry.

He smiled. 'Oh, you're going to make an honest man out of me, are you?'

'I certainly am . . . well, as soon as you propose, that is.'

'When a man proposes to the woman it's tradition to do it with a ring, so until I can afford one you'll have to wait.'

She laughed. 'Then I'll just have to be patient, won't I? Oh, Ben, I want to hug you but I daren't because I'll hurt you. But there's nothing wrong with your lips, is there?' she said, looking at him meaningfully.

'There certainly isn't, thank goodness.'

CHAPTER TWENTY-SEVEN

'I swear these gates get heavier every year. You've finished closing yours so come and give me a hand with this one, Rhonnie,' Drina asked her.

A short while later, both the huge iron gates were chained shut and would remain that way until Jolly's Holiday Camp was reopened at the start of the next season.

Both women were leaning their backs against the gates, looking towards the now empty courtyard that up until a couple of hours ago had been teeming with campers buying last-minute souvenirs before their coaches rolled into the courtyard to take them home.

'Another successful season, Rhonnie,' said Drina, looking pleased.

'Yes, it has been, but not without its worrying times. Do you think we'll ever have a season when we don't have campers stealing the sink plugs and costing us a fortune to keep replacing them? Or much worse than that, people seeing Jolly's as a means of making money for themselves, like Jeff Sampson did? I should say Ronald Hickingbottom, as that's what the police found out his real name is.'

Drina shook her head. 'As long as we humans walk the earth there will always be those amongst us constantly on the lookout for ways to make a few pounds for themselves, not caring who they hurt in the process. We just need to keep vigilant for that type here, which thankfully up to now, through good management and loyal staff, we have managed to do.' She laughed and added tongue in cheek: 'And, of course, we mustn't forget . . . with the help of a tramp too. The main thing, Rhonnie, is that Jolly's has once again given thousands of people a wonderful holiday and next year even more will experience that thanks to the renovations. Now I have the bank's approval, I can't wait to get started.'

Rhonnie smiled at her. 'You'll never fully retire, will you, Drina? However much you try to back away, the camp keeps pulling you in, like a magnet, and while you live and breathe it always will.'

She nodded. 'You're right. Jolly's is like my baby and I shall never want to stop making it grow and prosper.'

Rhonnie mused, 'I wonder what your father would say, if he was alive today, to see how the camp had grown and changed?'

Drina smiled distantly. 'I can picture him now, standing here beside us, bursting with pride.'

'Just like his daughter is doing now,' said Rhonnie. 'And from the bookings we've already taken for next season, I don't think I'd be tempting fate to say that this time next year you'll be feeling even prouder.'

'Well, as long as we never forget that the world is constantly changing and we must keep up with the times to ensure that people will never want to stop coming here for their holiday, you and I will be standing here together for many years to come, celebrating the fact that we've had another good season.' Drina stood upright, clapped her hands together and announced, 'Right, well, time waits for no man, Rhonnie. Before we know it next season will be on us and we have a lot of work to get through first. For the rest of the afternoon, though, all my efforts will be directed towards my wedding to your father in two weeks' time. I've an appointment with the dressmaker this afternoon. Oh, it's so wonderful that everyone I care about is making such an effort to come to the celebrations. You and Danny, of course, I couldn't get married without you two being there, and Ben too. I'm delighted to tell you that Jackie is coming up and bringing her boyfriend for us to meet . . . "introducing him to her other family" to use her words. Then Ginger and Paul, Harold and Eileen, Eric and Ginny, Jill and Martin . . .

'Oh, that reminds me, I must get cracking on knitting her baby a layette. To be on the safe side I'm going to knit two of everything – one in blue, the other in pink. And what's this I heard through the camp grapevine that a clairvoyant told her she was expecting before she had any idea she was? Never mind, you can tell me about that when I've more time. There are other people coming that I'm very fond of but the ones I've just mentioned are the ones I especially want to share our big day with.' Drina flashed a look at her watch. 'Oh, I really must dash or I won't have a dress to wear on the day. By the way, I haven't forgotten that your father and I are babysitting for you tonight when you and Ben go out. We'll be over about seven.'

Rhonnie smiled. 'He's taking me to the pictures to see *Butch Cassidy and the Sundance Kid*.'

That's what you think, thought Drina. Ben was in fact taking Rhonnie for a special meal where he planned to propose to her and cement the engagement with the ring he had bought. Drina smiled at the memory of a very nervous Ben coming to see Artie and asking for his permission. He had readily granted it to Ben's delight, but then he'd asked Artie to keep it a secret until he had surprised Rhonnie with his proposal. Ben had taken Drina into his confidence too, to ask her advice on what style of ring she felt Rhonnie would like. Her answer was something simple and not ostentatious as Rhonnie was not at all the showy sort, and nothing too expensive either as she knew that Rhonnie would be very cross if she thought for a minute that Ben had spent money on her that he could put to much better use, like starting up another business for himself. In the meantime he was doing an admirable job of managing the caravan park and had moved out of the old hut in the woods – not without a great deal of sadness – and into the caravan Jeff Sampson had been forced to vacate, to take up his new residence in a prison cell.

Rhonnie and Drina trusted each other completely, so of course she had taken Drina into her confidence and told her just how Ben had come to be living as he was. Drina's attitude had mirrored Rhonnie's own, she too being of the opinion that if a mistake had been made then Ben had more than paid for it now. Drina had taken a liking to him when she had first met him that foggy morning back in late December. Her instincts about him had proved to be correct and the better she was getting to know him, the better she liked him for his honesty, intelligence, conscientiousness and sense of humour. She knew he'd make Rhonnie a good husband and be a loving father to Danny, and she was certain that Dan would have approved of him too.

Rhonnie watched Drina hurry off to attend the appointment with her dressmaker. She was really looking forward to having a night out with Ben tonight but her sixth sense was telling her that he wasn't taking her to the pictures or why would he have suggested to her earlier that she wore the new dress she had bought recently, which was far too dressy for the local flicks? Dare she hope that he was taking her somewhere romantic and, while they were there, planning to propose to her as he'd finally managed to save up the money to buy her a ring? She would just have to have patience and hope the time passed quickly until she found out.

But meanwhile she had work to do, making sure that for years to come Jolly's continued providing people with the best holiday they could possibly have.